Praise for Sherryl

'This novel is a page-turner and the action is pretty much full on; kidnap, murder, gangster wars, a McGuffin and a decent cop' – ***NB Magazine***

'On show in *Trust Me, I'm Dead* is finesse with character development and plot, in this case thermostatically synced to the reader's imagination' – ***The Westsider***

'Gripping and disturbing, Clark delves into dark places close to home. *Trust Me, I'm Dead* will linger in your mind after you have read it' – **Leigh Russell**

'This felt like an impeccably planned treasure hunt with tension interwoven into the story to lasso my attention right to the end. I'll be watching for the author's next crime fiction offering!' – ***A Knight's Reads***

'*Trust Me, I'm Dead* is an intense, addictive read with enough action to get your heart beating and characters to die for' – ***Chocolate'n'Waffles***

'Readers will be intrigued by many red herrings, and their interest maintained by the various twists and turns before the narrative reaches its unexpected and tense conclusion' – **Nan Van Dissel, *Blue Wolf Reviews***

'*Dead and Gone* is a classic whodunnit that is a fast-paced, thrilling and exciting read that will keep you glued to the pages' – **Once Upon a Time Book Blog**

'a jolly good read and a series with plenty of potential' – **Cheryl M-M's Book Blog**

'I really like the character of Judi. She is feisty, fiery and forthright' – **Leah Moyse, Reflections of a Reader**

Also by Sherryl Clark

Trust Me, I'm Dead
Dead and Gone

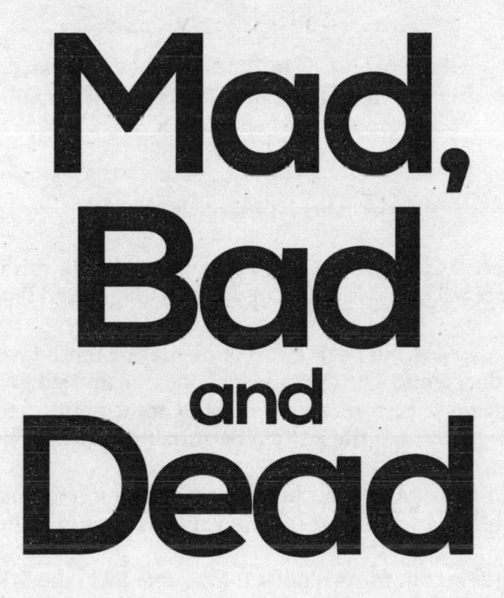

SHERRYL CLARK

VERVE BOOKS

First published in 2022 by VERVE Books,
an imprint of The Crime & Mystery Club Ltd,
Harpenden, UK
vervebooks.co.uk

A CIP catalogue record for this book is available from the British Library.

ISBN
978-0-85730-820-7 (print)
978-0-85730-821-4 (epub)

2 4 6 8 10 9 7 5 3 1

Typeset in 11 on 13.5pt Minion Pro
by Avocet Typeset, Bideford, Devon, EX39 2BP
Printed and bound by CPI Group (UK) Ltd, Croydon, CR0 4YY

For Karen –
it’s so good to be home.

1

My head was ringing. I shoved a pillow over it, which muffled the sound a bit, but not enough. It wasn't my head; it was the phone. The landline phone which hardly ever rang these days. Nobody had the number other than Connor.

Connor. Something must be wrong. I leapt out of bed, caught my foot in the sheet and half-staggered across the bedroom, making a grab for the chest of drawers at the last moment. Shit. One more centimetre and I would have brained myself on it.

The phone was still ringing. I lurched out into the lounge room, heading for the noisy damn thing, praying it wouldn't wake Mia.

'Waahhhh! Juddy.'

Too late. I snatched up the receiver. 'Yes!' Poor Connor. As the local cop, he'd probably get more polite answers to his calls. Still, he was used to me. We'd been mates long enough.

Silence for a couple of long seconds.

I took a breath. 'Connor? Hello?'

'Fuck you, bitch. You're going to be sorry.'

Click. The receiver was a dead thing in my hand, so dead I flung it away from me like a smelly fish. Then I stared at it lying on the floor, looking all innocent and cream-coloured.

'Judd-eeeeee.' Mia sounded very cranky. What a great way to start the bloody day. A vicious, anonymous phone call and a grumpy three-year-old.

I picked up the receiver and put it back in the cradle. I'd been thinking for ages that I should get it disconnected, but there was still no decent mobile phone reception here in my house.

The nasty voice clung to my brain like a sticky echo, and goosebumps ran up my arms. I picked up the receiver again. I should call Connor and make a police report. But the clock on the oven said 5.39am and I hated to wake him. Even good friends don't like being woken before dawn.

It would have to wait. The cranky three-year-old wouldn't.

'Coming, Mia, don't get your knickers in a knot.' I found her sitting up in bed, clutching Bum, her once-white stuffed rabbit, and chewing on one of his ears. Bum was supposed to be called Bunny but Mia had other ideas, despite my best efforts.

'Who was that?' she said, screwing her face up into a massive frown.

'Nobody,' I said. 'Maybe it was a mistake.'

'What's a mistake?'

'Er…' She caught me out like this a dozen times a day. My brain scrambled to retrieve its dictionary component. 'When you do something by accident when you don't mean to.'

She regarded me seriously for a moment, then nodded. 'Bum wants breakfast.'

'It's really early. You could go back to sleep.'

She scrambled out of bed, dragging Bum behind her. 'It's OK, I can watch TV.'

'All right.' At least that way I could lie down with her and get a bit more shuteye, perhaps. Then I definitely would call Connor. Even though I felt paranoid, I double-checked the doors and windows were locked before I joined Mia on the couch. She'd mastered the remote control long ago and now had found the kid's shows. How the hell she did it was beyond me.

Who had made that call? The voice sounded vaguely familiar, but only vaguely. Whoever it was had deliberately made themselves sound grating and harsh. And threatening, like they really meant it. *Fuck you, bitch. You're going to be sorry.* I lay there, staring at the TV screen and badly wanted to call Heath. Even the sound of his sleepy voice would make me feel better, and I could imagine him in bed. Sigh. Better not.

Finally at 6.30am I made Mia some cereal and called Connor. He sounded wide awake.

'How long have you been up?' I asked.

'Ages. I've just got back from a run.'

'Ugh. You need to give this fitness thing up. It might… never mind.' I sighed.

'What's up?' When I didn't answer straight away, he added, 'I know something is. Come on, spit it out.'

'I got this phone call. It was a voice. It said…' I couldn't get the words out. Mia sensed something was wrong and blinked up at me, so I turned away. 'It sounded weird. And threatening.'

'What did they say?'

I repeated the words I'd heard, for some reason feeling sillier by the moment. 'It's probably nothing. Forget I mentioned it.'

'It's not nothing,' he said patiently. 'It's pretty scary for you. And nasty. Did you recognise the voice?'

'Not really.' I heard it again in my head and swallowed hard. 'It was kind of metallic. But I couldn't even guess who it was.'

'OK. You need to come in and make a report. After breakfast is good.'

'Really? Can't we just, I dunno, make a note and see what happens?' I twisted the phone cord around my fingers so tightly that I cut off circulation, and had to flex them to get some feeling back. I wished I'd never called him.

'No, we can't. I want it on record.' A noisy slurp echoed down the phone line. 'Sorry, coffee's a bit hot. I'll see you about 9.30, OK?'

'OK. Thanks. I think.' I hung up and went to make some

coffee of my own. I was due at the pub at 10am, for a meeting with Andre, and I had to get Mia ready for childcare. We were in a routine now, which made it all a bit easier.

By the time I'd dropped her off at the centre and driven back to Candlebark, it was just after 9.30 and I met Connor coming out of his little police station, 4WD keys in his hand.

'Sorry, Judi,' he said, 'there's been a farm accident. I'll catch up with you later. I won't forget.' He jumped into his police vehicle and roared off down the street, leaving me standing next to my old blue Mercedes, feeling a bit deflated. I'd psyched myself up to make the statement and now it wasn't happening.

As I drove to the pub, I thought about the call again. Was it someone I knew? Clearly, yes. Why would a complete stranger threaten me? I pictured all the regulars in the public bar, their cheery beer-flushed faces and chuckling banter. None of them, surely. Then I thought back to the events of a few months ago when Macca, the pub owner, had been murdered. I'd got up a few people's noses then, but none of the key players were around much anymore. The ones who were had escaped prosecution, so they had no real beef with me.

The bikies did though. The police had descended on our little town of Candlebark and eventually rounded up half a dozen of them and charged them with dealing chop chop and illegal tobacco. A couple of them had threatened Andre and me and caused a lot of trouble for us. I'd been so glad to see them hauled away, but those guys were like fungi. More of them popped up to fill the gaps in the rotten wood. I shivered. That was the last thing I needed, the return of bikies to the town, the pub and my life. Connor was right. The threatening call needed to go on record.

At the pub, I parked around the back as usual and went in the side door, relocking it after me, and headed for the office. Andre was banging around in the kitchen, doing chef things.

I'd printed out the latest bank statements so Andre and I were ready for the online call we'd have to schedule with our co-owners. After Macca had left the pub to Andre, Suzie and me, Suzie had insisted we buy her out.

Three of Andre's mates in Melbourne had all chipped in to buy her share, but we'd had a lot of quiet weeks lately and the takings were pretty miserable. With winter looming, we needed to do more with our marketing or we'd all go down the gurgler.

I took all the bits of paper through to the bistro where Andre was sitting with a steaming mug by the open French doors. We'd renovated the courtyard with tubs of grevilleas and banksias and heritage green wooden tables and chairs. It had proved very popular over summer with the locals as well as the tourist trade we'd attracted with Andre's trendy new regional food menus. But that rush of interest had faded and things weren't good.

'Long face there, Judi,' Andre remarked. 'Don't tell me they're about to cut off the gas.'

'No, the bills are paid, thank God,' I said. I nearly told him about the phone call, but forced it back. We needed to focus on the pub. 'We're going to have to seriously tackle our marketing.'

'We could ask Bronwyn for some marketing advice.' His face twitched and he couldn't stop a grin from spreading.

'Bronwyn? I'd rather cut off my hand than ask that nasty bitch for help!'

Andre burst out laughing. 'Don't hold back, will you!'

Bronwyn Castille was the bane of our lives. Not long after we'd taken over the pub, she and her husband had opened a very expensive, fancy health spa about ten kilometres up the road. They'd bought an old farm, renovated the rambling house and built five yurts, all behind a thick row of shelter belt trees. The health spa was apparently all about being a 'Spartan', a 'warrior for your body', according to their website. We'd been hoping some of their guests might come to the pub for lunch or dinner, or just to sample our local wine list.

No. It was like they were in prison, placed on strict organic or paleo diets, woken at 5am to meditate and exercise, and alcohol was banned. The problem was that after a few days of this, most of their guests started sneaking out and coming to the pub anyway, and then Bronwyn would descend like the wrath of God and demand they return 'for their own blessed good'. Her hissy fits when she found them eating Andre's desserts would have been hysterically funny if it didn't also mean she frightened off some of our own guests. Bloody woman.

'We've got two options,' I said. 'We're either going to have to drop staff hours, or we have to come up with a way to attract more customers.'

'Honestly, we've done bugger all about marketing,' Andre said. 'We have to remember we're in competition with every other pub around here, as well as the ones on the Melbourne-Bendigo routes.'

I pushed a couple of the bigger bills over to him. 'These are due next week.'

'Shit, it's worse than I thought,' Andre said. His face was thinner these days, his eyes hollow. He was losing as much sleep as me over this. Why had we ever thought we could make a go of the pub as a gourmet attraction?

I pointed at one item on the most recent statement. 'We're going to have to cancel Murdoch Gate's orders. Their goat's cheese and olive oil are divine, but the cost is out of our budget now.'

Andre nodded. 'OK, I'll talk to the meat supplier tomorrow about doing a better deal. If he knows it's reduce the price a bit or lose our order, he might come around.'

'Hiya!' Kate, our waitress and kitchen hand came in. She was a tall woman, freckled and blonde, who usually wore a smile.

Today she looked worried, as if she'd already guessed what we were talking about, and I pointed to the coffee.

I wondered for a moment what was making Kate frown. She'd seemed a bit 'off' in the last few days, and I'd meant to ask her if everything was OK, but she was guarded at the best of times, not a chatterer. I liked her toughness, and her willingness to work hard. She'd been a lifesaver for the bistro, able to help Andre with the cooking as well as manage bookings and wait on tables.

Kate glanced at the stack of bills and statements as she sat down. 'Problems?'

'Same old,' Andre said. 'Know anything about marketing?'

'No, sorry. Your food gets lots of good reviews.' She grinned at Andre. 'Even that gross dish with gorgon's cheese. Doesn't that help?'

Andre laughed. 'Gorgonzola, you peasant. It's a start, but it's not enough. Marketing is an art, really.'

'Wish I could help,' Kate said. 'I avoid social media like the plague!'

Marie arrived for her bar shift and came to pour herself a coffee as well. She looked like she needed it. She slouched her way across the bistro, rubbing her forehead, her face a pasty colour. Another hangover. It was a trap, working in a pub, if you tended to drink too much. Suzie had been a master at collecting tips without actually drinking the freebies she was shouted. Marie, not so much.

'You need to go virussy,' Kate said.

'Viral,' Marie said grumpily over her shoulder. 'That's not likely. Most people who go viral do it by accident.'

Kate shrugged, and I frowned at Marie's retreating back. If it wasn't that we really needed two bar workers, I'd have cheerfully let Moaning Marie go and done a bit more myself, but it wasn't possible. I didn't want Mia to become a 'pub kid'.

After a few moments of silence, Kate said hesitantly, 'I know you want to get rid of Marie. If you do, I'd like to take over her bar shifts.'

The woman was a mind reader. 'But then you'd be working virtually seven days a week. Maybe fifty hours.'

'I could do with the money,' she said, her gaze on her worn, stained shoes. 'You know I work hard. And it'd only be for a few months, maybe until September. Then you can look for someone else when things pick up again.'

'What about Emma?' Emma was her fourteen-year-old daughter, a sensible, capable young kid if ever I'd seen one. But it'd mean Kate was leaving her home alone five nights of the week.

'Emma will be fine,' Kate said. 'She knows the situation.'

Something told me 'the situation' wasn't just about money. The temptation to get rid of Moaning Marie was pretty strong.

'Can we think about it?' Andre chipped in.

'Sure.' Kate got up and began gathering up the cups. 'How many in for lunch today?'

'Ten,' Andre said. 'Unless we have more escapees from Bronwyn's health farm.'

Kate laughed. 'I'll make sure I offer them the rum cheesecake then. What about tonight?'

Andre shook his head. 'Only two booked, sorry. Tuesday is pretty quiet at the best of times. But you're definitely on for lunch tomorrow – I have to go and see about a meat order in the morning so you'll need to do all the prep.'

'Cool. I'll get started then.' She went into the kitchen and the sound of slicing and chopping soon echoed through to us where we sat staring at the bank statements.

No point waiting for a miracle. I gathered up all the papers and stood. 'By the way...' I debated telling him about the threatening phone call. It'd feel good to tell someone.

'Yeah?' He sounded so dispirited, I couldn't load anything else on to him.

'Let's think seriously about letting Marie go and giving Kate her bar hours, OK?'

'Sure.'

Tuesday was my day off, so I locked the office and headed home. I swung past the police station on my way but Connor's 4WD wasn't there. I wondered briefly whose farm the accident had been on. Probably another quad bike mishap. They seemed to happen regularly, with disastrous consequences.

The day passed without me hearing from Connor, as did the night. Maybe he thought I'd overreacted to the call, even though it was him who insisted on a report. I woke briefly around 5am and tensed, thinking I'd heard the phone ping, but it was just my imagination. I was at the pub again by 10am, and spent some time upstairs trying to fix the leaking tap in Room 3. I really didn't want to call a plumber and be socked with yet another bill.

When I came back down, Charlie called out from the bar, and I went in to see what the problem was. Half a dozen locals were in, drinking beer and chatting, and I realised it was almost lunchtime.

He waved an order slip at me. 'I've got two steak sandwiches and chips, and nobody to cook them.'

'What? Kate can do those. She doesn't need Andre to supervise.'

'That's just it,' Charlie said. 'There's nobody in there at all. The kitchen is dark.'

I gaped at him for a moment. Surely Kate hadn't slept in? 'I'll find out what's going on. And I'll ring Andre. He should be on his way back by now.'

Sure enough, the kitchen was in darkness, and so was the bistro. No tables laid, no veggies prepped, nothing. I pulled out my phone and called Kate but it just rang out. Andre's went to voicemail. He was probably out of range somewhere.

'Hold the fort,' I said to Charlie. 'I can't help with the food. I'm going to go and get Kate out of bed.' But as I drove my old Mercedes above the speed limit down the back road to Kate's rental house, I kept thinking. And worrying. This wasn't like her at all. Something must have gone wrong for her to not even call me.

I pulled up in the driveway and got out. The house was a small white weatherboard, in need of painting, with sagging gutters. The cypress hedge at the front was overgrown, branches heavy with nuts leaning out at odd angles. I shivered, feeling like someone was watching me, and turned. Up on the hill on the other side of the road, a man stood by an old Land Rover, watching me.

Len Greenhall, farmer and owner of this rundown mini mansion. I turned my back on him and went to the front door, banging on the frosted glass. No response. I jiggled the handle, but it was locked. All the blinds were down so I decided to try the back door. As I rounded the corner I spotted Kate's car under the carport. So she was home! Damn it. I hoped she had a bloody good excuse lined up.

My footsteps echoed across the wooden verandah. The back door was unlocked; actually it was half-open, and for the first time, it occurred to me that something really was wrong. 'Kate? Hello? Are you home?'

Silence. That feeling of being watched again. I turned and stared up the slope behind the house, into the bracken and gum trees at the top. Shadows and gum leaves falling. Nothing more.

I pushed the back door fully open. It led straight into the kitchen, with dirt-brown lino and olive-green cupboards. Dreary as hell. Everything was clean and tidy though. Even the old stove was pristine.

'Kate? Are you there? It's Judi.' My voice seemed to be swallowed by the strange silence in the house. Then the old fridge clicked on and rattled, and frightened the crap out of me. I put my hand on my heart, like that'd somehow help to slow it down, and stepped through the kitchen to the hallway. Bathroom, a glimpse of an old pink iron bath and a shower curtain with birds on it. Two doors; the one on my right was Emma's bedroom, judging by the stuffed toys on her bed and a cheery blue and pink rug.

So the one on my left must be Kate's. The door was almost closed; through the small gap I could see slippers on the floor, a cheap white bedside table and a couple of books. I lifted my hand to push the door open and couldn't make myself do it.

'Kate? It's Judi.' *Fuck, please wake up and answer me.*

OK. Push the door open then. Come on, deep breath, push.

The door swung back and bumped the wall. Kate was in bed, yes, but she wasn't asleep. The two holes in her forehead told me clearly she was dead.

2

I stood there frozen for what seemed like an hour then my guts started churning and I knew I had to get outside, fast. I ran down the hallway, through the kitchen and down the steps. There was an outside toilet tucked under the back verandah roof, door gaping open and I ran for the bowl. I heaved a few times but managed not to vomit, taking lots of deep breaths until my hands started tingling.

'OK, OK,' I said, out loud. 'Stay calm. It's OK.' But it wasn't OK. It was as far from OK as it could possibly get. This was worse than Macca being found in the pub's dumpster because I hadn't had to actually look at his dead body.

Kate had been shot! I had the picture in my head now. Her eyes closed, dark blood around her head on the pillow like a halo, her face angled towards the door as if she'd woken and realised what was about to happen – too late.

I was shaking too much to stand up. I reached for my phone but it was in the car. I had no idea how I was going to get to it. So I sat on the wooden verandah in the sun, my hands gripping my knees until they ached, until I felt able to get up and walk without falling over.

In the Benz, I huddled in the driver's seat and fumbled with my phone, hitting the dial icon for Connor. 'Please, please answer.' I didn't know what I'd do if it went to his voicemail.

'Judi, sorry, I meant to get back to you about that call.'

'Connor… I…'

'Judi?' His voice went from apology to instant concern and worry. 'What's wrong?'

'You have to… you have to come to Kate's house. Now. It's Kate. She's dead.' I could barely get the last word out but he heard me.

'You're there now?'

'Yes.'

'Stay right where you are. I'm about ten minutes away. Don't move.'

'OK.' He'd already disconnected and I dropped the phone into my lap and sat there. No way was I going inside again. Just as well Emma was at school.

Or was she? What if she was in the other bedroom, behind the door, or in the bathroom? Why hadn't I checked? She could just be injured and praying for help. I pounded the steering wheel. I should go and look. I should.

But if she was only injured, surely she would have heard me calling and said something, cried out? No, she could be close to death, and me sitting here wasn't helping, it was being useless. Tears were rolling down my face and I palmed them away. *Get out of the car and go and check, you idiot. You have to. Don't look at Kate. Look for Emma.*

I levered myself out of the car and walked around to the back door again. 'Emma? Emma!' Nothing. Not even any birds singing. Why would they? Only the sound of a distant tractor. I forced my feet up the back steps again, stopped in the kitchen and listened. Now I could smell what I hadn't noticed before – metallic, fleshy… A large blowfly careened past, banging against my head and I swallowed hard.

I can do this, I can do this. I kept my head turned away from Kate's room, used my elbow to push open the bathroom door and Emma's bedroom door as fast as I could. Bang. Look. Bang.

Look. Nothing. No body lying anywhere. I ran outside and doubled over, sucking in air. I'd been holding my breath since the blowfly.

The sound of a vehicle filtered through to me. Engine, brakes, engine off, door opening and closing. Connor's voice. 'Judi? Where are you?'

'Round the back,' I called. To my amazement, my voice sounded almost normal, but the sight of Connor nearly undid me. I struggled to stay upright, to breathe and pretend to be calm. 'Thank God you're here.' I pointed at the back door. 'She's… inside. In her bedroom.'

'You're as white as a sheet,' he said, and pointed at the verandah. 'Sit there. I need to see what's going on.'

I hadn't said how Kate was dead. Maybe he thought it was a heart attack or stroke. I couldn't tell him. He'd have to find out for himself.

From inside, his voice floated out to me. 'Oh Jesus, no.' That was all he said. He was back outside with me in a matter of seconds. 'Did you touch her?'

I shook my head. 'I could see… I checked a couple of the rooms. Emma isn't here. Except… I didn't look in the lounge room. Sorry.'

'Hey, not your job.' He sat next to me and put his warm, comforting arm around me. 'I checked. Nobody else here.'

'Emma must be at school then,' I said.

Connor cleared his throat. 'It looks to me like Kate has been dead for quite a few hours.'

'What do you mean?'

'Unless Emma was staying with a friend, she was very likely here when it happened.'

I gaped at him. 'Where is she then?'

'Bloody good question,' he said grimly. 'Look, I have to call this in, get things moving. Homicide will have to attend.

There'll be detectives and police from Bendigo as well. They'll need a statement.'

Everything else in my life flooded back in around me and I said wildly, 'I can't stay here. The pub. Andre. Lunch.' Like that was even important.

'I'm sorry, Judi, you can't leave yet,' Connor said. 'Call Andre and let him know. But you can't tell him any details. Just that Kate is deceased and you have to stay here for a while.'

I couldn't answer. I nodded, and then listened as he called it in, using his official police voice and all the official words. Deceased. Suspicious. Daughter possibly missing. Crime scene. Cordon.

Finally his call ended and he turned to me. 'You'll have to move your car. Do you want me to do it?'

'No, it's OK.' He followed me to the Benz, waited while I reversed it out on to the road and parked, then got a reel of blue and white tape from his 4WD and began to cordon off the house.

I couldn't put it off any longer. I called Andre and he answered immediately.

'What's going on? We've got lunch bookings and nothing's been done.'

'Are you OK to keep going on your own?' Why couldn't I just tell him?

'I'll manage, but... something's wrong, isn't it?'

'It's Kate. I'm sorry. She's...' *Don't say deceased.* 'She's dead. I found her.'

'Oh, fucking hell.' Andre went silent but I could hear him crying, then his phone clattered as if he'd put it down and his voice was further away. 'Yes, I'm sorry. It'll just be a few more minutes. Drinks on the house.' He came back to me. 'I can't... I have to cook. I...'

'Can you hang in there on your own a bit longer? I'll be back as soon as I can.'

'OK.' He sounded far from OK. 'Hurry, will you?' That plea had nothing to do with customers and lunch orders.

I tried to talk past the lump in my throat. 'I'll try.' I hung up and went over to Connor. 'Can you take a statement from me now? Andre is desperate for help.' And I wanted to get the hell away from this house.

He thought for a moment and then nodded. 'I'll probably get into trouble, but yes.' He pulled out his notebook and wrote down everything I told him, which wasn't much really. It didn't even fill a page. How pathetic. A woman's death in less than a page. I blinked hard and signed and dated what he'd written.

'Do you know if she had family?' he asked. 'Where they might be?'

My brain still wasn't working well but I told him she'd never mentioned anyone. 'Where's Emma? Are you going to look for her?'

'I've had a quick look around the property. No sign of her. The detectives from Bendigo are bringing some officers with them. We'll start searching properly as soon as they get here.'

'Right.' I rubbed my stinging eyes. 'Do you really think she was here when…'

'It's likely,' he said grimly. 'Look, I'm on to it. There's nothing more you can do at the moment. Go and sort out the pub.'

I thanked him and got into the Benz, drove mechanically to the pub and went inside. I felt a million years old, caught between wanting to help Andre and wanting to run away and live on a desert island somewhere.

Andre had just plated up two lunches – he muttered the table number and I took them to the customers who were clearly enjoying their free wine. Luckily for them, they didn't complain about anything or even ask for tomato sauce.

Back in the kitchen with Andre, and his drawn face was a horrible shade of grey. His mouth opened but no words came out. I couldn't speak either. We just stared at each other for a few long seconds.

Finally he said woodenly, 'You said you found her?'

'Yes, she hadn't turned up for work. I thought she'd slept in. Wasn't answering her phone.'

'Right.'

'The thing is…' It felt like the words were burrs stuck in my throat. 'She was… it was murder.'

He closed his eyes and swayed so much I thought he was going to faint. I rushed into the bistro, grabbed a chair and took it back, making him sit while I found the brandy he used for desserts and poured him a glass. He swallowed obediently and then sagged in the chair. 'I can't deal with this,' he said. 'It's not real.' He took a breath and stood up, his jaw jutting, a steely look in his eyes. 'I need to work on lunch. All right?'

'Good idea.' It was. Both of us could think about it later. Customers happy, that came first. That's what I told myself anyway.

He picked up a knife and started cutting up mushrooms, muttering to himself, and I went out to clear tables and reset. Busy work. Served the two customers some coffee. Glasses polished, cutlery lined up exactly straight, salt and pepper shakers arranged either side of the little vase of flowers. No, they were going a bit brown. I threw them out and cut more from the garden around the pavers.

All the little jobs kept me moving, my hands busy, but they didn't help my brain. *Shot in her bed, shot in her bed. Where the fuck was Emma? Why? Who did it?* I shuddered so violently that I dropped the ceramic vase. Thank God it bounced on the carpet, but water spilled and the grevilleas ended up under a chair.

As I scrabbled to mop the water with a serviette and pick the flowers up, all the while whispering, 'Fuck, fuck, fuckity fuck', two pairs of expensive, high-heeled shoes stopped in the bistro doorway.

'Hello?' sang a plummy voice.

I pulled myself up on a chair, my hip twinging, and greeted the two women at the door. They beamed at me and one of them giggled. 'Two for lunch? We don't have a booking, sorry.'

I guessed straight away. Escapees from Bronwyn's health spa. I hoped to God she wasn't going to follow them down here. The last thing I needed right now was her coming in and creating a fuss.

'Sure,' I said, forcing a smile on to my face. 'Take any table. One that's set, I mean.'

'You're a darling,' the other one said, tripping across the carpet.

It took every ounce of willpower to keep the smile on my face as I fetched menus.

Soon after, a group of four that had booked came in – they'd been to a work seminar nearby – and I took their orders as well. Thank God Charlie had the bar sorted out, as I waitressed and ferried food orders for both areas and kept the drinks flowing.

But all the while, my brain kept bouncing back to Kate and Emma. It seemed Andre was the same. The next time I was in the kitchen with a pile of dirty plates, he said, 'Listen, I know this is going to sound…'

'Just say it. It's fine.'

'Do you know what happened?'

I took a breath. 'She was shot while she was asleep, I think. I don't know any more than that.'

'Shot?' He shook his head in disbelief. 'Who the hell would want to shoot her?'

'I don't know. Connor doesn't know either.' My bones felt like they were made of cake icing. 'It's all bloody horrible.'

We stood there, lost for words again, the misery on our faces like mirrors to each other.

'Hello? Can we order dessert please?' Giggling Gertie's face appeared in the food hutch opening, tinged with curiosity.

'Of course,' I said. 'Be with you in two ticks.'

She gave us another look and disappeared back to her table.

'The show must go on, I suppose,' I said.

He didn't reply, just turned away and picked up a knife. A second later, he threw it at the back door. It clanged, bounced and landed somewhere under a cupboard.

I bit my lips together until they hurt and then went out to take the dessert order. I could tell the two health farm escapees sensed something was wrong, but like most people involved totally in their own lives and issues, they decided it wasn't worth spoiling their lunch by asking.

When the bistro was finally empty and the tables cleared and cleaned, I sat by the French doors and stared out at the garden.

Was this pub jinxed? Once upon a time I'd have laughed that off as ridiculous. Now the very thought sent crawly things up and down my spine. Andre slumped into the chair next to me and rubbed his face.

'Are we ever going to catch a break?' He sucked in a sharp breath. 'God, I didn't mean it like that.'

I grimaced. 'I know. It's other people who are dying, or having their lives fucked up, not us. But.'

'I just…' He scrunched up his face and I realised he was trying really hard not to cry.

'She was a great person, and so good to have around,' I said. I pictured her face. 'She was tough, but she loved Emma so much. I dunno, I just felt like she was a fighter. Trying to make a good life for them both, work hard, you know…'

Andre let out a strangled sound and I turned to find tears running down his face. He waved his hands but he couldn't speak. I pushed my chair next to his and hugged him as close as

I could. Tears filled my own eyes and spilled out. Kate… it just didn't make sense.

Andre was saying something against my soaked shirt. 'What was that?'

'We need to bring Emma here, look after her. Kate would want that.'

I swallowed hard. 'Andre… nobody knows where Emma is. She's disappeared. Connor and the team from Bendigo are out looking for her now.'

His face was grey with shock again, and it suddenly struck me that this was a hell of lot more than a normal reaction to a workmate's awful death. 'Listen, mate,' I said, grabbing his arm. 'Did you and Kate… were you in a relationship?'

He nodded, his lips pressed together hard. Then, 'Sort of. Well, maybe I was being hopeful…'

'God, I'm so sorry.'

'She… you're right. She was trying to create a new life here for both of them. There were lots of things she wouldn't talk about though.'

'The last few days I thought she seemed…' I struggled to describe it. 'Not scared. But worried. Like she was looking over her shoulder.' I tested the words in my head before I spoke. 'Have you got any idea who would kill her?'

He started shaking his head and then it was like he couldn't stop. 'No, no, nothing. She never said anything like that. And yet… I was sure she was hiding stuff. Why wouldn't she tell me? Or you? Maybe we could've helped.'

Too late now.

I gave him another hug and let him go. 'Look, if you want to talk, just let me know.'

'Yeah, OK. But…' He looked at me bleakly and his mouth twisted. 'Where the hell is Emma?'

Another huge question I couldn't answer. I was still trying to deal with the picture in my head of Kate shot in her bed, lying there in a pool of blood. I knew it would keep me awake for quite a few nights.

3

We finished all the cleaning up and agreed that the bistro could stay closed for the evening. If anyone in the public bar wanted food, they'd have to bring a picnic box. I didn't want to go and tell Charlie about Kate, but by the time I spoke to him, he already knew. The local gossip network on the ball already. Someone had probably already posted it on the bloody Candlebark Facebook page. I debated about closing the whole pub for the night but we couldn't afford it. I'd have to come back later and do the closing with Marie. What a joy that would be.

Normally she didn't bother me that much. I had to get over it, otherwise if she left, we'd be totally stranded. I told Charlie I'd be back to relieve him at seven, and went home, picking Mia up on the way. At the top of the road where Kate's house was, I hesitated, then kept driving. Connor would find me if he needed me.

It turned out that was only half an hour later. He pulled up outside the house in his police 4WD and sat in it for several minutes, talking on his mobile. Mia and I were in the garden; she was helping me pull out several scraggly cherry tomato plants that had failed to produce much in the weird summer we'd had. Mia was eating three tiny fruits she'd picked while I yanked each plant free and knocked the soil off its roots before throwing it into the compost. As I worked, I kept an eye on Connor's vehicle.

Finally, he emerged and walked slowly down the garden to join us.

'Long, horrible day?' I said.

He nodded. 'The worst.'

'Sorry you had to deal with that.' I searched his face but all I saw was exhaustion and sadness. 'Did you find Emma?'

He shook his head.

'Shit.'

'The good thing is we didn't find her body, but…'

I frowned, trying to work out what he was saying. 'You think she's hiding? Too scared to come out?'

'No. I'm bloody worried whoever killed her mother has abducted her.'

I gaped at him. That had never occurred to me. 'Was there any evidence to suggest that?'

'Not so far.' He huffed out a big breath. 'To be honest, we've got no idea. Emma…' He looked at me for a moment.

'I won't tell anyone,' I said. 'You know me. Mouth zipped tight.' Connor had often unloaded with me in the past – he knew I didn't gossip – so his reticence now bothered me.

'I know. It's just the Bendigo guys. Barney made a big point of saying, "Don't you go and blab to that nosy friend of yours". Like I was a bumbling dickhead who didn't know any better.'

'Barney?' I snorted. 'He of the pea-sized brain and the elephant-sized ego?' Detective Constable Barney had been a pain in the bum when Macca had been murdered. As useless as tits on a bull, as the farmers around here would say, but he still tried to show off every chance he got.

Connor smiled. 'Yeah, him.'

'Stuff him.' I put the gardening fork away and called Mia back from chasing the cat behind the shed. 'Let's go inside – are you up for a beer?'

'Better not. The homicide detectives from Melbourne are due

any minute. I'll probably have to go back to the scene and help.'

Homicide detectives from Melbourne. My skin prickled and I tried hard not to smile. That might just mean I'd see Detective Sergeant Ben Heath again.

'Yeah, not Heath, Judi. Sorry.' He patted me on the shoulder. 'They've already told us who's coming and it's not him.'

Bugger. I could really have done with one of his strong, warm hugs. And the rest. 'Oh well,' I said, trying to sound nonchalant and failing miserably. Maybe I'd call him later.

When we were sitting down in the kitchen and Mia was chomping through her dinner, I said, 'So where are you at?'

'There's got to be a motive. Something we can't see.'

'What did Master of All Police Arts Barney say?'

He smothered a grin. 'It's an ex hunting her down. The fact that nobody around here really knows her background, or where she came from, is a flag.'

'Well, there is some truth in that.' It nearly killed me to agree with Barney, but Kate hadn't said much to me either. 'I employed her based on references and, I have to confess, I never got around to checking them.'

'Fake?'

I shrugged. 'Could have been. They were from Sydney restaurants I hadn't heard of, but it wasn't like she'd claimed to be working somewhere really swanky. No point if you're applying for a job in a little country pub.'

Connor drank some tea and made a face. 'Can't I have proper coffee?'

'Not if you want to sleep tonight.'

'So why didn't you check?'

'She was a great worker right from the start.' I thought back to those first days in the kitchen with Andre. 'Knew her stuff, she clearly had some kind of cooking experience, even if there were no pieces of paper. Andre was happy, and then she also took over the waitressing when Kelly went off to uni.'

'So she made herself indispensable.'

I frowned and thought about it. 'I guess so. You mean so I wouldn't bother with the employment check. Hmm, makes sense.' Mia shoved some cucumber in her mouth and chewed while picking through the peas and throwing them to the cat. 'Mia. Eating, not throwing.' She checked the cat, who was ignoring the peas, and was forced to agree.

'The name she gave everyone here was Kate Brown, right?'

I nodded.

'They've found no Kate Browns in Sydney or Melbourne that match her.' Connor rubbed his eyes. 'Did she have a tax file number?'

'Yes. She filled out the form and it all looked fine to me.' The more Connor talked, the more Kate became a mystery woman. 'Are you saying that there's no Emma Brown either?'

'Not so far.'

'You're the cop here,' I said, leaning my chin on my hand, suddenly tired. 'Why do people change their names, fake who they are? Was Kate hiding from an ex, like Barney says?'

'It's a real possibility,' Connor said. 'Women on the run from violent partners have to change their whole lives sometimes. Names, ID, move interstate. Sole parent payments, like Kate might have been getting, can be tracked.'

'What the hell happened to confidentiality?'

'Anyone working at Centrelink, or a few other government departments, can access records if they really want to, if someone pays them enough. There's also the possibility of hackers via the dark web.' He shrugged. 'It's also possible that's where she got a fake ID, if it is fake.'

'So even if she was in hiding, somebody could track her down.' I sat back, fuming. 'I could have put her at risk by registering her as an employee.'

'Look, don't blame yourself. If someone was that bloody determined, they'd find her no matter what. This is the cyber world we live in.' He tapped his fingers on the sides of his mug. 'And if she was hiding – if – she'd be on the lookout for anyone from her past life.'

'Yeah, well… none of that answers the most important question, does it? Where the hell is Emma?'

Neither of us could answer that. Connor said, 'We've searched about a two-kilometre radius around the house so far, checked the neighbours' houses and sheds, and got nothing.'

'Do you know what time Kate was killed?'

'The acting coroner here, Dr Smythe, said his initial estimate was she'd been dead about twelve hours. He examined her body about noon, so that means around midnight.'

'She was killed while she was asleep?' I blinked away the image of Kate's head. *Will I ever get rid of it?*

'Looks like it. Probably used a silencer.' Connor got up and lifted Mia out of her chair, giving her a hug. 'What did you do today, Mia?'

'Painting,' Mia said. 'I made a picture.'

'Cool. Where is it?' Connor asked.

'On the wall,' she said proudly. 'I bring it home later.'

She ran off to find the remote and Connor sat down again, checking his watch. 'I need to go soon. Liaison to do, and all that stuff.'

I was still deep in thought, imagining what might have happened. 'So if Kate was shot, even with a silencer, did Emma hear it and climb out of her window maybe?'

'Windows were all closed and locked. But the back door wasn't.'

I frowned. 'Was that how the killer got in? Was the lock broken?'

For a moment he just looked at me, then he sighed. 'Why did

you never train to be a police officer? A detective? You could have Barney's job.'

I was in the middle of swallowing some tea, and half of it came out of my nose. I laughed and coughed, and laughed again. 'Oh my God. Surely you're kidding.'

'Nup.' Connor regarded me for several long moments, as if debating something in his head. Then he spoke slowly. 'The killer might have got in the back door, because the front door wasn't forced. But the rest of the house was like Fort Knox. Well, compared to ninety-eight per cent of houses around here.' He waved a hand. 'Do you lock up when you go out?'

'Yes. But I always thought that was my city girl habit.'

'Mm-hmm.'

'Fort Knox?'

'Yep. Proper locks on all of the windows and doors that were new. Len said he didn't put them in. So why was the back door open?' He had a glint in his eye like a challenge.

'Emma left it open?' I ventured.

'Why?'

'No idea.'

'They have an outdoor dunny.'

The one I'd heaved over. 'So… you think Emma was in the dunny?' My voice went up two notches. 'Really? What did Maestro Barney say?'

'Nothing. He and Hawke left it all to the crime scene technicians. *They* let me put on a suit and walk around and ask questions. I said I wanted to learn, being a country copper and all.'

'I see.' I could just imagine the crime scene, Connor's face red with Barney's scathing comments, and then him sneaking off to have a look around for himself. 'Seems to me like you're the one who should have Barney's job.'

'Don't want to live in Bendigo,' he said. 'I like doing a variety of things and knowing people. Helping them. I wish…'

'What?'

'If someone was after Kate, and she'd told me, I could've helped.'

'Maybe.' I thought about what he'd said. 'This all sounds… I dunno. Professional?'

'Mmm.' He sighed. 'Now, what about this phone call you had?'

I'd completely forgotten about it. 'Don't worry about it. It's nothing compared to what happened to Kate.'

He eyed me stonily. 'You're not getting away with that.' He pulled out his notebook and asked me a bunch of questions and made notes. 'You're sure you didn't recognise the voice?'

'I was thinking about it earlier, until… No, I didn't.'

He tapped his pen on the table. 'OK. I don't think it's connected to Kate, not that I can see.'

'Connected because she worked for me?'

'It was possible somebody rang you by mistake, instead of her, but she didn't have a landline.'

'Time doesn't line up either,' I said. 'By the time they called me, she'd been dead for a while.' Saying it out loud made me shiver.

'See? The Bendigo detectives wouldn't have worked that out.' He grinned. 'Detective Constable Judi Westerholme. Has a nice ring to it.'

'Oh, piss off,' I said, laughing.

His phone pinged and he checked the text. 'Homicide guys have arrived. I'd better go.'

4

As Connor reversed out of my driveway, Mia came and grabbed my leg. 'Unca Connor coming back?'

'No, sweetie. He's working.' That reminded me I had to return to the pub and close up. I sighed and got Mia ready for bed. She'd be asleep in the car before we came home again and it would be easy to carry her in already in her PJs.

My heart sank when I pulled up outside the pub. The car park was more than half-full. I went inside, Mia in tow, and found Marie in the bar, red-faced and snapping at someone.

'No, you can't have a bloody Carlton Draught, Bill. I told you the keg's run out. When the hell have I had time to put a new one on?'

Bill looked very disgruntled and accepted a stubby instead.

Marie spotted me and, if anything, her scowl got worse. 'I thought Wednesdays were quiet,' she snarled.

'They are.' I took a breath and willed myself to stay calm. 'This is very unusual.'

She turned away from the customers lined up along the bar and muttered at me. 'All they want to talk about is Kate. What the hell am I supposed to tell them?'

'Nothing.' I glanced around. 'Look, why don't you take a break, go and make yourself a sandwich in the kitchen, and I'll take over here for a while?'

'I feel like going home, I'm so exhausted.'

That was all I needed. 'I'm sorry it's been so busy. You should have called me.'

'Well, I hardly had time to scratch myself, let alone make phone calls,' she huffed.

I guessed that in fact she had been coping quite well, despite the empty keg, and wanted to play the martyr. Oh well. I gritted my teeth, forced a smile and waved her off. Mia had already made herself at home in the corner with Joleen, who often babysat for me, and her husband so that was one less thing to worry about. I served the four people waiting for drinks, brushed off questions about Kate with a simple 'Sorry, no idea what's going on' and started collecting glasses for the dishwasher.

Just as most of the locals had decided to call it a night and wander home, two more people strolled into the bar, gazing around with sharp eyes. I'd seen that look before. They were journalists. And they'd get even less out of me than the locals had. When they asked for two rooms for the night, I was sorely tempted to refuse and tell them our accommodation wasn't available, but yet again, I could hear a little cash register zinging in my head.

'Sorry, there's no food though,' I said. 'Kitchen is closed.'

'Oh right,' the thin-faced woman said, examining me. 'Is that because Ms Brown worked in your kitchen?'

'Chef's night off,' I said shortly, handing them the registration forms to fill in. Then it dawned on me – we had no night manager at the moment so I'd have to stay. Unless Marie agreed to do it.

'Nup,' she said. 'Gotta get home and feed my dogs, sorry.'

I nearly reached out and throttled her. 'Fine. I assume you don't want to stay for an extra hour on the bar then?'

She mumbled something about 'hours up and down like a…' and I cut her off. 'I'll close up early then.' I could feel my face all tight and hot, and I probably looked like a thunderstorm. I nearly kicked her out the door, and went back to cleaning up.

Just then, someone else stalked into the bar like a woman on a mission and I groaned out loud. Bloody Bronwyn from the spa. The last thing I needed. At least her whiny other half wasn't with her. She spotted me and headed over like a heat-seeking missile honing in on a target.

'Judi, I really can't have this,' she started in a loud, bossy voice.

Over her shoulder, the two journalists perked up. Just fucking great. 'Bronwyn, if you have something to say, you can come to the office and speak to me.'

'I'd rather get it out in the open,' she said. 'Literally and metaphorically.'

Oh God, really? 'You're not doing your business any favours with a tantrum.'

'You are deliberately undermining the whole philosophy of what I'm trying to do!'

I tried to keep my own voice down but even the locals still in the bar had noticeably perked up, too. 'It's not our problem if your guests come here for a decent meal.'

'You deliberately tempt them!' she spluttered. 'I've seen your fliers.'

'My what?' For a moment I couldn't think what she meant, then I remembered some photocopied brochures we did back at Christmas. We'd brainstormed words like delectable, delicious, irresistible – and used every one of them along with photos of Andre's food. 'Those are several months old. How could your guests possibly have any?'

'They've been hiding them,' she hissed. 'Wendell found them when he was cleaning.'

I stared at her for a couple of seconds, then realised what she meant. Past guests had been stashing the fliers as a 'gift' to future guests. Probably they had secret stashes of chocolate and wine, too. A laugh exploded from my mouth.

'Really? Like distress messages?'

Her face turned such a deep shade of enraged red that I thought the top of her head might explode. 'It's not funny!'

Now everyone in the bar was watching us like we were the latest episode of *Married at First Sight*. I forced my face into some kind of serious, commiserating expression. I hated to think what that actually looked like from the other side of the bar. Probably as if I was severely constipated.

'I'm sorry, Bronwyn. I know it's a problem for you. But I can't stand at the door and bar entry to them. It's not legal.'

She leaned across the bar and shook a finger in my face, which only made me angry. 'You will be very sorry about this, you mark my words!' She turned and stormed out, just before I was about to tell her what I thought of her in no uncertain terms. I stood, head bowed, for a few moments, trying to calm down, and getting even angrier at the trembling in my hands. Bloody woman!

'Judi, are you OK?' It was Joleen, her round face full of concern. Mia was with her husband still, but staring at me with big eyes.

'Yep, good as gold,' I said, gripping the dishtowel with both hands and wringing it into the sink. It served at least to get my hands under control.

'How the hell she has any customers at all is beyond me,' Joleen said. 'You look like you need a drink.'

'Bloody good idea,' I said, and managed a grin at her. Then I noticed everyone else still watching me. 'It's fine, no worries.' I waved a hand at them all and tried not to scowl at the two reporters who were now huddling together, muttering. 'Do you two journos want a drink?'

That made everyone in the bar take a good squiz at them, as if imprinting their faces for future avoidance. The journos, who didn't dispute my outing of them, ordered wine, one red and one white, and I poured myself a Jack Daniels, straight. One good swallow and I started to feel better, going back to putting glasses in the dishwasher. I couldn't wait for this horrible day to end.

'Excuse me. Do you have any rooms?'

What now? Not more bloody journalists… I swung around, ready to fire off some terse words and stopped, mouth open. It was Detective Swan, who'd last been in Candlebark investigating Macca's murder. I glanced hopefully behind him, but it wasn't Heath. It was a pants-suited woman whose dark eyes flicked around the bar, taking in all the regulars and narrowing at the journalists. My heart resumed its normal thump, albeit a bit skippier.

'Sure. How are you, Detective Swan?'

Like an orchestrated wave, every head in the bar turned again and stared at him. Tonight was certainly giving everyone plenty of wood for the gossip fire. He ignored them all – years of practice – and smiled thinly. 'Fine. Didn't expect to find myself back here though.' He'd never been very friendly, just efficient and a bit impatient.

'I have two rooms free – I guess you want two?'

The woman arched her eyebrows.

'Yes, thanks,' Swan said. 'Any food?'

'Sorry, no.' I was about to offer a sandwich and remembered I'd refused the journalists. 'Come and sign in, and I'll give you your keys.'

They followed me to the reception desk, filled out the forms and I handed over the two key rings, explaining the two marked keys were for the front door. Then I added, 'You should probably know that the other house guests tonight are journalists.'

Swan grunted and the woman just nodded, then they took their small bags and headed upstairs. I checked the second form. 'Detective Constable Lauren Chandler.' She was as unsmiling as Swan. Perhaps it was catching.

Why couldn't it have been Heath?

I shook myself, returned to the bar and swigged down some more JD. At this rate, I'd finish the bottle. What else could go haywire tonight? But instead Joleen came over, carrying Mia, and asked if I would like her to take Mia home and look after her for the night.

I nearly cried with relief. 'Thanks a million. I'm stuck here all night now, with guests in. There's not even anyone I can call to fill in.'

'You need a new night manager,' Joleen's husband said from behind her.

I couldn't remember his name but I forced a smile. 'Yes, I'll add that to my list.' Along with a new car and a holiday in the Bahamas. But I knew what he meant. Macca had had Bob to help out, but Bob was in an aged care place now.

I retrieved Mia's bag of toys and spare clothes from behind the bar and handed it to Joleen, then gave Mia a cuddle and a kiss before they left. My shoulders sagged. It was great to have Mia taken care of, but I still had a night's work ahead of me.

Naturally, the journos were the last to leave the bar. I'd served them two more wines each, plus four bags of chips, but thankfully they'd stayed in their own corner all evening and not tried to approach any of the locals. I couldn't detect a stagger, or even a small totter, in them as they made their way up to their rooms. I did the till, cleaned the bar and all the tables, and then headed for the bistro to set up for tomorrow morning's breakfast. Finally, close to midnight, I crawled into bed.

Even though I felt exhausted, I lay awake for ages. Had Kate said anything I'd missed? I could have helped somehow, if only… Where was Emma? I couldn't bear the thought that she was hiding in the bush somewhere, cold and distraught, with nobody to turn to. My hip ached and I tossed and turned again, trying not to let the image of Kate creep into my head again. I was almost too scared to go to sleep, in case I dreamed about it.

Thankfully, I finally dropped off and my phone alarm woke me at 6am. I dragged myself out of bed, had a quick shower and found a clean polo shirt in the laundry cupboard. Downstairs, the first thing I did was put on the coffee, and nearly jumped out of my pants when Swan loomed up behind me.

'Fuck, can you at least warn me?' I snapped, my heart like a mad racehorse.

'Sorry.' At least he had the grace to actually look apologetic. 'I'm starving, and desperate for coffee, too.'

'We do have one of those capsule things.' I pointed to the little machine in the corner.

'No, percolated is good, thanks.'

We both stood in silence and watched the last dribbles into the carafe, then I seized it and poured us both full mugs. I fetched the milk from the fridge for mine, while he piled in three spoons of sugar. He gestured at a nearby table so I decided to join him and get the questioning over with.

'Kate Brown worked here?' he asked.

'Yes. Since before Christmas. She was really great.' I suddenly remembered her big laugh and the way she snorted sometimes and made us all laugh even harder, and gulped my coffee. 'Have you got any idea…?'

'Not yet. Did you know Brown wasn't her original name?'

'Um, no.' I wasn't going to dump Connor in it.

'How did you check her credentials?'

'She had written references and some certificates that she said were in her maiden name. And a valid tax file number.'

'Mmm.'

'Was she in witness protection or something? Because if she was, it all went to hell for her.'

'Mmm.'

I sat back and folded my arms. I'd been here before. *You want something, you give me something.*

'What time did she leave here on Tuesday evening?'

'Afternoon. She worked the lunch shift but we had no bookings for dinner so she went home.' I thought back. 'I don't know the exact time. I wasn't here. Probably about 2.30. Check with Andre.'

'Mmm.' He wrote something in his notebook.

I leaned forward and tapped the table hard. 'Listen, have you found Emma yet?'

'Ms Brown's daughter?' He gazed at me for a long moment. 'No. Do you know where she might be?'

'No, and I'm bloody worried. Aren't you?'

'Of course.' He managed to look slightly affronted.

'You don't think she's hurt and lying in the bush somewhere? Did Kate's killer take her?'

'We do take all of those possibilities into consideration.'

I glared. 'I forgot about the stick up your arse. You know, people around here will be a lot more helpful if you treat them nicely.'

His face reddened but he glared back. 'And I forgot about your entrenched hostility. Vinegar and honey, Ms Westerholme. Works both ways.'

There was a brief standoff and then we both seemed to give up the bullshit at the same time. 'Sorry,' I said. 'Old habits.'

'You're right,' he said. 'Country people are often more willing to help.'

I went and fetched the carafe and poured us more coffee. 'Cereal is over there. I'll go and get the fruit and stuff for breakfast. You did say you were starving.'

He actually smiled. 'That'd be great. Er…'

I waited.

'Did she ever say anything about someone harassing her? Trouble with anyone, local or otherwise? Any problems at all?'

I thought for a few seconds. 'No. She was quite reserved.

Didn't really talk about herself or Emma at all. She seemed... hardened, as if something had happened and she'd got through it by being really tough and just gritting her teeth.' It made my skin prickle to say it out loud, and the echoes of my own life made it worse. 'She was protective of Emma, but Emma was a tough cookie, too, from what I knew of her.' It was true, and I hoped like hell that toughness was helping her survive out there.

Swan flicked through his notebook. 'I have Andre's mobile. I'll ring him and ask him to come earlier.'

I nodded and went to gather up all the breakfast food from the fridges. It didn't take long to fill bowls with tinned fruit and jugs with juice and milk. All the while, I thought about Andre and his reaction to the news of Kate's death. I'd had no idea they were moving into a relationship, but then these days I wasn't in the bistro much. How much of her life had she revealed to Andre? Maybe very little. Maybe they hadn't progressed to the tell-all life story stage. And now they never would.

I sighed heavily. There were times when I really had to wonder why life was such a bowl of shit for some people. I stood in the kitchen, leaning against a bench, and quickly ate some muesli while I went through the day's jobs in my head.

By the time I went through the bistro, Lauren Chandler had joined Swan and the journos were just staggering in. They didn't look impressed with the cereal and toast on offer, but they weren't getting bacon and eggs. I went to the office to double-check I'd locked away the takings last night. I'd been so tired I could have forgotten, but they were in the safe.

I stood by the desk, rubbing my hands on my shirt and wondering why I felt so... antsy. Was it because Mia was at Joleen's? No, that was fine. She loved it there. It was Emma. I looked at my watch. More than thirty hours since her mum had been shot, and she was still missing. I pulled out my phone to call Connor and put it away again. Connor couldn't tell me any more than Swan just had.

I came out of the office just as Swan and Chandler were leaving. 'Are you going to be staying tonight?' I asked.

They glanced at each other. 'No, probably not,' Swan said.

'That was a quick investigation.'

Swan grimaced and Chandler stared at me impassively. 'We have to go back to Melbourne to follow up on information and do reports. The others in the team will be staying close by and monitoring the search for Emma. We'll probably be back in a day or so.'

'No leads?'

'Maybe when I talk to Andre. I'll be here at 10.30. Tell him not to go anywhere.'

'Sure.' I went into the bistro and found the journos sitting over toast crumbs and empty coffee mugs, madly tapping on their phones. 'More coffee?'

'That'd be great,' the woman answered.

The man looked up from his phone. 'Have they found the girl yet?'

'Her name is Emma,' I said. 'No.'

I wasn't in the mood to be questioned for the next edition of either paper, so I put the coffee pot back and started cleaning up. Andre would be here in half an hour and I wanted the kitchen to be ready. He had enough to deal with without me leaving a mess. Above me, I heard the faint sound of the vacuum cleaner – so Joyce and Margot were on the job already. I could always rely on them, thank God.

Andre arrived, looking awful, like he hadn't slept at all. I poured him a coffee and shoved it into his hand.

'Have you had breakfast?

He shook his head.

'Right, sit down there and I'll make you some toast.' I

virtually had to push him on to a chair and he watched with dull eyes while I toasted and buttered some of the Vienna bread from yesterday for him.

'Thanks,' he said, but he didn't pick it up.

'Eat,' I urged. 'Or else I might have to cook something.' Not that I was a terrible cook, but Andre had high standards.

He managed a little smile and picked up the toast, eating it like it was poisoned. I sat with him and stayed silent, making sure he kept eating.

'Swan is coming soon to ask you some questions.'

'Yeah, he called me.'

I updated him on what had been happening, including the four guests overnight, and he nodded. 'Swan knows you and Kate had got friendly. He thinks you can shed some light on her past.'

'Friendly. Huh.' He drank some coffee and stared down at his shoes. 'She said very little. I was hoping she'd open up a bit more. Now, it seems ominous, doesn't it? That she was clearly hiding stuff from me, from you, too. And it has to be something in her past that got her killed. You don't just walk into someone's house and shoot them because you feel like it. Not around here, anyway.'

'You're probably right.' Swan suddenly appeared in the doorway, making me jump, and I wondered how long he'd been eavesdropping. 'Can I talk to you now?'

'Sure,' Andre said. 'You probably heard me say Kate didn't tell me much.'

'Anything will help at this point.'

I took the hint from Swan's glare at me and retreated to the kitchen, making a bustling noise with plates for a few seconds and then standing still so I could listen.

Andre usually told me everything. Was there something he was holding back, something so bad about Kate that he couldn't even tell me?

5

Swan started with all the usual questions about Kate, how long she'd been working here, what she did, and then, 'What time did she leave that day?'

'About 2.30. She wanted to be home for Emma getting off the bus. She always met her at the stop.'

'Do most parents do that for high school kids?'

'I don't know. Probably not.'

'So she was careful about stuff like that. Her house was well locked up.'

'Not well enough,' Andre said bitterly.

'No. Did you see her later?'

'Yes. I went over to her house for dinner, since the bistro was closed here. She liked to cook for me. Said it gave me a break.'

I frowned. He hadn't mentioned that to me.

'What time did you leave?'

'About nine.'

'You weren't in the, er, habit of staying over?'

'No.'

'What time did you get home? Can anyone verify you were there?'

My mouth dropped open. Surely they didn't think Andre did it? That was ridiculous!

'I live alone,' Andre snapped. There was a small silence. 'I looked up some recipes on the net. My computer history should verify that.'

'We'll check it, to be sure.'

'Knock yourselves out,' Andre said. 'You already know I have a record. Is that what this is about?'

I wanted to rush out there and shout at Swan to stop being so stupid, but it would just make things worse. I knew Andre. He would never do something like this. He'd been inside for drugs, and that was a long time ago. As he'd told me: when he was young and bloody stupid.

'You know how it works,' Swan said. 'We have to eliminate you. Standard procedure. Same with your DNA.'

Andre didn't reply.

'What did Ms Brown tell you about her past? Where she'd lived before, worked, who Emma's father was? That kind of thing?'

Andre sighed heavily. 'Not much. She'd been living in Sydney. Her certificates and references she gave Judi were from Sydney. They were old, though, in her maiden name. Well, that's what she said.'

'NSW police have told us her original name was Lisa Silverson. Brown wasn't fake – she'd changed it legally.'

'Oh. Well, she never said anything about that.'

'She was married to Emma's father, Craig Silverson, divorced when Emma was two years old. At some point she got into a relationship with a Mikey Koslov, also known as Mikhail Koslov. He's got a record in Sydney, been in gaol on and off, hung out with a bad crew. She'd reported him once for domestic abuse and then dropped the charges.' Swan ruffled pages as if checking back through his notes. 'That's common. Women get threatened with worse if they don't.'

I stood, fuming at Swan's tone. It might be an everyday event for him, but for others, abuse was soul-destroying, and often life-destroying. To think that Kate had endured that and probably had to run away was bloody appalling, even worse that she wasn't able to tell us. Too bloody scared, probably. I thought of Connor wishing he'd known more so he could've done more to protect her.

'So you think it was this Mikhail who killed her?' Andre sounded like he was choking.

'No. He's inside again at the moment, has been for ten months. Another four years to go.'

'Good. He no doubt deserves it. What's he in for?'

For a moment I didn't think Swan was going to answer him, then he said, 'Drug dealing. We think Ms Brown, or Mrs Silverson, left not long after he went into gaol. That was back in September last year. We don't know where she was between then and when she arrived here. She didn't say anything to you? No family mentioned, or friends she could have been in contact with?'

'No. I actually saw her phone contact list once. It only had people on it from Candlebark. I thought that was a bit odd, but I didn't ask her. She…'

'Yes?'

'She didn't like questions. She'd change the subject.'

'Emma never chatted to you about moving, or friends or school?'

'She was like her mum.'

'Like she'd been warned by her mother not to say anything?'

A pause. 'Yeah, I think so. She was a really quiet kid. Strong, like Kate. Just got on with things, like starting at a new school and enduring it. Not sure she'd even made any friends there yet.'

'In case they asked questions?'

'Maybe.'

'So you left her house at 9pm, and did you hear from her again?'

'No.'

'She didn't call you for help?'

'No.'

'She sounds like a very unfriendly woman, for her own reasons. What made you become friends?' Swan sounded purely curious now.

Another pause. 'We just got on really well. She worked hard here, and she really liked that Judi and I were trying to make a go of this place. She said she wanted to help that happen. Not many people are like that. They just want to do their hours and take home their pay.'

Like Moaning Marie. I shifted on my feet, easing my hip, and wondering if we had any bookings today. If we did, Kate would have written them in the book in her neat handwriting. I swallowed the lump in my throat.

Noises in the bistro told me the questioning was over. Swan said an officer would be around to check Andre's computer. Then Andre asked, 'What are you doing about looking for Emma?'

'We've got another search of the area going now, widening it out. But we also have to find who was responsible for Ms Brown's murder. That won't be easy.'

'Why not?'

'It was… there's no evidence so far.' Swan cleared his throat. 'Ms Westerholme?'

I emerged from the kitchen and Swan told us a technician would be there shortly to take swabs from us for elimination, since we'd both been in the house.

After Swan left, Andre grimaced at me. 'That wasn't much fun,' he said. 'Did you hear all of it?'

'Yep. I agree with you. Kate was really unwilling to talk about anything in her past. I didn't worry about it too much, because I don't either.' I waved an arm around. 'Candlebark has great people in it, but I hate the gossip network.'

'The Facebook page is the worst,' he agreed. 'But maybe they can use it to get the word out about Emma.'

I pushed my fingers into my temples, trying to force back a headache. 'Where the hell is she? Why would this maniac take her with him?'

Andre clenched his hands. 'Fuck, I can't even think about that. I just pray she's in the bush, hiding, and they'll find her soon. Surely with the dogs…'

I took a breath. 'They'll find her. They have to. Now, we have to sort lunch.'

'Six bookings for lunch, six for dinner. Unless the house guests are staying?'

'Cops have checked out, but not the journos. They still might, though. Not much to report on here now.' That reminded me and I filled him in on Bronwyn's tirade.

'You're kidding. She'd better not come in here and start on me.' He opened the fridge and pulled out the tray of fresh vegetables and then switched on the fryer. 'Swan has put me way behind. I'd better get my arse into gear.'

'And I have to change a keg over, or else get Charlie to do it. See you later.' I left him to his peeling and chopping and went to see how the other staff were going.

Joyce and Margot had finished the two rooms Swan and Chandler had been in and Joyce smiled at me sympathetically. 'How you going, love? That was shocking news about Kate.'

'Yes.' I took the laundry from her. 'I'll take that down. I have no idea if the other two are staying another night or not.'

I left them to it, dealt with a huge pile of laundry, then met Charlie in the bar, went through the stock and did a hundred other small pub-running jobs.

Connor arrived just on midday and ordered a steak sandwich and chips from Andre before sitting down with me.

'No news about Emma?' I asked.

'No. God, I don't want to think about the killer grabbing her.'

I didn't either.

'One little possibility though... We found a bag in Kate's bedroom. Packed and ready to go, like pregnant women do when their baby is due.'

'And?'

'I mean, packed and ready. All her ID, copies of papers, two changes of clothes, a toilet bag with spares of everything.'

'A running-away bag, you mean.'

He nodded. 'But Emma didn't have one in her room. I reckon she used hers.'

I sat up, a small flutter of hope in my stomach. 'But that means she's on the run.'

'Yeah.'

'What do the others say?'

'They say it's unlikely. She would have been seen hitch-hiking or catching a bus. Someone would've seen her by now.' He scratched his arms. 'I think I got caught out there in poison ivy while we were looking for her.'

'We don't have that in Australia,' I said. 'Probably nettles, or maybe spurge. They both irritate the skin.'

'I bow to your greater gardening knowledge,' he said with a grin. Andre came in with the food ready and Connor stood, taking the bag. 'Thanks. Can you put it on my tab? I'll pay it later.'

'Keep us up to date about Emma, will you?' I said.

'Sure.' He glanced at Andre. 'And let us know if you remember anything else Kate told you, please.'

Andre nodded. After Connor had left, I asked him, 'Did you ever see Kate or Emma with a packed bag in their rooms? Or the lounge?'

'No.' He frowned. 'They were leaving?'

I explained what Connor had said, and added, 'The thing is, if Emma was OK, she might've managed to get back inside the house later and grab her bag.'

Andre shrugged, like it was all too much for him to think about right now. 'Yeah, maybe. I'll get on with lunch, OK?'

'OK.' I stared after him. I didn't like the way his shoulders bowed, or the despair in his voice. Andre was usually my shoulder to lean on. I straightened and gave myself a mental shake. Well, now I'd just have to be his for a change.

I set up for lunch while I thought about our staffing issues. I had no choice but to stick with Moaning Marie for now, and if the bistro picked up, I could look for a waitress. In the meantime, I'd have to do a bit of everything. After a quiet lunch period, Andre finished in the kitchen and sat at one of the tables, a half-full glass of beer in front of him, shredding a paper serviette. I sank down on to the seat opposite him and we sat in silence for a couple of minutes.

I kept thinking about the bush around Candlebark, how thick and dark it was even when the sun was shining. It had clouded over around midday and the paved area outside was full of gloomy shadows. Would Emma really have run into the bush? She was a city girl. If she was lost…

I owed it to Kate to give it a decent try.

I said abruptly, 'I don't know about you but I can't sit here like this. I need to go and look for Emma myself. There's no reason the guy who killed Kate would have taken Emma. I just have this gut feeling she's out there somewhere. Hiding.' I'd said on the run before. *Or lost*. I liked hiding better.

'How are you going to find her when the others couldn't?' He sounded skeptical.

'No idea. But I need to get out of the pub for a while anyway, so I might as well look for her while I'm out.' I searched his drawn face for signs of interest but there was nothing, which actually made me more determined. 'You have to come with me.'

'What?' He stared at me. 'I'm not a bush walker. I'm not even a normal walker.'

'Do you want to help me find Emma or not?' No reply. 'Don't we owe Kate a damn good try, at least?'

'Fine!' he snapped. 'I suppose it's not going to kill me.'

I nearly let fly with a few choice insults about his childishness, but I knew that underneath this rudeness was a heap of grief and pain. Nothing I could say would help just yet, but maybe walking and feeling like we were at least trying would make a difference. The sun had emerged again, but the air held a crisp autumn-like chill, promising a cold night.

I decided to take my binoculars and drive up to the lookout a few kilometres outside of Candlebark. It would be a start. I followed a gravel road that passed a lot of paddocks and a few houses, some of which looked quite new. The land was mostly small acreage blocks, probably bought by tree-changers who thought life in the country would be relaxing. At one point we had to stop for a farmer who was moving a flock of sheep to another paddock. The sheep streamed across in front of us like a woolly wave, three busy dogs nipping at their heels while the farmer leaned on a long stick and let out the occasional whistle.

He nodded hello at us, then shut the gate and followed the sheep and his dogs across the grass. I put the Benz in gear and kept going to the turnoff, then followed the signs up the hill to the small parking area. For a moment I thought Andre was going to refuse to get out, then he joined me and we walked up the rough steps to the lookout.

The hill wasn't very high but it gave us a view across the valley and up to the bigger hills in the distance. From here, the farms were undulating patchworks of brown and green, and

Candlebark was a toy town. The bush, however, was a dark, brooding stain that spread across the landscape in all directions. I'd never realised how much of it there was.

Andre was silent and I glanced at him, but his face was turned away. I reached out for his hand; it felt cold and lifeless. 'Are you OK? You look terrible.'

'I feel like it's my fault,' he finally said.

'How can it be? She never told you what was going on!'

'No, but I knew something was. I've known a few crims in my time, not so much now but when I was younger.' He rubbed his eyes. 'There were a couple of things she said that made me wonder, but she shut me down really fast. I didn't want to upset her. If she was starting a new life, you know, the last thing she'd want was nosy questions.'

Andre knew about nosy questions, prying people. He was a trained chef now, and one of my best friends. I'd never cared that he had a record, but it was like anything – it marked everything, one way or another. Like abusive parents did, or any abuse. You never quite scrubbed it away.

'You didn't tell Swan what she said, though.'

His mouth thinned. 'It was nothing concrete. Anyone else probably wouldn't have picked it up. He just would have made assumptions.'

'Can you tell me?'

'What for?'

'Humour me.'

'Well,' he said, frowning, 'once she said she could never go back to Sydney. Not would, could. And another time, when I said something about all the locks on the house, she said something about how they didn't stop eyes.'

'You mean she thought someone was watching her?' I shivered, thinking about the guy who'd been staking out the pub with his rifle a few months ago.

'I don't know. That time, I did ask, and she just laughed and said she'd been watching too many horror movies, but Emma rolled her eyes, and not in a funny way.'

I pulled out the binoculars and scanned the hills and valley slowly, thinking and remembering. One of the worst gangland murders in Melbourne had been a woman who'd been shot in her driveway in front of her kids. It took years before the detectives discovered it had been a mistake, and the wrong woman had been killed. Had that been what happened to Kate? But you could hardly get a house wrong out here. There weren't enough of them. Kate's house wasn't even in town.

All the same, shot in her bed. That was pretty damn cold-blooded. Not the result of an argument, or a love affair gone wrong. Would a demented ex come and kill her like that? Usually there was a big fight first, or attempts to force the woman to return, or make amends, or… It just didn't feel like the ex-husband.

If Heath could read my mind right now, I knew what he'd say. My hands tightened on the binoculars. *Stay out of it, Judi. You could get hurt. What about Mia?*

But it was too close to home.

And I couldn't let it go.

6

There was no sign of movement below us. The bush was like an impenetrable lumpy grey-green blanket. I let out a huge sigh and Andre said, 'Emma will turn up. She's a tough kid.' He pointed at the swathes of dark trees across the hills. 'She's not lost in there anywhere. I reckon she's hitched to Melbourne. I have a feeling she said they have friends there.'

It was the first I'd heard of it. 'Do you know who they are? How to get in touch?'

'No idea.'

We both subsided into silence and made our way back to the car and drove to the pub. The journos' gear was still in their rooms, so I assumed they were staying, and had it confirmed when they bowled in a little later. My opinion of them rose a little when I heard they'd been helping the search teams.

Just before I was about to pick up Mia from childcare, Charlie called to me from the bar. 'There's a guy here wants a room for a couple of nights.' His voice sounded a little odd so I went straight in to see what was going on. At the far end of the bar, chatting with Scottie and Old Jock, was a young guy, early thirties, with curly brown hair receding at the temples and a round, cheery face. He was drinking beer and laughing, while Scottie and Jock didn't seem quite so amused.

I went over to them. 'You all know each other?'

'Nup,' Old Jock said. 'This fella just arrived.' He was a bit too quick to deny it.

I glanced at Scottie and got a stony glare in return. I knew he still held a bit of a grudge about what happened to Macca, but I ignored him.

'I'm after a room,' the stranger said with a grin. 'Coupla nights, if that's OK?'

It actually wasn't. I'd have to stay over again. Although since the journos were still here… He was perfectly friendly, almost charming. I couldn't very well refuse. 'If you come out to the front desk, I'll get you to sign in and give you a room key. Will you want dinner?'

'I can eat at the bar, I guess?' he said.

'Of course. Bar menu is just the basics, though. Bistro food is good.'

'Great.' He followed me out to the desk and filled in the registration form, giving me his credit card to run through the machine. I handed him the keys for the room Swan had been in, which was away from the journos. I'd found it was better to separate guests if possible, in case of noise. After he'd filled in the form, while I was fiddling with his credit card, I could feel his eyes on me, watching intently. When I finally glanced up, he didn't look away, just smiled. 'Thanks a million,' he said. 'Nice little place, Candlebark.'

'It is. Very quiet most of the time, although we're hoping to attract a few tourists.' I was used to this kind of pointless chit-chat by now.

'What's with the health farm up the hill? Full of trendies?'

Trendies? 'I'm not sure who stays there really.'

'Are you the pub owner?'

'Part owner,' I said. I was liking the chit-chat less and less. Underneath, this guy reminded me a little of Swan. Hard as galvanised nails. Although, come to think of it, this guy in front of me was happy Ronald McDonald in comparison to Swan. 'Thank you,' I said, handing the card back, 'Mr...' I glanced down at the registration sheet.

'Winter, Chris Winter.' He thrust out his hand and I had to shake it. He had a hard grip but he eased off as soon as he realised he was overdoing it. My hand was released, but it tingled a bit.

'Nice to meet you,' I said. I kept the smile fixed on my face, wondering why he made me uneasy. 'I'm sure you'll enjoy the food. We have a night manager if you need anything after hours, but no room service.' I didn't tell him I was the reluctant night manager. It seemed better not to. I'd asked both Charlie and Marie about taking the job over tonight, but Charlie's wife was very pregnant and he didn't want to leave her. Marie always said no to anything extra.

'Beauty!' Winter said, and went back into the bar.

I wiped my hand on my jeans and checked the form. Christopher Winter, address in Balwyn in Melbourne, mobile phone number and car rego supplied. The credit card with Christopher Winter on it had gone through so it wasn't overdrawn or stolen. I had arranged for Mia to stay with Joleen again, and I suddenly wanted to go there, too, and crawl into the little bunk bed with her.

I picked Mia up and we went home for a while to eat and watch some TV and play with the cat. All the things we usually did. But when I said she was off to Joleen's again, she dug her heels in. 'Bum wants to stay with you!' Her eyes filled with tears and she glared at me.

'Just one more night, I promise.' I couldn't bear the look of betrayal on her face. It reminded me all over again that Emma was out there somewhere, alone.

'No, I want you to stay here.' The tears spilled and she wailed so loudly that the cat scarpered out the door. 'Don't like Jolly's bed,' she sobbed.

Shit. I knew I should put my foot down, but I just couldn't. The poor kid was in childcare most days and sometimes it felt like we hardly had any time together. Most working mums were stuck with the same problem. Knowing that didn't help. I had a wailing three-year-old and I felt as guilty as hell. So I called Andre.

'Three guests?' He sounded surprised. He hadn't been taking much notice of anything outside the kitchen, I supposed.

'Do we legally have to have a night manager sleeping there?'

'Er… probably. What if there was a fire?'

'True,' I said glumly. I could hear things crackling and boiling in the background. 'Look, don't worry, I'm sure she will calm down. I'll bring her to the pub with me and drop her off at Joleen's later.'

'No,' he said quickly. 'I'll stay. It's fine. It's only one night. Means I can put my feet up after the bistro has closed and have a couple of drinks. No driving, Mum!'

'Thanks, Andre, you're a life saver. I'll be there shortly to do the dinner shift.' I smiled at Mia who seemed to magically pick up that she'd got her way and turned off the water tap. She still gave me a suspicious look though.

The dinner shift went quietly and I left by eight, then as soon as Mia had a quick bath and about two hundred stories, I put her to bed with Bum and the night light. I collapsed on the couch and poured myself some wine. My brain jumped from one thing to another – Kate, Emma missing, bills at the pub, my brother's death. I wanted Heath there beside me to tell me I was worrying too much. My mobile phone sat there silently. I could send him a text, or stand by the back door and call him.

Why hadn't he called me? It was times like this I ached for him, wondering why the hell I didn't move back to Melbourne where we could have dinner or just hang out like a normal couple. He'd understand how I felt about seeing Kate dead.

A patter of little footsteps and Mia came trotting into the lounge room, dragging Bum by the ears. 'Juddy, crying.'

I dragged myself upright. 'You're crying, Mia? What's wrong?'

'Somebody crying,' she said. 'Not me, see?' She put her face close to mine and pointed at her eyes.

'Right, well, it's good you're not crying. Did you have a bad dream?'

'No!' She glared at me. 'Somebody crying out there.' She pointed at her bedroom.

'You mean outside your window?'

'Yes!'

'It's probably the wind, or maybe it's a possum.'

'Possums cry?' She scrunched up her nose. 'Why?'

Actually, possums growled and had fights and made all kinds of weird noises. They would do well in horror movies. 'I'll come and chase it away, all right?'

She glanced at the door. 'You going *outside*?'

'Just for a moment, with a big broom.'

'You sweep possums away?'

I laughed, and leant over to give her a cuddle. 'Very gently, all right? You hop back into bed and I will fix the possum.'

'OK.'

I got her back in bed, tucked her in with Bum, and promised to sweep really quickly. I slipped on my gumboots in case the grass was wet and grabbed the broom and the torch on the shelf by the back door, going out and shutting the door behind me. The torch beam was bright and illuminated the yard and trees with a large circle of light. I swung it around as I edged along the side of the house, across the grass and past Mia's window. The fruit trees there showed no signs of possums, not even scats underneath, but I checked the apples twice since they were close to ripening. Nothing.

I aimed the torchlight around the rest of the area, checking the shed door was shut, nothing was in the compost pile and the back gate was also shut. Strange. I didn't doubt Mia had heard something, but what it had been was a mystery. I shivered, and scuttled back inside as fast as I could, locking the door after me. That still didn't satisfy me. I reassured her first, showing her the broom and saying I'd swept away the possums for her so she could go to sleep now, then I kept the heavy torch in my hand as I went through the rest of the house and checked every cupboard and wardrobe, and under my bed. Only then did I relax.

Sort of. I drank more wine, fidgeted, tried to put my feet up on the couch and do some deep breathing. What a waste of time that was. I should've brought home the accounts to go through again, so I could decide who we'd pay and who I could persuade to wait a bit longer.

When the phone rang, I almost gasped with relief. Something to stop me going around the bend. 'Hello.' Hoping it was Andre or Connor.

'Think you're fucken smart, eh?' a harsh, metallic voice snarled. 'You'd better watch yourself. Accidents happen.' And then a low laugh that made all the hair on my arms stand up like spikes.

I couldn't even say, 'What?' or swear at whoever it was. I was still standing there in disbelief, long seconds after he'd hung up. I was sure it was a *he*. Then I came back to the room and wanted to smash the phone against the wall. Fuck!

Instead I found my mobile and pressed the screen with shaking fingers. Thank God Connor answered in a few seconds.

'Judi, hi.'

'He… it… they…'

'Another call?'

'I… yes. Shit!' I nearly screamed it, then clapped a hand over my mouth. The last thing I wanted was to wake Mia when I was in this state of panic.

'OK, OK, take a few breaths.'

'I don't want to –'

'Judi, breathe. Take a breath, suck it in, let it out. Come on, you're tougher than this. Breathe.' His calm voice was like a hand on my head, settling me down. I dropped on to the couch.

'It was him again. I'm sure it was a him.'

'Tell me what he said.'

I related the words, near enough, and added, 'And this time he laughed, like threatening me was funny.'

'You have all your doors and windows locked?'

'Yes, I just did it before the call. I made sure.' I was still trying to breathe normally, and sat on my free hand to settle it.

'Good. I'm coming over, all right? I'll be there in five minutes.'

'Oh God, thanks.'

'No worries.' He hung up and I kept hold of the phone, ready to call him again if I heard anything at all and watching the time tick over. Finally, I heard his 4WD and then a light knock at the door. I checked it was him before opening.

'You took six minutes and thirty seconds,' I said.

'But who's counting?' He smiled and finally I smiled back.

'OK, I'm being neurotic,' I said.

'Hey, no, you're not!' He had on his solemn police face, which made me feel safer. 'Calls like this have to be taken seriously. Never think you're overreacting. And really, out here in Woop Woop, someone who goes to the trouble of threatening calls has to be dealt with. It's not going to a random prankster.'

I made a face at him. 'You are *not* making me feel better.'

'Um, yeah, sorry.'

'Who do you think it is?' I asked, watching his face closely. I can usually tell when he's dodging the question or fibbing.

'Who have you had trouble with in the pub lately?'

'Nobody! Not even any fights in the bar. Oh, hang on…' Bronwyn yelling at me in front of everyone. 'Bronwyn from the health spa place. But she's always upset with me. And besides, I'm sure it wasn't a woman.'

'What about her partner, Wendell?'

I tried to remember what he looked like, hovering behind his wife. 'He's pretty skinny and small. Not much of a threat.'

'Those are the kinds of guys who might try other ways to frighten someone.'

'He's good at glaring.' I recalled his buggy eyes and smiled a little. 'But why would he bother?'

Connor shrugged. 'Their business hasn't been doing too well, I've heard.'

'Bronwyn definitely blames me for that.' I thought about the voice again. 'I want it to be him, to make it simple. But the level of hate was… horrible.'

'Well, at this point I would say don't answer your landline anymore. If I want you, I'll call your mobile, or send a text if I can't get through.' Connor got up with a groan.

'You sound in pain.'

'I overdid the jogging yesterday, and then we were climbing hills and gullies, looking for Emma.'

'Any sign of her? Anything at all?'

He shook his head. 'They brought a dog in this afternoon but I think any scent would have gone by now. It rained last night.'

I rose to see Connor out, all the while wishing he'd stay longer. Guard the house all night. I tried to shake it off. 'I'm really worried about Emma. It's weird how she's just disappeared. Have you heard any more about Kate's past in Sydney?'

'Apparently her ex-husband was working for a guy who's known to police but they've never been able to get enough on him.'

'Drugs?'

'Guns more than anything.'

'And Kate was shot.' I stared at him for a moment. 'Was she in witness protection?'

'Not from what we know,' he said. 'And she'd never been arrested, or even suspected of any crimes. She kept a really low profile.'

'On purpose maybe. What if she did know stuff and was on the run?'

It was his turn to stare at me. 'How did you know that was one of the theories the homicide guys were discussing?'

I shivered. 'Surely the police up there would have told you.'

Connor frowned. 'Yes, well… It was just something they were throwing around as a possible motive. They're also looking closer to home, of course. Relationships, that kind of thing.'

But Kate's only relationships here were with people at the pub. Andre? Swan and Chandler were so serious, and such hard liners – I could imagine them suspecting him. It explained the way Swan questioned him. Well, I knew Andre had nothing to do with Kate's murder, and I'd make sure Swan knew it, too. Even if he did see it as interfering again. Too bad.

'Look, I have to go, Judi,' Connor said. 'Like I said, don't answer that phone, and keep your mobile on all the time. You've got me on speed dial, right?'

'How do you do that?' I asked. My lack of techno ability was famous.

He took my phone off the bench and fiddled with it for a few minutes, then gave it back to me. 'OK, I'm Two. All you have to do is tap the phone, and then tap the number two. Here, I'll do it on your landline receiver as well.'

'Thanks.' It didn't seem any simpler than using my Contacts but I didn't argue. I shut the door after him and locked it, then went around the whole house and checked every window and door again. I wasn't paranoid, no, not me. On the other hand, if it was Wendell harassing me, I might bring the garden fork inside and keep it handy in the cupboard with the vacuum cleaner. The vacuum was a wet-and-dry so I could quickly suck up any blood.

That made me feel a whole lot better, and I finally went off to bed.

Of course, my mobile rang about 3am. I jerked upright in bed and saw Andre's name on the screen. 'Hello?'

'Judi, it's – I thought – door – footsteps –'

What the hell was going on at the pub? Was Andre OK?

7

I glared at my phone and the one tiny reception bar that was showing. 'Hang on, Andre, you're breaking up.' I raced out to the back door, my feet cringing at the cold bluestone floor, and stood on the mat, shivering. 'Say that again?'

Andre's voice was quiet and a bit clipped. 'That guy, Winter. He's walking around the pub.'

'Inside or out?' If he was inside, he was probably stealing drinks. Bastard.

'Both. Wanted to let you know. Should I talk to him?'

I thought for a moment. What if Winter had a gun? No, why would he? Stop panicking. 'Can you go down and ask him what he's doing? Nicely. In case he's sick, or delirious or claustrophobic or something weird. But if he's just being a pain in the arse and nicking drinks, you might have to call Connor.'

He muttered something and said, 'Hadn't thought about him stealing stuff. Like we don't have enough trouble.'

'I know. Listen, hang up and go and find out what the fuck he's up to. If I don't hear back from you in five minutes, I'll ring Connor. All right?'

'Got it.'

I went to find my slippers, clutching my mobile phone, waiting. Wondering if I should just call Connor anyway, and, for some reason, listening hard for anything strange around the house. I mean, it wasn't like weirdo Chris was going to run all the way out here to... whatever. Mia's complaint about the possum noise niggled at me. But as usual, all around me was deep, dark silence. I'd always loved that: total silence – apart from chainsaws and tractors during the day – and being able to look up at the night sky and see thousands of stars.

Now, it felt threatening.

I pushed the thought away and checked my phone. Four minutes.

Five seconds before it hit five minutes, the phone rang. 'Andre?'

'Yeah,' he said. 'It's OK, he's gone back to his room and promised to stop wandering around. Said he was an insomniac and found that walking helped. He's a bit claustrophobic, too. I suggested he open the window instead.'

'I suppose an insomniac is better than the drunks who can't find the bathroom.' That wasn't actually true. The killers who wanted to shoot you were the worst, but I wasn't about to go there. 'Go back to bed. But if you have any more problems with him, ring Connor straight away, OK?'

'Yep. Will do.' He sounded a bit more confident, and I hung up. Maybe we'd have to employ a night manager, or stop taking guests. The last thing I wanted was to have to move into the pub. I couldn't, not with Mia.

I tried to go back to sleep, but without much success. It was almost a relief to see dawn glowing over the top of my curtains, giving me an excuse to get up and make some ginger and lemon tea while I sat and made a To Do list for the day.

While I sat there, it all started to crowd in on me. The never-ending responsibility of the pub, dealing with staff, trying to pay the bills, wondering how the hell to get more customers in... Not for the first time, I wondered if Andre and I had taken on a huge bloody millstone that might end up drowning us. There was no way to deal out the jobs other than how we already had –

Andre had control over the bistro, the supply orders, the menu and how it all ran. I did the bars and the guests. His sleeping partners in Melbourne had no say in operations.

Ideas of putting the pub on the market were creeping ever closer, and some days all that was holding me back was Andre, and his hopes for a business that would make his name and see him through to retirement.

I sat there for too long, staring at the wall, hoping to be struck by some brilliant idea that would solve everything. Fat chance. By the time I got up to have a shower, my bad hip was aching from the hard wooden chair and I hobbled into the bathroom, cursing. We hadn't had enough decent rain for me to soak in a bath, so I stood under streaming hot water for a few minutes and then hopped out.

Saturday I was due to take Mia down to visit her grandparents, her mum's parents, and I'd decided to stay overnight in Andy's house that was my house now. It would be the first time they'd had Mia to stay for the weekend and I didn't want to be too far away. I'd rostered Charlie and Marie on with Andre, but that had been when Kate was still with us. Shit. Maybe I'd have to come back for Saturday night.

I felt like pulling my hair out and screaming. Instead I made the mistake of glancing at myself in the bathroom mirror. Bags under my eyes, sagging chin, lines in my forehead. That was not how a relaxed country woman was supposed to look. I came to Candlebark to get away from all the crap, not to find more of it.

I shook my head and went to get dressed, pulling on tights under my work pants. The mornings were getting damn chilly. Mia woke up and dragged Bum in to find me sitting on my bed, staring at the wall again.

'Good morning says Bum,' she announced importantly.

'Good morning.' I gave her a kiss and then had to give Bum

one, too. Ugh. He was getting a bit smelly, but there was no time to wash him before the grandparent visit.

We had breakfast, Mia chattering and talking to both Bum and I. Neither of us said much, but she didn't notice. Once she'd finished, she wanted to go and look for the cat so I opened the back door for her, checking around outside first. She came back in a few minutes later, muttering to herself.

'No cat?' I asked.

She frowned and said something I didn't catch. I pulled her jacket out of the cupboard and helped her put it on, then collected up snack food into a container for her. This morning we'd go to the pub first, and I'd take her to daycare a bit later. That way we'd have a bit more time together.

She was still chattering when I put her in the car seat, and I thought she was talking to Bum. 'Look at his poor ear,' I said. It needed stitching back on. 'Don't keep pulling on it, OK? It'll fall off.'

She grabbed his arm instead and held him close, kissing his poor, tattered ear. At the pub, as we went inside to the office, I glanced into the bistro. Only Chris Winter was there, eating alone, reading a newspaper. 'Good morning,' he called when he spotted me.

'Hi,' I said. I wondered where Andre was, but when I checked my phone, there was a text from him. *Gone home to shower and change. Done breakfast, the two journos left around 6.45am, Winter hasn't emerged yet.* It came into my phone at 7.02am, while I was in the shower. Maybe he shouldn't have left Winter here alone after last night, but the guy was eating breakfast calmly enough.

I felt like, more and more, the pub was getting away on me, small things going haywire or just not working smoothly the way they should. It was the same bad feeling I'd had with the pub in Melbourne. Back then, I hadn't known about Max's drug dealing and how he'd been helping himself to cash from the till all the time. Once I'd realised what was going on, it was too late.

Kate's murder increased the feeling tenfold.

I waited until Winter had finished his breakfast and gone back upstairs before I took Mia in with me while I cleared the table and put the breakfast stuff away. I didn't want her around Winter – I didn't like the negative vibe I got from him. I wished he'd pack up and leave today. She asked for a piece of toast and Vegemite, and when I'd made and given it to her, she said, 'Keep for the girl.'

'Pardon?'

She gave me back the toast. 'Why didn't the girl have breakfast? She was hungry.'

I stared down at her little, worried face, my tired brain churning until a few cogs managed to finally slot into place. Mia had seen a girl outside. She'd heard someone crying. Maybe, just maybe, it meant Emma was hiding at my place. If so, she had to be in the shed. It had a bolt on the inside as well as the outside, something the previous owner had done. I'd assumed he'd wanted to hide out there from his wife, or maybe she from him.

I grabbed my phone, ready to ring Connor, and then stopped. If Emma was there, a man's voice would probably freak her out worse than she already was. I'd have to go. She knew me a little from being at the pub with Kate. But I wasn't about to leave the pub for Winter to wander around in again.

I rang Andre instead. 'Can you come in now? I know it's a bit early for you, but there's only me here, and I need to do something urgent after I drop Mia off.'

'OK, no probs.' But he sounded as exhausted as me.

In return, I spent the waiting time setting up the tables for lunch for him, while thinking we really would have to replace Kate after all. Otherwise I could see we'd be here all hours again. When Andre came in, I basically yelled, 'Hi, bye!' and rushed past him, whisking Mia into the car and dropping her at childcare a few minutes later.

Outside my house, I sat in the driveway, trying to breathe slowly, thinking through what I'd say. Then I got out of the car and went through the side gate to the garden shed. As I went, I checked around the garden for any signs. We seemed to be missing a few carrots but the apple tree had lots of fruit on it so it was hard to tell. Anyway, half-green apples might give her a stomach ache. Closer to the shed, I finally saw scuff marks and the print of a runner, nothing like the gardening boots I wore.

The shed door was unbolted on the outside, but tightly closed, so I was right – she'd bolted it from the inside. I knocked gently. 'Emma, Emma? It's Judi. Only me. Nobody else here.'

Silence.

'Emma.' I knocked a bit harder in case she was asleep on the cold, hard floor. 'Please come out. You're safe. It's just me, I promise.'

A bit of scuffling and then the bolt sliding slowly. Finally the door opened a few centimetres and I could see her grimy, pale face through the gap.

'Hi. Are you OK?'

A sniff and a little nod.

'You want to come and have something hot to eat? Or coffee? Milo? I can make you porridge.'

'Yuck,' she whispered. 'Milo'd be good.'

'Good, I can do that.' I didn't pull the door open – I let her do it at her own pace. Very slowly the door opened further and she poked her head out, checking all around before coming all the way.

'You sure no one's here?'

'Positive.'

'No one can see into your house?'

'No. My neighbours are a long way away.' I stood back and let her walk tentatively with me, an old backpack over her shoulder. 'Weren't you cold out there?'

'A bit. Mum told me...' A little sob escaped and she pressed her lips tightly together.

'I know. You'll be all right now.'

'No, I won't,' she whispered, but she followed me into the house and watched as I locked the door behind us.

'Would you like a hot shower first?' When she nodded, I showed her the bathroom and gave her a clean towel. 'It'll have to be short, sorry. I'm on tank water.'

'I know.'

I shut the door and sagged against the wall. The poor bloody kid. She looked like a little waif that would be whisked away in a strong wind, but to get away from her house, knowing what had happened, and hide out in my shed all this time took guts. I had a feeling she was a lot tougher than she looked.

I boiled the kettle and got her Milo ready, plus put the Weet-Bix packet and some bread ready for whatever she wanted to eat. Then I sat and thought about what to do next. I needed – wanted – desperately to tell Connor, but I didn't want to frighten her into running again, and I thought she might. The waif part came from deep fear, the kind that sapped your spirit, and probably her tough part was pretty exhausted, too. I'd have to tread carefully.

She emerged a few minutes later, wet hair brushed back and wearing clean clothes. 'Do you want me to put your other clothes in the washing machine?'

She shook her head. That convinced me she was ready to run again. She wasn't even game to hand over what was probably her one change of clothing.

'Weet-Bix or toast?'

'Toast, please.'

I put bread in the toaster and laid out margarine and a range of spreads for her, then filled her mug with boiled water. She hid her face in the mug for a few seconds, then she looked straight at me. 'Where's my mum?'

There were several things I could say, those euphemistic things like 'passed on' or 'gone to a better place', but they stuck in my throat. And I couldn't say her mum would be fine. I was pretty sure she'd known what was going on and heard the gunshot. I took a breath and let it out.

'I would say by now she's in Melbourne. Being looked after.'

'In the morgue? Fuck off.' She banged her mug down on the table.

'They're looked after in there. With care. I know.'

'What? You saw it on TV?' The scorn on her face was palpable. She shook her head and looked away, blinking hard.

'My brother was in there, not that long ago.'

'Yeah, right. Pull the other one.'

I kept my voice deliberate. 'He'd been murdered in Footscray. Shot. I didn't know, then someone rang up Connor and he came and told me.'

That silenced her for a few long seconds. 'Did they cut him up?'

'Possibly. I didn't ask. But they needed to know what had happened, so they could catch whoever did it.'

'Yeah, sure.' The scorn wasn't quite as dripping. The toaster popped, which made us both jump. 'Did they… did they catch him?'

'They… they actually both died before they were properly charged for the murder.' I placed the toast on her plate.

'Good,' she said fiercely. 'The bastard who killed Mum deserves to die, too.'

I wasn't sure what to say. It was obvious she'd feel that way, but I like to see a bit of justice served myself. I settled for 'Mmm' and put more bread in the toaster before sitting down again. I watched her scrape the margarine across her toast and do the same with the Vegemite. Old habits. She'd been brought up in a house with very little spare cash, I'd say.

'Look, I didn't call Connor before I came to –'

'You can't tell anyone!' she spat at me.

'But he's a –'

'I don't care! If you try to tell anyone, I'll run away again.' Despite her threat, her hands shook and her chin trembled.

'Everyone is looking for you,' I said gently. 'They're worried.'

'Sure they are. And they'll all lead that guy straight to me.' Tears rolled down her face. 'You don't understand. My mum…'

'I understand you're terrified that the man who killed your mother will find you.' I thought for a moment. 'Why do you think he'll hurt you?'

'Not hurt me, kill me.'

'Why? Bec –' Something dawned on me. 'You saw who it was?'

She nodded.

'But if you know who it is, the police –'

'They won't help,' she said bitterly. 'Why do you think we were living here in the middle of fucking nowhere?'

'Hiding?'

'Fat lot of good it did!' She suddenly let out a huge sigh, that sounded as if she'd been holding it in for days, and slumped in her chair. It was as if all the life had just drained out of her and, for a second, I thought she was about to faint.

'Listen, drink your Milo and eat. I'm sure you'll feel better after some real food.' I tried a smile. 'Our carrots aren't really that filling, are they?'

She shook her head but at least she sat up a little and ate her toast. Once she started eating properly, there was no stopping her. Five pieces of toast and two Milos later, she had a bit of pink in her cheeks, and I felt I could try again.

'What am I going to do with you?' I said, as caringly as possible. I wasn't used to being this nice but apparently my months with Mia had improved my disposition a bit.

'I can stay here,' she said quickly. 'I'll be no trouble. I'll do all the housework, and I can cook a bit, too. I won't be any trouble.'

She wasn't to know I'd been on my way to becoming a certified hermit, at least before Mia came, and I'd been loving it. The thought of having Emma here sent shudders through me that I tried to hide. 'Hmm, I don't think that's going to work.'

She stood up, pushing the chair back with a screech. 'I'll go then. Thanks for the breakfast.' She grabbed her backpack and turned.

'Hang on a minute!' I said sharply, and she froze. 'Sorry, didn't mean to snap, but you're not giving me much of a chance to…'

'Find an excuse to get rid of me?'

'No, damn it!' I sucked in a breath, let it out slowly. She was as bad as Mia having a tantrum about putting Bum in the washing machine. 'I want to help, but I can't just hide you here indefinitely.'

'Can you hide me for a couple of days? Just until I figure out how to get to Melbourne without being seen. Pleeease?' From anyone else it might've sounded wheedling, but from Emma it just sounded bloody desperate.

I thought about it. It would mean lying to Connor, which I wasn't sure I could do. I'd have no trouble lying to Swan and Chandler. On the other hand, if I avoided Connor… Then I remembered what was happening on Saturday.

'I'm going to Melbourne tomorrow.' As soon as I said it, I regretted it.

Her face lit up. 'Cool! I can come with you.'

'Why? What will you do when you get there?'

'Mum's brother is there. Uncle Sam. If I can get to his place, I'll be fine, truly I will.'

All kinds of questions and doubts jumbled inside my head until I thought my eyes would pop out. 'I'll think about it.' As she tried to protest, I held up my hands. 'I'm not saying yes yet, so don't push me, OK?' I checked my watch. 'I have to get back to the pub. Will you be all right here on your own?'

She nodded. 'I'll keep it all locked up, no lights, no TV, no phone.' It sounded like something she'd learned by heart, which raised another question. No time to ask now. I left the house, full of misgivings, and even after I'd given her my mobile number and made sure she double-locked the door after me, none of them went away.

At the pub, I found Andre cooking fish and chips in the kitchen, saying the detectives and Connor had pre-ordered for an early lunch. 'Problems with Mia?' he asked, eyebrows high.

'No, she's good. Just something to sort out at home.' I could feel my face heating up, and I thought I might confide in Andre later, if only so he could tell me what a dickhead I was being. Then I could agree and call Connor.

Except Emma would run, and then anything could happen to her.

In the bar, Moaning Marie was pulling beer for a couple of the locals, and ensconced at a corner table at the other end was Chris Winter with Scottie and Old Jock. Either they were getting all matey very quickly, or Scottie had been bullshitting me the night before. I knew which one I would pick. It also explained why Winter gave me the willies – if he was associated with Scottie, I could pretty much guarantee they were up to no good.

The question was – what kind of no good?

Stay out of it, Judi. Heath's voice was an echo in my head, reminding me I hadn't heard from him for a few days. Since I was going to be in Melbourne tomorrow, maybe we could have lunch, at least. Dinner would be better, but if I had to come back for the pub, that'd wreck everything. Including... my face warmed up. No, don't even think about sex, I told myself.

I checked Marie was OK on her own, which she should've been, given it was a normal Friday lunchtime, and went into the office to call Heath.

'Heath.' Clearly, he hadn't checked his caller ID.

'It's me. Judi.'

'Hi!' His voice warmed by about fifty degrees. 'Is this your weekend to bring Mia down?'

'Yes, it is. Are you busy?' I'd learned not to fluff around with him on the phone – he was always in the middle of something.

'Hopefully not. Unless somebody dies and we get called out. Not our turn though.' A car horn and a faint siren sounded in the background. 'Dinner?'

'I hope so. I need to talk to Andre first, make sure he'll cover for me until Sunday evening.'

'Are you still being a control freak?'

He laughed so I knew he was joking, but it still rankled. They say the truth will do that. 'No, it's just... we've had a death here.'

'I heard. A murder. A woman in her thirties. Did you know her?'

Suddenly, his matter-of-fact words hit me, and I had to bite the inside of my mouth for a couple of seconds until I could speak. 'She worked here at the pub.'

'Aw, shit, you did know her then. I'm sorry, Jude. That's awful.'

I took a few deep breaths, then said, 'Yes. It's been a shock.' I left it there, in case he knew any more about it – I didn't want to get into questions about Emma. 'Shall I call you tomorrow, before I leave here? I'll know about dinner by then.'

'That'd be great. See you.'

I hung up and thought about going to help Marie, deciding she could damn well cope on her own for the whole shift. I was sure if there was a sudden rush, she'd come and get me. I pulled out the sheaf of bills and set to work with the calculator, putting them in piles of Urgent, Needs a Chat by Phone, and Can Wait for Second Notice.

Going over the accounts again was doing my head in. I needed food, and I needed to talk to Andre. He was the one person I could trust not to throw a hissy fit about me hiding Emma. Or not a very big one, anyway.

I was surprised to see half a dozen tables in the bistro full of chattering people, and Andre running around like a mad chicken. 'Why didn't you call me?' I said, grabbing an order pad and pen.

'I haven't had time to do any more than run fast,' he said. 'Plus they all just arrived at once!'

'Sorry. I'll start taking orders.'

'Great. Marie has only been in once for drink orders. I've had to tell people to go into the bar to get served.'

I ground my teeth. By now, Kate would've had everyone sorted, drinks on the tables and be back in the kitchen helping Andre. I tucked the thought away and got busy with greeting people and taking orders for drinks first, then shoving the order pad at Marie in the bar. 'Get these ready asap, please, and take them into the bistro. Table numbers on top.'

'But I'm busy,' she protested.

I glanced around the public bar. There had to be all of eight people in there. 'No, you're not. Get a move on, please.'

Her face looked like a sucked lemon, but I was past caring where she was concerned. I hurried back to the bistro and checked the menu board to see what Andre had listed, then started taking food orders. It soon became apparent that half of the tables were people escaping from Bronwyn's health farm.

Uh-oh. I hoped she wasn't going to burst in and berate them all.

Two hours later, a lot of happy customers had left with full stomachs and praise for the chef, and I'd finished cleaning up. I sat at one of the tables and put my aching feet up on a chair.

'Here you are,' Andre said, putting a plate down next to me. It was the spinach and parmesan gnocchi I'd been drooling over as I served it to half the customers.

I ate a mouthful and sighed. 'Oh, this is the best. Thank you.'

'You're welcome. You made a great waitress today.' He grinned.

'It was worth it to see the money coming in,' I said, 'but I can't keep doing it.' I nearly said something about Kate but kept my big mouth shut, and Andre stayed silent. He was drinking a cold beer and contemplating his shoes, and I wasn't sure how to broach the subject, but I really needed an understanding ear.

'So... you know how the police are still searching for Emma?'

He knew me better than anyone, even Connor, and gave me a death stare. 'What are you about to tell me? Or should I say, do I really want to hear it?'

I'd put Andre in danger before, but this was different. 'I... I kind of know where she is. Well, not kind of. I do know.'

'Let me guess. At your house, probably watching *Big Brother* or *Home and Away*, right?'

I squirmed in my chair, and the gnocchi wasn't going down so nicely. 'Not quite. But you can't tell anyone.'

'Judi, what have you done?' His face was stern and his tone even more so. I really regretted saying anything now.

'I didn't actually do anything.' I made my voice firmer. 'I found her this morning, hiding in my shed. Until then, I had no idea where she was. Truly.'

'So have you let Connor know?'

'That's where it gets tricky.'

He heaved a loud sigh. 'It's not tricky. You ring him up

and tell him. Let them deal with it, and look after her.'

'If I do that, she'll run. She's terrified.'

'Of course she is. Tell Connor.'

I couldn't work out how to get through to him what Emma was like, how I knew she'd disappear as soon as anyone came to the house who wasn't me. I was sure she'd have an escape route plotted, and that she'd be out the back door and into the bush before anyone even got out of their car. But I tried anyway. And I kept trying, until finally his face changed a little.

'You really think she'll bolt like that?' he finally said.

'Yes. I wasn't able to ask her what was going on, but from the way she's acting…' A realisation broke through. 'I think she knows the guy who shot Kate, and she knows he's either a cop, or is connected to cops somehow.'

'That's a bit unlikely.'

'Yeah, I guess.' I thought some more. 'But she does know enough to make her far more terrified than you'd expect. I mean, sure, her mother was killed and she was there. That'd frighten the crap out of any kid. But this is more than that, a lot more.'

'Like?'

'Why was Swan asking you about what Kate might've told you?'

He shrugged. 'Don't know. I couldn't help.'

'But Connor told me that Kate, and very likely Emma as well, had bags packed and ready to go. Like emergency running-away bags. Who does that if they're leading a normal, ordinary life in a little country town?'

'Well, I did wonder…'

'What?'

'She was always losing her phone,' he said slowly. 'Like every few weeks. And instead of getting it replaced and keeping her number, she'd go and buy another one with a whole new number.

She said it didn't matter to her. She only had a few people she called, plus the pub and me. Easier just to get another cheapie.'

'But it's not really. You think she was buying new phones to make sure nobody could find her?'

'It's a bit excessive, but...' He spread his hands. 'What would I know about being on the run?'

'Did you ever see Emma with a phone?'

He frowned. 'Come to think of it, no. And you know what teenagers are like with mobile phones. Like they're permanently attached to their hands. I just thought maybe Kate was really strict about it. Some parents are.'

We sat in silence for a while, thinking, and I finished the gnocchi. Just as I opened my mouth to speak again, Marie came in.

'I've finished my very onerous shift,' she announced pompously. 'And I won't be continuing in this position. You will need to find someone else to be your slave labour.'

A dozen extremely rude rejoinders ran through my mind, but before I could get myself into trouble for employee harassment, Andre jumped in. 'Sorry to hear that, Marie. We were about to offer you a pay rise in appreciation of your hard work since Kate died.'

I managed to stop myself just in time. Marie glared at us both for a moment, then decided to take Andre seriously. 'How much of a pay rise?' she asked suspiciously.

'Two dollars an hour,' Andre said. 'Interested?'

I stared at him in disbelief. 'Two dollars?'

He ignored me. 'If that's OK with you, we'll see you for your lunch shift tomorrow.' He smiled at her in a way that I knew was totally fake but I was speechless.

'Um, yeah, yeah, OK.' Marie left, still looking flummoxed and I poked Andre in the arm.

'Are you kidding me?'

'We need her, Judi, much as I hate to say it. And two bucks is really only another fifty dollars a week. Do you really want to have to try and find someone else right now?'

'No,' I said. 'I guess not.'

'Right then. So now we need to finish this chat about Emma.' His face was furrowed and his eyes troubled. 'I know you. You've already decided what to do. You just want me to say it's OK, and I'm not sure it is. Whatever you have planned.'

He did bloody know me… too well. But I also wanted him to tell me honestly if I was being an idiot, despite Emma's terror, and I knew he would. I explained about taking her to Melbourne, to her uncle's house. 'Once she's there, if she still won't tell the police, I will tell Connor.'

'It all sounds way too shaky to me,' Andre said. 'How do you know she's even got an uncle?'

'I don't, I guess.' I rubbed my face with both hands. 'God, I don't know. Maybe you're right. I'll go home and see if I can persuade her to talk to Connor.'

'That's the sensible thing to do,' Andre said, smiling at last. 'Go now. Because you know you'll have to be my waitress again tonight. We've got six bookings.'

That was all I needed. It meant I'd have to call on Joleen for childcare, too. Thank God Charlie was on the bar – at least I'd get drinks service in the bistro.

The front door banged and I jumped, whirling around to see Chris Winter give us a wave and head up the stairs to his room. One more night and he'd be gone, thankfully.

I called Joleen first, then drove home under the speed limit for a change while I thought about how to convince Emma to let me call Connor for help. I pulled into my driveway and got out slowly, wanting to give her time to see it was me on my own, and not be scared. The house looked exactly as I'd left it this morning, quiet and isolated, with paddocks on two sides and the bush on the other. I shivered, noticing for the first time how the bush I loved so much actually gave someone a good place from which to watch me.

I unlocked the front door and stepped inside. 'Emma? It's just me. Hello?'

Silence. I went through every room, checking places she might be hiding in or under. When I reached my back door, I found it unlocked. The garden shed was also empty.

Shit! She'd made good on her threat and run away again.

And I'd have to explain to Connor and Swan why I hadn't told them she was there.

8

I'd have to call Connor to tell him Emma had been here. And was now gone again. If I didn't, he'd be in the bad books with higher up, and I didn't want that to happen. I remembered just in time I now had him on speed dial. Fat lot of good when I hadn't called him this morning.

'Hiya,' he said. 'Not another abusive call, I hope.'

'No, it's not that. I need to let you know something.'

'Ye-e-es.'

'I found Emma here at my house this morning, hiding in the garden shed, and I didn't know she was here, I promise, but I gave her some breakfast and then I had to go to work and when I got back just now, she was gone again. Sorry.'

He took a moment to unravel my garbled report. 'She was there this morning? Safe and sound?'

'Yes. Cold and hungry, but yes. Not dead.'

'That's good. But… why didn't you call me this morning? Where is she now?'

'I…' This was the hard part. Andre hadn't been convinced so why would Connor be? 'She was terrified. She begged me not to tell anyone. She doesn't trust the police.'

'That's not the point, Judi. You still should've called me. I could have come on my own to talk to her. Shit.' He sounded stressed now. I wondered if Swan or Chandler were there.

'No, she would've run away, I'm sure. She said if anyone

came to the house, she'd bolt again. She meant it.'

'No doubt she did, but…' He let out an exasperated huff. 'I'm coming over now. Don't move.'

'I have to pick up Mia soon.'

'I'll be there in a few minutes. Don't. Move.' He hung up and I was left to dread what he'd say next. Or do. At least he wasn't bringing Swan with him. I gazed out at the bush, hoping I'd see a flash of movement, or signs of Emma still hanging around near the house, but there was nothing. She must've left as soon as I'd disappeared down the road – she could be almost to the main road by now, if she walked fast. I doubted very much she'd try to hitch a lift around Candlebark.

Connor arrived soon after and sat in my kitchen with his notebook, taking down all the details. Time, appearance, everything Emma had said that I could remember. Then he checked out the garden shed, but there was no sign of her even being there.

'Have you looked to see if she's taken anything from the house?' he asked.

'No, I'll do it now.' It turned out she'd taken tinned food, had made herself sandwiches, and also nicked one of my sweatshirts, the thickest one with a rabbit on the front that Mia had insisted I buy. Emma would swim in it but really, if it kept her warm, I didn't mind that much. Bunny rabbits weren't exactly me.

'You're sure she didn't say anything else,' Connor repeated. 'Nothing about the shooting?'

'No, but I got the distinct feeling that she knew who'd done it.'

His eyebrows shot up. 'Why?'

'Just the way she was talking, and her terror about being found.' I eyed him, pursing my mouth. 'She doesn't trust the police at all. Have you found out what Kate's involvement with New South Wales police might have been?'

'Swan said none at all. No record. This guy Mikey was the one with a police record and gaol time.'

'What are you going to do now?'

He flipped his notebook closed with a loud slap and stood. 'Report this and wait to be told what action to take.'

'Will they resume the search for Emma?'

'Probably.' He frowned down at me. 'I really wish you'd called me straight away. Even when you left the house. She wouldn't have known.'

'I know. I'm sorry.' But the thought of Emma running through the bush with half a dozen cops and police dogs after her sent a shudder through me. Hunted like a young deer. A part of me was glad that hadn't happened, but I still wondered where she was. It was easy to get lost out there, even though there were tracks. All the gum trees looked the same and you could end up just walking in circles. I'd followed the track through almost to the main road once, and it had taken me hours, but if I'd veered off and walked south into the state park, I could've been lost for days.

Time to leave it to Connor. He knew the bush around here far better than I did. I picked up Mia from the childcare centre and spent some time with her at home, playing outside with the cat and planting broad beans, even though it was a bit early. The large seeds were easy for her to handle and grew fast enough to make her happy.

I had frozen quiche that I microwaved for her, then cut up to cool it down. She ate so slowly that I had to put it in a container to take to Joleen's. I was waiting for another refusal, but she seemed fine tonight. After dropping her off, I was back at the pub, facing another night of waitressing. Whoopee.

Andre greeted me with the news that we now had eight tables booked. 'I think a few of them are from the health spa.'

'Oh God. Surely Bronwyn's going to notice when they disappear?'

Andre shrugged. 'It's not like we stand at their front gate with a bribe.'

'Well, if she comes in all shouty, I'm going to let you deal with her this time.'

'Sure.' He grinned wolfishly. 'I'll keep a meat cleaver handy.'

I went into the bar and checked Charlie was doing OK, and told him about Marie threatening to quit. He made a face. 'I know we're short-handed but…'

'If you hear of anyone good looking for a job, just let me know.'

'Will do.' He went back to serving the pair who'd just come in – Scottie and Old Jock. Jock was smiling and cheery for a change, but Scottie had a face like he'd smelled something rotten. He was staring across the room and I guessed before I turned around that his focus was Chris Winter. Winter gave me a wave and then came over.

'Ms Westerholme, can I buy you a drink? This pub is such a great place, it's worth celebrating.' He was ignoring Scottie and beaming at me like he'd won the lottery. He'd obviously just showered and his longish hair curled damply on his neck.

'Thanks, but I need to go and help in the bistro.' I started to edge away but he wasn't about to let me go.

He dropped his smile into a sombre expression. 'Terrible thing, this local murder, isn't it? I see the journos left. Must've found a juicier story somewhere else.'

'I guess so. If you'll excuse me…'

'And the police still haven't found that poor girl.'

He looked at me expectantly, and I had a horrible feeling he knew Emma had been at my house – but how could he? I remembered the front door banging earlier. Maybe he'd been just outside the bistro all the time, eavesdropping, and just pretended to be coming in, making a big noise. I shook my head. I was being ridiculous because I didn't like him.

'It's very distressing,' I managed to say. 'If you'll excuse me, I have tables to set.'

'Save one for me,' he said with a laugh. 'Love the food here, just love it.'

God, now he had me wondering if he was secretly a food critic or something. Or maybe he was just plain fucking weird all round. I forced a smile and went to the bistro, setting tables and getting everything ready for dinner. Andre wrote the menu on the chalkboard and said, 'I've kept it simple. If they don't like what's on here, they'll have to have the public bar menu.'

I gave the board a quick squiz and asked him to tell me what was in some of the dishes, since people always asked. 'I'm trying to use up what's in the freezer,' he said. 'But fresh local produce is so much better.'

I pointed at the Moroccan pulled lamb. 'That's new.'

'I started it last night so it would look after itself. Limited servings, so check with me about how many are left if you get a lot of orders.'

Oh, the joys of running a restaurant. I also checked the wine on the list to make sure we had enough and made a mental note about the local Shiraz we'd got a good deal on. If I pushed that a bit more, the profit would be handy. Maybe I'd shove some down Chris Winter's throat and charge him double.

It wasn't long before the public bar started to fill. I helped Charlie for a little while, but by 7.30 I had eight tables filled and was running back and forth at a hundred kms an hour. Charlie helped with the drinks orders and I was grateful yet again for Andre's limited chalkboard menu. I couldn't have dealt with a full menu and waiting for ditherers to make up their minds. When Chris Winter strolled in and took a table in the corner, I cringed a little, but in the end I was too busy to take much notice of him. He spent most of the time on his phone, watching what looked like YouTube videos and chortling to himself. It wasn't until later in the evening, after Connor had done his usual walk-through, that I heard the news.

They'd called for volunteers to help the police and SES search for Emma, now they knew she was definitely alive, starting at first light. And apparently Chris Winter had put his hand up, saying loudly it was the least he could do.

I managed to talk to Charlie as he brought me the takings to go in the safe. 'What on earth did he volunteer for?'

'Dunno.' Charlie shrugged. 'Seems like an OK guy. A lot of the others didn't say yes, like Scottie.'

I decided I was letting a personal dislike get in the way. Not even a dislike. How could you dislike someone you didn't know? Charlie's wife was still a few weeks away from giving birth, so he'd agreed to sleep over as night manager, just the once. I'd made sure Marie was doing lunch on Saturday, but after seeing four large table bookings for Saturday night, I knew I'd have to return from Melbourne by 6pm. Bugger. I sent Heath a text to explain and suggested lunch. No reply. Double bugger.

I picked up Mia on the way home and put her into bed in a silent house. I kept thinking about Emma, where she was, and whether the search in the morning would find her. If only I'd told Connor as soon as I knew she was at my place. But I kept seeing her face and hearing her voice, and something still made me feel I'd done the right thing, even though logically I hadn't.

I poured myself a large glass of wine and settled down with Andre's lamb leftovers reheated. Yum. I watched TV for a while but my brain skittered around, and eventually I stood under the shower for a few minutes, wishing fervently that it was a deep, hot bath instead, and then went to bed.

Mia and I were up early, and left for Melbourne by 8.30am. Saturday traffic was light until we got to the Ring Road. I was glad to turn off at Williamstown Road and make my way to the house Geoff and Lucy were renting in Newport, near the power station. They both came to the door to greet me warmly, and yet again I was glad I'd come to my senses and allowed them to share Mia with me. They loved her to bits, and she loved them now, even though she'd been a bit wary at first.

This would be her first sleepover with them, so I made sure they had my phone number at the pub as well as my mobile, and told them about a dozen things to remember that they already knew, before I finally tore myself away and got back in the car. For one horrible moment, I imagined them waiting until I left, then piling Mia into their car and driving back to Sydney, never to be seen again.

OK, so I had trust issues. Sue me.

I drove straight to Andy's house in Ascot Vale, wondering why I still called it 'Andy's house' instead of my house. I guessed because I'd always associate it with his turned-around life, his few years of happiness there, and his death. How I wished he was still there, bringing up Mia and being happy. I shook off the gloom that threatened to smother me and went into the house where I put on the kettle and searched fruitlessly for biscuits. One empty container. At least I had some sachets of long-life milk for my coffee.

Time to call Heath. I didn't even get a hello. 'Sorry, I'll call you back in a minute or two.'

A minute or two stretched into twenty before my phone rang. By then I was out in the garden with my coffee and a hat and gardening gloves on, weeding ferociously, imagining I was pulling hair out of Heath's head.

'Hi, sorry about that. I was just about to get a forensics report we'd been waiting on, and then I had to brief the team about it.' He sounded like always – rushed and busy, with a bare surface of calm.

'No problem.' I couldn't afford for it to be. We both had our constraints. 'I'm in Melbourne. I just dropped Mia off. Are we still…'

'Definitely lunch. I'll be finished here by twelve at the latest.'

That probably meant one or one thirty. It'd give me time to do a bit of grocery shopping and visit Margaret Jones next door. 'OK. Will you pick me up?'

'Um…' He spoke to someone in the background and then came back to me. 'Yeah, I will. No point you waiting in a restaurant somewhere if I'm late.'

Yes, been there, done that. 'See you then.'

He was gone again, leaving me with my errands and more time for weeding. I drank some lukewarm coffee and threw it on to the garden, but before I could go back inside, my phone rang again.

'Ms Westerholme?'

'Yes.'

'It's Mary Miller from Gentle Haven Rest Home.' I recognised the lilting Irish accent and immediately felt guilty. I hadn't been back to the nursing home for months. 'I'm calling about your mother.'

'Oh.' The one person I didn't want to hear about.

'She's had a fall, dear, and she's very poorly. I think you need to come and see her.'

'What – is she dying?'

'No, dear, I don't think so.' She didn't sound very certain though. 'It's just that she has taken a tumble, and now she's asking for you.'

'Me? She doesn't know who I am.' I could hear myself almost screeching and tried to calm down.

'Oh yes, she does now and then.'

That was being way too generous. Maybe once a year, my mother might be lucid enough to remember she had a daughter. 'I live two hours out of Melbourne. It's a bit difficult to get down there.' An outright lie considering where I was right that moment.

'Well, it's up to you, dear. But I'm sure it would do her the world of good to see you.' She waited and the silence grew.

Finally, I said, 'I'll try. It's just very difficult right now.'

'Certainly, dear. Whatever you think.' Her now-frosty tone was finished off by her hanging up on me. I was sure lots of people left their elderly parents in homes and never saw them from one month to the next, just because they didn't care enough. I wondered how many of them did it because they loathed the sight of their parents.

I shoved my phone into my large handbag, found a couple of shopping bags and went out to the Benz. Margaret was in her front garden, cutting some beautiful deep apricot and red roses. I went over to say hello.

'Those are amazing. David Austin?'

She beamed. 'No, but such fascinating names. Red Intuition and Tuscan Sun. I'd have my own Victorian rose garden if I had half an acre somewhere.'

'I'd just like to be basking in the Tuscan sun, full stop,' I told her.

'You and me both.' A little frown creased her forehead. 'I think there might be a problem with your car, Judi dear.'

'Oil dripping on the road?'

'No. It's making strange noises, even though the engine isn't running.'

My first thought was that Margaret was losing her grip, but I dismissed the idea when I heard the noise myself. *Thump, thump, thump.* I went closer. It was coming from the boot. I'd guessed before I even pushed my key into the lock.

The lid sprung open and Emma sat up, fuming. 'Took you freaking long enough!'

'To do what exactly?'

'Let me out, of course!' She scrambled out of the boot, hauling her backpack after her. I heard my stolen cans of food clunk, and no doubt there would be sandwich crumbs in there.

'How was I supposed to know you were in there? I thought you'd run away again.'

'Well, duh, I have.' She slung her backpack over her shoulder. 'Where the fuck are we?'

'Ascot Vale,' I said acidly. 'Were you thinking maybe I'd driven to the Gold Coast?'

'Course not!' She started walking away.

'Hey!' I yelled. 'Where are you going?'

She turned. 'To my uncle's place. I told you, he'll look out for me.'

'What's his name?'

'What – so you can tell the cops?' she sneered.

'They probably already know.' I took a breath and huffed it out. Bloody kid. 'Do you want me to drive you there?'

'No. Definitely not.' The fear was back. 'Don't you tell anyone I was here.' She turned and ran down the street, the backpack thumping against her spine. Fuck my life, honestly. I was caught between being worried to death about her and wanting to give her a good smack around the ears.

'What on earth was she doing in your boot?' Margaret asked.

'It's a long story,' I said heavily. 'Her mum just died and she's… a bit mixed up.'

'You can say that again,' Margaret said.

'I'm off to the supermarket,' I said. 'Do you need anything?'

'No, thank you, Judi. I made a banana cake this morning – maybe later you can pop in and have a slice with a cup of tea?'

I heard the loneliness in her voice. 'I'll try. I have to go back to Candlebark and work tonight, but if I don't see you later today, I'll come down and visit soon, OK?'

'All right, my dear.' She sounded like she didn't really believe me, but I vowed I would do it. I owed Margaret a hell of a lot more than I owed my demented mother, that was for sure.

I got into my car and stopped before I turned the key. This time I'd do the correct thing. I called Connor and he took unusually long to answer.

'Hey, Judi, are you in Melbourne?' He was puffing.

'Are you out running again?'

'No, I'm in the bush beyond your house, searching for Emma. Argh!' There was a sound of breaking branches and a thump.

'Connor?'

Swearing in the background, then, 'Sorry, tripped on a branch in the undergrowth.'

'I know where Emma is,' I said.

Silence. 'Really? Because I'd love not to be here. I've ripped my pants, too.'

'She's in Melbourne. The little bugger was hiding in the boot of my car.'

'So you've got her there? I can let Swan know so he can –'

'No, she's gone.'

'What?' he shouted.

'She climbed out, more or less told me to get fucked and ran off. Said she was going to her uncle's house.'

'So she's not terrified anymore?'

'Yes, she is, but it's coming out as anger now, I think.' I stared down the street, willing Emma to come back, but it remained empty apart from three large black crows on the phone pole.

'Shit. No one said anything to me about an uncle.'

'She could've been lying.' The crows all nodded as if agreeing with me. 'Anyway, I'll leave it with you.'

'I'll notify Swan and the others. Let me know if you hear from her,' he said. 'I don't like the sound of a fake uncle at all.'

'Me neither.' I hung up just as one of the crows let out a long, harsh *Faaaaaarrrrrkkk*.

'You and me both,' I muttered.

9

It was a quick drive to the supermarket where I stocked up on a few things, mostly non-perishables, stuff I could freeze and long-life milk. I had no intention of staying at the house anytime soon, but an ominous feeling in my guts made me keep piling food into the trolley, and then I added several bottles of wine to the haul before taking it back to the car. I'd just finished packing it all away in the freezer and kitchen cupboards when there was a knock at the front door.

Heath was early. I tried to wipe the smile off my face with no success. He looked just as happy to see me, and had his arms around me before I'd even got the door closed. He breathed in deeply. 'You smell good.'

I didn't like to admit I'd put on my favourite perfume just for him, in places I didn't usually spray it. 'You're nice and early. We've got time for coffee before we go.'

'Coffee?' He pulled back and made a face. 'I had something else in mind.'

So did I. I'd remembered to pull the doona back and air the bed a bit when I'd first come into the house. Just in case. A woman has to be prepared.

I wondered if I'd be able to put aside the horrible events of the last few days and focus, but the feel of Heath's warm hands on my skin, his mouth on mine, the way he looked into my eyes as if he could see right into my mind and soul – the world receded into the distance and all I knew for a while was him and me. We started gently and ended up hard and fast and passionate, as if together we were racing away from demons.

It wasn't until we were lying together afterwards, arms and legs entangled, that I asked if he was OK. 'I am now.' He kissed me and didn't say anymore so I let it rest. I didn't want to spoil this precious time together either.

Suddenly my stomach let out an enormous gurgling rumble and Heath laughed. 'I think that's a hint we need to eat lunch.' But before either of us could move, the familiar plinkety-plink of his phone echoed around the room. 'Damn it,' he said, reaching for his jacket that he'd tossed on to the chair.

'Heath. Yes. Yes. No, not my case. Oh, you mean…' He glanced at me, mouth half-open as if he wasn't sure whether to go on or not. 'Yes, she's here. Hang on.' He covered the phone with his hand. 'It's Swanny. Wants to talk to you about someone called Emma.'

I made a face. 'I've already told Connor what happened.'

He just held the phone out to me. I took it and said, 'Yes?' Not very politely.

'I believe you brought Emma Brown down to Melbourne this morning.' Accusingly.

'Not intentionally,' I said. 'She was hiding in the boot of my car.'

'And you let her run off.'

'She's a teenager with longer legs than me and was a lot more determined to run away than I was to break a leg trying to catch her.' I tried to calm down but it didn't work. 'Do you think I should have brought her down with a rugby tackle?'

Heath made a funny choking sound.

'Not at all,' Swan said stiffly. 'What did she say?'

I wasn't going to repeat the general 'fuck you' part of the conversation. 'She said she was going to her uncle's. I believe it's her mother's brother.'

'Where does he live?'

'No idea. Isn't that your job?' Heath frowned at me and I ignored him. 'She just said she'd be safe there. That's all I know.'

'All right, thank you. We'll be in touch again, no doubt.'

Rather than tell him not to bother, I simply pressed the red circle and handed the phone back to Heath. 'He sure knows how to destroy a good mood.'

'Just doing his job,' Heath said.

Yeah, but did he have to do it so grumpily?

Not that I could talk. And I didn't want to. Bloody questions, and I never had an answer they wanted to hear. I didn't want it to affect the rest of our time together so I used the shower to wash away my irritation and we headed for the café down on the Maribyrnong River, opting to sit outside under the pergola and look at the river. Conversation was strained – I could tell he was dying to ask what Swan had wanted, and I didn't want to admit I'd held back information about Emma's whereabouts.

Finally I just said it. 'That was about the woman who was shot. One of my staff.' He nodded, his expression curious. 'Her daughter went missing and it turned out she was hiding in my garden shed. Not that I knew.'

'And then?' He always knew when I was holding back.

'She was terrified. She thought the guy was still hunting her. She wouldn't let me tell Swan, or even Connor.'

'But you did, of course.'

'Sure.' I drank some wine. 'After a little while.' I ignored his look and went on. 'By the time I went back, she'd gone anyway.'

'So what was the bit about her hiding in your car?'

'She did. I didn't have a clue she was there. When I got to the house here, she jumped out and ran off.'

He shook his head, and I bristled. If he was about to lecture me, I was leaving. Great sex doesn't make up for being patronised or scolded like a five-year-old. He should know that by now.

'At least she told you where she was going,' he said mildly.

Good, he did know. We were back on safer ground. 'I wish she would accept help. She seems convinced that the police can't be trusted. That must come from something that happened to them in Sydney, surely.' I eyed him trying to work out if he knew any more. 'Do you know anything?'

'Not my case. You'd have to ask Swanny. I'm up to my ears in several others.'

Our food came and we started eating. I think we were both ready to let the subject drop. I was halfway through my fish when my phone rang. As always, I ignored it at first, hoping whoever it was would go away. Then I realised it might be Emma.

It was. 'Judi? Where are you?' She sounded almost hysterical, her voice in the high registers.

I pressed the phone closer to my ear to try and block out the chatter around me. 'Emma, I'm still in Melbourne. What's wrong?'

'My… my… they're both… Oh God, it's my fault. I never should… oh God. Help me.'

A dozen questions rose up but I tried to focus on her. 'I can come and get you. Right now. Where are you?' I could see Heath nodding and ducked my head, listening hard. 'Tell me where you are. Please, Emma.'

'In… in the shopping centre.'

'Highpoint?'

'No, no. The one… the one near his house. Oh shit, I don't know. It's…' She was moving, talking to someone. 'Airport West.'

I knew of it but had never been there. 'I'm coming now. Where are you in the centre? You need to be somewhere I can find easily.'

'I'm near Coles supermarket.'

I had no idea where that was. 'Is there a public toilet nearby?'

'Um… yeah, yeah, just up a bit. Hurry. They might come looking for me.'

'Listen, go into the women's toilet and into a cubicle. Lock the door and wait for me. You'll be OK in there. All right?'

'All right.' She sounded like she was crying. I would be, too.

'I'll be there as soon as I can.' I hung up and looked at Heath. He was already pulling out his wallet to pay the bill and gathering up his jacket. 'You're coming?'

'By the time I take you home to get your car, she might be gone again.'

'OK.' We raced to his car and he drove fast. It paid to have a souped-up car sometimes. I leaned forward in my seat all the same, urging him on.

'Here.' He shoved his smartphone at me. 'Google the shopping centre and find a map of all the shops. Then you can tell me which entrance to park at.'

I found it in a couple of minutes and told him, 'Westfield Drive, entry next to Kmart.'

'Great, thanks.'

'When I find her and bring her out to the car, she's going to panic.'

'Tell her I'm your fiancé or ex-husband or brother or something. Don't tell her I'm a police officer.' He glanced at me. 'Can you convince her?'

'Of course I can. I don't want her running off again.' His phone rang in my hand and I could see it was Swan calling. 'Are you going to answer him?'

'Sure. Hit that green one and then put it on speaker, please.'

I did as he asked and held the phone up closer to him.

'Heath, you still with Madam Trouble?'

Heath suppressed a smile and said, 'Yes, mate, and we've got you on speaker.'

Swan made a strangled noise and then carried on. 'We've just got to the uncle's house. Emma's not here. Not that we've found so far. But the uncle and his partner are both dead.'

I nearly dropped the phone. 'Shit, no wonder –' I snapped my mouth shut.

'Cause of death?'

'Both shot. She was at the front door, he was out in the garage working on his car. No witnesses.'

My hand holding the phone started trembling and I closed my eyes. Fuck.

'Sounds like the girl has good reason to be on the run.'

'Has Ms Westerholme heard from her?'

Heath looked at me, then back at the road, but he didn't answer.

'Heath? What's going on?'

'Sorry, mate, we're in the car and you're dropping out a bit. I'll call you back in a few minutes, OK?' He nodded at me and I disconnected.

'What are we going to do?' I asked, my voice raspy.

'Find Emma in this place and get her somewhere safe. Really safe.'

'What if she refuses? What if she tries to run again?' I was trying hard not to imagine what she'd seen at her uncle's house. Then another thought struck me. 'If the uncle was shot because they guessed Emma was heading there, wouldn't they have been waiting for her? What if she's right? What if they have followed her to this shopping centre?'

'That's why I'm going to come in with you,' he said grimly. 'And I'll be armed.' He hesitated. 'I should call for backup.'

'You can do whatever you like but I'm not waiting.'

'What if they're in there looking for her?' He swung the wheel and tyres screeched as we hurtled around the corner.

I grabbed the edge of my seat. 'I'll think of something.'

'If they start shooting?'

He was trying to frighten me into doing it his way, and I knew he was right. Sort of. But if someone was in that shopping centre with a gun, hunting me down, and I knew that people who said they'd help me were outside 'waiting for backup', well… 'They won't be expecting me. They'll be looking for a girl on her own.' I looked over at the back seat where he'd tossed a worker's high-vis orange vest. I hooked it with one hand, bundled it up and shoved it in my bag. 'Are we there yet?'

'Next street.' Two minutes later we pulled up outside the centre, parking across the doorway. He put a sign on his dashboard and said, 'I have to call in. I'll be in deep shit if I don't.'

I opened my door. 'You go right ahead. If you're not outside the women's toilet by the time we come out, I'll bring her out here. As fast as I can.'

He looked thunderous but he didn't argue, just tapped his phone and put it up to his ear.

I went in through the entrance doors and looked around. So many shops, and crowds of people on a Saturday afternoon, but I just had to find Coles. Thank God supermarkets were big and had large signs. I spotted it along the row and headed towards it while searching for the WC sign with male/female symbols. There! *Please let her still be in there.*

The toilets were busy, too. Two women and a young girl stood washing their hands at the basins, and most of the cubicle doors were closed, showing red Engaged signs. I went to the furthest away. 'Emma?'

No reply. The women had revved up the hand dryer machine and didn't take any notice of me but the girl stared. She wasn't Emma so I ignored her. 'Emma.' I rapped on the cubicle door 'Emma.'

'Judi?'

'Are you OK?'

'I guess so.'

'Can you come out?'

'I don't want to. I'm too scared.'

'Can you open the door a little bit, just so we can talk without shouting? Please?'

I waited and finally the latch clicked to Vacant and the door opened a few centimetres. Emma's face was a white mask, and she stared at me mutely.

'I've come to take you somewhere safe.'

'Where?'

'A friend is setting it up for us.'

'What friend?'

'My boyfriend.' I felt my face burn but it was kind of true.

'I don't want to come out.' Tears rolled down her cheeks.

'I know, love. But you can't live in here.' I could see she was wearing my rabbit sweatshirt. If she'd been wearing it when she went to the house, it would give her away. 'Have you got anything else to change into?'

'No. I dropped my backpack when I ran away.'

'OK.' I doubted the work vest would be any good as a disguise. 'Can you wait here for about five minutes?'

'Why? Where are you going?' Her voice rose into panic again.

'Just to get you a hat and another top to wear. I'll be really quick, I promise. It'll be like a disguise, all right?'

She nodded.

'Lock the door again. I'll let you know when I'm back. I'll call your name. Ignore any knocking.'

'OK.' She shut the door and latched it again.

I went out into the centre again and looked for Heath but he was nowhere in sight. How long does a bloody phone call take? Cotton On looked promising for cheaper clothing. I raced in and found a black hoodie almost straight away, debated about a cap and put it back. Strangely they also had fake reading glasses with blue frames so I bought them, too. Another check for Heath before going back into the toilets – nothing. Bugger!

Emma was ready to swap clothing, handing me my sweatshirt and pulling on the hoodie. After she'd tucked in her hair and I'd made sure the hood covered it all, I gave her the glasses. Deep in the recesses of my bag was a lipstick, one I rarely used that was covered in fluff. I brushed it off and gave it to her. She made a face. 'Trust me, lipstick will make you look different, give you colour.'

She came out of the cubicle to put it on using the mirror. 'Horrible colour. Doesn't even suit you.'

'That's probably why I don't wear it.' I checked her again. 'That's good. Now, when we go out, I want you to put your arm through mine. Like we're best mum-and-daughter friends. The final part of your disguise.'

I thought that would be the one she'd baulk at, but she obeyed without a word. My heart was thumping so hard by the time we came out of the hallway leading to the toilets that it was almost deafening me.

Still no Heath. I wanted to kill him. The surge of anger was good though – it got me moving through the shopping centre, pretending to point clothes out to Emma, faking a cheery smile, and walking quickly but not rushing in a panic. If Heath wasn't outside waiting with the car, I'd never ever speak to him again.

Halfway down the aisle of shops, Emma's fingers gripped my arm like pincers. 'That guy. I know him! It's him.'

Oh fuck. My legs wobbled. 'Which – no, don't tell me. Don't look. Do as I say.' I forced a bigger smile on to my face and stopped by a shop window, pointing at something even though I had no idea what it was. I couldn't see it. All I could see was faint reflections of people moving past us.

'Was he looking at you?' I said in a low voice.

'No, but he was looking around. Looking *for* me. I know he

was.' She was dragging at my arm now, like I was all that was holding her up.

'Emma! Focus. Don't look around. He's looking for a girl on her own. We have to act normally, all right?' She nodded, and I could feel her shaking against me now. 'Take a deep breath, come on, breathe in. Let it out slowly. Do it again. Keep looking in the window.' I could see now it was a menswear shop and we were both staring at a mannequin in a suit. Too bad. She was breathing, and felt a bit steadier against me.

'OK, now we'll turn and keep walking. We're almost there.' I nudged her around and half-pulled her with me. My own breath felt stuck in my throat and I coughed, then waved my arm around and let out a weird little laugh. It didn't matter, as long as I looked happy. Despite feeling like I had a huge arrow painted on my back with the words *Here she is!*

The exit doors were five metres away now, four, three... A crowd of teenage boys bowled in and nearly walked right into us. 'Sorry, sorry,' they shouted, laughing. I smiled and kept moving, making them split and flow around us. They were camouflage. The doors slid open and I desperately scanned the road. Heath's car was there, but where was he? Fuck, why had he...

Suddenly he was there in front of us, opening the rear door of the Commodore. 'Hello, ladies. Hop in.'

Emma tried to stop, pulling away from me but I snapped, 'Emma. It's my boyfriend. Come on, get in, hurry.'

Heath's eyebrows rose fractionally at the 'boyfriend' but he didn't say a word. Just as well for him. I pushed Emma across the seat and got in next to her. Heath slammed the door behind me and jumped behind the wheel. In a few seconds, we were accelerating away, and my bones turned to jelly as it hit me all at once.

'What happened?' Heath asked.

'Emma saw the guy – said he was looking for her inside the centre.'

'Right.' Heath called someone on his mobile – probably Swan – and reported what I'd said, then asked me, 'Can she describe him? Did you see him?'

That was when I realised Emma was crying, silent sobs shaking her whole body. I don't do hugs much but I gathered her up and let her cry it out on my shirt front, snot and all. Heath passed a large white hanky over from the front seat, which helped a lot.

'I didn't see him at all,' I said.

Heath nodded and muttered into his phone. I heard 'identify… possibly work… artist… safe house…' before he hung up.

'Where are we going?' I asked.

'Not sure yet. I'm waiting on Swan and his team. They're at the shopping centre, but they don't know who they're looking for.'

'You want Emma to do an identification thing, like a drawing?' She stirred in my arms and wiped her face.

'The FACE tool. It's our only option if we want to catch him. Nobody in Candlebark saw a thing.'

Over Emma's head I stared out through the front windscreen, past Heath who glanced at me occasionally in the rearview mirror. Emma sat up and turned away from me, clutching Heath's hanky. I wondered who'd taught her to cry like that, without making any noise.

Heath's mobile rang again and we both jumped. 'Heath. Yeah. Yeah. Now? Then what?'

After he'd disconnected, I said, 'You need to tell Emma what's going on.'

'I know what's going on,' she said bitterly. 'Your boyfriend is a cop. I told you they can't be trusted.'

'Why not?' I asked. 'You must have a reason.'

'Mum said it was the cops' fault we had to leave home and hide like we did. She said she should never have asked for their help.'

I looked at Heath and asked, 'Are you talking about the police in Sydney?'

'Yeah, but they're all the same, she said. Being paid off by the bastards running everything, letting people go.'

I had my own beef about certain police detectives, but that was irrelevant. 'Emma, if that guy had seen you, I wouldn't have been able to protect you. Heath and the other police can.'

'Sure they will,' she snapped and moved further away from me, huddling up against the passenger door.

We were going fast on the Ring Road, whizzing past cars on both sides, but I was still worried she'd jump out if we slowed down somewhere. As if reading my mind, Heath turned his head and mouthed, 'Child lock' at me, and I relaxed a bit. As we flew over the Westgate Bridge, the suicide fence a blur of grey-black, I gazed at the soaring city skyscrapers and the apartment blocks in Docklands. It'd be like human battery chooks in one of those. My hands twitched and I wanted to be in my garden with Mia, planting broad beans or thinning out the parsley.

At the police building in Spencer Street, we drove underneath to the car park, stopped by security for a few minutes to prove we were legit, and around to the area near the lifts. As Heath put the car in Park, I leant forward and said softly, 'I have to get back to the pub for tonight's shift.'

'I know. Let's just get Emma safe upstairs first.'

He opened the back door and I slid out, then turned to Emma. 'Come on. I could do with a strong coffee. How about you? I'm sure they can find you a sandwich at least.'

The lift doors opened and Swan and Chandler stepped out.

Great. The last people I wanted to see. Swan looked predictably grim, but Chandler came over first, her face friendly, and shook my hand. 'Detective Constable Lauren Chandler. And this is Emma?'

Emma was still climbing out of the car, head down. She barely muttered, 'Yeah.'

Lauren smiled at Emma even though the girl wasn't looking at her. 'Great. We're really glad you got here safely.'

Emma gave her a disbelieving look, but when Chandler asked her when the last time she'd eaten was, Emma muttered, 'Dunno.'

'Let's go and find you some food. Would you like coffee or hot chocolate?'

'Hot chocolate,' Emma mumbled.

'Great. I'll even share some of my stash of marshmallows.'

The detective was trying too hard, but at least she was trying. She led the way to the lift, Emma shuffling behind, followed by me. Heath had gone to park his car and I didn't look at Swan – I didn't want to give him an opportunity to launch into questions or criticism of my decisions. I'd done my best. If they didn't like it, they could shove it where the sun didn't shine.

In the end, we all crowded into the same lift, and my heart sank. Swan wasn't letting us out of his sight. I was loath to leave Emma in their clutches, even if Chandler seemed friendly. Upstairs, she led us to a bland room with some decent looking beige couches and chairs, which I assumed was the kind of place where they dealt with families or witnesses. She offered me coffee and went off to get our hot drinks, and I was glad to see Swan leaving us alone for now. He paused outside the door, making a phone call, and then disappeared down the hallway.

Emma perched on the edge of a couch and I sat next to her. 'You won't leave me here, will you?' she said, her voice trembling.

'I do have to work tonight,' I said.

'No! You have to stay!' Her eyes were wild and she looked around for an escape route.

'Emma, it's fine. They'll keep you safe.'

'You don't know *anything*,' she said. 'Just because you're sleeping with one of them.'

'That's nothing to do with it. They've helped me before. You can trust Heath.' My words weren't making any difference.

She jumped up and started pacing around the room, shoulders hunched, biting her fingernails. I wanted to tell her that the police had saved Mia, saved me from gangland thugs, solved Macca's murder – but in all honesty, I couldn't.

All the same, I wasn't playing detective this time. This time I really was going to leave it all to the police.

'I can't stay here,' Emma said.

'I know it's not very homely, but… where else have you got to go?' I almost offered to let her stay with me, but if someone really was after her, it would put Mia in danger, and I wasn't having that.

Chandler came back with two steaming cups with another woman following close behind, carrying plastic-cased sandwiches and a chocolate muffin. I thought longingly of my abandoned lunch, not to mention my abandoned glass of very nice Sauv Blanc. Emma just stared at the food and made no move to open it. Chandler and the woman sat opposite us, making themselves comfy on the other couch like we were in a book club or something. I guessed the woman was some kind of family liaison officer.

'Emma, do eat something,' Lauren urged. 'You look like you haven't eaten for days.' She kept glancing at the chocolate muffin as if she wouldn't have minded eating it herself.

'How would you know, *Detective* Chandler?' Emma said. She shoved herself back on the couch and pulled her legs up, hugging her knees.

'Call me Lauren,' Chandler said. 'It's easier.' And a bit more friendly. They both watched her, looking concerned. I wasn't sure how genuine it was. Lauren leaned forward. 'How would you feel about helping us create a picture of this guy?'

Emma shrugged. 'What's the point? You won't find him.'

'I think we will,' Lauren said. 'According to what we know so far, he's responsible for three murders, including your mother. Don't you want us to catch him and put him away?'

'How are you going to do that?' she said. 'He isn't even from down here.'

Lauren stiffened. 'You mean you know who he is? His name?'

Emma laughed a bit hysterically. 'Stop looking at me like I'm going to save all your arses and do your fucking job for you!'

Lauren frowned. 'I don't know what you mean, Emma.'

Emma hugged her knees harder and refused to answer, but I could hear her muttering under her breath. 'You know nothing, you know nothing.'

Stalemate.

10

Lauren opened her mouth again to question Emma but I jumped in. 'Emma, if you were able, what would you do? Where would you go?'

Tears spilled down her cheeks. 'I'd turn back time. I'd make my mum move to Bali or America or Siberia. Anywhere but staying here.'

I could see by their faces that the two cops thought she was being ridiculous, but there was more to it than a teen tantrum. They needed to get their shit together and stop treating Emma like a criminal for not cooperating.

'Why did you have to move?' I asked gently. 'What happened?'

'It was his fault. Mikey. Mum should never…'

'Do you mean your stepdad?'

'Mikey? Shit, no!' She glared at me. 'That loser was never my stepdad. He was just a moron, a leech. He had Mum twisted up and doing whatever he wanted.'

I didn't want to let on I already knew a lot of this. 'But he's in gaol now. In Sydney?'

'Yeah. Serves him right.'

I glanced at Lauren but she sat impassively, waiting to see what I would ask next.

'Is your dad still alive?'

She shrugged. 'Dunno. He dumped Mum when I was little. I don't even know where he is.'

'So Mikey caused you both a lot of trouble. Is that why you had to leave Sydney?'

It seemed like a pretty straightforward question, but she froze and then jerked her whole body away from me. 'I'm not talking to any of you anymore.'

And she meant it. All three of us tried for about ten minutes but she never said another word. I saw Heath hovering outside and went out to talk to him.

'Is she going to help?'

'Nup.' I checked my watch again. Shit, it was nearly four. 'I have to go. Can you take me back to my car?'

'You're leaving Emma here?'

'Happy to take her with me,' I snapped. 'Except, if this guy really is after her, we might all end up dead.' Oops, that was a bit over the top, but the whole day had stressed me to the limit.

His face tightened and he took a breath. 'Chandler's not getting anywhere, and I think maybe Swan will make her worse.'

'You think?'

'Judi, you're not helping either.'

OK, that was it. I'd had enough of all of them. 'Fine. No problem. I'll go back to my pub then.' I spun around and went back to Emma, bending down to whisper to her. 'I have to go back to Candlebark. I've got to work at the pub. Do you want me to come back here tomorrow morning and help you? Yes or no?'

She stared up at me with big red-rimmed eyes. 'Yes, please.'

I moved up to a murmur. 'All right. If you can help these guys, great, but I'm not going tell you what to do. You have to think it through and make your own decisions about what's right for you. I'll see you tomorrow morning, unless you call me and say don't come, all right?'

She nodded and then launched herself off the couch to hug

me, her thin fingers digging into my shoulders. I hugged her back, wishing I could take away some of her pain, but first of all she had to let me in more. Tomorrow.

The atmosphere in the car going back to my place was a bit frosty, but there was nothing I could do about it. He was being a cop, and I was being me. I wasn't going to make it worse by saying anything. When we arrived, I said, 'Thanks for the lift. I'm sorry our lovely lunch got hijacked.'

'Are you coming back down tomorrow?'

I nodded. 'I don't pick Mia up until the afternoon, but if Emma still wants me with her, I'm happy to do that. Unless Swan doesn't want me to. He might think I'll be a bad influence on her, but I'm trying to help.'

'Hopefully she'll agree to assist with identifying her mother's killer.'

'Yes, hopefully.' But I was convinced she wouldn't, and I spent most of my trip back to Candlebark wondering why not. Not that I came up with any answers, just a lot of possibilities. My main theory was that she knew the guy somehow, as in *knew* him, not just knew who he was. An old boyfriend of her mum's perhaps, or someone in their family, or more likely a good mate of Mikey's.

I was running late so didn't bother to go home and get changed. Andre would be champing at the bit, trying to get ready for the dinner bookings, and I had to check on Marie and Charlie to make sure they were both OK working the Saturday night shift. Chris Winter should have left, so I wouldn't need to be the night manager at least. A dozen tasks awaited, but I started with Andre.

He was tasting something bubbling on the stove top, and screwed up his face as he thought about whether it was 'right' or not, then added a couple of ingredients. Finally, he noticed I was there.

'Hey, how was your lunch?' He waggled his eyebrows and smiled lasciviously.

I laughed. 'It was great, thanks, until it got interrupted.' I gave him a quick rundown on Emma hiding in my car, her uncle and aunt's murders and then rescuing Emma from the shopping centre. Even to my ears, it sounded ridiculous, like a terrible TV drama, and his face reflected my thought.

'God, Judi, can't you just go to Melbourne and shop, like normal people?' he said.

'I know.' I sighed. 'And I'm supposed to go back in the morning early and be there for Emma. I think she's going to be in a bad way after a night with the police.'

He shook his head. 'Even when you want to stay out of it, you get dragged in.'

'Maybe you could go,' I said. 'You know Emma better than me. You must've talked to her a bit when you were seeing Kate.'

'Not really. She didn't seem very impressed with me.'

'Shock, horror! How could she not like you?' I was more than half-serious.

'I don't think it was me so much.' He frowned. 'Looking back, I suspect it was just that she didn't want her mum to be with anyone.'

'Jealousy?'

'Mmm, no. More… worry and annoyance.'

I was tempted to run all my theories past him, but there was no time.

'We've got bookings for a lot of tables tonight,' Andre said. 'I've persuaded Marie to run the drinks for you.'

'How on earth did you manage that?'

Andre grinned. 'Believe it or not, she wants to be a chef, so I've promised to teach her some basics and, if she works hard, to help her get into the course in Melbourne.'

I shook my head in amazement. 'Now I really have heard everything.'

I went into the bar to talk to Charlie and, after a quick check on how everything had gone in the afternoon – which was pretty slow as nobody wanted to come in and watch the cricket – I turned to find Chris Winter at the end of the bar with a beer in front of him. I could feel my mouth turn down and I tried to summon a smile but it wouldn't come out even with coaxing.

'Hey,' he said, with a big smile. 'I didn't think you were working tonight.'

'We've been a bit short-staffed for one reason or another,' I said shortly. I wasn't going to mention Kate, but his face fell.

'Yeah, sorry. Didn't mean to be tactless.'

I found myself warming to him a little. 'Are you still staying with us?'

'Yes, I did ask Charlie here, and he said it would be fine.'

Charlie knew our financial situation and that we weren't able to turn away any customers. Damn it, I'd have to sleep here myself.

'Er, you look like you'd rather I left,' Chris said, his forehead creased in dismay.

'Sorry,' I said quickly, my face burning. 'Nothing to do with you, truly. I just have a lot going on and my mind was on other stuff. It's perfectly OK.' I tried to be a bit friendlier. 'You seem to have taken a liking to Candlebark.'

'I love it here,' he said. 'Really needed a break, and now I'm thinking I should look around for a place, like a weekender. Where do you live?'

'Over that way.' I waved my hand vaguely. No way was I telling him my address. 'I don't know of anywhere for sale at the moment, but you could ask around.' I hoped he wouldn't, but he did seem keen. Unfortunately.

'I'll do that,' he said. 'I'm getting to know a few of the locals already.' He looked past me. 'Jock, my man, speak of the devil.'

Old Jock had plonked himself down, three bar stools away, and grunted a reply.

'What'll you have?' Chris said. 'My shout.'

I'd never known Old Jock to reject a shout from anyone. I thought he'd probably accept one from Lucifer, even if his pitchfork was on fire.

'Beer,' Jock said, and Charlie poured him his usual. I excused myself and went back to the bistro to set more tables, then hid myself in the ladies toilets for ten minutes, having a wash and trying to look a bit more presentable and bit less like a seedy actress in a terrible TV drama. Dinner was over within two hours, thanks to Andre's smaller menu, and I was able to pop into the bar as well now and then. Scottie turned up a bit later and joined Old Jock, and Chris seemed to be doing his best to make friends with them. I could've told him not to bother. After Macca's death, and their being questioned about the illegal tobacco dealing, they'd both taken on an aggrieved air in the pub, as if seeing Andre and me in charge gave them chronic indigestion. I had no doubt that if there was another pub here, they would've decamped and I would've helped them.

By the end of the evening, Chris Winter had either sat at the bar or been eating in the bistro the whole time, and he was still on his bar stool. I don't think he'd drunk much, and he certainly didn't appear to be inebriated. He spent a lot of time on his phone, reading and tapping, and glancing up at the races on the TV, so I assumed he was betting online. As the last race at Moonee Valley finished, he let out a little whoop and waved me over.

'Had a good win on that one,' he said. 'Can I shout you a drink? You've had a long night.'

I was about to refuse, then stopped myself. He was a customer, he wasn't that bad, and it wouldn't kill me to accept a drink. 'Thanks, much appreciated.' I poured myself a Jack Daniels on ice and took a large sip. It burned all the way down and perked me up, making me almost forget my aching feet. I continued to load glasses in the dishwasher while Charlie went around collecting them. Marie had left at 9pm after the bistro closed. She'd worked a full day with hardly any complaining. It was a miracle.

'I had a look online for a place to buy,' Chris said. 'There isn't a lot around, is there?'

'It's a small place,' I said.

'I could rent, I suppose.'

'What – just for occasional weekends?'

He frowned a little. 'I could use it as a base for my business.'

I didn't want a conversation, but I also didn't want to upset him. Who knew how long he'd be staying at the pub? 'What do you do?'

'I'm a small business adviser. I help people with financial problems. We're expanding outside of Melbourne metro.' He handed me a card that had someone else's name on it, and I frowned at it. 'My partner,' he said quickly. 'I've run out of my own cards.'

'Right.' Odd, but it happened. I slammed the dishwasher door shut and pressed the button. 'I would've thought you'd be better off in a big place like Bendigo.'

He pursed his mouth. 'I don't like Bendigo much. Phil's going to cover that area. By the way, I guess you know about my little problem at night.'

Uh-oh. I pretended I knew nothing and waited impatiently for whatever BS he was about to try on me.

'I, ah, I sleepwalk.' He drank down the last of his beer. 'Tried everything to control it, but the doc says if I won't take medication, then I just have to put up with it. Try to de-stress my life.' He shrugged. 'Just thought I should tell you. I think I gave your night manager a bit of a scare.'

'My concern is that you might fall down the stairs.' I knew the damage that could do. But I also knew he'd told Andre something different.

'I seem to be OK with things like that,' he said. 'But if I wander in strange places, I can get lost. Weird, I know. Hopefully, it won't happen tonight.'

I bit my lip, then said, 'Thanks for telling me.' I forced a smile and went through to the office, checking that the takings were in the safe and all was right with the pub before Charlie went home. By the time I returned to the bar, Chris Winter had gone upstairs and I let out a relieved sigh. I topped up my JD, turned out all the lights and sat in the darkened bar for a while, staring out the window at the main street of Candlebark.

I checked my phone and discovered I'd missed a call from Geoff and Lucy, but they'd sent me a video instead – it was Mia, waving me goodnight and kissing the screen. Suddenly, I wanted her right there with me so I could hold her close and smell her little girl scent of soap and biscuits. I wanted to look at her and think of my brother and remember the good times we'd had. And I wished I'd heard the call tone and answered it, instead of running around the pub looking after other people.

My thoughts skipped around and back to Emma. What would happen to her? It sounded like her uncle had been her only family. Without him, would she end up in foster care? It seemed so unfair, so wrong. I pictured her pale, thin face. What had their life been like in Sydney? Kate had seemed happy here, enjoyed working at the pub, but I'd never had any inkling about her personal life.

What was there in her past that had led to her murder? A violent partner? Mikey was inside, so… Didn't stop him from seeking revenge though. It wouldn't be the first time. Yet why would the killer also want to get rid of Emma? Sure, she was a witness, but all he had to do was wear a ski mask or something.

The highs and lows of the day gradually took their toll and my body started to sink further into the chair. I'd fall asleep there if I wasn't careful. I levered myself up, checked the doors again, and went upstairs to find the old PJs and bag of toiletries I'd left in the linen cupboard. Within a few minutes I was in bed and drifting off.

It was the front door that woke me up. It was almost directly beneath my room and, even though it hadn't banged, the click of it closing was loud enough to filter through to me. Either that or I was on edge anyway. Bloody Chris Winter and his stupid sleepwalking! I really didn't want to have to see what was going on, but if he'd gone outside and then woke up somewhere strange, he wouldn't be able to get back in. Nobody goes sleepwalking with their keys in their pocket. I groaned and crawled out of bed, going to the window.

Nobody in sight. No, wait, there he was, coming out of the shadows under the trees by the pub car park. I didn't know what a sleepwalker looked like. I was half-expecting him to have his arms out ahead of him or weaving around like a drunk. Instead he was ambling casually up the street.

'Shit, shit, shit.' I pulled clothes on over my PJs, grabbed my keys and ran downstairs, letting myself out quietly. Something told me to be stealthy and hide, rather than barge up the street like a banshee, waving and shouting at him. At the other end, at the entrance to the old mechanic's workshop, he disappeared.

Had he fallen in the drain there, or wandered into the workshop? I was pretty sure the doors were locked. The place hadn't been used for years, although it still smelled of old oil and metal filings. I scooted along the street, patting my pocket for my phone in case I needed to call Connor. I didn't like this at all. If Winter really was sleepwalking, I might just shout in his ear and frighten the crap out of him to teach him not to do it anymore.

When I got close to the workshop entrance, I stopped at the corner and peeked around it. The concrete apron was empty, dark with shadows from the surrounding buildings, and there were no lights showing in the workshop. Well, why would there be? I could see the padlock on the main roller door from here. Then I heard voices.

People who were sleepwalking didn't carry on conversations.

The voices were muffled; they were coming from a narrow walkway down the side of the workshop. At least two people were in the parking area at the back, having a meet-up. No way was I going down there to see who it was. Instead, I backed away and checked around me. Across the street was an old shop that had once sold craft stuff and wool like a few other places in Candlebark, it was empty now. But it had a deep porch, away from the streetlight, and it would make a good spot to watch from.

I ran across to it and hid, keeping my back against the dusty old wooden door, hoping there were no spiders that would get narky about me disturbing them. Just when I was starting to shiver with the night chill and thinking about going back to the pub, there was movement at the workshop. Winter came out of the walkway and headed back to the pub, striding quickly. Sleepwalking, my arse!

He was halfway down the street when I heard the sound of a vehicle starting up. I stayed where I was, scanning the area and caught a glimpse of a ute as it rumbled to the corner, turned right and headed out of town. I'd know that fluorescent-green thing anywhere – it was Scottie's son, Brendan. Now why had he been meeting up with Winter? I was pretty sure they weren't convening the inaugural Candlebark Sleepwalkers' Club.

Except, at the sound of the ute, Winter had stopped and

moved back into a doorway, like me. Strange. When the street was silent again, I followed Winter back to the pub, not at all surprised he went back inside without any trouble. Clearly he'd taken his door keys. I did my best to close the front door without making any noise – just a faint click. I sat in the bar for about ten minutes until I hoped he'd be asleep again, then I crept back up to my room. I'd think about whether to report the midnight walk to Connor or not in the morning. This day had been long enough.

I was up early, and at 7.01am I called Connor. As always, he sounded awake and alert. He must train himself to be like that every time his phone rang, like a guard dog. 'Judi. Emergency?'

'No, an update. Thought you might like one.' He listened as I described everything that had happened yesterday in Melbourne, minus Heath and I and you-know-what, and that I was heading back down there shortly.

'Can't believe it,' Connor muttered. 'Poor kid.'

'Yes. I don't know how I can help her but I feel like I have to try. Plus there's this.' I told him about Winter and the middle of the night meeting. 'What's Brendan been up to lately?'

'Good question. Lying low, like his dad, I would have said. But this sounds like they're planning something.'

'More chop chop dealing?'

'I doubt it. The Customs people are keeping an eye on this area now.'

'Do you have anything on Chris Winter?' I asked. 'Have you checked him out?'

'I didn't have any reason to,' he said. 'I will go and have a look at him though.'

'Can you tell me if you find anything, please? If he's going to stay here any longer, I need to know what I'm dealing with.'

Connor cleared his throat. 'You realise I'm not supposed to do that.'

'Pro quid whatever it is. I've provided you with plenty of info over the last few months.'

'True.' There was a long pause. 'You're not getting into anything, are you?'

'It wasn't my fault that Emma was hiding at my house,' I said impatiently. 'And I had nothing whatsoever to do with Kate's murder. It was a huge shock.'

'Yeah, OK. Sorry. Look, if I find out he's dangerous or wanted or anything, I'll tell you. But if he just owes for a few parking fines, no deal.'

'Fine. That works for me.' I stood up, wanting to be on the move now. 'I'll talk to you when I get back tonight.'

'Drive safely.'

Like I ever did anything else these days!

It looked like Winter was sleeping in so I didn't have to be nice to him until Andre arrived. Andre said he had plenty to do in the kitchen and waved me off. After a shower and change of clothes at home, I set off on the road to Melbourne again. Halfway there, I stopped for coffee and a bacon and egg toastie at a café that advertised 'monster brekkies for truckies' and had a parking area the size of the MCG, and called Swan.

'How's Emma?' I asked as soon as he picked up.

'Good morning to you, too, Ms Westerholme.'

'Yeah, sorry. Is she OK?'

'Can't fault you for your focus. She's fine. She has spent the night in a hotel with Detective Constable Chandler to look after her. Was that all you wanted?'

Just as well we weren't on video phone. My facial expression would've given him nightmares. *Calm down.* 'I'd like to see her this morning. And find out what's going to happen to her.'

'You're not her guardian. Or even a relative.'

'I'm a friend,' I snapped. 'Her only one at the moment. I'm looking out for her. Is that such a bad thing?'

He sighed loudly. 'I suppose not.' A short silence. 'She still refuses to do any identification work with us. Do you think you could persuade her?'

My turn to stay silent while I considered it. I wanted him to grovel but I'd be wasting my time. 'I can try. You do realise how scared she is?'

'Yes. I'm not completely heartless.'

I didn't dare answer that.

He went on, 'It's going to be difficult to guarantee her safety if we don't know who to look for. Putting this guy away is her only hope.'

I finished my coffee and threw the cup in the large black bin at the side of the parking area. A huge semi roared past me so I had to wait for it to go before I could talk. 'I get that. I'll be at the police HQ in less than an hour. Will you be there?'

'No, but I'll make sure Chandler and Emma are here by the time you arrive.'

Great. I hung up and got back in the Benz. Despite my annoyance at Swan, I wanted the guy caught, too. There was no way I wanted Mia or me to be caught in the crossfire. I spent the rest of the trip south trying to think up various ways to convince Emma to do the ID thing.

I didn't get very far.

11

I had to wait for a while in the reception area at police HQ before an officer came down to get me. I used some of the time to call Geoff and Lucy, who were at the park near their house. Mia was on the swing, Geoff said. Did I want to talk to her?

'No, I'm just checking that pick-up time is still one o'clock.'

'Yep, all good.'

I disconnected, ignoring the little niggle that said maybe I wouldn't make it in time. I signed in and was taken upstairs, back to the same beige room to find Emma sitting in the corner of a couch, knees up as usual. But she wasn't as hostile as yesterday, and it looked like Lauren Chandler had been allowed to buy her some new clothes. Emma sported new jeans and a long-sleeved T-shirt, and her fingernails sparkled with blue polish. Lauren had been playing girl stuff with her then. Probably a good thing – it might've helped make Emma feel more normal.

Emma greeted me with a casual 'Hey', but didn't offer any conversation. I was beginning to wonder why I was there.

Until Lauren sat down next to Emma. 'So, we'd really like to work on the ID picture with you now,' she said.

Emma immediately pulled in on herself, but she didn't refuse outright. I shut up and let Lauren do the work.

'Are you into computers much?'

Emma shrugged.

'Instagram? TikTok?' She didn't wait for the girl's reply. 'This computer program we have is pretty cool. It's a bit like a jigsaw puzzle. You take a bit of this and a bit of that and stick them together until you have a face.'

Emma picked at her new nail polish.

Lauren glanced at me. 'I think Judi has used it before. Haven't you?'

That was my cue. 'Yes. It's really interesting. And helpful.'

Emma sent me a snaky look. Then she said, 'For your brother, yeah?'

I nodded. 'Well, not exactly. It was for the two guys who attacked me.'

'You? You didn't tell me that.' She was wide-eyed.

I didn't like bringing it up again, or using it to manipulate Emma, but this was important. They really did need to find this guy. He'd now killed three people. I tried not to think of my desperate escape with Emma from the shopping centre.

I held up my hand, turning it 180 degrees. 'The scar has faded a fair bit now. But the guy's knife went all the way through.'

'Really?' But Emma didn't lean forward to look closer.

'I did the computer thing and found both guys. It helped a lot.'

'Yeah, sure it did.' She sounded scornful, but not hostile.

Lauren looked kind of bland, like she was backing right off and leaving it to me. Clearly Swan hadn't given her a heads-up about me. I was done with patient coaxing.

'Well, you've got two or three alternatives here, Emma,' I said. 'One is that you just keep refusing to help the cops identify the guy who is after you, and eventually they'll palm you off into foster care, because that's their only alternative.' I could see Lauren stiffening, but I kept my eyes on Emma. 'Another one is that you walk out of here and make your own way. To somewhere. God knows where. Have you actually got anyone you could call on for help that you don't think will be murdered if they get in the way?'

'Hey, hang on a moment, you –'

I overrode Lauren and kept going. 'Or you can pull your finger out and help these detectives. Because, whether you believe it or not, they are actually trying to help you. As am I. You think I really wanted to come into that shopping centre and rescue you from the toilets? I came because I cared. I really liked your mum. I like you. But for fuck's sake, help us out here.'

Emma got a mulish look on her face, one that every teenage girl in history has probably perfected, but after a long silence, she muttered, 'All right, if I have to.'

'That's great,' Lauren said, jumping in too fast.

'But you have to come with me,' Emma said to me. 'Or I won't do it.'

'I can stay for a little while,' I said, 'but then I have to pick Mia up, and go home.'

'You're leaving me here?' Her face was filled with panic now, her eyes shiny with tears.

'I can't...' I looked at Lauren who looked blank for a moment, then finally got the hint.

'Judi isn't allowed to take you with her. She's not a registered foster carer.'

'I don't care,' Emma shouted. 'I'm not going to go to some stranger's house like a piece of fucking garbage nobody wants.'

'It's not like that,' Lauren said. 'You won't be going anywhere, for a while at least. You're under our protection. You're in danger. You said you were. We know you are. Do you want to put Judi and Mia in danger, too?'

Tears ran down Emma's face. 'It's not fair. We just wanted a normal life.'

I leaned forward and took her hand. She tried to pull away but I gripped harder. 'Emma, everyone wants you safe. Your mum would want you safe. When they get this guy, you will be. If you want to, I bet they'll put you in witness protection.'

'As if I care about that! I want my mum back.' She sat there sobbing her heart out, and nobody moved for a few seconds until I jerked my head at Lauren to get her to move and I sat next to Emma, hugging her again. It seemed like this was my main job, to be her shoulder to cry on, but that was OK. She badly needed somebody in her corner. I knew what that felt like.

Finally, when her sobs had stopped and she'd used a bunch of tissues to blow her nose and wipe her face, she whispered, 'Better get this shit done then.'

I wanted to hug her again for being so tough and strong, even when she least felt like it, but right now she did need to do the ID. I stayed with her long enough to get her talking to the technician and sorting out how it all worked, and then said goodbye. 'I'll try to come back to Melbourne in a couple of days,' I promised. 'All going well.'

As I left the police building, guilt flooded through me. I knew I had to put Mia first and protect her, but I felt bloody awful leaving Emma behind. Lauren had said she or another female officer would be with Emma twenty-four hours a day, and they'd take good care of her, but I still felt like I was deserting her. My hand shook as I put the key in the door lock of the Benz, and I sat in the driver's seat for a few minutes to pull myself together before I went to collect Mia. I didn't do a very good job of it.

Geoff and Lucy both picked up that I wasn't my usual self, but I faked it well enough for Mia that she didn't notice. She talked at the top of her voice, pulling me through the house to her bedroom and showing me her new books. 'Take them home,' she demanded.

'But if you do that,' I said, 'they won't be here for you next time.'

'Oh. Take Bum home?' The rabbit was next to her little bag of clothes and toys.

'Of course. Bum has to help with the garden.'

'Carrots,' she said. 'Bum said we have carrots, like Bunny Bug.'

I glanced at Lucy who laughed. 'Bugs Bunny.'

Soon, we were in the car and heading back to Candlebark and, by the time we passed Calder Park Raceway, she was asleep, leaving me with my own thoughts and a twisting gut as we got further and further away from Emma. I kept looking at Mia and telling myself, 'She comes first, she comes first.' It helped, but not a huge amount.

Back at the pub, chaos awaited. I walked in to find Bronwyn in full hysteria, berating Andre. Sunday lunch was over, and all the tables were cleared, so I had no idea how many customers we'd had, but apparently some of them were Bronwyn's guests. Andre kept trying to get a word in, his jaw set and his eyes angry, but she was in full flow.

'You are doing this deliberately!' she shouted.

'Bronwyn,' I snapped. 'Calm down!'

She swung around, flinging her arms out and nearly hit me in the face. I ducked just in time, and the stress of my weekend began to morph into a cold anger.

'They're leaving!' she shrieked at me, her face dark red with fury. 'It's all your fault. Neither of you have ever supported me. You're going to be the ruin of me!'

I was in no mood for this crap. 'Bronwyn, get out! Now!' I shouted.

To my horror, Mia, who'd followed me in, burst into frightened tears. I scooped her up and glared at Bronwyn, who'd actually shut up for a second, but her mouth was already opening to object.

'I mean it,' I threatened in a lower voice. 'I'll give you five seconds or I'm calling the police. How dare you blame us? Try looking in your own backyard.'

She wasn't backing down that easily. 'My guests come to me for rejuvenation and health. Not for the fatty, fried rubbish you serve here!'

I didn't bother answering. 'Andre, call Connor, please. This woman is disturbing the peace. I might even get her arrested for child abuse.'

Andre pulled out his phone and tapped it quickly, then put it up to his ear.

Bronwyn's face turned an even deeper shade of purple-red. 'How dare you!' she spat. 'You'll pay for this. Wendell and I are going to sue!'

'Give it your best shot,' I gritted out. 'Now get out before Connor arrives or you'll be very sorry.'

She turned in a swirl of peasant skirt and stalked out, slamming the front door behind her.

Andre said, 'Can I hang up now?'

I almost said yes, then changed my mind. Her threats sounded ominously like the phone calls I'd had. That Wendell could easily have made at her command. 'No, ask him to come here and we'll make a report. I want a record of her behaviour. I have a horrible feeling this won't be the end of it.'

When Connor arrived about fifteen minutes later, I'd calmed Mia down, assuring her the nasty woman would not come back and frighten her or Bum again. Andre had told me four of today's lunch customers were from her health retreat, and all four had packed their bags and were calling in for lunch before they made their permanent escape. Apparently they'd regaled Andre with horror tales of quinoa and brown rice and yoga sessions in the freezing cold at 4am. More worrying were their promises to give the health retreat terrible one-star reviews so nobody would ever be tempted to go there again. That's what would kill Bronwyn's business, not our bistro menu.

'Bronwyn has no idea,' Andre said. 'She's got so much competition – Daylesford isn't that far away, and there are luxurious health spas galore in that area.'

Connor was in civvies and explained he wasn't technically on duty, but he came anyway. He listened to Andre and shook his head. 'She's a difficult woman. I've had her into the station several times, complaining about the speed limit on her road, and also about the smell from the farm next door. A pollution complaint, she said.'

'She was shouting and threatening Andre when I got here,' I said. 'It made me wonder if she was responsible for those phone calls I've been getting.'

'You said that was a man though.'

'She could've been faking a deep voice,' I said. 'But I think she got her partner, Wendell, to do it.'

'Yes, that's possible,' said Connor. 'He seems quite under her spell.'

Andre and I glanced at each other in disbelief.

Mia came running across from the play area. 'Unca Connor, I went on a swing today with Nanna and Poppa. I went up high to the sky.'

He grinned at her. 'That's great, Mia. Did you go on the slide, too?'

'Yes, I did. I was a big girl.' She checked my expression, which was probably grumpy, and tugged at Connor's shirt sleeve. 'There was a lady here and she shouted. And Juddy shouted, too.'

'That's not very nice, is it?' he said.

'Not when their faces are like this.' She screwed up her little face, looking remarkably similar to when she was trying to do a poo. I immediately tried to smooth my face out and paste on a smile.

'It's all fixed now, Mia,' I said. 'We can all be happy now.'

She checked me out again and seemed satisfied that she could go back to the toys.

Connor made some notes and confirmed the time that Bronwyn was in the pub, then stood. 'OK, I have a record of it all. I've got to go, sorry.'

'Hot date?' Andre asked.

Connor's face went pink. 'No, just dinner with Leslie.'

'You're bringing her here?' I said, astonished.

'Er, no, she's coming to my place and I'm cooking.'

Before I could say anything about Connor's cooking consisting of phoning for pizza, Andre chipped in. 'I've been helping him. He's just about perfected my chicken and white wine dish.'

For a moment I was stuck for words. 'That's, er, great. Have fun. Don't burn anything.'

Connor checked his watch. 'I'd better go or I will burn something.' He got halfway to the door and turned back. 'Listen, can you give me a hand in the morning? Len Greenhall wants Kate and Emma's stuff cleaned out of his house they were renting.'

'Sure.' I'd be able to collect it all for Emma. 'He's in an unseemly hurry.'

'Yeah, well, now the crime scene techs have finished, he's already rented it to someone else.'

Before I could ask who, he'd gone. Andre made Mia a toasted sandwich, and I cleaned and vacuumed the bistro and set tables while he sorted Sunday night dinner out. He'd made Sundays roast days, to pull in the locals who couldn't be bothered cooking their own, and as the beef and pork were already cooking, he had a million spuds to peel.

I was just about to call Joleen for childcare when it occurred to me to ask Andre about Chris Winter.

'Yeah, he had breakfast just after you left, and that's the last I've seen of him all day. He did say he's staying tonight, though.'

'Bugger. I don't want to have to stay here with Mia.' I explained about the so-called sleepwalking and the green ute.

Andre frowned. 'He's meeting up with Brendan Scott? He's bad news.'

'Brendan refuses to drink here. I think he goes to Heathcote.'

'Just as well. Scottie's bad enough.' Andre sighed. 'Maybe we'll have to close the accommodation for a few months.'

'I think you're right. It's not worth it for one person, and there's never a way to say, "Yes, we can take your room booking if you bring more people".'

'I know what we can do.' He waved his hand around his head. 'We can run health weekends here on a theme. Once we put Bronwyn out of business, we can take over. We could offer a French weekend – lots of butter and wine. A Spanish weekend – I cook a mean paella. Piece of cake!'

'Your cakes are very good,' I said. 'How about we run fake Government House afternoon teas, like they do at the Windsor? High Teas, that's what they call them.'

We both laughed and went off to do our own work on getting the pub ready for Sunday night trade, but the conversation stuck with me. Maybe nobody here would want a High Tea, but now the outside area had been cleaned up, we could run kids' birthday parties with cakes and sausage rolls and stuff. Maybe parents would love a venue where they could have wine and beer with their sausage rolls. I made some notes and decided I'd give it serious thought. And I kind of liked Andre's theme weekends, too. Why the hell not? It was worth a try.

I dropped Mia in at Joleen's and promised myself yet again that this had to stop. Andre was right – we had to close the accommodation.

Just after six, Chris Winter turned up. I was serving in the bar alongside our Sunday barperson, a woman called Bev who normally worked at the aged care home. The pay there was pretty crap, so the Sunday lunch and night shift with us earned her enough to keep her head above water, and gave Charlie Sunday and Monday off.

Chris sat quietly at the end of the bar, tapping on his phone as usual, and ordered wine when I asked him what he wanted. 'A good local red. What do you recommend?'

I offered him a Shiraz from Sanguine Estate and he smiled. 'Sanguine, eh? Ironic, but I do always believe in being positive.'

I squashed down my surprise that he knew what sanguine meant and poured him a little bit to try.

'Very nice,' he said, gesturing for me to fill the glass. 'I heard it's roast night tonight.'

'It is. I'd get in early if I was you,' I said, putting the lid back on the bottle. 'Once it's gone, it's gone.'

He smiled again and went back to his phone, leaving me wondering yet again who he really was and why he was here. I couldn't recall getting a straight answer out of him but his late-night meeting made me uneasy, and I was glad I'd mentioned it to Connor. I didn't want to be the town snitch, but running a pub put me in the position more than I liked. Oh, for the days when I was determined to be a hermit and stay in my little house all the time.

Roast night was becoming a hit, and even the public bar was busier than usual. Bev and I were kept running, and I helped Andre with orders and food delivery. I was very glad when he said both roasts were sold out, even though it meant I missed out. After the bistro had emptied and the tables cleared, he brought me out a plate and flourished it in front of me.

'You are bloody brilliant,' I said, my mouth already watering. 'How did you know I was desperate for the roast pork?'

He tapped his nose. 'Just a really wild guess.'

After everything was closed and Bev had left, I waved Andre off and grabbed my room key. This was becoming far too much of a habit. I sat in the darkened bar and sipped some JD, thinking this was becoming too much of a habit as well. But it was treasured quiet time, and I pondered birthday parties and theme weekends. I really thought we were on to something. And why wait to see whether Bronwyn went under? We'd be doing something very different from her, although she might not see it that way.

I fell asleep in my usual room, hoping Chris Winter wouldn't do his pretend sleepwalking trick again. I was tired enough to think maybe this time the door wouldn't wake me anyway.

It wasn't the door that made my eyes spring open. It was a noise that I thought for a moment I'd dreamed, until I heard it again.

A gunshot.

12

I'd heard hunters' gunshots around my house often enough to know they weren't firecrackers.

Three more echoed down the street. Shit! I jumped out of bed and went to the window, then stopped myself. Last thing I needed was the shooter noticing me staring down and being a witness.

Where was Chris Winter? Dead on the footpath?

I grabbed my phone and pressed the contact listing for Connor's mobile.

As always, he sounded totally alert. 'Judi. Where are you?' He was on the move.

'At the pub. I heard shots fired.'

'Yes. I'm on my way. Stay in your room.' Rustling and murmuring. 'I'm walking from my place, taking it quietly. Don't want to alert anyone I'm coming. Talk soon.'

There'd be no time to put on his uniform – I hoped he had a vest or something for protection. He'd certainly take his gun and badge. But what if it was something to do with Kate's murder? Had her killer come back? Or was this Chris Winter's doing? Was he out there? Was he the shooter?

I sat by the window, my phone on my lap, and finally got up the nerve to peer out the window, pulling the curtain back half a centimetre. The street was empty. Not even a stray cat. I kept imagining Connor being shot at, lying on the footpath, someone attacking the pub. Were the doors all locked? Yes, I'd double-checked like always. But had Winter gone out and left one open?

I should go down and check.

But someone might have already come in. I couldn't sit there, thinking a killer might be roaming the pub, looking for me or Winter. I felt like a trapped rabbit. The only thing missing was the headlights. I got up and crept to my door, listened hard. Nothing, not even the usual creaks of an old pub. I eased the door open and peered out. The hallway was dimly lit, nobody in sight.

I left my door open and crept along to Winter's room, then put my ear to his door. Snoring. Regular, real snoring that went on and on. Nobody could fake that. So it hadn't been him out in the street. The front door would still be locked then. Thank God.

My feet were freezing and I was wide awake. I went back to my window. The street had an eerie pulsing glow now, Connor's 4WD parked down the other end, blue and red lights strobing around. That meant he'd stopped sneaking and was in full police mode. I was desperate to know what was going on, but no way could I call him.

I used the little kettle in the room to make tea and kept watching. An ambulance had arrived and parked next to Connor's vehicle. Another dark-coloured car arrived, along with a police car – Bendigo cops probably. It was now 3.30am and I needed some sleep. What did the experts say about sleep debt? I was well overdrawn. Next thing I knew, my alarm was beeping in my ear. I'd gone to sleep lying on my phone.

I pulled myself upright. My head was aching and my neck was stiff. I'd slept crooked. A great way to start the day. A hot shower eased my neck a bit, then I scooted downstairs to make coffee and set up for one breakfast. I ate mine standing in the kitchen and kept checking the clock. How long before I could ring Connor?

Joleen was dropping Mia off at childcare, so I ventured out for a walk to satisfy my curiosity. The corner where I'd seen Winter walk past the workshop to meet Brendan Scott was taped off. I craned my neck and caught a glimpse of a white-suited crime scene tech squatting on the concrete apron in front of the workshop roller door, and some tag things on the ground.

Was Brendan the person who'd been shot? No sign of the green ute. Maybe there'd been a shoot-out on Main Street, Candlebark. Maybe the next thing would be more journos turning up, bloodthirsty for stories of gore and mayhem.

Maybe I needed to get a grip.

In the bistro, Chris Winter was finishing his breakfast, tapping on his phone yet again.

'You'll wear that thing out,' I said brightly.

'Best way to get the news,' he said. 'I seem to be in the middle of all the drama here, but I never heard a thing.' He looked up at me. 'Did you hear anything?'

'Yes, I heard shots, that's all.'

He shook his head, as if marveling at the events. 'Crikey, I slept through it all.'

I found that very hard to believe, but then I'd been sure his snoring wasn't faked. I smiled and drank my coffee, then decided it was time to call Connor. I had the excuse that I was supposed to help him with Kate's belongings this morning.

I went into the office and closed the door before calling.

'Hi, Judi, sorry I didn't get back to you. And thanks for calling about the shots you heard. Are you OK?' He sounded rushed, which was unlike him.

'I'm fine. What about you?'

'Flat out here. The crime scene techs are here now. By the

time I found the person who'd been shot, the perpetrator was long gone.'

'Is it another murder?' Somehow just saying the word sent a chill through me. I tried to shake it off.

There were voices in the background, one I recognised, and I sank into the office chair. Swan was back. I should've expected it – they probably thought the two things were connected. Yet again, I wished Heath had caught this case. 'Has anyone been around to check on Brendan?'

'Yes, the detectives from Bendigo have. He was fine, reckoned he'd been home all night.'

'Barney isn't there again, is he?'

Connor snorted. 'No. But Detective Sergeant Swan is back with some of the same team.'

I made a noncommittal noise. 'So who got shot?'

'No ID yet. He's in intensive care.' There was muffled talking again, Connor said, 'Just going there now', and a car door slammed. When Connor came back to me, I could tell he was inside his 4WD. 'I'm coming to the pub now to talk to you. See you shortly.'

That was a surprise. They usually gave Connor the crap jobs like standing on the tape and shooing away the nosy locals, or fighting his way through the bush in the search team. Perhaps because this was only attempted murder, they had fewer people on the case. I shrugged and put my phone in my pocket, then cursed because I had forgotten to ask him about the house cleaning.

It didn't matter – he arrived a few minutes later and, when I asked that question first, he rubbed his head. 'Yeah, I know, but I'm not going to get there. Len will be ropeable.'

'Can I do it without your supervision? If it's no longer a crime scene...' Then something icky occurred to me. 'Er, what did they do with Kate's bed?'

'It's OK, Len told me he'd burned it yesterday. The crime scene guys had cut quite a bit out of it, so it had to go.'

Thank God for that.

'Yes, it should be OK for you to do it. I'll double-check though.' He called up Swan, who gave the go-ahead. 'You might need some boxes but there isn't much there. Len rents it out furnished, which is probably why Kate leased it.'

'No doubt he'll keep the rent that was paid in advance?' I said wryly.

'Yes, but Emma will get the bond back. The rent should've covered the mattress replacement.'

I shook my head. Murder was bad enough, but having to deal with this kind of thing just added to the pain. I was glad I could help Emma by collecting their things. Connor's questioning was standard procedure, since I hadn't seen anyone, and I headed to the rental house after getting a few wine cartons out of the storage room.

As I drew closer to the house, my stomach started flipping around. I had no idea what to expect. I kept remembering what I'd found and then visualising what Kate's bed must've looked like, then telling myself not to be so stupid. That damn image of her lying there with bullet holes in her just wouldn't go away. I hated how it rose up when I least expected it. By the time I pulled up in the driveway, I'd managed to tamp down the worry and get myself under control a bit, but I had to take a few long breaths before I went into the house.

It was a bit of a mess in one bedroom, where crime scene people had left fingerprint stuff all over the place and somebody had searched through all the drawers and the wardrobe. Kate's collection of clothes was small, and most of them were worn. The only things that looked relatively new were what she wore to the pub, including her pub polo shirts. I put them aside and found an empty suitcase in the wardrobe that I packed her clothes into. Another check and on a shelf I found the bag Connor had mentioned – the one Emma had also had, filled with the items you'd take if you had to make a run for it. The documents were gone, taken by the police, but I found two changes of clothes, a spare phone still in a packet and basic toiletries. I put it in a box as it was.

Kate had no jewellery or souvenirs, no photos in frames, nothing personal at all. In the bathroom I found a small bottle of Beautiful perfume – perhaps a gift or something she'd treated herself to. The rest of the things in there were everyday deodorant, shampoos and soap. I took every single thing and boxed it, then added the few things from Emma's room. She at least had some teen stuff – costume jewellery, cheap perfume, makeup and notes from friends at school. I didn't read the notes. I felt like I was intruding enough already.

I added her sheets and doona, thinking I'd wash them, a few other bits and pieces including a daisy alarm clock, a mauve stuffed toy monkey and some hair ties, and then started on her clothes. Like Kate, Emma had the bare minimum, but lots more newer, cheap stuff. Clearly, Kate's money had gone on Emma. I guessed every mum wanted their kid to be happy.

I had one box left, and I hoped it was enough for everything in the kitchen. I'd forgotten to bring a cold container for the food. Just as I opened the cutlery drawer, a gruff voice frightened the crap out of me.

'That all stays in the house, missus.'

I swung around – it was Len, probably checking I wasn't stealing anything. When my heart rate slowed a bit I said, 'That's good to know, thanks. I wasn't sure.'

Len stared at me balefully from under his faded, green John Deere cap. 'Where's his lordship?'

I guessed he meant Connor, but I said, 'Who's that?'

'The local copper.'

'He's not coming. There was a shooting in town last night.'

'Holy hell, what's this bloody place coming to?' he growled.

I couldn't disagree with him there. 'I said I'd collect Kate and Emma's things. You've got someone moving in already?'

'Yep. Beating them off with sticks.' He didn't sound happy about it though.

I wondered if it was someone who liked ghoulish houses. 'I'll just pack the food that's here then, and get out of your way.'

'The wife will be over shortly to clean. Thanks.' He thumped out of the house in his gumboots and left me to it.

The fridge was almost empty. Some milk, yoghurt, margarine and store-brand orange juice. One packet of mince in the freezer compartment. Some bags of pasta and rice, various other bits that you'd use to give bland stuff a bit of taste, and half a loaf of bread. I stood, staring down at the box I'd barely half-filled. Did they live on takeaways? Out here? I checked the rubbish bin. No takeaway containers or pizza boxes.

That told me they were living on the bones of their arses. And Andre and I had had no idea. No wonder Emma looked so thin and pale. When was the last time she'd had a decent steak or something like fish? How had we not realised the way they were living, with barely enough food? Had Andre never really looked? He's a chef. Surely he'd notice the lack of food in the house?

I called him. I described what I'd found.

'I had no idea,' he said. 'I feel bloody sick. Kate insisted they were doing great. The night I had dinner with them, she made me spaghetti carbonara and we had red wine. Well, actually I brought the wine. I just... fuck, really? The cupboards are bare?'

'Worse than Mother Hubbard.'

I doubted he'd know who she was, and he didn't reply anyway. Just made some noises into the phone that sounded like groans. 'OK,' he finally said. 'Bring it all back here. No sense throwing it out, I guess. But we need to give Emma some money for it.'

'Sure, of course. I'll see you soon.'

I hung up and found Mrs Len standing in the doorway behind me. Both of them were very good at creeping up on people. Her lank grey hair was cut in a severe bob that matched the thin line of her mouth.

'Are you ready for me to clean now?' she asked.

'Yes, of course. I'll take the boxes out to my car and get out of your way.'

She nodded and looked around. 'What's that black powder stuff?'

'For fingerprints, I think.'

'Len'll take some off the bond for the cleaning.' She sniffed the air.

I almost said the dead body was gone so no need to make a drama out of it. Instead I said, 'You do realise that Kate's daughter has got nobody. She'll need that money.'

'Won't be much left after we pay for a new mattress.'

'Christ, it's not like she got murdered on purpose!'

Mrs Len sniffed again and pretended she hadn't heard me, dragging in a large bucket and mop and a box of cleaning cloths and spray packs. I took the things I'd collected out to my car and got out of there, wondering if Len and his wife had spied on Kate, and if Connor or anyone had questioned them. It was highly likely they had, but had they asked the right questions?

Back at the pub, I unloaded the food and gave it to Andre, and then stacked the other few boxes in the corner of the office. I'd have to find a way to get them to Emma, when they found her somewhere to stay. Guilt stabbed at me again, but I wasn't going there. I had to think of Mia.

Apparently, Chris Winter had checked out, which was a

relief. No more night manager issues. And Andre had closed the bistro until Wednesday, as usual.

'I'm off now,' he said. 'See you Wednesday.'

The public bar had half a dozen regulars sitting with their beers – *quiet as the grave* came to mind, and I shivered. I tidied up, served a few more beers and sold some potato chips, and someone asked if they could go across to the takeaway for hot chips, and I said sure. If we stopped offering food, who was I to make them starve? Just as he was leaving, I grabbed him and added some money of my own. Hot chips sounded like just what I needed.

We all agreed they weren't as good as Andre's, but they were hot and freshly cooked. By 3pm, the bar was empty and I doubted anyone would come in now until after 5. I decided to bring Mia back to the pub – it'd save money not to have her at Joleen's and besides, I could spend time with her for a change. When I went to pick her up, the crime scene tape was still up but the techs and detectives seemed to have all gone. Connor's 4WD wasn't at the station or his house. The town felt deserted and I checked around for random tumbleweeds as I drove.

Back at the pub, we had time for play and book reading and before I knew it, it was after 5pm and the first couple of locals wandered in. I served them their beers and when I turned around, Mia was right behind me.

She patted her track pants importantly. 'I did a wee.'

'I can tell,' I said.

She frowned. 'How?'

I bent down and pulled the long strip of toilet paper out of the back of her pants. 'You have a paper tail.'

'I'm a pussy cat. They have long tails.' She bared her teeth and made a meowing noise.

'Are you ready for some soup?' Andre had left some for us.

'Soooouuuuup! Tomato soup!' she shouted.

No, it wasn't, but I wasn't going to get into that here either.

I gave Mia her soup and made myself toast, then waited until she'd settled into her folding bed in the office before calling Connor. He answered quickly and said he was on his way over. I was surprised to see him turn up in jeans and a black short-sleeved shirt. He seemed to always be in uniform. He sat at the far end of the bar and ordered a beer, another step out of the ordinary.

'Long day?' I asked.

He rubbed his face with both hands and sighed. 'You aren't kidding. I've been on the go since the shooting last night.'

'Do you know yet who the guy is?'

'Still waiting. No ID on him, no idea how he got to Candlebark. No idea who was with him.'

'Can you ask him? He's in hospital, isn't he?'

'In the morgue section, yes.' Connor swallowed half of his beer in one go and burped. 'Sorry.'

'He died?'

He nodded. 'So now it's a homicide. If it turns out this is connected to Kate's death, Swan'll expand the team and send a couple more up, I think. No way will they all fit in my station. It was a tight squeeze when Macca got killed.'

'They could move into the old scout hall,' I said.

Connor stared morosely into the last centimetre of his beer. 'I don't get it. Macca's death I could understand. He was a local and he got in over his head with the chop chop. But this... it doesn't make sense. Kate killed in her bed and now Mr Nobody on the street.'

'What makes you think they were shot by the same person?'

'It's Candlebark, not Carlton or Kings Cross. Two shootings so close together not being connected is highly unlikely.'

'But possible.'

'I guess so. That's not what Swan thinks though.' He watched me collecting glasses off the tables. 'Will you get a new staff member?'

'Not much point at the moment.' It was only 8.30pm but the bar was almost empty. 'If things don't pick up, I won't be able to give anyone shifts anyway. I might have to come and live here for a while to save us some money.' I shuddered at the thought.

'When's the next race day?'

We'd always done well on country racing weekends. 'There's one in about three weeks, but Carl doesn't stay here anymore.' Macca's old mate used to bring half a dozen friends and make a weekend of it, but that was the old days and he avoided us now.

Connor finished his beer and nudged his glass at me. I filled it again and said, 'This is unusual for you.'

'Yeah, I've got a lot of thinking to do,' he said. 'A couple of beers always de-stresses the brain cells.'

'Sounds serious.' I studied his face but he wasn't giving anything away.

'Yeah, could be.'

I wondered if it had anything to do with Leslie's visit on the weekend. She worked in Melbourne and, if things were getting serious with them, Connor might be persuaded to move to the big smoke. A thick sadness settled inside me, a feeling I didn't like at all. I'd had so much change in my life in the past year, most of it uninvited and unwanted. I was coping, and Mia was the big positive, but I'd had enough. Connor had always been a good friend here, one I relied on a lot, and he was someone I could trust. It was totally selfish, but I didn't want him to leave.

Connor focused on me. 'Hey, how did you go with picking up Kate and Emma's things this morning? Sorry I couldn't help, after all that.'

'I think you had other more important jobs to do.' I trailed my finger through some spilt beer on the counter, making it into spirals. 'It was a bit weird all round really. I mean, they had bugger all. I talked to Andre about it. Hardly any food, bits and pieces, a few clothes.' I described what I'd collected and then Len and his wife. 'I get that they didn't really know Kate, but she was murdered! They acted like she'd caused them a major inconvenience!'

'Yeah, Len and his wife are... not terribly community minded.' He drank more beer. It didn't cheer him up. 'I just hate that someone really nice like Kate was killed in cold blood like that on my patch. It's not right.'

'Have Swan and his mates in homicide got no idea at all who did it?'

He shook his head. 'They're still waiting to hear from the police in NSW. Swan is getting pretty irate with the lack of information, I can tell you.'

Mia appeared in the doorway, dragging Bum by the one ear that looked in danger of falling off. 'Unca Connor. It's me!' She ran across to him and he picked her up, balancing her on his knee.

'Aren't you supposed to be in bed asleep, Mia Moo?'

'Bum had a bad dream,' she said. She looked at me. 'Bum said chippees would make him feel better.'

Connor laughed and, just for a microsecond, I imagined what it would've been like if I'd been in love with him and we had settled down with Mia. No, impossible. It was never going to happen. Connor was a total pushover – he bought some chips and shared them with Mia. I noticed that Bum never got a look in.

I closed everything up by 9, Connor helping me to put Mia's stuff in the car. With all the doors locked, I waved goodbye to him and drove home. My house, usually a haven of quiet and cosiness, seemed empty and dark tonight. It was too easy to put Mia to bed, pour myself some wine and sink into maudlin thoughts.

What was Heath doing right now? Was he missing me, like I missed him? I sighed. Probably not. The silence closed in on me and a sharp sense of loneliness made my throat ache. And poor Emma. Was she lying alone somewhere, thinking about her mum?

That led my brain into the puzzle Connor had mentioned. Poor Kate had died at somebody's hand, either via her husband or someone she knew. Nobody was tracked down to a small country town and murdered for no reason. There was nothing in her house worth stealing. Or was there? Maybe Mikey had robbed a bank and she was hiding the proceeds.

I went online on the laptop I used for pub work and searched for information about him and his background, as well as what he was inside for. Nothing about banks or armed robberies connected to him in the past five years at least. His thing seemed to be drugs.

As Swan had said, there was nothing about Kate Brown either. I tried to remember what he'd said her real name was. Lisa... something like a metal. Gold. Copper. Silver. Silverson. I googled her as well but found almost nothing. I tried a search on social media specifically and found her in Facebook. I couldn't friend her, so was limited to the basics that showed up. It was her, but it wasn't her. One photo with Emma as a primary school student in a maroon uniform, Kate/Lisa bending low next to her, and another on her own next to a car. I couldn't see who the driver was very well but I suspected it was Mikey.

I searched for Emma instead – trying Emma Silverson first and there she was. A lot more active than her mum, as young teens tended to be, but what I could see was also limited. Emma looked happy, arms around a group of her friends, laughing, and another in her netball gear.

What was I expecting? Someone to post on their pages *I am coming for you*?

Emma clearly thought the guy was after her as well. So was it him that was shot in the street last night? If so, why? Did Emma have a protector? No, that was ridiculous. I was reaching for stupid ideas now. I was pretty sure the dead man would be connected to Brendan somehow, or Scottie. It still rankled that Connor had never been able to get any evidence to put Scottie away.

I thought Swan and the rest of them were wrong. It was a horrible coincidence, and the two crimes had nothing to do with each other. Which meant it still wasn't safe for Emma to come back here.

I slammed the laptop closed. I had to stop obsessing over this stuff. I had no information, just a lot of questions, and I knew Swan wouldn't answer any of them. Neither would Heath.

As if thinking of him made it happen, my phone pinged with a text. *If you're home, I can call.*

Heath knew I had to stand by the back door to get a signal. I texted back and went through the house to wait, not bothering to turn the lights on. The phone jingled like a constipated piano accordion and I resolved to find something worth being summoned by. The theme music to *Bosch* perhaps. Or *Wallander.*

'Hello.'

'Hi. Are you OK?'

Why was he asking? 'Yeees.'

'You didn't call me.'

I racked my brains over why I should have called. Oh right. He rescued me and Emma from the shopping centre. Had I not spoken to him since? I couldn't remember. Oh dear. No wonder I was bloody useless at relationships.

'Sorry. It's just been one thing after another.'

'I heard.' His voice was stiff and a bit cold.

'Did Swan tell you about the shooting here last night?'

'Yes, I did have to hear it from him.' Not so much stiff as shitty.

'I wasn't involved. I was safe inside.' I had a feeling no matter what I said, I'd make it worse. Why hadn't I called him? I didn't want to be a bother? 'I'm sorry. I've been trying to help Emma, and this morning I had to go and clear out their house. On my own.' A bit of a plea for sympathy.

'So that shooting was nothing to do with the pub?'

Was he grilling me on Swan's behalf? I bristled. 'I should bloody hope not. Connor said nobody even knows who the guy is.'

He made a non-committal noise.

'I've got Mia to think of. I don't want anything to do with it.' Never mind my insatiable curiosity and my desire to figure it out. The sooner it was solved, the sooner we could return to peace and quiet.

'Good.'

'Have you heard anything about Emma? How is she?' It wasn't his case but…

'She's being looked after. Swanny said you persuaded her to work on the ID. They've got a pretty good image of him now.'

'But I'm guessing they don't know who he is yet.'

'No. They've sent it up to NSW – it's more likely they'll be able to identify him.' He fell silent and I waited, not sure what else to say, then the silence suddenly felt like a huge abyss I was desperate to fill.

'What case are you on now?' I asked.

'A home invasion that ended in the homeowner's death.' He made a grumpy noise. 'I wish people would give up their BMW and their TV without a fuss. Nothing is worth dying for. Anyway, we've arrested the three who did it. They've been responsible for half a dozen break-ins like that, as well as assaults.'

'Well, it's good you got them.' I wanted to tell him I missed him, but I'd just completely ignored him for nearly three days, so would it be honest to say it or not?

A persistent ringing broke through my thoughts. 'Is that your landline?' Heath asked.

'Yeah, but I'm not answering it.'

All the same, the ringing went on and on. 'Maybe you should.'

'It's after eleven. I've had some threatening calls. Connor said not to answer it anymore.'

'Who's threatening you?'

'If I knew that, he could go and arrest them!' *Oops, calm down.* Another thing I hadn't told him.

The phone stopped. Heath was frosty again. 'I'd better let you go then, since it's late.'

'But...' I took a breath. 'This is hard. I'm not good on the phone, you know that.'

'True.'

'Maybe we should do those video call things that everyone is doing.' I had second thoughts immediately. 'When I'm having a good hair day.'

He laughed. 'We could try that.'

After a couple of minutes, we said goodnight and I hung up. Standing at the back door, looking out across my dark garden at the paddocks and the edge of the bush, I wondered for the first time if where I lived was too isolated. Bad phone reception, no neighbours within shouting distance, and too far to walk to Candlebark. Was I going to have to move somewhere where Mia could play with friends after kinda or school? Go to sleepovers?

But I loved it here. I loved my gardens, growing veggies, walking out of my back door and hearing nothing but birds and sometimes the faint sound of a tractor or a mower. To have to put up with other people's TVs, parties in their backyards, cars roaring past... no, I couldn't do it. I craned my neck and saw the full moon rising above the far hills, glowing white and round. A movement caught my eye and I glanced towards the bush again.

Was that someone walking along the tree line? I shrank back

a little and peered out, my heart banging in my ears. There it was again, not human-shaped though. It wove in and out of the shadows, following the track and then veered across the open grass. In the full moonlight, I could see it better – it was a large dog, patched with white, not in any hurry, occasionally dipping its nose to the ground. I didn't recognise it. The farmer over the back of me had kelpies, and he wouldn't happy to know a stray or roaming dog was making itself at home in his sheep paddocks.

My phone jangled suddenly into the silence again, and I jumped. 'Bugger it!' I went through and grabbed the receiver up but didn't say anything. As soon as I heard the dreaded voice start, 'You'd better –', I pressed the button and disconnected, then pressed again for a dial tone and shoved the thing under a cushion on the couch. 'Now try and call me, you bastard.'

I was glad I'd cut him off and dealt with the phone, but as I stood there alone in the darkness, I started shivering and the horrible image of Kate's head came to me again.

Stop it, you're fine. It's not about you. You and Mia are safe. I didn't stop shivering until I'd wrapped myself in the fluffy rug on the couch and done some deep breathing. But it felt as though a mist of 'wrongness' still hung in the air. I made myself get up, checked all the windows and doors twice and then climbed into bed. My microwaved heat bag was my sole source of comfort and it took me quite a while to get to sleep.

13

My mobile rang the next morning as I was driving Mia to childcare. I pulled over and answered, and it was Swan. No hello or good morning.

'Have you heard from Emma?'

'No, but I was thinking of coming down today to see her.' I had kind of promised Tuesday and here I was.

'Don't bother. She's gone again.'

I tried to assess his tone. His usual abruptness, along with a definite hint of panic. 'She's run away?'

'Yep. Bloody kid.' He huffed out an angry breath. 'If she calls you, can you please let me know asap?'

I could tell he was about to hang up on me. 'Hang on a minute. How did she "run away"? I thought you had her in protective custody? In the hotel? With a minder?'

'Yes, well, she nicked off from the hotel. Waited until the constable was asleep and sneaked out.'

I shook my head. 'Boy, she really doesn't want to hang out with you guys, does she?' Far too much levity. I knew it as soon as I said it and waited for his cutting reply.

Instead he said, 'I don't get it. For a kid who's being hunted down by someone who's already killed three of her family… what the hell's wrong with her? Other people would be demanding a new identity and a plane ticket to Hawaii!'

Good point. Emma had been terrified. No, on second

thoughts, she'd swung between terrified and angry. Why was she so angry? And if she was genuinely terrified, why wouldn't she accept police protection?

'Do you think there's a good reason why she doesn't trust you? What have you been told by the NSW police?'

There was a short silence on his end that told me I was asking questions I wasn't allowed to again. 'Just call me if you hear from her, OK?'

'Yes, I –' He'd hung up. I wondered if he spoke to his wife like that. Nah, he'd be divorced, for sure.

A little voice piped up from the back seat. 'Are you mad, Juddy? Who you mad with?'

'No, I'm not mad.' I put the car in gear again. 'Just confused.'

'What's confoosed?'

'Like a big puzzle,' I said. 'You know, when you do your puzzles and you can't see where the pieces go.'

'That's because Bum hides them,' she said.

'Somebody sure does,' I muttered to myself.

Would Emma come all the way back to Candlebark? She had no reason to, except… I had all of her stuff, and her mother's as well. With nowhere else to go, that might be enough of a reason for her to return. If she had money for a bus ticket, the V/Line bus would get her as far as Heathcote and maybe she'd hitchhike. Surely Swan would check the buses first? But a clever girl would get a train out of Melbourne to the airport, perhaps, and catch the bus from there.

Not your job to work this stuff out, Judi.

No, it wasn't. All the same, after I'd dropped Mia off, I called in to the police station to talk to Connor. His face was drawn and he was slumped in his chair, barely raising himself to say Hi.

'Have you slept since Sunday night?' I asked.

'Not much.' He grimaced. 'Are those bloody journos back at the pub?'

'No.'

'They're probably staying closer to Bendigo, where they can hassle the police and the media liaison person there.'

'So do you know who the dead guy in the street is yet?' I leaned against the counter, dumping my bag on the floor. Usually I'd go in and sit with him, but something held me back.

'He hasn't been identified, no. They're still waiting for –'

'The police in Sydney to get back to them.' I found myself fidgeting with the pen on the counter and put it down. 'That's what Swan said about the information on Kate – still waiting. I thought inter-state cooperation was a bit better than this.'

'Yeah, well…' He stood and stretched, then came over to the counter. 'Any more of those phone calls?'

'No, well, yes, but I hung up on them. Last night.'

'Hmm. I'll make a note. How many have you had now?'

'Three? Or is it four?'

He nodded. 'Have you talked to Emma?'

He wasn't going to like this. 'I got a call from Swan about half an hour ago. Emma's run away again. Sneaked out of the hotel last night.'

He stared at me, his face full of consternation. 'Why the hell would she do that?'

I shrugged. 'Something is going on with her, something she's not telling anyone – me, you or Swan. I feel like it's more than her mum getting killed. It's… more serious, if that doesn't sound strange.'

'I wish I knew what.' He reached out for his phone that was lying on his desk under some papers. 'Have you seen this guy? This is the ID thing that Emma created with the FACE officer.'

He brought up a digital image of a man's face that was so

clear it could have almost been a photo. I peered down at it.

'You're kidding, aren't you?' I said. 'That's Chris Winter.'

Connor's frown deepened into something like pain. 'The guy staying at the pub?'

'You've never seen him?' I tried to remember if Chris had ever been around when Connor was there.

'No. You asked me to check him out, remember? There was nothing.' He stared down at his phone. 'Fucking hell. Kate's killer was here under my nose the whole bloody time.'

'He's not at the pub now,' I said. 'He left yesterday morning. God, he could be anywhere by now.'

'He's not,' Connor said grimly. 'He's renting Len's house, where Kate and Emma were living. The guy's obviously as cold as they come.'

'What…' It didn't make sense. 'But he didn't arrive here until…' I racked my brains. 'Thursday evening.'

'Cold as well as a bald-faced con man. He killed Kate and then turns up pretending he knows nothing about it.' He went back to his desk and found a business card, flipping it over. 'I'd better call Detective Sergeant Swan right now.'

I'd chatted with Chris a few times – I hadn't liked him much but that hardly made him a killer. It didn't feel right. But the image was definitely him, and how else would Emma have created it if she hadn't seen him at their house? And why the hell would he hang around, let alone rent the house where he'd shot Kate?

Connor was answering a lot of questions from Swan. 'No, I don't know. He rented it yesterday. I haven't seen him.' He glanced at me. 'Judi said he arrived at the pub last Thursday and stayed there until Monday. Yes, all right. At least forty minutes. Yes, sir.' He hung up.

'You're going to arrest him?'

'When Hawke and Barney get here. He's calling them and telling them to leave now.' He checked his uniform and flicked bits of paper off his trousers, then started trying to tidy up his desk.

'Right, I'm going to the pub then,' I said, picking up my bag. 'Can you… can you let me know what happens, please?'

'Sure.' He gazed around his office as if he'd lost something.

'Connor, it's not your fault the guy was here and you didn't know. Nobody knew. Swan was at the pub talking to Andre and he never put two and two together either.' I bit my lip. 'I'm not convinced you're actually getting four, but if that's what Emma gave them, I guess you have to go with it.'

'Yep.'

I had one more go at cheering him up. 'How was dinner with Leslie the other night? You didn't burn anything?'

He brightened for a second. 'Yeah, good.' His face fell again. 'This long-distance thing is hard work though. How do you and Heath manage it?'

I let out a harsh laugh. 'Bloody terribly. Whatever you do, don't use us as your example.'

'Oh. OK.' The phone behind him started ringing and he waved at me as he went to answer it. I escaped and drove to the pub, parking around the side and sitting in my car for a few minutes, looking at the old building with its stonework, rusty iron lace and sagging guttering. Years ago there'd been a movie called *The Money Pit* that I'd seen on late-night TV. Maybe that's what we had here – our very own money pit.

I sighed heavily and got out of the car. That kind of thinking was defeatist. All the self-help gurus would have a field day with me. *Just believe and it will happen*. I was more a *get off your arse and do the hard yakka* person, but some days the hard yakka was beyond me.

In the office, I pushed the boxes of Emma's and Kate's things as far back in the corner as I could. It was Tuesday, Charlie was back on deck today, and no bistro to worry about. I pulled out a notebook and a decent pen and started making notes about my ideas for kids' parties and theme weekends. By the time Andre came back tomorrow, I might even have something ready to run by him.

By the time I picked up Mia and went home, leaving Charlie in charge, I was ready for a bath with Mia and an early night. I found the phone still under the couch cushion and put it back on the bench but not in the cradle. I was in no mood for late-night threats. I didn't even check my mobile phone until after dinner and Mia was in bed.

There was a text from Connor, sent just after 4pm. *Winter in custody. Says he has an alibi. We'll see.*

That was a relief. One less thing to worry about. I texted him back. *Had a thought. Emma might head up this way to collect her and Kate's things. Go to their house?*

He replied a few minutes later. *Yes. Thought of that. Will swing past there shortly.*

Then just as I got into bed – *Nobody there. No sign of her.*

Thanks for letting me know.

I lay in bed, trying to read some best-selling memoir that everyone had raved about but that seemed self-involved and bland to me. I tossed it aside and turned off the bedside lamp; the darkness outside my window slowly changed to moonlight and shadows as the full moon rose. We'd put in broad beans already, so maybe it was time for beetroot and parsnips. By the next full moon, I could start planting bulbs. I drifted off to sleep trying to decide between more daffodils or splurging on tulips.

I woke the next morning thinking of Emma. Had I been dreaming about her? Not sure, but I could see her pale, thin face as if she was right in front of me. All through breakfast and dressing Mia and answering questions about why Bum didn't talk much (much?) and why was my car blue and why didn't I make bread, I kept seeing her face.

At childcare, as soon as I undid the clasps on Mia's car seat, she was scrambling to get out of the car. 'Don't forget your bag,' I said, but she was heading for the front door and I followed, marvelling at her ability to charge straight in and make a beeline for the play area out the back. I signed her in and put her bag in her little locker. *Forgotten in a second.* But right then, she turned and came back to me, putting her face up for a kiss.

'Bye, Juddy.' Then she was off again, and my throat had a funny little ache in it that I tried to swallow away before anyone noticed.

At the pub, I counted the previous day's takings that Charlie had put in the safe and added them to the banking. We'd made just enough yesterday to pay Charlie's wages for one day. When Andre arrived, his face lined and bags under his eyes, I said, 'You look terrible.'

He grimaced. 'My mates thought getting drunk would help me. Cheer me up. Like that was an answer to everything.' He sighed. 'I'm getting too old for hangovers.'

'Me, too.' I'd already made coffee so I poured him a mug. 'I've been thinking…'

He held his head. 'Oh God, don't ask me to think too much. I think I've blown a few fuses.'

I fetched the packet of paracetamol and handed it to him. 'Have a few of these. All you have to do is listen.' I laid out my ideas for kids' parties, pointing to the patio and the cleared space, and the notes I'd made on food ideas as well as the two locals who did party tricks. One was a fairy, one was a magician. 'No idea how good they are but at least they're close. Probably parents will have their own plans for entertainment.'

'No miniature pony rides,' Andre said. 'I don't like horses.'

'And I really like your idea of French weekends, or at least dinners. Look, we can even hire a French musical trio.'

'Expensive,' he said. 'Would we make our money back?'

I shrugged. 'Maybe at first we focus on food and provide recorded music, and if we get it going, we can have live music later.'

He stared at me. 'You're really keen on this, aren't you?'

'I just… I don't want to give up. I know we can make a go of this, but our marketing is shit. We need a point of difference.'

'I thought that was my cooking.' He grinned and nudged me. 'Only kidding. But how do we tackle the marketing properly? That's not my thing at all.'

'I'm going to have to learn, starting with Facebook.' The thought still made me blanch, but it had to be done.

'Let's do what we said and find some money for a professional.' He stood and stretched. 'I'm making a bacon and egg sandwich to get me moving – you want one?'

'You bet.'

While we ate, I filled him in on the ID, the arrest of Chris Winter and Connor's long hours. Andre shook his head about Chris. 'Can't say it surprises me. There's something about him, isn't there?' All I could do was agree.

There were lunch bookings but no escapees from Bronwyn's health spa today, and I wondered if maybe she had no guests this week. Initially she'd seemed busy – I'd driven past a few times and seen people outside doing yoga or sitting in the spa surrounded by ferns. It would be so much better if we could cooperate somehow. Maybe Andre could come up with some good brown rice recipes.

No bookings for dinner, so I dropped Mia off at Joleen's and said I'd pick her up by ten. The bar was busy; I spent the evening in there helping Charlie and let Andre work on his own for the few drop-ins. Scottie and Jock came in before dinner, Scottie scowling as usual so I let Charlie serve them. About 8.30pm, I'd just loaded glasses into the dishwasher when someone hailed me from the far end of the bar. I turned and froze.

Chris Winter was waving at me, a smile on his face. It took me a couple of seconds to get my legs working and go over to him.

'H-hi.' I had no idea what else to say. *Why are you here? I thought you were in gaol? Did you kill Kate?*

'Good evening. A glass of that local red, thanks.'

'Sure.' He was pretending like nothing had happened. Maybe he just assumed none of us knew he'd been arrested. But this was a small place and the gossip… I placed the glass in front of him and took his money, returned his change and tried to escape.

'I suppose you heard the cops took me in?' he said breezily, like they'd taken him in for a cup of tea.

'Um, yeah. Word gets around here.' I swallowed and forced a smile. Why the hell was he out? Why the hell had nobody told me? Why hadn't Connor called me?

'Oh yeah, small town. No worries.' He bent towards me. 'I can understand the worry. Stranger in town. A murder. That's bloody serious stuff.'

'Yes, it is.'

'But when she was killed, I was still in Sydney. Just leaving actually.' He spread his hands. 'So it sure wasn't me.'

Clearly, he'd been able to prove that to Swan and the rest of them. 'That's good,' I managed to get out. 'If you'll excuse me…'

His face fell. 'I thought you might have a drink with me.'

Was he hitting on me? For God's sake. 'Maybe later.' And then wished like hell I could take it back. Hopefully he'd leave before closing.

As I brushed past Charlie on my way to the bistro, he said, 'You need any help with that guy?'

'No, I'm fine, thanks.' I wasn't, but I wasn't sure why not. If Chris Winter had an alibi, that was an end to it. Wasn't it?

Andre was cleaning the kitchen, having just finished some prep for tomorrow. He wiped down the last bench, then leaned against it and eased his back into a stretch. 'God, I miss Kate. She was so capable, could do anything, just got stuck in.'

I ignored that. 'They let Chris Winter go. He's in the bar now.'

His mouth dropped open. 'You're kidding.'

'He had a solid alibi. Was still in Sydney.'

'Don't you think that's odd? Why did he come here in the first place?' He rinsed the cloth and folded it over the drying rack. 'I assumed he'd come up from Melbourne.'

'He had a Melbourne address on his room registration. And the guy who got shot – they still don't know who he was or what he was doing here.'

'I guess Winter had an alibi for that, too – you said he was snoring his head off.' He led me out of the kitchen and turned off the lights. 'I was thinking about your kids' party idea. Let's sit down tomorrow and cost it.'

I felt a little stir of excitement, or maybe I was tired and imagining it after days of worry. 'Yeah, let's do that. See you tomorrow.'

Another hour and I could leave. Charlie closed the place at 10.30 on a weeknight, or earlier if everyone had gone. I collected the takings and put them in the safe, then locked the office. Back in the bar, Chris was stuck on his bar stool like a toad on top of his toadstool.

Don't be nasty. That's what I told myself as I went over to be nice and chat. Really, I wanted to find out more about how he wriggled out of the potential arrest. As usual, he was focused on his phone but sensed immediately that I was heading his way.

'Hey, ready for that drink now?'

'That's very nice of you, thanks.' I poured a small glass of Sauv Blanc, since I'd be driving home soon.

There was a small awkward silence while he looked at me

expectantly, but my brain had gone blank. Eventually I said, 'What did you say you did again?'

'Business adviser.' When I raised my eyebrows, he added, 'I also broker the sale of small businesses. Things that could be a going concern but the owner has given up or not managed it well, or just had enough and wants to move on.'

This time the silence was longer. I was sure he could hear my brain clanking and churning into gear and then puttering. 'You're here to see if we want to sell the pub?'

He burst out laughing. 'No, not at all.' Then serious. 'Unless you want to. Do you?'

I wasn't admitting anything. 'No, we're doing OK, thanks. Not bailing out.' Yet.

'There are a couple of businesses in Heathcote I'm meeting with, and a winery up the road further, and an art gallery.' He drank some of his Shiraz and wiped his top lip. 'It's hard work running a business. Bloody hard work.'

You can say that again. 'You haven't been talking to Bronwyn, have you?'

He shook his head. 'Who's she?'

'The health spa woman. Her place is up the road there.' I waved a hand.

'No. I probably wouldn't, even if she wanted to sell. Those places tend to rely too much on the people running them so the goodwill is not transferable. Kind of guru stuff.'

I spluttered, some wine going down the wrong way. Bronwyn, a guru? Goodwill? 'So… I was a bit surprised to hear you'd rented Len's house.'

'Cheaper than staying here.' He put up his hands. 'Absolutely no complaints about the pub. But I also guessed I was costing you money – the night manager issue.'

'Yes, well…' He'd just gone up in my estimation. 'It didn't bother you that…'

His face stilled and he looked away from me, his mouth tight. 'Yes, it did. Can't deny that.' He breathed in and out through his nose, like a calming thing. Odd to watch someone so closely but I really wanted to know what was going on with this guy.

Something rang a little clear bell in my head. 'Did you know Kate?'

He blinked, more than once. 'No. But she sounded like a lovely lady.'

That was a lie, I'm sure of it. 'She was.' I nearly said something about Emma but I didn't want anyone to know she was out there somewhere alone. I glanced around and saw the last two customers making moves to leave. 'We'll be closing soon.'

'Right.' He looked down at his beer. 'Can I have a bourbon? Straight.'

'Sure.' I got it for him and placed the glass next to his wine. 'Enjoy.'

'Yeah, yeah,' he said, but he didn't look at me and he didn't touch the glass.

'You OK?' I was being polite but also curious.

'Yeah, I…' He glanced at me and away again. 'I told you a bit of a fib just then. I did know Kate. I was coming here to see her.'

'Why?' My tone was verging on rude.

'We were… friends. In Sydney. I was worried about her.'

'Did you know someone was coming to kill her?'

'No!' His tone was shocked but I would've bet the pub he was lying again. 'If I had, I would've done something about it.'

'Do you know who did it? Or why?'

'Not really.'

I'd had enough. 'I hope you told the police all of this.'

He stared straight at me this time. 'No, I didn't. And I don't know why I'm telling you now.'

'You expect me to keep quiet about it?'

'No.' He let out a strangled laugh. 'I'll go and talk to your cop mate tomorrow, but I can't tell them anything useful.'

Can't or won't? 'Why exactly are you in Candlebark, Chris? You could easily stay in Heathcote or south Bendigo.'

'I told you, I like this area.' He swallowed down half the bourbon without even a slight grimace. 'I like this pub.' A small pause. 'I even like you, despite your rudeness. Or perhaps because of it.'

I snorted. 'You need to get out more.'

Another swallow, the empty glass placed back on the bar and he stood, collecting his phone and patting his back pocket for his wallet. 'I'll get out of your hair so you can close up. And Judi?'

'Yes?'

'Be careful. I mean it.' He was out the door and gone before I could answer.

14

I stood there for a few moments after Chris left, staring at the dark window opposite and my reflection in it. Portrait of a Shocked Woman. What was that about? We'd had two murders in less than a week. Did he think I was next? My skin felt clammy and I rubbed my arms. That was all I needed – someone else threatening me. Except it hadn't sounded like a threat – it had sounded like a plea.

Weird. I shook myself and turned around. The bar was empty and Charlie was collecting the last glasses and wiping tables. Normally I would've left him to it and gone to pick up Mia, but tonight I helped him and left when he did, getting into my car and locking the doors before he drove away.

At my house, having collected Mia, I carried her inside and held her awkwardly while I locked the door behind me. I didn't go out to fetch my bag and a bottle of wine from the car until I'd checked the rest of the house was locked up and looked all around outside. It gave me the shits that I felt compelled to do this. I'd long considered my little house to be an oasis and a retreat, safe and quiet. Now, yet again, I was questioning its isolation.

'Bugger it,' I said out loud. 'Nobody's bloody chasing me away from here!'

My heart rate slowly settled, I poured myself some wine and turned on the TV to watch the late news. As usual it was boring politics and weaselly politicians, a husband killing his wife, a massive car crash near Cranbourne and boring footage of footballers training. I was deep in thought about Chris Winter and what he'd admitted to me when the phone rang – I picked it up without thinking.

'You want to be very careful,' the harsh voice began.

'Oh, fuck off,' I said.

'In the car park at your pub alone? Nobody would miss you.' Click.

I put the phone down very slowly, trying to breathe without gagging. Why the hell had I answered? After everything Connor told me. The voice echoed in my head. Something about it was... Well, it wasn't Chris Winter, I was pretty sure of that. Too ocker, not cultured enough. Not that Chris was cultured, but he spoke with a bit of a private school edge.

Car park at the pub? Whoever it was had been watching me leaving work. Thank God tonight I'd waited for Charlie. This was getting personal – and close.

I took the landline receiver off the hook, shoved it under the couch cushion and used my mobile to call Connor from near the back door, making doubly sure it was locked first. As soon as he picked up, I said, 'That guy called again. A definite threat. Talked about me in the car park at the pub after work. Should I hire someone for security?'

'Slow down, Judi. What time was the call?'

'About four minutes ago. I –'

'Same voice?'

'Yes.'

'You recognise it yet?'

'I'm pretty sure it's not Chris Winter. How come they let him go?'

He cleared his throat. 'Let's do one thing at a time. Is your house locked up?'

'Yes. You think he'll come here?'

'No. I think he's still mostly trying to frighten you, but I'm worried that he's getting more specific.'

Mostly. 'God, what if he does come here? What should I do?'

'Do you want me to come over?' His voice was kind and supportive, not annoyed and short at all, and I loved him for it.

I hesitated, wishing for the impossible. Heath. 'No, it's OK. Not like you can stay the night every night to make me feel safe, can you?'

He laughed. 'No, not really. I can come now though.'

'No, it's all right.' Even though it wasn't.

'You come in first thing and make another report, eh?'

'Yes, OK.' Report it again. No use really. Neither of us knew who it was.

'By the way, they let Winter go because he had a solid alibi. And no motive.'

I slid down the wall and sat on the stone floor, wincing at the cold that seeped through my pants straight away. Maybe we were going to have an early frost tomorrow morning. 'He told me he knew Kate.'

'What? When?' That was clearly news to Connor.

'Tonight, at the pub. Said they were friends, and he was coming to see her.' I shifted around on the floor but my bum was already going numb. 'He said he didn't tell Swan.'

Connor whistled through his teeth. 'Great. I wasn't given all the details, just that his alibi checked out and he had nothing to do with it. Detective Sergeant Swan will not be happy.'

Is he ever? 'Winter said he's coming to see you in the morning and tell you.'

'I bet he doesn't. I'll have to go and find him.'

'Mmm, you might be surprised. He sounded like he meant it.'

'Yeah. Now, you're sure you're OK?'

'Yes, thanks. I'll keep you on speed dial, don't worry.'

'Make sure you do.' He said goodnight and we hung up. It took me a couple of minutes to get up off the floor, and my hip ached. I contemplated a bath and couldn't be bothered. I caught the weather as I was turning the TV off – no frost, but late storms and hail tomorrow. I was keeping Mia home with me tomorrow – I wasn't seeing enough of her. She loved childcare but I was worried she'd start calling the woman there 'Mum'.

I crawled into bed and tried not to think about the phone calls, but my brain kept replaying tonight's words. Why didn't I recognise his voice? It was familiar somehow. Was it someone who came into the pub? I tried to replay some of the regulars' voices but none of them sounded right. It was bugging the hell out of me, but eventually I dropped off into an uneasy sleep, dreaming that someone was ringing me and shouting at me through the windows when I didn't pick up.

I jerked awake suddenly, unsure if the cracking noise was in my dream or for real, straining to listen. The house was silent, but the longer I lay there, the more certain I was that the noise had been real. I slid out of my bed and tiptoed to the door, which I always left open for Mia. Freezing cold air slid around my calves. Somewhere, a door was open.

I could hardly breathe and my heart felt like it was lurching against my ribs. Mia! I had to protect her, but how? Lock us both in her room? It had no key. Grab her and lock us both in the bathroom? The lock was too flimsy to be of any use. I almost let out a whimper and put my hand hard against my mouth. Think!

Phone Connor. Then I'd try and work out how to get us both out safely.

I turned to grab my mobile phone off the side table. An arm slid over my shoulder and pulled back on my neck, forcing me against him. It had to be a him – no woman smelled like that. Sweat and cigarette smoke and some kind of alcohol. Scotch.

I'd recognise that stink anywhere. His arm was cutting off my breathing and I clawed at it. 'I can't breathe,' I choked out.

'Good.'

I struggled to get free, pulling against his arm but I couldn't feel skin. He was wearing a leather jacket. Then something hard and cold was jammed against the side of my neck, just under my ear. I froze.

'That's better.' The arm relented a little and I sucked in air.

This was what happened when you ignored threatening phone calls. The bastard eventually came to get you. *Stupid.* That was all my numbed brain could offer.

He didn't say anything else for a few seconds, then, 'Where is she?'

Mia? I tried to twist away but his arm clamped again, and the gun barrel dug harder. Why did he want Mia? He wasn't getting her. He'd have to fucking shoot me first, and I'd fight him.

'Stop it!' His voice was like a slap and I stopped, getting another strangled breath in. 'Where's the girl? You've got three seconds to answer.'

The girl. Maybe not Mia. The girl? Emma.

'I don't know.'

'Bullshit.'

'I don't know,' I wailed. 'She ran away. In Melbourne. The cops don't know either.'

'You must know. She was hiding here before.'

How did he know that? Who the fuck was he?

The killer.

I couldn't match the phone calls with Kate's murderer. Nothing made sense. 'Let me breathe,' I gritted out. 'I'll tell you what I know.' Which was nothing.

His arm loosened again but the gun was still there, painfully hard, forcing my head at an angle. 'She'll come back here. She's probably here now. Hiding with you.'

'She's not. Search the house. Search anywhere. She's not here, I promise. I haven't heard from her.'

Just then, a sound came from Mia's room. Oh God, exactly what I didn't want. 'Juddy! Juddy!'

'Is that her?' he asked.

'Does that sound like a fourteen-year-old?'

'Don't be a fucking smartarse.' He released me and pushed me away from him. 'Turn around.'

I turned slowly. He was a black shape, with a balaclava over his head. The yellow night lamp in the hallway lit his eyes with a weird glint. He was like something out of a nightmare. Mine.

'Juddy!'

'I'm coming,' I called. 'Stay there!'

He pointed the gun at me. 'Go and shut her up. I'll be at the door. Don't do anything stupid.'

I took a step forward and staggered, my legs wobbling. *Come on, keep it together. Protect Mia.* I kept going, into her room, aware all the time of his shape just outside the door.

'What's the matter, Mia?' I tried to make my voice sound soft and soothing, but it was a bloody struggle.

She was sitting up in bed, blankets back, ready to hop out. 'Is Ben here?'

'No, sweetie. What made you say that?'

'Heard his voice.' She looked at me suspiciously.

'No, that was… Connor on the phone.'

'Unca Connor! Can I talk, too?'

'No, he's gone now. Come on, lie down and go back to sleep. We've got a big day tomorrow, remember?'

'Do we?' She lay down but her face was puzzled.

'We're going to the bank, and then we can have ice cream!' My voice was too loud, but I was trying to block out the sound of his feet scuffing outside her door. 'We might even buy you a new book.'

'Ice cream for Bum?'

'Only if he's very good and goes to sleep straight away.' I bent and kissed her goodnight.

'Kiss Bum, too.'

Anything to get her settled again. I kissed the grubby rabbit face and pulled her blankets up around her shoulders. 'Nighty-night.'

'Bug bears bite.' She closed her eyes and I backed out of the room.

He was right there, and the gun was shoved into my ribs. 'What's in that cupboard?' he whispered. Good, he didn't want her awake any more than I did. It was Mia's little wardrobe, across the room.

'Clothes and toys. There's no room for anything else.'

'Show me.'

I opened my mouth to object and snapped it shut again. *Do what he wants and get him out of the house.* I tiptoed across the room, swung both doors open and stepped back so he could see, then closed them again and walked out, pulling the bedroom door shut. 'See?'

'Other rooms. Now.'

'She's not here!'

'Do what you're fucking told.' He pushed me towards the lounge and I stumbled. 'Get in there.' He pointed with the gun towards the couch. 'Sit down. Shut the fuck up. If you move off that couch, I'll shoot the kid. Got it?'

I nodded frantically and sat, hunched over, watching him. I didn't recognise his voice at all. It had a faint accent, that was all I could discern. He took something out of his back pocket, which I realised was a torch when he flicked it on. It was one of those small ones with a powerful beam that he shone straight in my eyes, blinding me.

'Remember what I said.'

'OK.' My heart was hammering in my ears, but I eyed the iron poker by the fireplace. If he went back to Mia's room, I was going to grab it and attack him, of that I was sure.

He moved away, scanning around the lounge room first, looking in and behind everything, even the wood box for the fire. I hoped a bloody big huntsman spider would leap out on to him, but no luck. Then he checked the kitchen, opening all the cupboards, the fridge, looking in places even Mia would hardly fit. Hall cupboards, then my bedroom. As soon as he moved out of sight, I scrabbled under the cushion and found the phone.

This one was programmed on speed dial, too. I kept it under the cushion to muffle the beeps and coughed at the same time. Press 2 for Connor. Even where it was, I could faintly hear it ringing at Connor's end, then his answer. Only then did I lift it up, whisper 'Help. Intruder.' I disconnected and shoved it back under the cushion, coughing as I did so.

He emerged from my room. 'What are you up to?'

'I'm scared shitless,' I said. 'It makes me cough.'

'Shut up.' He moved towards the laundry and bathroom area, checked in there and came back. 'So she's not here. Yet. She will be eventually.'

'She's got no reason –'

'Shut up! Fucking gabby woman.' He breathed heavily through his head covering. 'She always calls on you for help. So I'll be watching you. All. The. Time. You tell the cops I was here and that little kid is dead. Remember that. I can get you or her anytime.'

He turned and walked out through the back door, and the cold draught swept into the lounge like it was filling the space he'd left. I waited, holding my breath, listening hard. Had he really gone? Could I get up?

I decided I could, then I wasn't able to. I started shaking and gasping for breath, feeling hysteria just below the surface, trying to hold it back. *Shut up, shut up, you'll wake Mia.* I grabbed the couch cushion and held it to me like a shield, like a comfort toy, until the shaking started to subside.

Then an old familiar feeling flickered inside and built in a few seconds to a burning rage. Fucking thugs, same all over. Frighten the woman, use force and threats. Use the kids. Fucking bastards. *No more. No more.*

'Judi? Hello?' Connor's voice floated down the hallway from the back door. I hoped he had his gun drawn.

'Here,' I croaked. 'Lounge room.' I swallowed hard. Breathed deeply. 'He's gone. I think. Be careful.'

Footsteps, careful and light, then, 'Can I turn the light on?'

I checked the curtains were closed. 'Yeah, OK.' I shielded my eyes from the glare and then blinked and focused on him. Gun in hand, he checked around, looking in the kitchen first and then in the other rooms. Finally, he returned to the lounge and sat with me, putting his arm around me. It felt warm and comforting and I sagged against him.

'I came as fast as I could.'

'I know. But he had a gun.' *He might've shot Connor.* I sagged further.

'Was it the guy on the phone? Could you tell?'

I shook my head. 'Pretty sure it wasn't. Different voice.' I closed my eyes for a moment. 'No. This guy was after Emma. Searched the whole place from top to bottom.'

'Emma? But...'

I let Connor's arm fall away and stood up but my legs still felt like overcooked spaghetti. 'I need a drink.' I poured half a glass of Jack Daniels and took a large mouthful, nearly choking on it as it went down. But the warmth in my throat and stomach helped to calm me further. 'Whoever this guy was, he wasn't from around here. He was a professional. Totally calm, ruthless, he meant exactly what he said.'

Connor looked at me for a long moment. 'So he could be the person who killed Kate.'

'That'd be my guess. More than a guess. Ninety-nine per cent sure.'

'Right.' He stood and added, 'I parked up the road and checked outside on the way in, but I'm going to do it again. You need to look at your back door.'

I followed him down the hallway and saw what he meant. The door had been forced open, with wood split around the lock. 'Used a small crowbar.' He turned on the outside light. 'There it is.'

I peered at it. 'That's mine.' The garden shed door was wide open. 'He's gone into my shed and used my own tools. Bastard.'

'You should keep it locked. But, I know, you don't usually have to.'

I didn't say that I'd been leaving the shed open in case Emma did come back.

'What did he touch in the house?'

'Everything. But he was wearing gloves. Thin ones. And a balaclava.'

Connor nodded. 'Look, the best thing I can do right now is take down everything you can remember, especially anything about him and what he said. The sooner I report it in, the better.' He paused. 'Then maybe you and Mia should move to the pub.'

I laughed shortly. 'Like that's any better.' I still remembered the guy who'd broken into the pub several times and tried to kill Carl and me.

'It's in town, and I can get there faster, plus there are people around you.'

Yeah, yeah. With this guy, I doubted that would make a scrap of difference. The rage bubbled up again and I took a breath. After I'd closed all the cupboard doors and made tea, we sat down at the kitchen table and I went through it all again in detail, even down to what he smelled like.

'Height?' Connor asked. 'Build?'

'About ten or fifteen centimetres taller than me, no more. Strong, but not fat or body builder type. No paunch on him.'

'Age?'

'I don't know.'

'Did his voice sound older? If he was a smoker, they're pretty raspy by the time they hit forty.'

'Oh, right.' I thought about it. 'Possibly early thirties? But it's a guess.'

'No problem. Good to get your thoughts on it now while it's fresh, like I said.' He wrote down more stuff. 'What did the gun look like?'

'Deadly. Like it would shoot bullets at me.'

Connor grinned. 'You're starting to sound more like yourself.'

'Hmph. It was… black. Fitted in his hand.'

'When he pressed it against your neck, what did it feel like? I mean, small and round?'

'No, I don't think so.' I closed my eyes, tried to feel it again. 'Kind of oval, like this.' I made an oval shape with my thumb and index finger. 'And the gun… this sounds weird but it might have had some blue on it. Paint?'

Connor wrote some more. 'It's possible. Worth noting.'

I could tell he had an idea what it was but he wasn't saying, and I didn't really want to know. 'Is that it?'

'Yes, for now.' He grimaced. 'I'll call Swan and fill him in. He'll probably come up tomorrow and talk to you.'

'Yay.' I yawned so wide that my jaw cracked.

'I'm going to stay here the rest of the night, OK?' He had his phone out and was scrolling through his contacts list, and looked up for a moment. 'I can't fix that door, although I can barricade it with a cupboard, and you probably don't want to wake Mia and move her in the middle of the night.'

'No.' It was well after 2am. 'Thanks, Connor.'

'No problem. Although if I get called out for a road accident or anything, I will have to take you both to the pub.'

I nodded and left him to it, checking on Mia and then crawling into bed. I couldn't get warm, my whole body shivering, and I tried to imagine Heath was there, holding me, but it didn't work. Tears kept welling so I tried deep breathing, then box breathing that I'd heard guys in the army used. Gradually the counting and slow breaths calmed me, and then I heard Connor's little puffy snores from the couch and smiled. With him and his gun there, I finally drifted off; before I knew it, it was morning, and Mia was shaking me.

'Unca Connor made breakfast!' she told me with a big grin. 'He said I could have choccy sauce in my milk. Ssshhh.' She put her finger to her lips. 'Don't tell Juddy.' She chortled with glee and then stared at me. 'You got hair like an echidna.'

'How do you know what an echidna is?' If I looked like an echidna, I clearly needed a decent haircut.

'Mrs Needham showed us. It has a looooong nose.' She stuck her fingers out to show me. If an echidna had a nose that long, it'd be an elephant.

'That's very interesting. Time for your breakfast.'

I gave her a kiss and headed for the shower. It was only when I was under the water, eyes closed, reaching for the shampoo that the feeling of the man's arm around my neck came back to me in full force, like a vision.

I gasped and dropped the shampoo bottle on my foot. 'Fuck.' I didn't want to close my eyes again so my hair got short shrift. Like anyone would notice. By the time I got to the kitchen, there was loud banging from the back of the house and Mia told me that Unca Connor was fixing the naughty door.

A few moments later, he came back, holding the hammer and some nails. 'I've had to nail it shut, sorry. I can't fix that lock. You'll need to get it replaced.' He put the hammer and nails on the bench. 'I'll leave this here in case you need it.'

I might need it to kill somebody. I shook myself, poured coffee and drank some, hoping the caffeine would stave off the headache that was looming above my eyes. Connor sat at the table and finished his toast. 'Mia, are you allowed to watch TV now?'

She looked at me.

'Just for a little while,' I said. When she'd found the remote and settled on the couch, I added, 'More questions?'

'Just wanted to go over what he said again.' He checked his notebook. 'He knew about Emma running away again.' I nodded. 'And that she'd been hiding here.' I nodded again. 'Tell me again the last thing he said?'

I tried to recall, word for word. 'She always calls on you for help. So I'll be watching you. All the time. You tell the cops I was here and the kid is dead. I can get you or her anytime.' I shivered, staring down into the murky depths of my mug. 'He meant Mia. I can't even…' I hoped Emma called me so I could insist that she stay as far away from here as possible.

Connor tapped his pen on the notebook. 'He knows a lot. Too much.'

'How many people would know all that about Emma?'

'Lots would know she'd run away. There's been an alert out for her. But…' His face was deeply furrowed. 'He was talking like he knew she'd been hiding in your shed. That has been kept under wraps. It sounds like he also knew you'd got her out of that shopping centre.'

'Did he see me there?' I thought back. 'Emma said she saw him before we got outside to Heath's car.'

'OK, but why did she then do an ID that looked like Chris Winter?'

We stared at each other, and neither of us had an answer that made any sense.

15

For the first time, I began to wonder how much of this was centred on Emma, not Kate. But that didn't make sense either. She was a kid. And surely the killer would have shot her first? My thoughts swung back to my own huge problem.

'I don't like it that he's watching me, waiting for her to turn up!' I couldn't sit still. I jumped up and started clearing the table, clattering dishes into the sink. All the while glancing out the window and hoping to God nobody was out there.

'Look, I…' Connor stopped and sighed again.

'What? Tell me!' I was wringing the tea towel so hard that I heard it rip.

'I can't raise the issue of an information leak with Swan. It's this country cop thing. And the Bendigo guys look down their noses at me, too.'

'Hey, you're a better bloody detective than all those Bendigo twits put together.' I sat down opposite him again. 'If you think there's a leak, say so. It's Emma's life at stake here. And mine and Mia's.'

'Yeah, you're right.' He managed a smile. 'OK, I phoned it all in after you went to bed. Got Swan out of bed, which didn't make me popular, but he agreed it was urgent. It's the first lead they've had.'

'But there'll be no fingerprints or anything.'

'Might be DNA, especially on that crowbar. So the crime

scene people will be here very shortly, and so will the Bendigo detectives.'

'Oh God, not Barney,' I groaned. 'I am not talking to him.'

'No, they'll be doing other things. One of Swan's team is coming up to interview you.' He checked his watch. 'He's coming to the station so he'll be here in half an hour.'

He could bloody wait. I gestured to the window. 'That guy said he's going to be watching me. He probably means the house. He could only be doing that from the bush.' The threats echoed in my head. 'He'll see your police 4WD.'

'He's a pro,' Connor said. He shifted in his chair. 'He could be in a hide, or even using a drone. I don't think you should stay here. You and Mia.'

I gaped at him. This was getting beyond ridiculous, and bloody scary. I was starting to feel like I was in a spy movie. Then a horrible thought struck me. 'If he's that much of a pro, he could be a long way away, and using a sniper's rifle. You know, with one of those scope things.'

Connor nodded, barely looking at me. That was a really bad sign.

I clenched my hands together. 'So if he had one of those, how far away could he be and still be able to shoot me? Or Emma, if she was here?'

'Well...' He cleared his throat. 'He'd have to be a really good shot.'

'How far?'

'He could be five hundred metres or more away.'

'Anywhere.'

He nodded.

'I could be getting into my car at the pub and he could shoot me from a car up the street.'

'I really doubt he'd do anything like that, Judi.' He looked like he was in pain, trying to reassure me with nothing really to offer. Then he said, 'You're sure he wasn't the guy threatening you on the phone?'

'Positive.' The answer popped out but I was sure I was right. 'The guy who broke in here last night wouldn't do stupid phone calls. He'd just kill me. Or Emma.'

'OK.'

It wasn't, but what the fuck. Nothing I could do right now. I went and turned off the TV and got Mia ready for childcare. She seemed to sense I was in a bit of a state and was quiet herself, not even fussing when I chose her clothes for her. When we came out of the house, Connor was talking to someone next to a white van. The crime scene people. I was glad to be out of there, leaving the house to them to deal with.

Just walking down the path sent crawly sensations up my spine. I ducked my head and kept going, Mia trotting behind me.

It wasn't until I reached the car that I remembered. I'd cancelled childcare today. I'd planned to spend the day with Mia. Bank in Heathcote and ice cream. I leaned against the car and tried to hold the tears back. One little bugger got out and rolled down my face and I swiped it away.

'Juddy?' Mia tugged at my jacket. 'Why you crying?'

'Something in my eye, that's all.' I put her in her car seat and drove to the pub. I didn't want to be anywhere near my house today. I hoped to God I didn't still feel like that at the end of the day. The pub didn't feel safe either, and I didn't fancy a motel in Heathcote in the slightest. Connor couldn't stay with us twenty-four hours a day. I felt trapped.

At the pub, Joyce had already been in and vacuumed downstairs – there was nothing to do upstairs with no guests. After I'd made sure every door and window was locked, I sat in the bistro with Mia, playing with her and noticing how worn out and old the play area toys were. Something else to add to the list for updating and improving. Mia wanted to go outside and play catch but I persuaded her that we could do it later. I didn't want to be out there feeling like I had to look over my shoulder all the time.

When Andre came in, he did a double take. 'Didn't expect to see you here.'

'My house is full of crime scene people.' I tried to make it sound like an everyday thing and failed miserably. 'Mia, how about a snack?'

That gave me an excuse to hide in the kitchen and tell Andre what had been happening.

'Fuck my life,' he said, and gave me a big hug. 'That is just completely shit.'

'Yeah, you can say that again,' I said shakily.

'That is just completely shit.'

'Ha ha.' But he did make me feel better. 'I've been going over and over everything, and the one thing I keep coming back to is Emma. Why does he want her dead? Badly enough to threaten me, and to hang around here when the cops will be looking for him. And who's leaking information to him about where Emma is?'

'Stuffed if I know,' Andre said. He was chopping up an apple for Mia and I was worried he'd take a finger off he was banging the knife down so hard. 'Don't you think it's time those cops in Melbourne told you what was going on? Surely they have some idea? Why aren't they protecting you?'

'The other thing I don't get,' I said, 'is why Emma did that ID thing and created a picture of Chris Winter.'

'Well… you said Winter admitted to knowing Kate before. Maybe Emma did it because she doesn't like him. You know, a teenage revenge thing?'

Mia banged on the kitchen door. 'You said snack!'

'Yes, sorry.' I took the apple out and she sat at the table with

Andre and me. He'd brought out coffee and orange juice. I was still thinking. 'Or maybe she's so scared she did it to put the police on the wrong track.'

'That's not very sensible if they're trying to protect her.'

'She's never trusted them, right from the start.' I absent-mindedly ate one of Mia's apple pieces and received a glare. 'When she was hiding in my shed, she was adamant she didn't want me to tell them where she was.'

'Didn't you tell me Swan was liaising with the NSW police?'

Before I could answer him, someone started pounding on the pub's front door, and I nearly jumped out of my underwear. 'That'd better not be Chris fucking Winter!'

'I'll answer it,' Andre said, and went to see who it was. He came back in a few seconds, the look on his face saying, *You aren't going to like this.*

He was right. I didn't. It was Detective Sergeant Swan.

'I was expecting the mon –' Oops. Do not use the organ grinder joke with this man.

'Ms Westerholme. You've had a stressful night, I hear.'

'That's one way of describing it.' Total shit would be another. 'Coffee?'

'Thank you.' He glanced at Mia. 'You may not want to talk about your experience in front of the child.'

'Probably not.'

'She can stay here with me,' Andre said hastily, 'and you can go in the office?'

I nodded and Swan and I carried our coffees, not bothering to make polite conversation. I had to fetch him a chair from the bistro, and he sat drinking his coffee while I described what happened. I stopped after a minute or two. 'You're not taking notes?'

'Senior Constable Byrne has given me a record of his interview with you, which was very detailed and helpful. But I want to hear it for myself and ask a few more questions.'

'Right, well…' I kept going but now I felt like he was waiting to trip me up on something. I was starting to understand how Emma felt. When I'd finished, we sat in silence for a little while, with me getting more and more irritated. 'I do have work to do,' I said.

'Senior Constable Byrne said you've been getting threatening phone calls.'

'Yes, but I don't think they're connected to this.'

He gave me a stony look. 'I think I can decide that for myself. Who would threaten you?'

'I've been having a problem with the woman at the health spa, and her partner is a man. She's been really angry with us.' I thought about my own list. 'Keith Scott, possibly. You remember him?' The one they'd never been able to pin anything on after Macca's murder. Swan nodded.

'Anyone else?'

Like I had a million enemies. 'If you really want me to push the possibilities, it could be someone connected with the bikies who were selling the chop chop. But the main guys are all in gaol, aren't they?'

He sipped his coffee. 'Not yet. I believe two are out on bail.'

'What?' I stared at him in disbelief. 'Well, that's just bloody lovely, isn't it?'

'The court system in this state is backlogged at the best of times. People are entitled to bail unless they're a flight risk, and until proven guilty.' He sounded almost happy to tell me that.

'Oh, good-o then,' I snapped. 'Never mind the rest of us who do the right thing and end up worse off.'

'There's no need for that,' he said. 'I don't run the courts.'

I took a long, slow breath, and it didn't work so I tried another one. Nup. 'No wonder Emma ran away from your so-called police protection. I'm bloody glad I helped her. I hope she's a million miles away by now. I know I would be.'

That got a reaction. His face was still a mask but his eyes were narrowed and angry. I couldn't give a shit. 'Did Senior Constable Byrne tell you what the guy said to me?'

Swan nodded slightly.

'So you know that he said stuff to me that was supposedly only known to police.'

No nod. Just a stiff neck, as usual.

'Who is passing on this information to him? This guy is a pro. Even Connor acknowledged I was right, after the way I was attacked last night. Inside information about Emma, things that nobody is supposed to know. You want to tell me what the hell is going on?'

'Senior Constable Byrne should not have commented on an ongoing case.'

'Oh, for fuck's sake, get the stick out of your arse, Swan!' I'd had enough. Been there, done this crap before. 'Get over yourself for a minute and look at this from my point of view. Is that remotely possible? You know, thinking about it from the victim's experience?'

He shifted in his chair. 'Your hostility –'

'Fuck my hostility! I have bent over backwards to help! How many times have I heard the police calling for help from the public? Witnesses, information – you basically ask people to dob each other in.' I folded my arms for a moment, but that felt too defensive and I unfolded them again. 'Look.' I took a breath, let it out. 'This is a small town. We've had stuff happen here that shouldn't happen to any place. It's starting to make us look like Snowtown.'

He jerked slightly at that, which was some kind of reaction at least.

'But what you forget is, at the most basic level, people here are great. They help each other. You came here to investigate

Macca's murder, but I don't think you ever understood why everyone was so upset. You didn't come to his funeral, and you weren't obliged to, but everyone Macca had ever helped came, and helped out with food and memories and donations to the footy club junior teams. That's what happens here.'

'We do care about justice and finding closure for…'

'Closure for some people is good,' I said. 'It's what they need. But for a lot of people, they want to know that someone cares. Cares enough to look after the ones who are affected, and try to make things right. Yeah, yeah, I know things can't be made right when someone dies. But it's the trying that makes the difference.'

He sat there like a statue and I couldn't figure out what was going on in his head so I just waited.

When he finally spoke he surprised me. 'Why do you think Emma doesn't trust us?'

'I just said someone in your lot is leaking information about her and –'

'*She* doesn't know that. She's out there in the wind somewhere. Why?'

He was asking me? Weird, but… 'Her past experience. Something happened to her and her mum in Sydney, something to do with the police up there.'

'Go on.'

I was struggling a bit, but since he was giving me his full attention without being sarcastic, I kept going. 'Her mum's ex is in gaol and has been for a while. Did her mum play a role in putting him there? What was he doing before he went inside?' I shrugged. 'I don't know – was he a police informant? You're kind of asking why Kate was killed as well.'

'That's true.' His face was unreadable.

'If he was a police informant, maybe he told Kate something he shouldn't have. Except… why wouldn't he have already told the police the same thing?'

'He might have been holding something back to bargain with.'

I glared at Swan. 'You know what this is about. Why ask me?'

'Actually, we don't. Carry on. You are surprisingly good at reasoning things out.'

Another glare. Bounced off him like he was covered in rubber. 'OK, well, if Kate put her ex in gaol, it could be revenge. And someone in the police up there has leaked that it was her. But it seems a bit far-fetched that he'd pay someone to hunt her down. How long did he get?'

'Sentenced to almost five years.'

'Not worth it then. Conspiracy to murder would get him a lot more.'

'True.'

'Why are you trying to get me to solve this for you? Did Heath put you up to this?'

His jaw dropped a little, and he snapped it up again. 'Detective Sergeant Heath has nothing to do with this case.'

'I'll take that as a no then.' Pity. 'He did come and help me get Emma out of Airport West shopping centre.'

'An unfortunate personal involvement.'

I got the distinct impression he was talking about more than the rescue. Arsehole. I'd fix him. 'All right then, it was Kate who had the information the NSW cops wanted all along, and they shafted her. How's that?'

He stared at me for several very long seconds until I wanted to fidget or stand up, but I sat there pretending to be a rock and stared back. He dropped his eyes first, reaching for his coffee. *Gotcha.*

'You think I'm right.'

'It's one of several scenarios we're looking at.'

'Why don't you know, one way or another?' I watched his face closely, and caught the jaw clenching. 'The cops up there are holding back, aren't they? Not sharing information.'

'How close are you and Senior Constable Byrne?'

That one caught me flat-footed. 'What? What kind of question is that?' He didn't answer so I went on. 'Connor and I have been friends for years. Since I started working in the pub, he has assisted me with police matters such as potential drunk drivers, fights and the occasional murder and arson. That's all.'

'I'm concerned that he is providing you with confidential information, outside of his remit.'

Now I was past being irritated and moving into bloody angry. 'He's a bloody good cop! Don't you dare accuse him of stuff like that. Jeez, he puts your dickhead detectives from Bendigo to shame.'

Swan's mouth thinned into a line that I realised was probably his version of a smile. 'He does at that.' He stood. 'Thanks for your time.'

'Hang on. What are you doing to find this guy? The one who attacked me last night? Remember him?'

'We're doing everything we can,' he said. 'But you might consider staying in Melbourne for a few days. We can protect you better there, and you'll be out of this person's range.'

I didn't believe him. Recent events had proven otherwise. 'And who's supposed to run the pub?'

'It's not a difficult choice if you consider your niece,' he said coolly, and left.

I spent a few minutes getting all the F words out of my system, then went to find Andre and Mia. They were outside on the patio, playing with a large red plastic ball. Mia kicked it so hard that she almost overbalanced. The ball shot past Andre and through the open French doors.

'Goal!' Andre shouted.

It hit my legs and I bent and picked it up. 'Don't tell me – you've got her signed up for the Melbourne Victory team already.'

'Of course.' He examined my face. 'I see you and Swan got on well as usual.'

I opened my mouth to swear and changed my mind. 'Let's not talk about him. Let's talk about children's parties.' So we did while we played soccer with Mia and evaluated the spaces and how many we could fit in and how the hell we were going to entertain twenty kids at once. All the most pressing, urgent stuff that stopped me thinking about guys with sniper rifles and whether I should take Swan's advice. In the end, I asked Andre.

'Maybe he's got a point. What if you moved in here for a couple of days, just until they catch the guy, or he's scared off? No way Emma is coming back here, is she?'

'I bloody hope not.'

He scuffed his shoe over a weed growing between the pavers and bent to pull it out. 'I was actually going to talk to you about something like that anyway.'

I raised my eyebrows and waited. It took another couple of weeds pulled before he said, 'I thought I could move into the pub for a while myself.'

'What's happened to your house in Heathcote?'

He made a face. 'The landlord has put the rent up – a lot. Said he really wants to run it as an Airbnb so I think he's trying to force me out.'

'Oh, bugger!' I'd been to Andre's a few times for dinner and the house was a lovely little miner's cottage, well restored with real character. Yeah, I could see it on Airbnb all right. 'Of course you can live in the pub. Macca used to.'

'I actually don't want to,' he said seriously. 'It's just not homely. I'll look for something else, but in the meantime, it'd be handy if we had guests. And let's face it, we need guests.' He took a breath. 'Which brings me to the next thing. Marketing.'

'Mmm.' That was my sole contribution. We needed it. I had very little idea how to do it.

'Our silent partners in Melbourne – my group of mates... I've been talking to them. They think we should get stuck in and pay someone to do really good marketing. Go for broke.'

Broke. That was something I didn't want to be. 'How can we pay for it though?'

'They'll put up a bit more money. I think they feel like if they don't, they could lose the lot.'

'No, they won't!' I frowned at him. 'We agreed that if we sold, they'd get their investment back first.'

'I know, I know.'

Mia had stopped kicking the ball and whacked Andre on the leg. 'You stopped playing.'

'Sorry!' Andre grabbed the ball and said, 'I'll teach you how to catch like a goalie.' He glanced at me. 'Let's talk about it later. It's a good idea, and so are the kids' parties.'

I nodded. 'I need to get the banking ready, then Mia and I are going to Heathcote for ice cream.'

She had ears like a bat. 'Ice cream!'

All the way to Heathcote, I pondered. Like Andre, I didn't want to move into the pub, but for different reasons. Mia made it difficult – there was nowhere for her to run around, and she and I would have to share a room, possibly a double bed. I'd have to move a mountain of stuff – clothes, toys, food – she and I liked. It wasn't just a matter of packing a small bag.

If only Heath could come up to Candlebark for a few days. Just thinking about that as a possibility made me go all warm and mushy, which was so unlike me that I realised I was under more stress than I thought. Still, going to bed with him every night... not to mention having him to talk to, in my house, like a normal couple. Now I needed a fan for my hot face.

It was all impossible. It didn't stop me from texting him when I'd parked in Heathcote. By the time we'd been to the bank and had found seats in the café and Mia had her ice cream in a dish with sprinkles and raspberry sauce, he still hadn't replied. Clearly the idea didn't appeal to him at all.

Time to head back to Candlebark. Moaning Marie was doing lunch as well as the night shift with Charlie. I'd been planning to take Mia to the little playground in the park, since it was a sunny day. I loved autumn, with the cool evenings and mornings and soft, hazy afternoons – such a relief after a hot, burning summer.

But suddenly the playground looked too open, too vulnerable. I shivered, glad I hadn't said anything to her. Swan had said they were going to 'protect' me, but he'd no doubt left by now, and I hadn't even seen Connor's 4WD around. Were they just humouring me? Swan said I had a choice – yeah, my choice was Mia and I in Cairns on the beach, or even Bali, where nobody could find us in the crowds.

Just as we walked into the pub, my phone rang. Mia ran ahead to see Andre, and I frowned at the caller name – it was Margaret, my neighbour in Ascot Vale. We went through all the hellos and how-are-yous and she finally got down to her reason for calling.

'I know this sounds like I'm being nosy, dear, but I just wanted to check that you did indeed have a guest staying in your house.'

'Um…' I couldn't put any sensible words together. 'Why?'

'It's the noise, dear, I can hear the TV through the wall. Oh, it's not loud or anything. It's just… after last time…'

Margaret had saved me a couple of times, once in particular when two thugs had broken in and attacked me, so I totally understood her caution. 'Maybe I left it on last time I was there?' I was pretty sure I hadn't but perhaps there'd been a weird power surge or something.

'It does go on and off. But it's also that I heard crying. Somebody out on your back porch, and she sounded quite upset.' Margaret clucked her tongue. 'I didn't like to put my head over the fence and upset her more. But I did want to check with you.'

I knew instantly who it must be. Emma. Shit.

16

How the hell did Emma get into my house? Surely I'd locked it up properly? 'Thanks for letting me know, Margaret. I really appreciate it. It's a young friend and she sounds like she needs someone there. I'll come down this afternoon.'

'Oh, that's such a weight off my mind, dear. Do pop in for a cuppa, won't you?'

'Of course. Thanks again.' Margaret as a neighbour really was worth her weight in gold.

I hung up and stood by the reception desk, running things through my head. Staffing, bookings, Andre, Emma, petrol in the Benz.

And Mia. Was it safe to take Mia with me?

The short answer was no. The longer answer was it was only Emma, and she wouldn't harm Mia. But the guy who was after her would, so I was back to the short answer.

Or I could just call Swan and tell him where Emma was.

I'd lost count of how many times she'd run away from the police. This time she might disappear completely. If this guy found her first, she really would disappear completely, and maybe her bones might be found in a few years' time by some dog chasing rabbits.

Andre's voice startled me. 'Are you OK?'

'Stuffed if I know. Whatever happened to a quiet, stress-free life?' I shook my head. 'I thought I had one of those once.'

'What's happened?'

I described Margaret's call, and he got it straight away. 'It's Emma, isn't it?' He examined my face. 'And you don't want to call Swan again. But you know that's the sensible thing to do.'

'I just want to talk to her first. If I can find out what the problem is, I think it would go a long way towards her trusting us more. Trusting the Victorian police. I can remind her that it was Heath who rescued us for a start.'

'Yeah, but… What if this guy who's after her is watching you? What if he follows you to Melbourne? Or maybe he doesn't have to follow you. Maybe he already knows where your house is down there.'

I shook my head. 'If he did, he'd go and check, either before or after he came to my house here. But you're right. He said he'd be watching me, so how do I get away?'

He was silent for a few long seconds, biting his lip, thinking it through. He was my mate, and he'd put Mia's and my safety first, no matter what. 'You could take my car. Wear a sort of disguise, and go the long way out past Bronwyn's health spa. But you can't take Mia. Absolutely not.'

'I know! I'd already decided that.'

'And you have to put her somewhere safe.'

'Joleen's house would be best. She only lives one street over from Connor.' I grimaced. 'Shit. I can't tell Connor where I'm going though. He'll insist on telling Swan and it'll all go to crap. Can you imagine the cops invading my house and frightening the crap out of Emma?'

'To be honest, I think far worse things have frightened Emma,' he said.

'True.' I hesitated. 'I know you still think I should tell the police, but Emma needs someone on her side. At her back. Whatever.'

'Their way of looking after her – and you – is to find this guy.'

'So let them do it. He's around here, not in Melbourne. I have to put Emma first. Kate…' I didn't want to go there.

Andre nodded slowly. 'All right, if you really believe it's the right choice. But there's one more thing.'

'Yes?'

'When you find Emma, you can't bring her back here.'

'But…' I huffed out a breath and closed my eyes for a moment. 'Yeah, you're right.'

'What will you do with her?'

'Try and persuade her to let the cops help, I think. If I call anyone, it's going to be Heath. She knows him and knows he helped, even if she can't separate that from everything else. I need to find out what the "everything else" is.'

Andre pulled me into a hug, and I hugged him back, hard. 'For God's sake, don't put yourself in danger again,' he said. 'It might be better if you don't know too much about Emma and Kate and what happened to them.'

'I'll be careful, don't worry,' I said, reassuring him. I should've taken more notice of the second thing he said.

As I sped away up the hill in Andre's sporty red Kia, cap pulled low over his trendy sunglasses, I felt momentarily guilty about not spending the whole day with Mia as I'd promised. Then I reminded myself of her excitement when she got to Joleen's and saw two other kids in the paddle pool out the back. I was ancient history in her mind from then on.

Andre had already parked his Kia around the back of the pub – I parked next to him and went inside to don my 'disguise'. He let me out the kitchen door, after checking nobody was around, and I kept up a watch as I drove out of town past the health spa and then followed the road east. Even when I hit the main highway south to Melbourne at last, I still didn't feel relaxed enough to stop looking in my mirror. I reached the city faster than I expected and spent half an hour driving aimlessly through the northern suburbs until I was convinced nobody was following me – then I had to stop and fill up Andre's car.

I finally arrived at the Ascot Vale house around 5pm and sat out the front, watching it. I had no real plan, other than to quietly let myself in and talk to Emma. I was half-expecting her to bolt out of the house and run off again – she was getting to be an expert at it – but I hoped I could keep her there long enough to make her see reason. There were no lights on, and I wondered if she sat there in the dark every night, watching TV with the blinds drawn, not realising Margaret next door was so alert to trouble in my house.

Finally, I eased myself out of the car, holding back a groan at the ache in my hip. If Emma made a run for it, no way was I going after her. I'd probably fall flat on my face. I unlocked the front door and let myself into the house as quietly as I could, listening for signs of life – no TV, no lights. Maybe she'd already gone. On the kitchen table was my spare key. She must've taken it from the hook at the Candlebark house.

I tiptoed around and finally found her, curled up asleep in my bed, two of Mia's stuffed toys in her arms. The brown bear stared up at me with its evil grin, reminding me of why I'd persuaded Mia to leave it here, and the pink dog looked very unconcerned about everything. Half its luck.

Even in sleep, Emma's face was pale and sad, her mouth drooping. I bent and rubbed her bare arm gently, whispering, 'Emma, Emma. It's me – Judi.'

She came awake instantly, rearing up and scuttling away from me, stuffed toys kicked away. 'Get away! What are you doing? Leave me alone!' Then she blinked at me as if only just registering who I was.

'It's me – Judi. I've come to see if you're OK.'

'I'm fine.' She moved to the edge of the bed. 'Sorry, didn't mean to be here without asking. I'm going now.' She began searching for her runners, which were at the end of the bed, along with her backpack.

'Hey, it's fine, you don't have to go.' I hesitated, not sure what else to say. 'I know… I know who you're running away from.'

'Yeah, sure you do.' She found her runners and tried to pull them on without undoing the laces, jamming her feet in hard.

'He came to my house last night.' That got her attention. She stilled for a moment, then reached for her backpack, pretending she hadn't heard me. 'He was looking for you. He stuck a gun in the side of my neck, and threatened Mia.'

'So now you know.' She stood and slung the backpack over her shoulder.

I put out a hand and she glared at it. 'You can't run away again, Emma.'

'Watch me.'

'Let the people here protect you.' I looked into her eyes and saw only fear and despair. The poor bloody kid. 'Please, let me help you.'

'Have they caught the guy?'

'No.'

'See?' She laughed hysterically. 'That's why I can't go to the cops. They have no fucking idea, and they also don't care!'

'I don't believe that.' She clearly didn't care what I believed. 'What are you going to do? Are you going to run away? Where to? With what? You're not old enough to work anywhere, you don't have a fake ID.'

'I'll find a way. I'll go to Western Australia.'

She tried to push past me and I held out my arms. No way was I going to physically grab her, but persuasion wasn't working.

'You know what happens to girls like you? They end up as underage prostitutes. You'd be perfect – on the run, no other way of earning money, you'd have to sleep on the streets, and they look out for girls like you with no other options. Is that what you want?'

'What difference would it make?' she shouted. 'I'm a slut anyway. Might as well get money for it.'

That was a weird reply. I tried to focus on what I thought Kate might say.

'You're not a slut,' I snapped. 'You're just desperate, you've made some mistakes, and for God's sake, you're grieving for your mum. That's an awful thing to happen to her, and you didn't even get to say goodbye.'

Her mouth opened and closed a couple of times and then she folded down on to the bed like a piece of wet tissue paper, wrapped her arms around herself and started sobbing. I sat next to her and held her, but I had no answers to her pain. I hadn't even managed to deal with my own. 'Shove it out of sight' was my strategy.

When her sobs had subsided to small gasps, I said, 'Let's go in the kitchen and have something to eat. I need a glass of wine. You can have a hot chocolate.'

She wiped at her face, but it didn't help. Her eyes were swollen and red and she'd smeared snot across one cheek. 'Hang on,' I said, and went and soaked a face cloth in warm water and brought it back to her, resisting the habit of doing the washing myself like I did with Mia. Emma sank her face into the soothing cloth for a few moments, then wiped away the tears and mucus.

'Thanks,' she whispered.

'Come on. I hope you like pasta and pesto in a jar because that's all I've got here.'

'Sure.' She followed me into the kitchen and sat at the table, watching as I melted chocolate and used my expensive mix to make her the promised hot drink. 'Yum,' she said, and stayed silent after that. I poured myself a glass of wine and tried to drink it slowly, but the day was catching up with me and the wine settled my frog-jumping brain a bit.

With a packet of linguine cooked and a jar of pesto added, I threw in frozen vegetables, found the parmesan cheese and dinner was ready. I thought Emma might pick at hers but, after a couple of slow mouthfuls, she cleared her plate before I'd half-finished. I guessed she hadn't been helping herself to food here then.

I poured more wine and sat across from her again. 'So, what are we going to do?'

'We?' But she said it resignedly rather than belligerently, so it looked like she might actually listen to me.

I decided to tackle it from the front. 'Why is this guy after you and your mum? Why did he kill her?'

She stared down at the wooden table and her finger followed the scar where the knife had gone in, after it had gone through my hand. I shivered. *Don't think about that.*

When she didn't answer, I said, 'OK, is it an object, money, drugs or knowledge that you have?'

Her head jerked up. 'Why do you ask that?'

I shrugged. 'It's got to be one of them. If your mum had done something that incited revenge, her death would've ended it. So whatever it is, you still have it.'

Her mouth opened but no words came out. Her face was so pale that her red eyes looked almost crazy. Finally, she forced out some words. 'I can't tell you.'

'That's not going to cut it with me, Emma. You forget – I've been down this road before. I know what happens when you have something they want.'

'You mean your brother?'

'Yes. Now what do you have?'

'I really, really can't tell you.' Her throat convulsed. 'Mum knew and look what happened.'

'So it's knowledge or information.'

She shook her head wildly. 'No, no, don't even try to guess! They'll kill you, too, and Mia.'

'OK, I don't need to know exactly what it is. Fine. Calm down.' I reached across the table and took both of her hands in mine. They were clammy and cold. 'Breathe.'

Her breathing slowed a bit and she blinked and said, 'You truly can't help me.'

'I'll be the judge of that.' Strangely, knowing what the problem was – or the basis of it – made it seem less scary. 'Can I make some guesses, and you tell me yes or no?'

'Maybe.'

I laughed. 'Fair enough. Now, you have something they want. But I'm guessing it's not something they don't know. It's something they don't want you to tell anyone else.'

'I – how did you…'

'I told you, I'm guessing, but I'm not stupid.' I thought a bit more. 'Whatever it is, there's also at least one person in the NSW police force who doesn't want you to tell anyone either.'

Her eyes went so wide I thought they were going to pop right out of her head. 'How did you…'

'I've been doing a lot of thinking. The big question is – what are we going to do?'

'Can you help me get away? If I could make it to Perth, I could…' Her face told me she'd remembered what I'd said about being on the streets and prostitution.

'I have no idea how to give you a fake new life, Emma,' I said gently. 'And you're not old enough to survive on your own.'

'Don't say witness protection,' she snapped. 'Mum said it wouldn't work, that somebody always knew.'

'Are you saying a cop up there leaked your location deliberately?'

'Oh yeah, he sure did! Bastard. I told Mum not to trust him.'

'Who are you talking about?' Wondering if it was Chris Winter.

Her mouth tightened into a thin line. 'Can't tell you.'

Should I push it? It probably wasn't necessary for me to know that either. I had to be careful. 'The Victorian police are different, surely. They're trying to solve your mum's murder. I know the guy in charge a bit.'

'Your boyfriend?' She smirked.

'No, thank God!' Swan in my bed? That would be the stuff of nightmares. 'Heath isn't on your mum's case – he's the guy who got us away from the shopping centre. But the detective in charge is called Swan.'

She made a face. 'The one whose face doesn't move.'

'Afraid so. But he is a good cop, even if he's not very... friendly.'

Her jaw set and she shook her head. 'Nup. He's the kind that would pass on stuff to NSW because those are the "rules".' She hooked fingers in the air. 'Nobody up there can be trusted. Not a single one of them. So no witness protection from anyone. Ever. I'd rather take my chances on the street, truly.'

I believed her. Which left me in a bloody awkward position.

'All right, how about we watch some mindless TV and get some sleep, and talk about it in the morning. But – ' I pointed my finger at her. 'Don't you dare sneak out in the middle of the night and run away again. I want your promise that you won't.'

For a moment, her mouth set in that stubborn line and then she relaxed. 'OK, I promise.'

I didn't believe her a hundred per cent, but I figured if she wanted to go, I couldn't stop her. I certainly wasn't going to stay awake all night watching her. I called Joleen to check on Mia – I'd already called once to let her know I was stuck in Melbourne – and said I'd be back tomorrow. 'She goes to childcare at nine, so I plan to be back by pick-up time.'

'That's fine,' Joleen said. 'It'd be good if you could pay me then. We're… a bit short.'

'Of course.' I felt guilty then but I'd make it up to her. And Mia. *Hollow promise*. No, I vowed silently that it wouldn't be.

When I woke up the next morning and checked the spare bedroom, I was a bit surprised to find Emma still there. After a shower, I called Joleen and talked to Mia for a little while – it was good to hear her happy voice telling me the dog had licked her face and now she didn't want a 'yucky doggie' anymore. Thank God.

Emma was quiet over breakfast and I was wondering how to start the conversation again when my mobile rang.

The number was blocked and I debated answering, then tapped the green circle. 'Hello?' A little silence. Probably a spam call. Just as I was about to hang up, an urgent voice reverberated in my ear.

'Judi?' The voice was vaguely familiar.

'Yes.'

'Listen. You've got about two minutes to get out of that house. Don't come out the front, don't go for your car. Climb the back fence. Now!'

'What?'

'Hurry! Fucking move, woman! He's coming.'

He's coming. Panic and adrenaline fired through me. I leapt up, grabbed Emma by the arm and pulled her towards the French doors at the back.

'What's happening?' she said. 'What's wrong?'

'No time. Let's go. Run.'

17

Emma didn't need a second urging to run. She pulled up the bottom lock of the French doors while I did the top one and opened them. Outside, she hesitated, glancing wildly around. I pointed left. 'Margaret's fence. Get over it. Stand on the pots.'

I shut the French doors and followed her. She was already halfway over the wooden fence, one leg kicking to propel her faster. I was right behind her. The fence seemed three metres high. I grabbed the top, hoisted myself on to the largest pot and half-jumped, half-pulled myself up. One leg over, rough wood scraping, other leg not high enough. Fuck! Emma got hold of my leg and yanked hard, and I was halfway.

I dropped my phone into Margaret's garden – I needed both hands. Swung the other leg, tried not to groan at the pain in my hip and the jabbing, splintering wood palings. Emma waited below, arms outstretched. 'Drop down,' she hissed, 'I'll catch you.'

I dropped, landing on her and she staggered, but managed to hold on to me and stop me crashing into Margaret's buddleia bush.

'Judi?' Margaret's voice came from her back door.

Emma and I crouched. 'Where now?' Emma whispered.

I checked Margaret's garden fences – both of the other ones were high metal panels, with no way of getting over them without a ladder. But we couldn't stay here. If he looked over the fence – I hoped to God I hadn't knocked any pots over to give us away – he'd see us. Beneath our feet was fresh pine bark, so no telltale footprints.

It'd have to be Margaret's house.

I ran to her back door and shepherded her inside. 'Quick, Margaret, we need to close the back door.' And lock it.

She obeyed without a word, backing quickly into her kitchen and watching us as I dealt with the door and Emma checked the windows were locked. Margaret had her TV on and I whispered, 'Can you turn it off, please?', then turned off the hallway light as well.

Margaret sat in her armchair. 'Can I do anything?'

She was a tough old bird, that was for sure. No panic, no carrying on. Yet again, I was bloody grateful she was my neighbour. I shook my head and pointed at her wall that adjoined mine, then I sat on the floor next to it and put my ear to the wallpaper.

Silence. Emma wiped my phone on her T-shirt and handed it to me. I hadn't even noticed she'd picked it up. I couldn't afford to dial 000 and talk or even let it ring. We had to stay completely quiet. I muted everything and then texted Heath. *Need police.* Just as I was trying to work out what else to say, I heard a sharp crack. I was pretty sure someone had just forced my front door. *Armed intruder. Ascot Vale house. Help!* Send.

The wall was brick under the wallpaper, but Margaret had told me she could still hear noise in my house – it was how she knew I'd had intruders before. I pressed my ear to the wall again. Faint footsteps moving around through the lounge, and to the French doors. I froze, pressed harder. Door being opened? Difficult to tell. I sensed he was out on the back deck, looking around the garden, possibly in the shed. Would he look over the fence?

The seconds stretched out agonisingly into a minute,

two, three. My heart was too loud and I wanted to shut it up. Footsteps coming back. Up the hallway. Gone.

Would he come into Margaret's? No reason to. We were as likely to be at the neighbour's on the other side or the back. I let out a breath, my lungs aching. Emma made a move as if she was going to the front window and I waved my hand frantically. Stay down and stay quiet!

Another endless minute and then there were sirens: distant, closer, really close. A screech of tyres. Someone banging on my front door, heavy footsteps in the house. Then I heard, 'Police! Come out now! Hands up!'

But I knew there was no one there. They'd missed him. Had he seen them? Did he know I'd called them? Then he'd know we had been here all the time, and he'd missed us, but it was really Emma he wanted.

I hadn't been able to look at her again, being so totally focused on listening, but now I did. She looked like a tiny, curled-up snail sitting with her knees to her chin and her arms wrapped around her legs, staring at me.

'Has he gone?' she whispered.

'Yes. The police are here now.'

'Too late. As usual.' But it was said sadly. I would've preferred her rage.

I knew I had to go and talk to the police in my house, but I left Emma in Margaret's care. 'I'll come back and explain, I promise,' I told Margaret. I shoved my phone into my jeans pocket and left via her front door, checking the street out front very carefully and then scanning the whole street once I reached her gate. There were only four cars parked and, as far as I could see, they were all empty, but the first thing I said to the officer who stood by the front door was, 'You need to check all of the cars in the street in case he's hiding in one of them.'

They must've been briefed on why they were there because

he spoke to the other cop standing by the patrol car and he did it straight away. I went to my front door and surveyed the damage. There was a clear mark next to the lock that looked like the one on my back door at Candlebark. Apparently all you needed to do to break in was jam a crowbar in that spot and push. I'd have to remember that if I ever decided to take up burglary as a profession.

The cop inside the house came down the hallway. 'You weren't here?'

I shook my head.

'How did you know you had an intruder?'

'My neighbour.' I wasn't being honest but Emma's paranoia was catching. I'd explain in more detail to Heath or Swan – if I was sure it'd be kept confidential. The last thing I wanted was for this guy to come back and threaten Margaret, or worse. 'Can I go in and check my house, please?'

'Not right now, I'm sorry. We're waiting for Detective Serg – here he is now.'

I turned and saw Heath pull up in his Commodore, and my body went to cotton wool. It was as if, once he arrived, I could stop being Wonder Woman and relax, except the relaxing was like totally giving way. I lurched sideways and grabbed at the verandah post.

'Are you all right?' The cop put out a hand to steady me.

'Yes, fine. Thank you.' I kept leaning against the post, trying to breathe normally. *Come on, don't be pathetic and hopeless.* But it was hard to pull my armour on again and straighten my spine. I bit the inside of my mouth, and did it anyway. By the time Heath came up the front path, I was ready with a smile. A very small one.

'You got here fast,' I said. 'Actually, so did they.' I waved my hand at the officers.

Heath frowned. 'They got a call. And not from me.'

'What? It wasn't me. I...' The person who called to warn me must have then dialed 000. Who was it?

Heath's phone jangled and he answered, mouthing Swan at me. 'Yep, yep. Hang on.' He asked me, 'Do you know who it was? Did you see him?'

'No, didn't see him but it was the same guy who broke into my house at Candlebark.'

'How do you know?' he said sharply.

'Trust me, I know.' Who the hell else would it have been? Anyone would think I had several killers after me and I might get them mixed up.

Heath turned away and muttered at Swan for another couple of minutes and then disconnected. The other cop had come back from checking the cars, shaking his head. It had been unlikely this guy would hang around, but I felt a tiny bit safer knowing he was definitely gone.

'They'll send the crime scene people but it might be a couple of hours.' Heath nodded at the cop by the door. 'Need to set up a cordon – keep anyone out of the front area here, and the house.'

'We – I – need to get my bag from the house.'

'You said you weren't here,' the cop said.

'I wasn't in the house when he broke in. But my bag was.'

He looked at me suspiciously but didn't say anything else.

'You've been inside?' Heath asked.

The cop nodded.

'Judi, tell him where your bag is, and he can get it.'

For fuck's sake. 'I was in the house all last night. I'm hardly likely to wreck any fingerprints or DNA – they'll all be mine.' And Emma's.

Heath huffed out an irritated breath. 'All right, but don't touch anything. You might overlay something.'

This killer wore gloves again, I'd lay money on it. There'd be nothing to overlay. But I agreed nicely and went in to get my bag from the bedroom and Emma's backpack. Had they given away how recently we'd been there? No, the unlocked French doors probably did that. My bag was actually hidden under the doona I'd pushed off the bed when I'd got up. There was some benefit to being untidy after all. When I returned to the front verandah, Heath raised his eyebrows at the backpack but said nothing.

We got into his car, but before he could start with the questions, I said, 'Can you wait a moment? I have to make a call.'

That earned me another frown, but he waited while I called Margaret. 'It's me – Judi. Can you hang on another few minutes, and then I'll call you back?'

'Of course, dear.'

When I'd hung up, I said to Heath, 'There are a few things you need to know, but I couldn't tell you in front of those guys.'

'All right,' he said slowly.

'I was in the house, and I got a warning phone call to get out. Probably the same person who called 000.'

'Who?'

'I don't know. I jumped the side fence into Margaret's. That's why the back doors are unlocked.'

'You jumped the fence?' His mouth twitched.

'Hey, I can be athletic when I want to be.' I didn't want to look at his mouth again. 'I didn't say anything about where I was – hiding at Margaret's – because I don't want to put her in danger. She was good enough to let us – me – in and lock everything up and hide. She doesn't need to be involved any more than that.'

'You think the officers attending would tell a killer that information?' His tone was so disbelieving that I wanted to give him a good poke in the ribs and remind him of past police fuck-ups I'd endured.

I took a breath and gripped my fingers together for safety, then matched my tone to his. 'Probably not.'

That didn't go down well.

'Why is this guy after you?' he asked.

'He's after Emma, not me. He thinks I know where she is.'

'Do you?'

This was my moment of truth or lies. One or the other. I wanted badly to lie, because I'd experienced Emma's deep fear first-hand and I believed she had grounds for it, even if she hadn't told anyone what they were. This man hunting her was evidence of that.

But common sense said I had to tell Heath the truth. I couldn't put Mia's safety and life ahead of Emma's. And ultimately I trusted Heath, but I had to get Emma to tell him everything, otherwise he couldn't help her.

'Judi?'

'Yes, I do know where she is.'

He let out a frustrated breath and went to speak but I held up my hand.

'For once, will you just listen – properly?'

'When do I not listen?' he snapped.

'When you're being too much of a detective following procedure and not enough of a person understanding someone's fear.'

He opened and closed his mouth a couple of times, and then said stiffly, 'Go on.'

'This man who killed Kate – Emma's mum – and is now hunting Emma is ruthless. And professional. You don't have a clue who he is, do you?'

I could see he wanted to protest and say it was all being investigated with leads and all that bullshit, but finally he said, 'Not really. A couple of possibilities.'

'It's likely he's from NSW?'

'How did you know that?'

'A logical guess. That's where Kate and Emma came from. And they were hiding. She'd changed her name. She had extra locks on the house. Both of them had an escape plan. That's how Emma got away, how she's been able to hide. Kate had it all worked out.'

'It's not my case so I've only heard some of this.' He scratched his head and sighed. 'Why did Emma do an ID pic of that Winter guy?'

'I don't know. I haven't had time to ask her.' I was trying not to look at Margaret's house, and concentrated on the dust on his dashboard. 'I do know Emma seriously believes that someone in the police is involved, and I think that came from Kate.' I gave him a brief rundown on my talk with Emma.

'This doesn't make sense. Why is this guy after Emma now? Revenge?'

'No.' I wrestled with myself, but in the end I couldn't do it. I couldn't betray the last crucial piece of information Emma had told me. Heath or Swan would have to earn it from her. Besides, I still didn't know exactly what it was myself. 'I think that if you prove you can protect her, Emma might eventually tell you what this is about. But I can tell you one thing – whatever it is, it's big. She's in such fear for her life that she said she'd rather run away and live on the streets than trust you.'

'Whoa.' He sat, deep in thought, staring out through the windscreen at the nature strip tree and tapping the steering wheel.

I waited until the tapping started to get to me. 'I can try and persuade her to talk to you, but really she's committed no crime so you can't hold her for anything.'

'She's underage.'

My frustration boiled over. 'See, that's the cop talking! You try to approach her like that, you'll get nowhere.'

'All right, all right.' He put his hands up. 'Sorry. Habit, that's all.' He cleared his throat. 'I'm guessing she's with Margaret.'

I didn't answer.

'And Emma helped you over the fence?' Now he was smiling.

'Nasty man. Yes.'

He took my hand in both of his and kissed it. 'Well, I'm bloody glad she did. I hate to think what would've happened if you hadn't got away.' He shook his head. 'Fuck.'

I gripped his lovely, warm hands with both of mine and tried not to think about it at all. 'It's all good. For now. But things can't go on like this. You have to find a way to get Emma to trust you. *You* do. Not Swan.' I kept talking over his protests. 'I know it's not your case, but she doesn't like Swan or any of the police she's talked to so far. You at least have done one good thing, getting us out of that shopping centre.' I hoped that was enough. That and the fact Emma knew he was my *boyfriend*. Ugh, I hated that word. *Lover* was no better.

'Swanny won't be happy.'

'Too bad. What's more important?'

He thought about it for a couple of seconds, and let my hands go. 'OK. How are we going to do this then?'

'I'll go into Margaret's and talk to her. Give me a few minutes and then knock on the front door. Hopefully by then she'll have agreed to talk to you. But no promises.'

'What if she runs away again? Out the back door?'

'I won't be able to stop her.' I gave him a hard look. 'And if you send those officers after her, it'll be the last time we see her. I'm sure of that.'

He thought about that plan a bit longer. 'All right. But I don't know how I'm going to explain it to Swanny.'

'If he's got any sense at all, and I think he has, he'll just be happy we finally found out what's going on.'

I got out of the car and went to Margaret's front door, giving it a few light taps and calling, 'It's me – Judi.' The door opened on the chain and Margaret's face appeared. As soon as she saw it really was me, she took the chain off and let me in.

'Is Emma still here?'

She nodded. 'I've made her some tea. Do you want some coffee?'

I accepted and followed her into the kitchen where Emma was hunched over her mug, a plate of digestive biscuits in front of her. She barely glanced at me, which wasn't a good sign.

'What's happening next door?' Margaret asked.

'The police are sending the crime scene people but I doubt they'll find anything.'

'They won't,' Emma said into her mug.

'I got your backpack for you, Emma.'

She managed a smile. 'Where is it?'

'It's outside. The police are looking after it, and my bag, too.' Inwardly, I cursed. I should've brought them with me instead of leaving them in Heath's car, although it might make her think twice about running again. I sat at the table and reached for a biscuit. They were nice and fresh. Margaret gave me my coffee and I inhaled it, then glanced at her bench. 'You've got a proper coffee machine!'

'Got to have some treats in life,' she said with a laugh.

I drank some coffee and watched Emma surreptitiously for a little while, then said, 'I have some thoughts on what we should do next.'

She didn't answer, just took another biscuit off the plate and crunched down on it. Crumbs flew across the table.

'Heath's here. My boyfriend.' Ugh. 'He's come to help.'

She made a face but didn't say anything.

'He's making you an offer. I think you should listen.'

Exaggerated sigh. But she didn't pick up on the obvious – that I'd told him she was here.

'I've explained a few things, the things I said to you, plus a few more. I think I've got a bit of a handle on this now.'

'You think?' Her eye roll was pure teenage scorn.

Right, miss, here goes. 'Your mother and you ran away from NSW, ended up in Candlebark. You were hiding. She changed your names. Somebody in the NSW police force tracked her down. Am I right?'

A flicker of her eyelids and the rest of the biscuit disappeared, but she didn't disagree.

'That led to your mum being killed. That's why you don't trust the cops. You know who the detective is and he's pretty high up, by the sounds of it. That means corruption, because whoever he told is a criminal of some kind.'

Margaret was sitting absolutely still. She was marvellous really – knew exactly what to do and when to shut up.

I was floating theories, but I'd had a lot of time during sleepless hours and driving hours to think it through. Her silence told me I was more than halfway right.

'So you don't trust police here, because you know they liaise, and if someone here tells someone up there where you are, you reckon you're a goner.' I was going to say something about Kate but I held back. 'However.'

She glanced at me.

'Heath is not on your mother's murder case. He's prepared to help you even if he gets into trouble for it.'

'Why would he get in trouble?' she asked.

'Because it's not his case and he'd be seen as interfering.'

'He's no use then, is he?'

'He's exactly who you need right now. Someone with nothing to prove and who wants to help you. Help you stay alive.'

She made a little scoffing noise in her throat. But she didn't say no.

'If you talk to him, and tell him everything, he can help. He knows about the problem with whoever it is in the NSW police, and he will do everything he can to keep what you tell him confidential, and protect you.'

'It doesn't matter what I tell him,' she said, 'he won't believe me. Nobody does.'

'If you're going to tell him that aliens landed and have implanted us with chips, then no.' That earned me a smile. 'But don't forget me. I will listen and I will believe you, and I'll help, too. I can be with you when you talk to him. I won't leave you with them on your own.'

She looked at me out of the corners of her eyes. 'You won't let them put me in foster care?'

Oh shit, she was basically asking if she could stay with me. Permanently. I couldn't commit to that, and I had to be honest about it. 'That might happen eventually. Do you not have any other family at all?'

She shrugged. 'Mum has a cousin somewhere. In Brisbane, I think. They went to school together.'

'There are always options. But I promise I'll make sure you're looked after properly, not shoved into care and forgotten about.' I drank some more coffee and waited while she thought it through. She'd pulled in on herself again, hunched over in that snail position, her face hidden. I glanced at Margaret and she frowned.

'Emma can stay with me for a little while, if that helps,' Margaret said.

'That's really kind of you,' I said. But Margaret had no idea about the guy who was after Emma. I didn't want to put Margaret in the line of fire – she'd done enough already.

Finally, Emma raised her head a little. 'I guess I can talk to him. But if he's mean, like the other ones, I'm not saying a word!'

'OK, good. Is it all right if I go and get him? Margaret, do you mind if we take over your kitchen?'

'Not a problem.' She got up just as there was a tap on the front door. 'Is that him?'

'Yes. But I'll sort it out.' I wasn't taking any chances. I checked who was at the front door first by looking through the curtains in the front room. It was Heath, alone, and I let him in. 'She's agreed to talk to you,' I murmured, 'on the condition that you believe what she says without being mean.'

'Mean? Me?' He looked surprised but I thought he was faking it.

'Yes, you.' I led him through to the kitchen, where Margaret made him a coffee with her machine and then left us to it. When I heard the TV go on, I closed the kitchen door. 'Emma, you remember Heath? His first name is actually Ben.'

'Uhuh.' She was trying to sound bored, like it didn't matter.

Heath sat down and took the last biscuit off the plate. 'Yum. Haven't had one of these for years.' His biscuit crunching filled the room. 'Emma, I want to say how sorry I am about your mum, and that we haven't been able to catch the man who did it yet. I know he's after you, and that must be really scary for you.'

She nodded a little but didn't reply and didn't look at him. I nearly said something but bit my tongue. *Let him do it. He has to get her to trust him on his own.*

'Do you know who this man is?'

She shook her head.

'But you've seen his face?'

Nod.

'OK. He seems to be a professional. Is he what you'd call a hitman?'

She hunched in a bit more, then she nodded.

'Right. This is a bit harder. Can you tell me what happened the night your mum was killed? Where you were and what you saw and heard? Take your time. It'll be really hard for you, I know, but we're both here to help you. Judi's not going anywhere.'

I laid my hand across the table and left it there, hoping she'd take it but she didn't. However, she did start talking.

'I… I was in the toilet. Mum told me not to have a big drink before bed, but I did. I had to have a wee, and it was really dark but the moon was out and it was so lovely outside. I didn't turn the light on in the toilet, just the one by the back door.' She took a huge breath and let it out. 'I was sitting there, kind of half-asleep. I heard these footsteps. The back concrete is rough, you know, and… Then the back door opened. I saw the light on the concrete. I thought Mum… maybe Mum had come out to see where I was.'

She didn't go on, so Heath said, 'But it wasn't your mum.'

She shook her head violently. 'No. I peeked through the gap in the door, saw him going inside. He was all in black and he had that hood thing over his head. I… I got out of the toilet as quietly as I could, and I ran. Mum and I had worked out where to run to, up the hill and into the hidey thing she made.'

'Hidey thing?' I asked.

'She pretended it was for birdwatching but I knew it was for us. For me. If someone came.'

'Did you hear any noises from the house?' Heath asked. I guessed he meant the shots.

'I'm not sure. I was running. Maybe sort of popping sounds but I was so scared that I just ran. I felt so bad, leaving Mum like that, but she told me I had to.' Emma started sobbing and I moved around to her side of the table, hugging her close. Heath fetched Margaret's tissue box off the bench.

'You're doing great, Emma,' he said. 'And you did exactly what your mum wanted you to. She would have been really proud of you.'

'Really?'

'Yes, I'm a hundred per cent sure.' He waited until she was calmer, then said, 'So he didn't come looking for you?'

'I thought he would. I was so scared. He came out the back door again and he looked around for ages. He was listening. I was nearly too scared to breathe in case he heard me.' She pulled some tissues out and blew her nose.

'Was that when you saw his face?'

She nodded. 'He pulled that thing off his head, I guess so he could hear better.'

'So if we asked you to do another ID, you'd be able to do one of his face then?'

'Yeah. I'm sorry about the wrong one. I was panicking then.'

It didn't answer the question of why she'd given the police Chris Winter, but Heath was apparently leaving that one for later.

'So you waited until he'd gone and then…'

'I waited for ages. I kept thinking he was trying to trick me, and I'd go into the house and he'd be waiting.' She shivered. 'I was so cold and finally I had to go and get some clothes. My teeth were, like, banging together. I put my jeans and a top on, and got my backpack, and then I…' She stopped, her throat working, her eyes filling with tears again.

This girl had so many tears inside her and, I sensed, for so many reasons. Maybe we'd never find out all of them.

'You had to go and check your mum,' Heath said gently. 'Anyone would do that.'

'She… she was lying there, like she was still asleep, but her head…' She looked at Heath, her red-rimmed eyes swollen and filled with grief. 'Would… would she have felt it?'

'No, I don't think so. She was probably asleep and never knew a thing.'

'Everything she was so scared of. It all happened.' Tears dripped down her face again. 'All because of me.'

Heath and I glanced at each other. What did she mean?

18

Instead of asking Emma outright what she meant, he kept the thread of the story going. 'So you left the house and went across the paddocks? Or into the bush? Towards Judi's house?'

'No, I didn't really, like, know where her house was.' Emma sipped some coffee and grimaced. 'Only that it was a bit more towards the pub. I went into the bush first, but I nearly got lost, so I came out and stuck to the edges. I was just walking. When the moon went down, I had to stop. I didn't have a torch.'

'Hmm, maybe I can help with directions.' He pulled out his phone and brought up Google Maps, honed in on Candlebark and asked for the name of the road where Kate and Emma lived. It was a bit hard to see on the phone, but the bush areas were green and Emma pointed out the way she thought she went.

'You walked a heck of a long way,' I said. 'I'm amazed nobody saw you.'

'I avoided people and hid,' she said. 'There was one place with a barn, or a big shed at the back of a paddock. I thought I could hide in it but there were two guys there, and it really stank. Yuck. Like there were rotten things inside. The windows were all covered up, so I thought maybe they were killing sheep or pigs in there. I kept going.'

Heath sat up, a strange look on his face. 'Can you show me where that was, by any chance?'

'Sure.' She bent over the phone and moved the map a little bit with her finger. 'About there, I think. Yeah, because after that I had to climb and I passed a thing like a mobile phone tower.'

Heath marked the spot somehow with the GPS settings and moved the map again. 'I see – so over this other side, you must have gone east until you got to Judi's.'

'Yeah, I recognised her house 'cause it's so cool, stone and everything. I hid in her shed. And then she found me.' She managed a small smile.

'OK,' Heath said. 'Are you all right to keep going, Emma? Or do you want a break? Maybe we should get pizza or something. You know, brain food.'

'Pizza would be great,' she said, and smiled properly for the first time.

'I can order on my app,' he said. He saw my look and added, 'Yes, I know I eat too much takeaway food.'

I put my hands up. 'I'm not saying a word.'

'Can I have one with lots of cheese and tomato?' Emma asked.

'Sure thing,' Heath said, and tapped away for a couple of minutes. 'While we wait, we can keep talking.'

'Mmm.'

'Can you tell me about Mikey?'

'Ugh. Mikey the moron.' She made a face. 'He was all charm at first. I hated him but Mum kind of fell for him. He was bad news.'

'Can I ask about your dad?'

'I think he went back to New Zealand, years ago. After him and Mum split up. I was about two. I don't remember him at all. He sent me Christmas presents for a little while, then they stopped. I don't know why, but...' She shrugged.

'Do you want to get in touch with him again now?' Heath asked. 'We can find him for you.'

'I... I dunno. I never, like, thought about it. He probably won't want me.'

'You never know. Just tell me if you want him found, all right?'

In spite of what we were hearing, I was fascinated by Heath's questioning of Emma. I was seeing a professional side of him that I'd wondered about – he'd shown me this softer side a few times, and Mia saw it, but the way he was dealing with Emma was a revelation.

'So Mikey was bad news.' He was back on track.

'Yeah, but his mates were worse. Mum had been going out with him for a few months, and he'd been coming around the house and staying.' Her face said it all. 'Double ugh. Then he'd bring his mates around. After a while, Mum found out they were in this gang. Not a kids' gang. A real criminal gang, like you see on TV.'

'Do you know which one? Did they have a name? Or a leader?'

She nodded, but she didn't answer. Then she said, 'Can we talk about this after pizza? And I need to go to the toilet.'

'Of course. Pizza should be here any minute.' He checked his phone. 'Four minutes, to be exact.'

Emma got up and went into Margaret's bathroom, which was next to the kitchen, and closed the door. Heath said, 'She's doing really well.'

'So are you,' I said.

'Don't sound so surprised!'

I laughed. Then I said, 'You're not taking notes or anything.'

'Not yet. I think that would freeze her up. There's something bigger coming, I can feel it, and I don't want her to avoid it. I think it's the key to everything.'

'Whatever it is, it's bad. As bad as her mum getting murdered.'

'Yep. And that worries me. Because it means they won't stop until Emma is dead.'

I wanted to protest, to tell him surely the police could protect her, keep her safe. But the words wouldn't come. The toilet flushed, the tap ran, Emma opened the door and Margaret called in a nervous voice, 'There's someone at the door.'

I went through to her. 'Join us for pizza, Margaret.'

'That'd be lovely, dear.'

We ate pizza around her kitchen table, and it felt a bit like a small party. Emma was safe, I was with Heath, and Margaret seemed to enjoy the company. After everything was eaten and the boxes cleared away, Margaret made a cup of tea and went back to her TV. Heath had gone next door to check what was happening and I followed him out, standing on Margaret's front porch, scanning the street. A police car was parked out front and the crime scene officers were working inside so he came back to me, saying they'd be an hour or so.

'I need to get back to Candlebark,' I said in a low voice to make sure Emma couldn't hear me. 'I have to pick Mia up. I'm not leaving her with Joleen two nights in a row.'

'If this guy is tracking you, you can't stay up there.'

'I thought I'd stay at the pub. With Mia.'

He shook his head stubbornly. 'Nup. You'll be an easy target there, too. You'll have to bring Mia back to Melbourne. And not stay in your house either.'

'Oh God, not another hotel.'

'It might be the safest option, sorry.'

'What about Emma?'

'You promised her you'd stay with her,' Heath said. 'You might regret that.'

'I can't dump her, I really can't,' I said. But another part of me was saying again – you have to put Mia first!

'We'll talk about it later.'

We went back to the kitchen and sat again, and there was finally some colour in Emma's face. However, her willingness to talk seemed to have faded.

'So, we were talking about Mikey the moron,' Heath said,

which earned him a slight relaxation of her shoulders. 'What made you think they were in a gang?'

'Money. And guns.' Emma blinked a few times, her gaze on Margaret's cat and dog salt and pepper shakers.

Heath had to prompt her. 'Handguns?'

'One. And I saw a couple of them with those big things, showing off in our backyard.'

'Mikey had a lot of money?'

'He kept it in this leather bag. It came and went. I watched him.'

'Why did you do that?'

'I wanted to tell Mum what was going on, make her break up with him.'

'Do you think maybe it was drug money?'

'I guess. It was like he collected it and then passed it on.'

'Who to?'

She shrugged.

'Did you tell your mum about it?'

'Yeah. She already knew. She was trying to pretend she hadn't got herself in the shit.' She took the cat shaker and let a dribble of salt fall on to the table, then dabbed her finger in it and licked it. Just like Mia did with the sugar when she thought I wasn't looking. Suddenly I longed to be back in Candlebark with her, doing boring everyday stuff and nowhere near all this shit.

I could sense Heath was getting a little frustrated with having to ask so many questions. I know I was. I asked her, 'Was that when she came up with the plan to change her name and take off to Victoria?'

'No, that was… She found out Mikey was seeing someone else, like, he had another girlfriend. Prick. She got really angry, and she was going to go to the cops and dob him in for the money and the gun and everything.' She dabbed more salt and kept her finger in her mouth for a few seconds. 'Chris told her not to.'

Hang on a moment. 'Chris Winter?' I asked.

She nodded.

'He was in this gang?'

Another nod. 'He was a mate of Mikey's, or he said he was. He came around a few times. More after Mum split up with Mikey. I saw the way he looked at Mum. He really liked her, but Mum was so mad about Mikey, she didn't want to know. She said she was going to dob anyway.' She smiled but it was wobbly. 'That was Mum – you didn't want to get in her bad books.'

'So did she? Go to the police?' Heath asked.

'Not then.'

'But later?'

Nod. 'She… something else happened. This guy, he was, like… he was the big gang leader. He… he came around one day.' It sounded like every word was having to be forced out of her, but she kept going. 'He threatened us. Me. He… he…'

I waited for Heath to ask what the threat was, although I guessed it was death. Drugs? Guns? But Heath left that one alone.

'That stopped your mum from doing anything?'

Head shake. 'No. It… it made her worse. She was so angry…' She sounded like she was choking.

'Emma, would you like a hot chocolate or a coffee?' I asked.

'No, I want to get this over with.' She swallowed a few times. 'That was when she changed her name. She said she had a plan, and Chris helped her, even though that man would've probably killed him if he'd known. We went up to Queensland for a while and stayed with a friend of Mum's, and then she must've found our house in Candlebark and paid the rent already. We drove there and just moved straight in.'

'That was how Chris knew where you were?' I asked. 'Why he went there?'

'Yeah. Too late.' She sighed heavily. 'The day before we left for Queensland, Mum went to the cops and told them everything. She said she made a "full statement".' She hooked her fingers in the air. 'Not that it made any difference.'

'Why not?' Heath asked.

'Nothing happened. Nobody was arrested. Mum waited, and then she decided we had to leave her friend's house. And then Mum was killed anyway.' She glared at Heath. 'She said the cops had promised her nobody would find out where we were. They were the only ones who knew our address, where we went, and what our new names were.'

'Didn't they offer you witness protection?' Heath asked.

'She didn't trust anyone, I told you. She said she would do it her way. As long as they kept their end of the deal. Bullshit! The cops in NSW told somebody. None of you can be trusted.'

There was a long silence. Heath sat with his elbows on the table, hands clasped, clearly thinking through what Emma had said. I got up and filled a glass with water from the tap, grimacing at its taste, and stared out at Margaret's garden, thinking as hard as Heath. Emma had told us a lot that filled in the gaps, but something was missing. The something that was as bad as her mum's murder. Yes, the death threat was bad, especially coming from this gang leader, and it had been carried out.

It still didn't answer the question of why the killer was carrying on his hunt for Emma. She clearly had the same information as her mother, had witnessed similar things that could potentially put gang members inside. Maybe that was the word I was sticking on – potentially. Would they take the word of a fourteen-year-old girl? Maybe not. But what did I know of police evidence? Not that much really. I had to leave that up to Heath.

I checked my watch – it was almost 3pm. 'I have to go and get Mia,' I said.

Emma swung around. 'You said you wouldn't leave me!' Her accusing face made me feel doubly guilty.

Mia comes first. I looked at Heath for help.

'Emma can't go with you,' he said. 'If this guy is watching you – this street, tracking you somehow – he'll attack you on the road.'

'What if I go on my own? I've got Andre's car.'

'It's not worth taking the risk.'

'I'm not staying with *you* on my own,' Emma snarled at Heath.

'F –' Heath clamped his mouth over the expletive.

'I have to get Mia,' I said. 'I'm not leaving her with Joleen indefinitely.'

'But where will you go then?' Heath asked. 'All of you will need to go into hiding, in a hotel probably. Somewhere we can guard you.'

Like the hotel they put me in while all the shit over Andy's murder was going on. I'd suffered it for a few days on and off, but this situation seemed never-ending. 'And how long would that last for? I've got a pub to run, and Mia trapped in one room for days on end will drive us all nuts.'

'Emma needs to do that ID pic for us as soon as. That's the only way we're going to get ahead of this guy. At the moment, we don't know who the hell we're looking for.'

I looked at her and steeled myself. 'Emma, he's right. You have to get that done now.'

Her eyes filled with tears again. 'Now you're being mean. It's not fair!'

God, it wasn't rocket science. Teenagers were rarely sensible, but I'd been hoping that she'd see the sense in this. I tried to make my tone nicer. 'Look, if you really want me to help you,

you have to help me. And Mia. I can't spend the next days and weeks too scared to go out, frightened that Mia is the one who will get hurt, or worse. Heath is right. The only way out of this is to find this guy and deal with him. That's the cops' job, not ours.'

She brushed away a tear rolling down her face and whispered, 'What about the next one he sends?'

Her words sent a feeling of suffocating black dread rolling over me and, for a few seconds, I couldn't breathe or speak. I wanted to run as far away from this girl as I could, or I wanted someone to take her away from me, take away the death and destruction she brought with her. I vaguely heard Heath say something, but I was too focused on my hands in my lap, fingers gripping each other so hard that bones cracked. *Take her away. Make us safe again.* And then I felt guilty all over again.

'Judi!'

My head jerked up on its own. 'What?'

'Emma has agreed to do the ID process again now. I'm about to call Swanny.'

'Yeah, good.' If she hadn't agreed, I would've probably forced her to anyway. I'd had enough. I was beyond caring if that was mean. *Mia.*

'If you drive Andre's car back to Candlebark, I'll follow you, and then you and Mia can come back to Melbourne with me.'

'What's wrong with my car?' The Benz was old but reliable, and it had Mia's car seat in it.

'Too noticeable. Too easy to follow.'

I gritted my teeth, and then decided he was probably right. 'Yeah, OK, then what? What charming hotel prison are we going to this time?'

'Same as before. My old mate is still head of security there.'

His eyes seemed to be apologising to me, but I just nodded and said, 'Don't forget Emma's backpack is in your car.'

'Will I see you at the hotel, Judi?' Emma asked anxiously.

I was about to snap a reply and took a calming breath. 'Yes, later on. And when you have that ID pic done, I'd like a copy, please. I want to see who to watch out for.'

'Of course,' Heath said. 'I'll make sure it's texted to you so you can keep it on your phone.'

Yay.

When we left, I gave Margaret a hug and said, 'Thank you. I'm sorry I seem to always be dumping my major dramas on you like this.'

'Oh, don't worry,' she said, smiling. 'It livens my day, dear.'

Hmm, she wouldn't have been saying that if the killer had jumped the fence into her backyard. But I couldn't think about that. Keep moving ahead, don't look back. That was my mantra right now. All the same, I'd be looking over my shoulder every few seconds for the foreseeable future, and I hated the thought.

The crime scene techs had finished and I went through the house, locking everything up again, straightening the bedding as I went and then checking there was nothing in the fridge that would go rotten in the next days and weeks. Who knew when I could come back here? Another question that made me grind my teeth.

Lauren Chandler and a male detective had turned up to take Emma back to HQ, along with an extra police car to follow them. Perfectly flagging that they had Emma with them, I thought, but didn't say so. Once they'd gone, Heath and I set off in tandem for Candlebark. It was already after 4pm, so I floored the little Kia and was a bit over the speed limit all the way, not caring whether it would result in a ticket or not. I couldn't see anyone that might be following us – hopefully the killer had seen Emma leave with Lauren and followed them instead.

The relief that rushed over me when I reached the turnoff for Candlebark made me gasp. *Coming, Mia.*

I'd have to go to the pub as well and explain to Andre and the others yet again why I was leaving them to do everything. If Andre was a bit less understanding, I would've been stressed out about that, too, but I knew he'd be like me – Mia was the most important one.

At my house, I packed bags for both of us, making sure I put lots of toys in for her and two bottles of wine for me. I had a feeling I'd be in the mood for a quiet drink or two late at night. Heath stayed outside and walked around the house a few times, watching and checking. I was glad to see the house was tidy and the lock on the back door had been replaced. No doubt I had Connor to thank for that.

Connor! I needed to see him, too, and explain what was happening. It felt like weeks since I'd last spoken to him. A horrible thought slimed through my mind – it was like I was packing, never to return.

No. I couldn't bear to think like that, not for a second. This was my home.

My mobile rang and I answered, even though I only half-recognised the number. 'Hello?'

'Ms Westerholme, it's Mary Miller again.'

Who? Oh, right, the woman from my mother's aged care facility. I quickly moved to the back door area to get a better signal. 'Yes, Mary, I'm sorry I –'

'Your mother has taken a turn for the worse, Ms Westerholme.' Her tone was no longer solicitous and caring. It was stern, to say the least.

'I'm sorry. I – things have been chaotic and I just…'

'If you don't come now, it may be too late,' she said flatly.

'Has she had another fall?'

'No, but she is in late-stage dementia, as you know, and is

now deteriorating quite quickly.' A short silence that I couldn't fill. 'I'm letting you know, that's all.'

'Thank you. I –'

'Goodbye, Ms Westerholme.' Click.

'Fuck.' I stared down at my phone, stuck between throwing it down the toilet and letting out a stream of four-letter words. Why now? Didn't I have enough to deal with? Obviously not. Someone on high had seen fit to add another turd to the pile I was already drowning under.

'Ready?' Heath called through the front door.

'Coming,' I managed to get out. I shoved the phone in my bag and hauled both bulging overnight bags to the door where he grabbed them and put them in his boot. Next stop was the childcare centre and then the pub. I'd think about my mother later.

Mia was quiet and didn't question why her car seat was now in Heath's car. I checked with Mrs Needham who ran the centre. 'Joleen said she'd had a bad night. She seemed very scratchy today, but better after her nap.'

'Scratchy?'

'She had a tantrum over someone taking the piece of banana she wanted this morning.' Mrs Needham shrugged. 'It happens. Just a bit unusual for Mia, that's all. Has she been unwell?'

'Not that I've noticed.'

I could see from the woman's expression that she thought maybe I hadn't been taking enough notice, and she was probably right. 'I'll keep a close eye on her,' I said. 'She won't be here for the next day or so. I've got urgent family business in Melbourne. I'll pay the fees for her booking, of course.'

That made Mrs Needham happy and she waved us off cheerily, although I noticed Mia hardly stirred, and just clutched Bum closer to her.

At the pub, Heath waited in the car. Mia followed me closely and, as I entered the bistro, she clung to my leg. She hadn't done that for ages. Andre was chalking up the dinner menu and going through it with Marie. The sight of Marie chatting and laughing, Andre explaining the difference between jus and sauce, Marie nodding, made my eyebrows shoot up in shock. Was this the same woman? Then my shoulders relaxed from their position up around my ears at last. Andre spotted me and waved. 'Here she is now. You can ask her yourself.'

Apparently Marie had a friend who was looking for work, and had done some waitressing before. I said she sounded good, and we'd organise a trial. Marie actually smiled again. I followed Andre into the kitchen, trying to talk to him while he stirred pots and checked oven and grill temperatures. Mia was still glued to my leg, and Andre glanced at her a few times.

'Is she OK?'

'Something's upset her, or else she's coming down with a bug.' I hoped it wasn't a bug that involved her bottom end. 'I need to keep an eye on her.'

'If you want to take time off, it's fine.' He tasted a sauce and nodded to himself.

'Things have got complicated,' I said. 'Emma was hiding in the Ascot Vale house, and… and…' To my horror, tears filled my eyes and I blinked them back. Mia wrapped her arms right around my leg as if sensing my upset.

'Judi, what's wrong?' Andre put down his spoon and came over to me, giving me a hug. That made me worse, and hot tears spilled down my cheeks.

'I need a paper towel,' I choked out.

He handed me one and kept one arm around me, the other one on Mia's head but she didn't look up. 'It must've been bloody scary when that guy broke into your house here.'

'Twice.' I coughed and dabbed at my face. 'Bastard came into the Ascot Vale house, too. We were lucky – someone called and warned me. We jumped over Margaret's fence.' Suddenly I knew whose voice I'd heard on the phone warning me – Chris Winter's. What the hell was he up to?

'Holy shit,' Andre said. 'This is all getting so bizarre. Is this all about Emma?'

'Seems so. Heath and I got her to talk to us at last.' Mia had started making a whimpering noise and I quickly explained the rest. 'Kate was running from some gang leader in Sydney. Now they're after Emma.'

'Did she explain why?'

'Yeah, mostly. I still think she's holding something back though.' Mia's distress was really getting to me. Even though she was bigger now, I could still pick her up if I was careful and lifted her the right way. I bent, knees braced and took her in my arms, then stood carefully. She put her arms around me and laid her head on my shoulder. At least her whimpering stopped.

'What are the cops doing about it all?'

'Heath's waiting outside for me. He's taking us back to Melbourne. Says they can't protect us here so we're hiding in a hotel.' I made a face. 'The last thing I want to do, but this guy frightens the shit out of me. Whether Emma will stay with us or not, I don't know. She keeps threatening to run away again.'

Andre shook his head, and then leapt across to the stove to stir again. 'Can't afford to burn anything. Fourteen in for dinner. I think half of them are from Bronwyn's place. Not that I care. I just want their money.' He looked at me through a cloud of steam as he took the lid off a pot. 'You need to stay safe and keep Mia safe. Leave this place to me, all right? We'll cope. Marie's doing well.'

I managed a wobbly smile. 'Thanks, mate. Hopefully the cops will catch this guy and life can go back to some kind of normal.'

After a few more back-and-forths about arrangements and hours, I left, stopping on the way to have a word with Charlie, and put Mia in the car seat. As soon as I went to close the door on her, she started crying, reaching her arms out to me, her little face all screwed up. Even Bum didn't help.

'I'll have to ride in the back with her,' I told Heath. Thankfully, that calmed her down, but she was still a lot quieter than normal. I stroked her face, testing for a temperature, but she didn't seem hot, so I relaxed a little.

The trip back to Melbourne seemed to take forever, and it was almost dark when we drove into the city, and then down into the depths of the hotel car park. Heath had called ahead and his mate was there by the lifts to greet us.

'Good to see you again,' he said to me, but I couldn't say the same. I muttered a hello and followed him into the lift, Mia in my arms again as she refused to walk. In the room, which was huge with two queen-sized beds and a bathroom almost as big as my lounge room, he gave me the swipe card and reminded me of the security lock on the door. 'The dinner menu is on the table, so just call me when you want to eat. I will bring the food up myself.'

'Thanks.' I started to relax. It did make a difference to have someone in charge who knew what they were doing and how to do it properly. Heath had told me once that famous people who wanted to be anonymous often chose to stay here, due to the top security offered. I could see why.

I sat on the bed with Mia and checked her over – she definitely wasn't hot or feverish, no coughs and when I took her to the toilet, all seemed OK there, too. But she was still very clingy so I stayed close and let her come to the door when Heath arrived. After checking the spy hole, I let him in.

'Sorry it took me a while,' he said. 'I've been on the phone to Swanny.'

'And?'

'Emma has done another ID with the software. Swanny put a rush on it – he contacted someone he knows in NSW who's in the gang task force and identified the guy.'

'You know who he is?'

'Yes.' He glanced at Mia and I took the hint, turning the TV on and sitting on the bed with her, but turning to talk to Heath.

'Who is he?'

'A guy called Aidan Solomon. Won't mean anything to you – or me. But he was in the army, and now he works for whoever pays well. He lives outside of Sydney in the bush somewhere.'

'I guess the question is who paid him to kill Kate and Emma.'

'Yes. Swan has sent the ID out to all the police around Victoria as well as Melbourne. But this guy will go to ground now.'

'You think?' I didn't think he would at all. 'I had a feeling today that Emma still wasn't telling us everything.'

'Yeah.' He checked his watch. 'She's being brought over from West Melbourne now. Are you still OK about having her here with you? I know you promised her but… it's a huge responsibility. She nearly got you killed.'

'I did promise.' I smoothed some hair off Mia's face and she snuggled closer to me. 'It's this one I'm worried about. There's no way I'll let her become collateral damage. If it's a choice between Emma and Mia…'

'Understood. Completely.' He leaned over and kissed me gently. Until he did it, I hadn't realised how much I had longed for him, for his touch. Just for us to be like always, and not struggling towards each other through so much crap. I kissed him back like I meant it, holding on to his arm, keeping him close. When we finally broke apart, he grinned. 'I hope that was a promise to me.'

'Absolutely.'

Whether I'd be alive to keep it or not was another matter.

19

The knock at the door made us both jump, and Heath went to answer it. It was DC Lauren with Emma; they both came in, Lauren being professional with Heath and me and Emma looking exhausted. Heath and Lauren left together, which sent a pang of jealousy through me, so I focused on Emma instead.

'I'm starving,' I said, grabbing the menu. 'Let's order some food.' Mia looked away from the TV and said hopefully, 'Pizza?'

'I'll see if they have any,' I said. 'Emma, what you do you feel like?'

She shrugged in the way all teens do, the one that says, 'Whatever, I don't care.'

I scanned the offerings and winced at the prices. My bet was the police wouldn't pay for more than the basics. Thank God there was children's pizza for Mia – I couldn't face two meals of it in one day. In the end, with a bit of nudging, Emma agreed to pasta and I chose a stir-fry that I hoped had real vegetables and chicken in it, not a bag of mix from the freezer. I phoned the order in, adding drinks for the girls, and pulled out one of the bottles of wine to pour myself a glass. Emma's eyes widened but she said nothing.

Once I'd settled in with my glass, I asked her, 'How did the ID go this time?'

She did that shrugging thing again. Had I done that to my parents? Not my dad – I would've got a slap for it – but probably my mother, when I bothered answering her at all. It suddenly struck me that I'd had a bag packed and hidden in my wardrobe from about the age of fifteen, ready to run away as soon as I felt really desperate enough. It had felt incredibly empowering at the time. All I had to do was pick up my bag and my bank card and go. Where to, I'd been hazy on.

Whereas Emma and Kate's bags had been real, vital and necessary, and Emma had had to use hers.

'You're very brave, Emma,' I said.

She jerked her head around to stare at me. 'No, I'm not. I'm useless.'

'Who told you that?'

'I just know.' Her mouth set into its familiar stubborn line.

'At your age, I thought my world was horrible but it was at least safe.' Sort of. More for me than Andy. 'You have been in a lot of danger, and you've been tough and strong. That's pretty amazing.'

'I don't feel amazing,' she muttered, but her mouth had curved up just a tiny bit.

The food arrived and we ate it all. I could've managed a meal double the size, but at least it was made with real vegetables. Mia's baby pizza was a bit too big for her so Emma finished it off after her pasta. It was good to see her eat well.

As I was collecting up the dishes to stack on the tray, my phone pinged with a message. Emma was sitting right next to it and she glanced down.

'It says your mother is asking for you.' She looked at me, puzzled.

'My mother has dementia and isn't very well,' I said.

'Are you going? It sounds kind of urgent.' She looked at the text again. 'They put NOW in capitals.'

My turn to shrug, and I waved my hand around the room. 'Bit hard to go anywhere. Mia will be asleep soon, and you're tired.'

'I can look after her, if you want to go,' Emma said hesitantly.

I don't want to go, that's the problem. 'No, I can't leave you both here.'

'We'll all go then. How far away is it?' She was sitting up, looking at me expectantly. 'It's your mum.'

I knew Emma had just lost hers, but she had no idea of my history with my mother, how much I loathed her, and how I knew if I went, she wouldn't have a clue who I was. It would be a wasted trip. And we'd just burrowed in here to hide from a killer who'd tracked Emma down three times already. We'd be pushing our luck, big time.

'It's too difficult.'

'Is she dying? It might be your last chance.' Emma bit her lip and went on. 'It could be really important. For you.'

Oh shit. I knew she was speaking from her heart, from her own experience of not being able to say goodbye to her mother, but… I contemplated for a moment trying to explain to her, but she was too young to understand, too much in the wrong place.

'I don't think…'

'Judi, you have to.' She stood up and looked around for her bag and handed me mine as well. 'We can put Mia in her PJs and a warm jacket. And ask for an Uber with a car seat. Come on.'

'I can't take an Uber. We're supposed to be in hiding.' *I'm not taking us outside to play targets, kid!*

'Ask your boyfriend then. *Come on!*'

Since when did a fourteen-year-old take control of my life and decisions? But she handed me my phone and urged me again to call Heath. In the end, I did it, because I knew he'd back me up and say we had to stay put.

'I'm just in Spencer Street,' he said. 'I'll come and get you. I know the way to your mother's facility.'

Of course he did. He'd taken me to the aged care place once

before. 'It's too big a risk for us to go out. I don't like it.' I glanced at Emma and muttered, 'I'm not putting us in danger for that old…'

'I think you'll be OK. This guy doesn't know you're in the hotel. Only I and one other police officer know your location. And he won't know where we're going, and I'll make damn sure nobody is following us.'

All very reasonable, but it was a stupid risk in my book. 'I really don't think I need to go.'

'I think you'll regret it if you don't.'

I bit back the words I wanted to say. *Why don't both of you stay the fuck out of my personal life?*

I sighed heavily. 'Yeah, all right.' I supposed it would get Nurse Miller off my back as well. But as I changed Mia into her PJs and found her jacket in the bag, dread curdled the dinner and wine in my stomach. I told myself it was fear of the killer, but I knew damn well it was all about my mother.

Maybe Heath and Emma were right, in a twisted way. I could visit the old vulture, do my duty and then leave her to die. Like she left me and Andy to suffer Dad's abuse for all those years.

We arranged to meet down in the car park, and I had to call the security guy so he could monitor the area. Heath turned up with a second police car that was going to tail us to make sure we weren't being followed. Overkill, just for my mother. I almost refused to go then. We left a few minutes later, me in the back with Mia. Mia clutched Bum and stared out at the bright city lights as we headed for the Nepean Highway. 'Who lives here?' she asked.

'Lots and lots of people,' I said.

'How many?' she said.

'Eleventy-hundred million,' Emma said with a laugh. 'That's what I used to say for big numbers.'

Mia gave her a puzzled look and then stuck her thumb in

her mouth. That wasn't a good sign. I felt her forehead but she was OK, not overly warm. I'd learned a lot during the time I'd been Mia's guardian and stand-in parent, but there were still plenty of times where I had no idea what to do, what to look for. I almost told her we were going to see her nana, but the words stuck in my throat. Besides, there was no way I was taking her in with me. Heath and Emma could look after her for the five minutes this ridiculous visit would take.

Everyone in the car was quiet. I guessed Emma didn't want to talk to Heath in case he asked her more questions. Heath was concentrating on driving and checking his mirrors every few seconds. I sat with my thoughts, which wasn't a pleasant experience but I couldn't stop things whirling in my head. After a while, Mia fell asleep; I gazed at her little face, seeing Andy in her all over again and wishing he was alive to watch her grow. She was such a little *person*, with her own very determined opinions on things – she made me laugh every day. And sometimes feel like I was going around the bend.

We arrived at the aged care place far too quickly. Heath parked in the visitors' area and turned off the engine. The support car had pulled up in the street.

'Ready?'

'You don't need to come in with me,' I said.

'I'm happy to.'

He was trying so hard to be there for me, but it was a wasted effort this time. 'No. Really.' I took a breath. 'This is going to be hard enough as it is. You know the history. I need to do it alone.' *Because I don't want you to see my reaction*. 'I won't be long.'

'OK, if you're sure.' He smiled at me like a teacher encouraging a nervous student, or that's how it seemed to me. It galvanised me into action, and I quickly got out of the car and headed for the entrance doors. It was after hours so I had to push a button and wait, but a woman in uniform let me in a few seconds later.

'Mrs Westerholme?' I asked.

'Just down that corridor. She's in a special care room.' She looked like she was going to give me a hug and I swerved away from her.

'Thanks.' I walked down the half-lit corridor, fast at first and then more slowly, stopping outside the door with her name written on the card in the holder. Maybe I could wait a couple of minutes and then walk back out, pretending I'd seen her. Too late. Another woman in uniform came out of the room, and her dark-skinned face beamed when she saw me.

'You can go in,' she said warmly. 'You're her daughter, right?'

I nodded.

'She goes in and out. If she opens her eyes, move close so she can see you.'

'All right.' The words came out in a gargle and I coughed. I so did not want to be here. I took one step, then another. Hospital bed, a couple of machines, tubes, breathing apparatus. My mother looked shrivelled and tiny, almost invisible under the bedding and all the stuff surrounding her.

Another few steps and I was there, beside the bed, looking down at her. I waited for the familiar surge of hatred to rise up, but it was a little ripple that died away. This woman lying in front of me held almost nothing of the woman I'd loathed for most of my life. With her eyes closed, the piercing blue orbs were concealed beneath papery lids, and the narrow, snooty nose covered by the oxygen mask.

I remembered what she'd looked like in the years Andy and I were growing up. Always made up, always immaculately dressed. Occasionally we'd get a dry kiss as long as it didn't smudge her lipstick. No hugs. We always had dirty hands, she said. At one stage I thought she'd gone deaf. How could a mother not hear her son being beaten with a leather belt? How could she let it go on and on and on?

Now the hatred was rising up in me, along with each painful, horrible memory.

But then a little voice said, "The only person this is hurting is you. She's beyond it. Stop wasting your energy on her.'

Besides, she was dying. The grey colour of her face and the little gasps behind the mask told me that. The nurse had glided back into the room and was checking one of the machines. She turned and smiled at me again. 'Has she opened her eyes?'

'No.'

She leaned over my mother and smoothed her sparse white-grey hair back off her forehead. My mother's eyelids flickered, and my heart jumped. *God, don't wake her up!* But she didn't come to, and the nurse looked disappointed. 'She's very poorly.'

'Yes.' I wanted to ask how long before she was expected to die, but I didn't know how to frame the words nicely enough.

'The doctor said just to keep her comfortable.' The nurse's brown eyes focused on me again. 'You know what that means, I guess.'

'She's dying. How...'

'How soon?' Her mouth pursed. 'We never know. Often they rally.'

Please, no.

'But I'm afraid she may not last the night. I'm very sorry.'

I'm not. I nodded at the nurse as a response. I'd stopped looking at my mother's face. I watched her hand instead, the one nearest me. It lay on the covers like a dead fish. Somebody had cut her nails short – she would've hated that. She'd always had long, polished nails, coated in a pale pink called Ballet Shoes. As soon as I was allowed nail polish, I chose fire-engine reds and blacks and iridescent blue that made her shudder and demand that I take it off immediately.

Her skin now was flaky, with pale freckles and fine wrinkles, and blue veins like a tracery underneath. One day my hands would probably look like that, although with all the gardening I did, they'd be rough and sun-damaged as well. As I watched, the fingers twitched as if they wanted to reach out, and I took a step back.

At the same time, the nurse leant over her again to adjust the mask. 'Oh dear, she's –'

I didn't wait to hear what she thought was happening. I turned and ran.

The front door of the place was locked but I found the green release button and jabbed it hard until the door hissed open. Outside in the cool air, I sucked in long breaths, feeling sweat roll down my spine under my shirt. I told myself it was the heating that they always turned up high for the tenants.

When I was calm enough to be able to talk and tell lies confidently, I walked over to Heath's car and got in.

'Did you see her?' Emma asked.

'I did.'

'Did she talk to you?'

'No, she's too ill. She wasn't… awake.'

Heath glanced at me over his shoulder. 'Is she…'

'She's still alive,' I said.

'Did you…' Emma's voice quavered. 'Did you get to say goodbye?'

Not in the way I wanted to. But I would never be able to explain what I meant, so I let it go. 'I guess you could say that.'

'Good.' Emma breathed out loudly, and brushed at her face. She was hurting, but it was taking a lot of effort for me to hold myself together in front of her and Heath. I had very little left for her right now.

'Time to go,' Heath said, starting the car. The trip back to the city was equally quiet. When we got out of the car by the hotel lifts, a different security guard was there, watching and waiting for us. Emma went straight into the lift and held it open with the button. Heath carried Mia into the lift, I joined them and the lift rose with a hum towards the eighth floor. I put Mia to bed in our room and Emma flopped on to the other bed, pulling her shoes off. I went back to the door with Heath.

'Thanks,' I said. 'I owe you.' He moved closer, as if to hug me, and stopped. I must've been giving off big waves of *leave me alone*.

'No problem. Are you OK?'

'Yeah. It was a bit… you know. Me and my mother.' I made a face and he nodded.

'I'll see you for breakfast, all right?'

'Are we going to have to stay in this room all day?'

'I'm not sure. Hopefully, we'll have some news by tomorrow.'

I managed to smile at him. 'Hopefully.' I touched his arm for a moment and walked back into the room. By now that bottle of wine should be lovely and cold in the little fridge. I poured a large glass and settled down to watch some mindless TV. Enough wine and I might sleep.

I did eventually drop off to the sound of American voices extolling the virtues of vacuum cleaners and fake diamond rings, but my dreams jumped around from Andy and me as kids stealing Dad's cigarettes and throwing them in the toilet to dark shadows walking around inside the pub chasing me to finally the killer's arm around my throat again. At that point, I woke up with a cry that sounded a bit like, 'Ferrkknggell'. Mia and Emma were still asleep. I got out of bed and went to the window, peering out through a gap in the curtains at a pink Melbourne dawn.

Other people would stand there admiring the colours and the light slanting across the acres of windows. I sighed and thought, *What kind of shit is today going to bring?*

Then I shook it off and stood under the shower for about twenty minutes, luxuriating in the wanton use of water for a change. As I dried myself with a large, insanely soft towel, Mia wandered in and I helped her on to the toilet. No little steps here. I thought she'd ask what we were doing in this hotel, but she was too interested in the array of little bottles on the bench, so I handed her the shower cap to play with, showing her how to put it on her head. 'But only when I say you can,' I warned. The plastic was a bit thin and dangerous, another thing I wouldn't have thought twice about a year ago. With her shower cap, she was happy to get under the spray even if her washing wasn't very efficient.

It was way too early to go down for breakfast to meet Heath, so I pulled a couple of books out of Mia's bag and we sat there for a while, me reading aloud and her pointing at the pictures and adding her own bits to the story.

When we got to the end of *The Very Hungry Caterpillar*, Emma said, 'I used to love that when I was little.'

'We have bufferflies in our garden,' Mia said. 'Naughty ones that eat things.'

'Well, their caterpillars eat things,' I said. We'd been through this before but Mia hadn't quite got to the stage of understanding real life versus the book. That was fine with me. 'If you have a shower, Emma, we can go and eat breakfast downstairs.' Might be the only time we get out of this room.

'OK.' She showered and was back in five minutes, dressed in the same clothes as yesterday. 'Can I get something different to wear? Or even some new undies?'

'Sorry, I should have brought clothes down for you. Everything from your house has been packed up.'

'What do you mean?' Her face paled and her mouth pinched up. 'Where's my stuff?'

'Safe, don't worry. It's all in some boxes and locked in the office at the pub.'

'You're sure?'

'Yep, I did it all myself.' I didn't remark on how little she and Kate owned.

My mobile rang and I answered, thinking it was Heath downstairs, waiting for us.

'Ms Westerholme, it's Mary Miller. I just wanted to let you know your dear mother passed away early this morning.'

'Oh.' I felt like all my bones had turned to concrete and I couldn't move.

'I hope your visit last night gave you some peace of mind.'

I rebelled inside at her smarmy, condescending tone and had to control myself. The urge to say *Fuck off* was overwhelming. 'Yes, well…'

'Do you have a preference for a funeral home?'

'I… what?'

Miller's tone tightened up a notch. 'I believe you are Mrs Westerholme's only living relative and have authority over her finances and possessions.'

'Yes, I think that's –'

'If you have no preference, then our local funeral director, Mr Gallop, is very good, and reasonably priced.'

And pays you a commission, no doubt. 'That will be fine. Thank you.' The words weren't coming out any easier. Not like the ones in my head.

'If you have a pen, I will give you his name and number.' She waited, letting the silence spin out.

'OK, hang on,' I said finally. The hotel had their usual notepad and cheap monogrammed pen on the side table. I wrote down the details Miller gave me, and said, 'Right, then. If there's –'

'We do require your mother's room to be vacated within three days. It may seem –'

'Three days? That's a bit excessive isn't it?'

'We have a waiting list, Ms Westerholme. Other families need places for their *loved* ones.'

It was pretty hard not to notice her emphasis. 'I'll see what I can do. Thanks for your call.' I hung up, all my nerve endings tingling. If the woman had been in front of me, I might have tried to strangle her. I paced back and forth a few times, trying to calm down, not even sure now why I was so upset. But words echoed in my head – *She's dead, she's dead, she's dead* – and my jaw was so tightly clenched that my teeth ached.

Suddenly, I remembered Mia and Emma. Mia was clutching Bum, her eyes huge, watching me pace. Emma watched, too, her brow furrowed. 'Is your mum...'

'Yes, she has... passed away.'

'Oh, that's so awful.' Emma's face crinkled further – she looked more sorry than I felt, although that wasn't saying a lot, since I wasn't sorry at all.

'It's fine.' I sat next to Mia. 'Are you ready for breakfast? What's Bum going to have to eat? Vegemite?'

She shook her head mutely. Uh-oh.

'He's not a very tidy eater. Maybe he can have some cereal, like you.' I tried to remember what was on the buffet from last time. 'They have lots of fruit here, and croissants and things. Are you hungry?'

She nodded and slid over to get down from the bed. I helped her put on sandals and brushed her hair, and away we went. I even helped her to press the lift button and pointed out all the numbers. We ended up stopping on 5, 4, 3 and 2. At the dining area entrance, I scanned the room for Heath but he hadn't arrived yet, so I chose a table at the far side from where I could watch everyone in the room as well as the hotel entrance.

As soon as we sat, a waitress came to pour me coffee. 'You're an angel,' I told her. 'Do you have any chocolate milk?'

'Sure.' She went away and came back with a small jug of it, and a melamine cup for Mia with teddy bears on the side of it. Mia had to have a good look at them before she'd accept any milk from the jug, then sipped cautiously as if she didn't want to upset the bears. Emma had already gone to the buffet – she stood in front of it for several minutes as if she couldn't believe how much food there was before picking up a plate and choosing what she wanted.

I drank my coffee and kept watching Mia, wondering how to find out if something was wrong. She was too little to ask. If she had a pain or fever or cough, it would be obvious. Emma came back with a plate of pastries, looking guilty, and I said, 'Eat as much as you want. It's the same price.' She smiled and offered a chocolate croissant to Mia, who shook her head.

I took Mia to the buffet and helped her put some fruit on a plate but then she spotted the bain-marie with baked beans and scrambled eggs and wanted them all on the same plate, threatening a tantrum when I expressed my doubts. 'OK, fine, but you've got to eat it.'

I helped myself to more bacon than was sensible, but I didn't really care. It was a treat and I made the most of it. Halfway through my second cup of coffee, feeling slightly more human, I looked up to find Heath standing by the table. His facial expression was unreadable, and I didn't feel like hearing any more bad news.

'Have some food,' I said, waving at the buffet.

'I'm fine,' he said. 'When you've eaten I need to take you to HQ.'

'Again?'

Emma kept her head down, dabbing crumbs off her plate.

'Swanny wants to brief you on where things are at.'

'What does that mean?' I searched his face for signs of something positive; he wasn't frowning or rubbing his jaw at least. 'They caught him?'

Emma's head jerked up, her eyes wide and hopeful.

'No, not yet.' He cleared his throat.

'You can tell us,' I said. 'I won't tell Swan that I know already.'

'Better not.' He finally sat down, but he seemed uneasy and we soon found out why. 'Swanny wants Emma to make a statement about what she told us yesterday.'

'Nup.' Emma glared at him. 'You can tell him what I said.'

'It doesn't quite work that way.' Now Heath was running his hand over his hair; not a positive sign.

'Look,' Emma said, with a heavy teenage sigh that usually came with an eye roll. 'It doesn't matter what I tell you, or him. Mum told me once that the police have no control over these guys. You can't stop them. If this Aidan has been sent to get me…' She swallowed and then kept going. 'You've found out who he is. Big deal. The cops in NSW know who he is. Big deal. Even if they found out who's paying him – or I tell you – big deal. You don't have anything on him. They're too clever for you. End of story.' She stood up. 'I'm getting some fruit.'

We watched her walk to the buffet and use the tongs to pick up the precisely-cut pieces of melon and pineapple. I sneaked a look at Heath – he was fuming.

'Is she right then?' I asked.

'Normally I'd say no. Most crims are stupid and that's how we catch them. This Aidan Solomon –' His phone rang and he picked it up, tapping the screen to talk. 'Heath. Yep. Yep. Hmm… Verified? By who? OK. No, she won't, and I'm not dragging her in. Talk to you later.'

'So you're not making Emma do a statement?'

'You heard her. If we try to force her, it'll be more trouble. We'll wait and see if she changes her mind.'

Emma sat down at the table and ate some pineapple, then offered a piece of orange melon to Mia who took it with suspicious care and left it on her plate.

'Emma, good news,' Heath said. 'Aidan Solomon is back in Sydney. Sighting of him in a café was verified this morning.'

Relief crackled through me. Did I get my life back now?

'Yeah, right,' Emma said. 'He'll send someone else.'

'Why?' I asked, my irritation rising again. 'What aren't you telling us? Why would this guy bother when Kate is already dead? Come on, let us in on what's really going on.'

'I told you.' She looked at Heath. 'Pay my fare to Western Australia and give me a new identity. That's all you can do. I'll go. Judi wants me to go.'

'I don't want you to go!' I said.

'Sure you do.' She gestured at Mia. 'You're worried about her. Like Mum was worried about me.' Her mouth twisted on one side and I realised she was biting it on the inside, trying to stay controlled and not cry. 'I have to look after myself now.'

I couldn't think what to say. Guilt seeped into every pore, but she was right.

'What about your dad?' Heath said. 'We think we've found him, but I won't contact him unless you tell me to. Or I can give you his details and you can call him.'

She stared at him in silence for a few seconds, then said, 'Where is he living?'

'Christchurch. He went to work there on the earthquake rebuilding, and he's stayed, apparently. He's an electrician.'

'Oh.' She seemed at a loss. 'I… I have to think about it.'

'OK, but we should move on this quickly. If you really think you're still in danger, we'll need to get documents and a passport for you. Start the processes now.'

'Yeah, I want to get out of here,' Emma said. 'Like, yesterday.'

'Good. But it's on one condition.'

She gave him the evil eye but didn't take the bait.

'You have to tell me the rest of it,' Heath said. 'The bits you left out yesterday.'

'It's got nothing to do...' Her voice trailed away. I started to say something but held back, like Heath, and waited. Finally, Emma said, 'If you call my father, and he says I can go there, I'll think about it.'

This girl could get a job as a hostage negotiator.

'If this Aidan guy is back in Sydney, then we can go back to Candlebark, right?' I sent Heath a pleading look.

'I'd rather you stay here,' he said, 'but I guess things are safe enough. The problem is that he would've reported back to whoever hired him.'

'Told you,' Emma muttered.

'So Candlebark is the obvious place to look for you both.' He drummed his fingers on the table. 'I'd recommend that Emma stays here while we sort out either New Zealand or some other safe option. I'd say you could go home, Judi, but...' He looked at Mia.

'Crossfire? Collateral damage? What's the trendy term now?' I finished my cold coffee and shuddered. 'I know what you're getting at.' I'd been thinking about another possibility for a while and now was crunch time. 'Give me a few minutes.'

I went out into the lobby and found a quiet corner. What I was about to do made me feel sick, but it seemed like the only real choice. I pressed my Contacts icon and found their number. 'Hi, Lucy? It's Judi.'

Within three minutes, it was all settled. Mia was going to stay with her grandparents for a couple of days, and I was going to be left with a child-sized hole in my life. After I'd hung up, I stood staring out at the busy Melbourne street, trying to get my feelings under control before I went back into the dining room. Despite Lucy and Geoff's love for Mia, she wasn't going to like being dumped there. She was already unhappy and reacting to me not being around enough. Now I was doing it all over again. That's what it felt like to me, at least.

But I was also angry. This time I hadn't done anything stupid – this had all been forced on me, and I hated that Mia and I were in a situation now where I had to give her into someone else's care to protect her. I wanted to punch or kick something, pulverise someone. Instead I had to tuck it all away and basically suck it up.

I'd do it for now. But something had to change. I'd make it change. I just had to work out how.

20

Back at the table it looked like Emma and Heath weren't speaking to each other and Mia was grizzling. Great. 'Emma, you'll have to stay here while I take Mia to her grandparents.'

'I have to go to work, sorry, or I'd take you,' Heath said.

'I'll go by taxi or something.' I frowned at him. 'This is why I wanted to bring my own car. Now how do I get back to Candlebark later on?'

'I'll organise you a hire car,' he said. 'How many days do you want it for?'

As if I had a crystal ball. I picked a number out of my head instead. 'Three.'

'I'm coming with you,' Emma said. 'To Candlebark.'

'No.' The word popped out and her face dropped into a major sulk. 'It's not safe, Emma. You were the one who said someone else was going to be sent after you.' And I was sick of having the target on my back as well, especially when the police were offering her protection.

'I want my things, and Mum's things,' she said mulishly.

'I can bring them back for you.'

'What if you forget something?'

'It's all packed up in boxes,' I said. 'All I have to do is put them in the car.'

I looked at Heath and could tell he was sitting there debating which was the better option. I didn't want him to say she should go with me so I narrowed my eyes and stabbed nasty silent threats at him. He finally caught on.

'You do need to stay here, Emma. We don't have the resources to send officers with you to protect you.' Two pings and he checked his messages. 'Lauren is coming to stay with you – she'll be here shortly.'

I didn't like the look on Emma's face. It said 'running away' again. Shit. 'Can Lauren take Emma shopping today? She's really short on clothes, especially underwear.'

'Sure.'

'I haven't got any money,' Emma said.

'We'll sort it out,' I said, getting up. I made a sign at Heath to follow us out and, while Mia and Emma were looking at the fancy gold fountain in the lobby, I muttered to him, 'Is there any victim funding Emma can use? My credit card isn't too healthy.'

'I'll ask Lauren to find some funds for her again, don't worry. And I'll get my security mate to organise the car for you.' He hugged me for a long moment but it wasn't nearly enough. In any way. 'Please be careful in Candlebark.'

My eyebrows shot up. 'You really think another hitman will come looking? Up there?'

'It's unlikely, but it's an easy place to check for Emma first, if they're looking.'

I scanned his face – it was drawn and tired, and he'd missed a bit on one side when he'd shaved. I touched it with one finger and tried not to wish for things I couldn't have right then. 'I may well stay at the pub with Andre,' I said. 'I'm not keen to be in the house on my own, to be honest.'

'Good idea.' He made a move forward, as if to kiss me, and then pulled back and turned a little. 'Hi, Lauren.'

'Hi,' she said cheerily. Today she looked like she'd just come from the gym, although she had a loose-fitting jacket on to hide her gun and holster. She listened to Heath's explanation and said, 'Sure. We had fun buying clothes the other day. But I'll make sure she's safe.'

'We've got verification the killer is back in Sydney,' Heath said, 'but Emma seems to think someone else will be sent. Whether she's right or not, we can't afford to take chances.'

Lauren lowered her voice. 'Does she realise she'll have to testify to seeing him at their house, going inside to shoot her mother?'

'Not really. She thinks the ID is the end of it.'

'Oh.' Lauren made a face. 'I won't say anything then. I'm already in trouble for her running off the last time.'

'Yes, keep her calm and having fun,' he replied.

Alone with Mia at last, after they'd all left, I went through the rigmarole of getting us over to Lucy and Geoff's house. Neither of them asked any questions about why I needed to leave Mia with them – they were too happy to have her stay. I bent down and gave Mia a hug and a kiss. 'I'll be back soon,' I told her. 'I have to go and fix a few things.'

That didn't wash with her at all. Her face crumpled and she started to cry. 'I wanna come with you.'

Just as she was brewing up a full-scale tantrum, Geoff scooped her up and said, 'Do you know what a swing set is?'

Tears rolled down her face as she shook her head and looked at me again.

'It's made just for little girls and their bunnies,' he said. 'All red and blue and green. Do you want to try out the swing first or the slide?'

That got her attention. I pasted a big smile on my face as Geoff took her off to the backyard where apparently they'd splashed out on a new swing set. Great bribe, Nanna and Poppa. Lucy gave me a wave and let me out the front door, but it was me who had tears on her face as I walked up to the main street near the station to get a taxi back to the hotel.

At least now, whatever you do, you know she's safe.

Yeah, but it still hurt.

The security man at the hotel had parked my delivered rental car, which turned out to be a 4WD. Or, as he pointed out carefully, after looking at my horrified face, a 'compact SUV' because I was 'going to the country'. Right. I didn't want to have to wait for a replacement so I sighed and got into it, trying to work out where everything was and what all the dials and lights were for. He gave me a little lesson, trying really hard to be helpful so I wouldn't yell at him, and finally I said OK and set off.

It wasn't until I was on the Ring Road that I realised I had my foot flat to the floor, just like in the Benz, and the SUV was doing 130 kmph. That way lay a big speeding ticket! I eased off and tried to use a light pressure, but old habits kept creeping in. Finally I noticed something that turned out to be cruise control. Saved!

Once I settled in, I enjoyed driving the thing so much that I started having dangerous thoughts about getting rid of the Benz. No, I couldn't afford it. I was back in Candlebark before I knew it, parking at the pub and going in to see Andre.

'Hey, stranger!' He gave me a big hug, keeping his garlicky hands off my clothing. 'How's Emma?'

'OK.' I gave him the rundown on what had been happening. 'And I've left Mia with her grandparents for safe keeping.'

'Safe keeping?' He raised his eyebrows almost to his hairline. 'You mean all this shit isn't over yet?'

'I hope it is,' I said, 'but Emma is convinced this gang boss will send someone else after her.'

He glanced past me. 'You didn't bring her back with you, did you?'

'No way.' I looked over my shoulder, too. Would I ever stop doing that? I hoped so. 'I need to take all of her and Kate's things back to Melbourne in the next day or so.' I made a face. 'Another trip up and down that bloody highway.'

'The highway to hell, eh?'

'You said it.'

'Talking about hell,' he said, 'we've got our first children's party booking.'

'Really?' I gaped at him. 'I never thought it would actually happen. When?'

He named a date about ten days away. 'The mum is booking a clown.'

'That's great for nightmares.' I laughed. 'Any more tantrums from Bronwyn?'

'No, but we have twenty in for dinner tonight – five tables – and I'm pretty sure at least one of them is from her place.' He grinned. 'I'm cooking pasta, organic chicken with a creamy wine sauce, and beef with super large spiced potato wedges.'

'I'll be here to help. And I'm staying here tonight as well.' I suppressed a shiver. 'I'm not quite ready to be home on my own yet.'

'I moved in last night. I hope that's OK.'

'Of course!' And I was relieved – I wouldn't be in the pub on my own after hours.

I bustled around at lunchtime, moving from bar to bistro and keeping an eye on things. As soon as the pub quietened down, I carried the boxes of Emma and Kate's possessions out to the rental 4WD. That made the office feel spacious again. Charlie went down into the cellar, as we'd had a beer keg delivery, to check all the lines and get the kegs sorted ready for replacement. I'd left the ordering to him this week, one less job for me.

The cellar trapdoor and stairs were in the hallway near the office. A lot of old pubs had the door in the floor behind the bar for easy access but apparently Macca, who was a large bloke, refused to use it after he got stuck one night in front of his mates.

He'd had it all moved into the hallway. Made no difference to me – I still wasn't going down there after my accident at the pub I'd had in Melbourne. The memory of someone shoving me from behind, and then lying on the concrete at the bottom of the steps for hours with broken bones... I'd put chairs on each side of the open trapdoor as usual, and hovered in the bar, checking on Charlie every now and then and heaving a sigh of relief when he came back up. However, I could hear him swearing and went to see what the problem was.

'The trapdoor lock won't go in and close properly,' he said. 'It's like the floor has moved out of whack.'

'As long as the door itself is sitting flat,' I said. 'That way I won't trip over it. We'll sort it tomorrow.'

Dinner in the bistro was busy – two of the tables were Bronwyn's clients and I spent the evening expecting her to barge in and harangue me again, but nothing happened. Perhaps she'd given up. I approached one table where a large, red-faced man had three women as his audience as he raved on about restaurants in Paris and asked, 'Hope you're enjoying your evening?'

'Gorgeous food,' he gushed. 'Isn't it, ladies?'

They nodded enthusiastically.

'Are you staying at the health spa?'

They looked at each other guiltily. 'Yes. But it's self-catering – they leave us plenty of food but sometimes you just don't feel like cooking.'

That sounded very odd to me, but I didn't pursue it. I was just happy they'd come to us for dinner instead. I was caught up in the bistro and when I finally returned to the bar, the sight of Chris Winter at the far end, perched on a stool, sent a small shockwave through me. What the hell?

'Hey,' he said, cheery as ever. 'How was Melbourne?'

'How did you know I'd been there?'

'Ear to the ground,' he said with a big grin. 'Part of my business to know what's going on.'

I didn't believe that for a minute. 'Were you in Melbourne yourself?'

'Me? No.' He waved a hand. 'I was doing some work in Bendigo, looking over a pizza restaurant that's going out of business.'

'So it wasn't you who called me yesterday morning, early?'

A tiny flicker around his eyes that I probably would've missed if I hadn't been watching closely, then he said, 'Not me. Why would I be calling you? You're not selling the pub, are you?'

'Not that I know of.' I laughed without any humour whatsoever. 'Although it seems like you'd know before me.' I tried one more jab. 'Have you ever heard of a guy called Aidan Solomon?'

This time his face was totally bland as he shook his head. 'No, sorry. Is he a local?'

Oh, Chris was good, all right. I didn't pursue it. If it had been him who'd warned us to get out of the house, I wasn't going to hassle him about it. He'd saved our lives. But it only served to make me triply curious about who the hell he was and what he was doing in Candlebark. I made an excuse about cleaning up in the bistro and left to wipe down the tables and make sure it was ready for lunch tomorrow. With no guests, there were no breakfasts to worry about.

Andre finished in the kitchen and poured us both a Sauv Blanc before we sat by the open French doors. It was a gorgeously warm autumn evening and two of the groups of customers had decided they wanted to eat outside – we had learned to supply insect repellent, but the mozzies had kept away tonight. I sighed loudly and put my feet up on a chair. Andre sipped his wine and sighed as loudly as me.

'Are we making any headway at all?' he said after a while.

'Let's not talk about finances tonight,' I said. 'Chris Winter is in the bar.'

'Good to have regular customers. Is he a problem?'

'No...' I told Andre about the warning call and how I was sure it came from Chris.

'That doesn't make sense,' he said. 'How would he even know the guy was coming for you? How would he know he was so close to breaking into the house?'

'The only way would be if he'd been following him. Or me.'

'Why would he do that?' Andre looked as mystified as I felt.

I drank some wine and pondered. 'I think he's some kind of cop. From NSW.'

'What the heck makes you think that?'

'Something Emma said, but I'm not sure what. Why –'

'Hello, hello, hello.' That could only be Connor, looming up in the doorway. 'Like my impression of a policeman?'

'Very funny,' I said. I went and gave him a big hug. 'You're in uniform so I'm guessing you don't want a glass of wine.'

'I'm actually off-duty, so yes, I'll have a glass.' He sat at the table and stretched his legs out, letting out a huge sigh that made us laugh. It seemed like the night for it. 'Did I hear you talking about NSW police as I came in?'

'Oops.' I winced. 'I need to whisper more often.' I was thinking of Chris Winter eavesdropping, not Connor. It took me ten minutes to fill Connor in on everything that had happened.

He rolled his eyes a few times and then said, 'Judi, you really do know how to land yourself in the middle of things.'

'Hey.' I held my hands up. 'Not my fault this time.' I was getting tired of defending myself.

'Tell Connor what your theory is,' Andre urged.

Before I said another word, I checked the bar from around the corner, but Chris had left and only a few old regulars were still drinking their beer and watching something on the TV. I came back and sat, debating with myself. I didn't want to lay it out for them and get rubbished for being ridiculous.

'All right,' I said, 'but don't shout me down until I've finished. It's just my ideas.' They nodded seriously and I went on. 'Like I said to Andre, I think Winter is some kind of police from NSW. Came here from Sydney, for no good reason, he spies on everyone, he's always where the action is. I mean, sleepwalking?'

'Yeah, that was a bit suss,' Andre said. Connor just contemplated me and waved for me to continue.

'Who would move straight into a house where a woman has been murdered? Who has a convenient job that means he can drive all over the place without it looking weird? And...' I sucked in a breath. 'I'm ninety per cent sure it was him who called to warn me about the killer coming for Emma and me in Ascot Vale.'

'Ninety per cent?' Connor said.

'All right, ninety-five. Who else could it have been, anyway? Nobody knew I was there except Andre.'

'A fair few people here knew,' Andre said. 'Joleen told them when she came and collected her husband from the bar.'

'Oh great. Still, it sounded like Chris on the phone.'

'But you're not sure,' Connor said. 'Did you tell Heath and Swan?'

'No...' Maybe I should have. 'Still, I think he's here for a reason, and it's more than being keen on Kate.'

'Whoa!' Andre said. 'Who told you that?'

'Emma. She said that's why she made the first ID picture of Chris. She knew him from Sydney.' Then I had to explain to them both what Emma had told me.

'Do the Melbourne police know all of this?' Connor asked.

'Yes. Emma finally gave them all the stuff she'd been keeping as a secret. I think Kate had drummed it into her that to stay in hiding was their only option. She's been trying to do what her mum said.'

'Let me get this right,' Connor said, scratching his ear. 'The killer has gone back to Sydney, Emma is under police protection in Melbourne and has told them what she knows at last, and you think Chris Winter is some kind of undercover agent.'

I nodded.

'And you haven't had any more threatening phone calls?'

'No. But I haven't been home really.'

'Everything should settle down then,' Connor said. 'If nothing is happening around here, Winter will leave again. It's a wonder he hasn't already.'

'Have you solved the murder of that guy in the main street yet?'

He grimaced. 'No. His fingerprints have identified him. He's from Melbourne, a low-level drug dealer. Nobody seems to have any idea what he was doing here.'

'Did Chris Winter know him?' I asked.

'No.' He stood and yawned. 'I'm off. Thanks for the drink. Don't forget to lock up properly.'

Andre and I chorused, 'Yes, Senior Constable Byrne, we will.'

By 11.30pm, the pub was empty and dark and locked up. Andre and I were in our rooms, in bed. He was probably fast asleep. I was so wide awake I could scream. I tossed and turned, stared up at the cracks in the ceiling, wished I was in my own house, fretted about feeling too scared to go back there. I hated the feeling of violation, that even though I hadn't been hurt, the house felt sullied, unsafe. It was horrible. It had been my haven for so long.

I turned over again and punched my pillow. Maybe I should get the local white witch in to cleanse the house with burning weeds or whatever they used. Not that I believed in witches and spells. Maybe I should… Damn it. If I kept lying here thinking stupid thoughts I'd never sleep. The best thing was to go downstairs and steal some of Andre's special hot chocolate mix, maybe read a book on my phone until my brain calmed down. Yep, that's what I'd do.

The hallway lighting was a dim glow but the stairs were in darkness. I felt my way down, hand on the rail, and by the time I reached the bistro I could see enough to dodge the tables. The various little lights on appliances in the kitchen meant I could make my chocolate without turning anything else on. It was peaceful, and I liked the sense of being in the pub alone. I was starting to feel a real sense of ownership, and partnership with Andre. Maybe we could make a go of the place.

I took my mug to a table near the French doors and sat, looking out at the patio area. There was enough moonlight to cast shadows and, as I watched, a small shape moved and a rabbit hopped slowly across, eating the grass growing between the pavers. I was so entranced by it that the sharp crack took a couple of seconds to penetrate my mind. It was followed by a sound I knew – one of the sash windows in the bar was sliding upwards.

Not again. I sat frozen while my brain's synapses zapped against each other in my skull like bouncing balls. Call Connor. Phone will light up. Burglar will hear me. Knives in kitchen. Could be used on me. Baseball bat. Don't have one. Could be a burglar, could be another killer. Emma was right? Do something!

I stood and immediately my legs shook so much I could barely stay upright. Then another thought flooded my brain. *I've had enough of this fucking bullshit! My pub. My friends. My life. Get the fuck out of my life!* I shoved my phone in my trackie pocket, went to the bistro entrance and listened. My breathing sounded way too loud and I tried to breathe slowly and lightly, but my chest was tight with fear. Do something. What?

Something scrabbled. He was climbing in through the window. Burglar would head for the office. Killer would… don't go there. Think! Charlie had said… I stepped into the reception area and tiptoed past the desk towards the office. Light footsteps now. He banged into a chair. No time to waste. Down the corridor behind the bar. Kneel. Find the latch and steel ring. Charlie had left the trapdoor unlocked. I lifted. Fuck, it was heavier than I expected. I strained and clamped my mouth against the urge to grunt with the effort. Lift! I doubled my pulling, feet braced, and the door rose, slowly then faster. Finally I had it open, the door lying on the floor, the cellar entrance a black hole.

Where was he? I couldn't hear a thing, then a small sound as he unzipped something. My heart was trying to climb out through my ribs. I stepped back, near the office door and tried the handle. It was locked. Shit! My only other option was the storeroom. It was probably locked, too. Nowhere to hide. I stood at the end of the corridor, back against the wall.

A shadow moved in the entrance to the bar. Stepped out, stood near the reception desk. He was listening, too. I reached out, hand shaking, and gripped the storeroom door handle. It rattled loudly and I snatched my hand away.

The shape turned my way, and I caught a glimpse of something in his hand. If that was a gun, I was in big trouble. But the rattle had caught his attention. A professional would check it out, surely.

If this guy had a torch and turned it on, I was dead. I had to hope he wouldn't, that he'd be worried about giving himself away. I gave the handle another nudge and it obediently rattled again. He moved. He was coming this way. My legs stopped holding me up and I slid down the wall into a terrified huddle.

Then he disappeared. There was a bang, a crunch, a panicked shout, and two huge crashes. I waited, eyes closed, praying.

Please let him be dead or broken. All I heard was a groan and then silence. I crawled forward on hands and knees until my fingers hit the edge of the trapdoor; it was much easier to lift now and I let it fall on to the floor hole with a loud, muffled bang. It had caught on the carpet edge. I had to get it properly shut.

I had no idea whether I'd get the sliding lock to work or not. I staggered into the bar and dragged out a table, tipping it over on to its top and maneuvering it over the trapdoor. That would have to do. I stood by the reception desk and called Connor's mobile.

He picked up after two rings. 'Judi, you've heard already?'

'About what?'

'Your car. Sorry, the CFA couldn't save it.'

'My…' I didn't want to know. 'You need to come to the pub.'

'I'm out at your house. What's going on?'

'Someone broke in. He's in the cellar. I…' What was that smell? I turned on the lamp on the desk. Some kind of liquid was flooding through under the front door. Was it petrol?

Breaking glass in the bar. More breaking glass in the bistro. Two horrible flares of light. Fire. God almighty, was the wraith back wanting revenge?

'Judi? Judi! Talk to me!' Connor was shouting through the phone. 'What's going on?'

'The pub. It's on fire. It's being… someone is attacking us. Petrol. It stinks!' I gasped, and whimpering sounds dribbled out of my mouth.

'Judi, get out! I'll send the fire truck. Get out now!'

'Water, I can get water.'

'Not for petrol,' Connor shouted. 'You'll spread it. Get the fuck out of the pub!'

21

I couldn't move. I put my phone down on the reception desk, picked it up again. Home screen. I'd cut him off. The flames were getting higher on both sides of me. If they reached – no, *when* they reached the petrol in front of me, the pub would become an inferno. I'd have to walk through the petrol and open the door. What if the killer was waiting for me?

Andre! He was upstairs, fast asleep.

That finally galvanised me and got my legs moving. I scooted around the desk and headed up the stairs, stumbling a couple of times, pulling myself up by the rail. I banged on his door and screamed, 'Andre! Wake up! Fire, fire!'

The door to my room was open, the keys in the lock still. I wrenched them out. Andre's door opened.

'What did you say? What's wrong?'

'Someone's set the pub on fire. We have to get out. Now!'

Then I heard an ominous whoosh and a blast of hot, petrol-fumed air swept up the stairs.

'Holy shit!' Andre shouted, suddenly aware of the danger. 'We can't get down the stairs.'

'Outdoor stairs,' I said.

'Don't have any. We have to get on to the balcony from Macca's old room. There's a ladder.'

The panic kept swamping me in dark waves, and my brain was struggling. Andre grabbed the keys from my hand

and opened Macca's door. 'In here.'

'My purse.' It was in my bedroom.

'Fuck your purse,' he said. 'Come on!' He dragged me into Macca's room and slammed the door shut, then raced to the window, flicking off the lock and wrenching it upwards. It groaned and squealed but it was up. He went out first and then helped me. The balcony here was rotten, and some of the boards had holes. The last thing we needed was to put a foot through.

Noises from below made my guts churn. Crackling and banging, like the pub was alive and in pain. Flames lit up the ground around the window and door cavities. But over the sounds I heard a distant siren, then another. The CFA were coming. Not in time to save anything though. Not in time to save us.

'Where's the ladder?' I asked.

Andre turned to me, his face white. 'Not here. It must be on the other side.' He looked over the iron railings. 'We'll have to jump.'

'I can't jump from here!' I shouted. 'If I stuff up my hip again...'

'OK, then maybe I can jump and catch you.'

'With *your* broken legs?' I glared at him and then laughed. And kept laughing. I felt totally hysterical and I couldn't stop.

He grabbed my arm, hard, and shook me. 'Judi, where is the fire?'

'Everywhere.' My laughter broke into a sob. 'Everywhere.' And I'd never see Mia again.

'No, come on. Where did it start?'

'Bar. Bistro. And petrol in the entrance by reception.'

'OK, OK. Listen. Sirens. Close. We can wait. We're on the other side.'

'We can?'

'Yes. Get ready to shout and scream as loud as you can.'

He leaned over the railing and said, 'Lights. Fire truck. And Connor. Another fire truck.'

Too late to save the pub though. If the wooden floors burned, it'd all collapse into the cellar.

Oh shit. The cellar. I thought I was going to vomit. 'There's someone in the cellar.'

'Have you got smoke damage?' he said. 'No one is in the cellar.'

'Yes, yes, they are. We have to get down there, open the outside doors.' Now it was me leaning over the railing, searching for Connor or the firefighters. 'Hey, hey! Up here, up here! Help! Help!' I screamed the words over and over until my throat burned and ached.

A firefighter in yellow coat and hat ran around the side of the pub and stared up at us. 'Where's your fire escape ladder?'

Before I could shout something rude, Andre said, 'Gone. We can't get down. Hurry!'

The man ran off around the side and was back in a minute that felt like an hour. Two of them carrying a long ladder that they put up to the balcony. 'Can you get yourselves down?' he shouted. 'We need to be on the hoses.'

'We'll be fine,' Andre shouted back. 'Come on, Judi, you first.'

I swung my leg over the railing, wincing at the familiar hip pain that was sharper now, and my phone slipped out of my pocket. I grabbed at it, and watched it fall into the garden below. 'Hurry up,' Andre urged. I managed to get my feet on to the ladder while clinging to the iron lace. Step by step, I went down, while Andre got on to the ladder above me. I was caught between wanting him safe and hoping to God he wouldn't fall on me. At the bottom, my feet found solid ground and I nearly dropped down and kissed it.

No time. I staggered around the pub, dodging the car park bollards and looked for Connor. His 4WD was there but no sign of him. I pulled the arm of the nearest firefighter who was wrestling a hose and directing a thick spray of water through the windows into the bar. 'There's someone else inside. You have to get him out.'

'Nobody's going in there,' he said. 'It's too dangerous.'

'No, he's in the cellar. You can get in through the outside door.'

'Shit.' He pointed to another firefighter further along. 'Tell George. He's the captain. Hurry.'

I went through the same explanation with George. 'Who is it?'

'I don't know. He broke in.'

'He set the fire?'

'I don't know.' Why would he? Why wouldn't he? I couldn't get my head around any of it. 'The guy down there is injured.'

'How do you know?'

Andre had come up behind me and was watching the fire. It had melted the lead in our beautiful stained-glass window, shattering the glass, and flames now roared out of the hole. Someone had rammed open the front door and was directing water through it, while another hose focused on the bar windows. 'I can't watch this,' Andre said, but he did, as if he was under a spell.

I tried to answer Captain George. 'He fell down through the trapdoor.'

'Shit, he might be dead then.' He shook his head. 'Where's the outside door?'

'I'll show you.' It was where the beer deliveries went and I hoped they had something to lever the padlock off with.

'Judi,' another uniformed firefighter said. It was Connor, doing double duty. 'Saw you were out. Is Mia still in Melbourne?'

'Thank God, yes.'

'Problem, Byrne,' George said. 'Judi says there's someone in the cellar, injured. Can't get themselves out.'

'Right.' Connor never wasted time on questions if there was an emergency. He ran and grabbed a fire axe off the truck and went straight to the cellar doors. They were a double-door, opening out, with a concrete rim to rest the boards on that they rolled the kegs down. Connor hacked at the padlock, severing it in two goes, and pulled the doors back.

'Don't you go,' George said. 'Marty! Put your mask on.'

A young man pulled off his hat, dragged a mask on and tightened the straps, then put his hat on again. Under George's directions he went down into the cellar, lighting the way with a large torch. Smoke puffed out of the cellar entrance, not as much as I expected, and I guessed the floors were still intact.

Marty was back. 'Found him. He's in a bad way. Broken limbs. Head injury.'

'Is he breathing?'

'Yes, pulse was hard to find though.'

'Right. We have to get a move on.' George went to the truck for his own mask and a folding stretcher. He was back in seconds and lowered himself into the cellar next to Marty. They disappeared from sight.

A duo of sirens sang out behind me and two more fire trucks arrived from CFA depots further south. I spotted one firefighter whose pyjama top was sticking out from under his jacket. Thank God for volunteers who came out at all hours. Within minutes they'd got themselves organised and were adding their hoses of water to the inferno. A couple of minutes later, an ambulance and another truck arrived and Andre and I were ushered quickly out of the way, forced to watch our pub burning from the other side of the street.

Gusts of heat blew ash and smoke at us, and sparks and flames whirled up into the sky. As I watched, part of the roof caved in with a *whoomph*. That was it then – the rafters and the beams underneath were gone. I pressed my lips together hard to stop myself from crying or letting out a string of four-letter words for the entertainment of the avid watchers lined up along the street.

I focused again on the cellar doors. George had just stuck his head out and called a paramedic over. There was a short, tense conversation, where George looked like he was reading the riot act, then he ducked back down and within seconds, the fire rescue stretcher was being levered up through the doorway and hauled out by a team of firefighters and the two paramedics. They bent over him, carried out a fast examination and then got him carried away from the building. George and Marty emerged and went back to the hoses. By now the cellar would be full of smoke as well.

'I can't believe this,' Andre said mournfully. 'You said petrol. Who the fuck would burn us down?'

All I could think was – who the fuck wouldn't? I had several suspects lined up. I glanced around, shocked to see how many of the people in Candlebark had turned out to watch the show. Some of the older people were in dressing gowns and slippers! The younger ones were all happily taking videos of it all.

'Right now, I'm just glad you and I got out,' I said. 'If I hadn't been…' The words stuck in my throat.

'Hadn't been what? And who's the guy in the cellar?'

I screwed my palms into my eyes, wanting to blot out the sight of the flames consuming our future. Trying not to throw a huge, ranting tantrum. *Look at the crowd again. Who's here?* Wasn't that what the cops did – see who turned up to the funeral of a murder victim? I scanned the people crowding the street.

'Judi!' Andre tugged at my arm. 'Who was in the cellar?'

'I was downstairs. I couldn't sleep.' I wrapped my arms around myself, suddenly cold. 'I was sitting there thinking, and I heard someone breaking in.'

'Shit – like last time?' He put his arm around me and gave me a hug. 'You didn't need another bloody lunatic breaking in.'

'I just thought, you know, with Kate and Emma and all that stuff – I thought someone was coming to get me.' I swallowed hard. 'I didn't know what to do. I… Charlie couldn't get the trapdoor to lock earlier on, so it was there and I opened it.'

Andre stared at me, his mouth open. 'And he fell down it?'

'Basically, yeah.' I wasn't going to explain the rattling doorknob. 'And then petrol came in under the front door and then flames in the… it all happened so fast!'

Andre hugged me closer, his arm comforting and strong. 'Why did this guy break in and then set it on fire? If he was still inside?'

I shook my head. 'It doesn't make sense. It must be two different people. But that is so bloody unbelievable that I have no idea anymore.'

Connor jogged over to where we were standing. 'Who owns the white 4WD around the back, do you know?'

'Oh no,' I said. 'It's my rental.' Did I take out the extra insurance or not? I was pretty sure I had, but… 'Is it burnt?'

'No, they've been spraying it with lots of water,' Connor said, 'and the back of the pub isn't too bad, but it's covered in ash and stuff. Have you got the keys? I can move it.'

I made a face and pointed at the upstairs of the pub. 'They're next to my bed.'

'Righto, I might get a tow truck in. We could use a fire truck, but better to do it properly, since it's not yours.' He gave me one of his looks, the one that said: I know you're going to give me a weird answer. 'Who was the guy in the cellar? Did he start the fire?'

'I have no idea, truly.' I got a flash of me huddling in the corner and the guy falling down the cellar hole and shuddered. 'He broke in. But…' I thought about that moment of smelling the petrol, seeing the shadow of it creeping across the floor. 'He was in the cellar already when the fire started.'

'The arson detectives will have to be called in,' Connor said. 'Maybe he had mates outside who were expecting him to run out?'

'Pretty tight timing then,' Andre said. 'Judi's talking about a matter of maybe a minute or two?'

I nodded. 'Why wouldn't they wait until he came out?'

Connor eyed me again. 'Who would want to burn your car and the pub then? It's too much of coincidence for it not to be the same person, or people.'

'Wait – my car?' I gaped at him. Could this night get any fucking worse?

'Sorry, I did try to tell you when you called, but the pub was more urgent.' He patted my arm. 'I know you loved that old car, but the Benz is history. It's lucky the fire didn't spread to your house really, but we got there in time to stop it. Your neighbours were coming home and saw the car burning.'

Loved that old car? Sometimes. Sometimes I hated it because it had been my father's favourite car. Whoever burned it had probably done me a favour. One more thing from my past I could put behind me. As soon they came and towed it away.

Andre's face was a picture of gobsmackedness. 'Her car *and* the pub? Who would have it in for you that badly?'

Connor scanned the watching crowd in the same way I had. 'I've got somebody videoing everyone who's here. Not that it's a certainty, but if there's anyone looking a bit suspicious… All the same, I may have a few ideas.' He checked his fire truck crew and said, 'Better get back to it. Listen, I think you two should stay at my place tonight. I don't want you going back to your house, Judi.' He pulled his keys out of his pocket and unhooked his house keys. 'Don't wait to see the pub burn. It'll be a while before we get it out completely.'

'Thanks, Connor.' I wanted to hug him but his jacket was covered in ash and crap so I smiled instead. As he walked back to take another turn on the hoses, I looked around the crowd again, and this time I was searching for a few in particular. Some of the culprits from the chop chop dealing, for a start. Not a sign of any of them, but Chris Winter was there, phone held up, taking photos. No, it was video by the way he was moving it. Was he Connor's 'spy'? At this point nothing would've surprised me.

'I've had enough,' Andre said. 'You realise all of my stuff was in the pub? I'd put some of it in the cellar and a lot of boxes in my room.'

'Oh shit, I'm sorry!' The loss of my purse and a few clothes seemed irrelevant. 'We can claim it all on insurance, surely.'

His face took on a pained look. 'Please tell me our insurance is up to date.'

'God, yes. I checked not long ago.' I'd always been anal about insurance, since WorkCover and insurance had paid for all my operations and medical bills when I was pushed into the pub cellar in Fitzroy. I've always thought one disaster was enough to ensure any sensible person kept their cover up.

'Let's go then. I hope Connor has a few beers in the fridge at least. I need a drink.'

'Can we have a go at finding my phone first?' He made a face but followed me around to the garden. This side of the pub wasn't burning, but it wouldn't be long.

'Here,' Andre said. He wiped my phone on his pyjama pants and handed it to me. Two cracks across the screen but it lit up OK. We went off, arm in arm, to Connor's house, found the beer and some wine, broke out the cheese and crackers and eventually crawled into bed about 3am after tossing for the spare bed and the sofa. I went to sleep with the pictures of the burning pub still playing in my head and kept waking up, seeing the dark shape disappearing again, hearing the noises he made. What if I hadn't remembered he was there? He'd be dead by now. Maybe he was dead.

I gave up on sleep when Connor came home around 7am; he disappeared into the bathroom and turned the shower on. By the time he came out, I had made coffee in his plunger and was staring out into his overgrown back garden. He looked exhausted, with dark rings under his eyes, and reached for a coffee mug with a sigh. 'Brilliant, thanks.'

'Is it out?'

'Yep. Some of the boys are still keeping the hoses on it to make sure. Probably means your cellar is full of ash and water by now.'

My mouth and chin were quivering and I put a hand over them, unable to speak. Finally I said, 'I can't believe it. Who would do that?'

'Doesn't look like it was the guy they dragged out of the cellar.' He cleared his throat. 'Marty… when he was down there with him, before George took the stretcher in, Marty picked something up off the floor. He said he doesn't know why, he just did, and then he threw it in the fire truck. He gave it to me this morning, when they were getting ready to take the truck back to the depot.'

I looked at him and waited.

'It was a gun, with a silencer. Clearly not yours or Andre's.'

A weird laugh spurted out of me. 'No.'

'Did you see this guy with a gun? After he broke in?'

'It was too dark. He was a shape. I… I thought he was a burglar, but really I guess I knew he was either that Aidan come back, or someone else who'd been sent. Either way, Emma was right.'

'In what way?' Connor pursed his lips. 'What's so important that they're still after her?'

I shrugged. 'I don't know and she's not telling. Heath and I both think she's holding something back, but we can't budge her.'

'Hmm. By the way, your rental is outside.' He reached for his pile of keys and wallet and stuff and extracted a black ignition fob, pushing it across the table to me. 'The towie is also the RACV mechanic and he organised a replacement for you.'

'Great.' I didn't touch it. I didn't know where to go. Home? It didn't feel safe now. And I sure didn't want to see my burnt-out Benz. I didn't want to see the pub either. I wanted to be on a desert island somewhere with only a Mai Tai cocktail and a little paper umbrella to cope with. Except I didn't much like rum. I finally picked up the fob and shoved it in my pants pocket.

'Judi?'

'Yeah?'

Connor frowned at me. 'You need to eat. There'll be people here to talk to you very shortly.'

'Why? They should be out there finding out who this fire-happy dickhead is!'

'They need to ask you some questions first, especially about the break-in and the suspect in the cellar.' He fed two slices of bread into the toaster and set about putting margarine and jam and Vegemite on the table. As the aroma of toast cooking drifted through the air, Andre wandered in, looking as bad as I felt.

'Thanks for the T-shirt and trackies, mate,' he said to Connor. 'Coffee, you beauty.' He poured the last of it and sipped. 'You need to buy a better brand than this.'

'Is this what I get for allowing a chef into my house?' Connor joked.

We carried on with a bit of banter while we ate and drank and tried to pretend Andre's and my life hadn't just been totally fucked. I felt like I was floating above myself at one point, looking down and wondering what the laughter and jokes were all about, and were we all going crazy. Then there was knocking at the front door and I crashed back into myself again. Connor went to let them in and I knew from the voices who it was going to be. That was all I needed.

Detective Constable Hawke and Barney the Master Arsehole.

22

DC Hawke was pleasant and polite, as usual. Barney swaggered in and surveyed us and the breakfast things on the table as if we'd all been having an orgy before he arrived. My hackles rose instantly and I laced my fingers together tightly to try and keep my shit together.

Connor seemed slightly taken aback at having them in his house – maybe he'd been expecting someone else. He offered coffee and they both accepted, sitting at the other end of the table while he boiled the kettle.

'Thought you'd be a capsule machine kind of man,' Barney said, smirking.

'Sorry I can't offer you a cappuccino,' Connor said, and I hid a smile.

Hawke had his notebook and pen out, as if he wasn't in the mood to waste time on Barney's jibes. 'Ms Westerholme, I'm sorry to hear about your car and the pub. We need to ask you a few questions and find out what happened.'

'Of course.' I decided to answer only him, and turned to face him squarely. 'Ask away.'

We went through the events of last night, a series of actions and reactions that seemed like a dream, or a half-remembered nightmare. When we got to the bit where I described waking Andre up, Barney butted in.

'You didn't hear anything?' he asked Andre.

'Why would I?' Andre said. 'I might have vaguely heard glass breaking but it'd been a long day. I was knackered.'

'So we've only got Ms Westerholme's word for what happened?' Barney said. 'And she doesn't know who broke in, and didn't see who started the fire.'

'Sorry I can't be your perfect witness,' I snapped, 'but I doubt you'd believe me anyway.'

'Can we stay focused on the events that actually happened, please?' Hawke said.

I kept talking like a robot, and finally got to the bit where we were standing in the street. I turned to Connor. 'Was it Chris Winter you asked to video the crowd?'

'Yes, he was there and he's already emailed me the file,' Connor said.

'We'll need that video,' Barney said.

Connor's face tightened but he said, 'Judi, you need to tell them about the phone calls.'

I caught Barney rolling his eyes. 'Do you need some eye drops, Constable?' I asked.

'No. Why?' His face reddened all the same, but maybe because I'd once again dropped the *Detective* off his title. He couldn't detect his way out of a paper bag.

I explained about the threatening calls and that Connor had logged them.

'It's possible they're connected to the arson,' Connor said.

'Leave the detecting and surmising to us, thanks,' Barney said.

Now Connor reddened, and I wasn't letting Barney get away with that. 'I think Senior Constable Byrne is right. It's too much of a coincidence that I get threatened and then my car and the pub are attacked.'

Hawke leaned forward. 'But do you know who's been making the calls?'

'Phone records show they've been coming from a pay-as-you-go phone,' Connor said.

'This area has become a real little hotbed of crime, hasn't it?' Barney smirked again.

'What do you mean?' Andre asked. 'This arson is personal. We don't have bikies or chop chop here anymore.'

Barney slanted a look at Connor. 'News hasn't got out yet then?'

'What?' I shouted. 'Stop playing bloody games and spit it out, for fuck's sake!'

Hawke stretched his head back and forth and his neck cracked in the sudden silence. 'We, er, the Drug Squad closed down a local meth lab yesterday.'

'What's a meth lab?' I said. 'Connor?'

'Brendan Scott and his mates have been manufacturing methamphetamine, what they call ice, in the machine shed up the back of Scottie's farm. They'd set up a meth lab, with all the gear, hidden inside.' He folded his arms defensively. 'I would've told you today, but then the fires happened.'

'Why would you tell *her* that information?' Barney snarled.

'Because it was Judi who gave me the initial information about who was dealing chop chop with Macca – Mr Macclesfield.' Connor jutted his chin out. 'It was confidential information and I was obliged to keep it secret that it came from her.'

'So?' I said. 'That was chop chop. What's it got to do with this meth stuff?'

Connor said. 'The phone threats you've been getting. I thought it was likely to be Bronwyn, given her verbal attacks on you, but I wasn't totally convinced. Then I found out that somebody leaked it was you who told me about Scottie.' His eyes slid sideways to Barney for a tiny microsecond, then he lifted one shoulder. 'This meth factory is something else though.'

'I knew nothing about that,' I said. 'How did you find out it was there?'

Hawke and Barney were following us back and forth like spectators at a tennis match. Barney opened his mouth to butt in again, but Connor kept talking. 'Heath told us. He said it came from Emma.'

My head was spinning as I tried to make sense of it all. Then I remembered – all the walking she did across the hills and paddocks to get to my house after Kate was murdered. Something about a barn with the windows covered and a disgusting smell – probably like the old science labs at high school, but a lot worse. Things gradually fell into place. 'So,' I said slowly, 'you arrested Brendan and his mate. What about Scottie?'

'Yes, he was arrested as well,' Connor said, 'but Brendan swore his father knew nothing about it, so he was released yesterday, late afternoon.'

'Of course.' And now I knew whose voice it was on the calls. *Brendan's*. Put up to it by his scumbag father.

'Look,' Barney said, 'there's nothing to say the two things are connected. You probably get people causing trouble at the pub all the time. I mean, look at that guy who was out there with his rifle last year.'

We all gaped at Barney in disbelief, even Hawke. He eventually said, 'This is a small town. Things like this are almost always connected.'

Barney's face flushed from his neck up to his hairline, and he muttered, 'Rednecks.'

The atmosphere in the room suddenly heated up; Andre looked furious and Connor's hands were clenched so tight I thought his knuckles would crack. I'd heard enough of Barney's crap. My mind was focused elsewhere.

'Excuse me,' I said as nicely as I could. 'Nature calls.' I got up and went down the hallway to Connor's bathroom, opened and closed the door loudly, and then sneaked out the front door. The rental 4WD was parked in the street and I was in it and driving away in seconds, trying not to speed and attract attention. I knew exactly where I was going. Once again, it felt like one of me was driving and the other one of me was sitting in the back seat muttering, 'Are you sure this is a good idea?'

'Shut up!' I said loudly and gripped the steering wheel harder.

I almost missed the entrance to Scottie's farm, skidding slightly as I threw the 4WD into a sharp right-hand turn, brushing past the overgrown hedge. It didn't look like it'd been trimmed since the last time I was here, thick branches of cypress hanging low and arching overhead. The road had a million potholes but I didn't bother dodging them – I drove straight through, splashing mud and water and bouncing through the bigger puddles.

Brendan's bright green ute was parked to one side and Scottie's old ute was angled across the concrete path, half in the straggly garden. It looked like he'd come home drunk and hadn't stopped in time. I slammed on the brakes and jumped out of the 4WD, checked the decrepit tractor shed in case he was in there, and then headed for the front door.

I knocked as hard as I could and nobody stirred so I tried the handle. It opened and I pushed the door inwards. A rotten smell of garbage, spilled beer and something dead wafted out to me and I quailed. Then I remembered that sneering, menacing voice and rage surged up inside me. *Frighten me, will you, you bastards? Burn me out? You'll be bloody sorry!* I stepped inside and checked the rooms, one by one, half-expecting to find Scottie still in bed, but the bedrooms were empty. Bedcovers lay in rumpled piles on top of filthy, reeking sheets, and piles of dirty clothes littered the floors. Ugh. My stomach lurched and I almost turned and ran. Almost.

I found Scottie in the kitchen at the back, sitting at the table, passed out, his head on his arms. For a moment I thought he was dead. I nudged his arm, none too gently, and he stirred slightly, so I punched it instead. 'Scottie! Wake up, you evil bastard!' Beyond the stench from the sink and a bench full of dirty plates and cups and an overflowing bag of garbage, I could smell something else. I bent closer to him and sniffed.

Petrol.

'Scottie!' I slapped the back of his head. That got a reaction. He tried to raise his head, sucked in a breath, let it out. The stink of rum sent me back a metre or so. 'Scottie! Wake up!'

'What? What d'ya want?' He forced his head up and gazed at me blearily. 'Fuckin' hell. You still alive? Fuckin' bitch. Go away.'

'Yes, I'm still alive, you prick!' I stepped forward and slapped him again; his head rocked to the side and back again.

'What're you doin'? Get the fuck outta my house.' He staggered to his feet, swaying.

'I'm going to get you for this,' I hissed. 'You burned down my pub, you bastard.'

'So what?' He stared at me with the same hate-filled eyes I saw in the bar every night. 'Pity you weren't in it.'

'I was in it, you shit-for-brains. So was Andre, and so was some poor bugger who'd broken in and was in the cellar. That's three counts of attempted murder. You're lucky they got the guy in the cellar out. Otherwise you'd be up for murder.'

'Yeah, yeah. Fuckin' bullshitter.' He let out a rank belch and rum fumes billowed across the table. 'Poor old Macca really got taken in by you.'

I suddenly saw red stars in front of my eyes. 'Poor old Macca? The only mistake he made was ever thinking a scumbag like you was a mate. It was probably really you that shot him.'

'You just waltz in and take the pub. Fuck me, talk about scamming an old man…'

The rage was burning like a bushfire and I could hardly get

the words out. 'You're fucked now, Scottie. You won't get out of this one. I'll make sure you go inside for years, and your stupid fucking son can keep you company.'

'Don't you fuckin' threaten me, bitch!' he shouted. 'You fuckin' deserved it, all of it.' He staggered around the table. 'Get outta my house. Now!' He swung a wobbly fist at me and I ducked.

The rage surged up and boiled over, and things went black for a millisecond, then it was like a mad person took me over. 'You'll have to do better than that, shithead.' I moved in and punched him in the chest with both fists, using all of my strength. He lurched back, his feet scrabbled on the greasy floor and he went down. For one horrible moment, I thought his head was going to hit the bench behind him, but instead he ended up on his back in the bag of rubbish. Potato peelings, wet cardboard and tea bags spilled out around him.

I had a sudden vision of his skull hitting the sharp corner of the bench and blood and brain matter splattering the floor. My stomach rolled up into my throat and I gagged.

'Judi! What the hell are you doing?' Connor shouted, grabbing me by the arm and pulling me back.

'Let me… I have to…' I jerked away from him and ran to the sink, vomiting over the food and mould-caked dishes, tears streaming from my eyes. I hadn't thought the kitchen stench could get any worse but I'd managed it. I ran the tap, rinsing my mouth and gasping, while Connor checked Scottie on the floor. He'd been slightly winded but apart from that he was just drunk.

'Fuckin' bitch,' he whined. 'Should be fuckin' arrested. 'Cept you'll look after her, won't you, you dog.'

'Shut up, Scottie,' Connor said. 'You're under arrest for arson and attempted murder.' Connor recited his rights and then hauled him to his feet and put handcuffs on him. Scottie was still cursing and muttering as Connor propelled him out of the house to his police 4WD. As he left, Connor said over his shoulder, 'Judi, get out of here and go home. Hawke and Barney will finish questioning you later.'

I'd never heard that tone of voice from Connor before – cold and angry and disgusted. It was almost worse than anything else that had happened. At that moment anyway. All the years of friendship with Connor and I'd wiped them away with one stupid, angry outburst. If Scottie had indeed smashed his head on the bench corner, Connor would have been arresting me for murder.

I turned the tap off and stood, leaning against the sink, feeling like I was up to my neck in shit and sinking fast. Everything I'd fought so hard to create here in Candlebark was teetering on the edge of a black hole, about to disappear forever. My peace and quiet, my haven house, building the pub business with Andre, my friendship with Connor – and my growing bond and love with Mia, the awe and fear of mothering, the sense of meaning she gave me.

I'd nearly thrown it all away.

For a moment, I thought there was another one of me again, shaking her head, wagging her finger at me, then she was gone. It was just me. Me and my fuck-ups. Me and my second chance to start again, because the man I'd attacked had landed in the rubbish bag instead of against the bench.

In my pocket, my phone rang and vibrated and I nearly jumped through the ceiling. I pulled it out and tapped to answer. It was probably Barney hassling me again.

'Hello.'

'Ms Westerholme? It's Alexander Gallop, from Gallop Funerals. How are you?'

How am I? Just bloody marvellous. I cleared my throat. 'I'm fine, thanks.'

'Good, good. I'm just calling about your mother, and her funeral arrangements.'

Oh shit. My mother. I'd completely forgotten about her. Which wasn't surprising – I'd spent years trying to deliberately forget her and my father. 'Oh yes, sorry. Things have been… a mess.'

'I completely understand.'

Really, he had no idea, but that wasn't his fault. 'I guess you want me to set a date and organise a service and things like that.' All the things I'd done for my brother. None of which I wanted to do for my mother, but I knew I'd have to.

'Well, yes, that would be good. Are you able to come and visit us? Soon?'

'Yes, I'll need to drive down to Melbourne. I'm not sure… Can I call you back in a couple of hours or so?'

'Of course. I'll look forward to hearing from you.'

So polite. His calm tone had helped to settle me down, and after I hung up, I laughed. Life was just one big ironic kick up the bum really.

I left Scottie's house, making sure to close the front door. I thought about wiping my fingerprints off everything but what was the point? Connor knew I'd been there, so if Scottie insisted on having me charged for assault, so be it. I drove to the end of Scottie's road and stopped. 'Go home,' Connor had said. I didn't have anywhere else to go. So I turned the wheel and headed for my house, steeling myself for the worst.

23

Despite knowing my car had been burnt as well, I still wasn't prepared for the sight of the Benz in my driveway. It was a blackened hulk, bare steel showing in patches where the paint had burnt off, the seats and interior reduced to melted frames and springs. I parked and stared at it for a while, and then sent a silent thank you to the CFA firies for saving my house. The paint on the nearest window frame looked a little blistered, but other than that and the front garden being a bit singed, it was all good. I went inside and made strong coffee and then sat at the kitchen table in the blessed silence and did some heavy thinking.

Funeral. Car insurance people. Pub insurance people. If we were really lucky, the old antique office safe would have survived, Macca's relic he refused to get rid of. Not that there was much inside it, but there'd be a week's takings and receipts. Would Hawke tell me if the guy who fell into the cellar had survived? Or who he was? Would Connor tell Hawke and Barney about my attack on Scottie? Well, Scottie was sure to. It'd be more revenge.

I snorted. Revenge for something that wasn't even my fault.

Emma. I'd have to call Swan and see whether Emma was heading for New Zealand. At least her and Kate's boxes of possessions were safe in my rental 4WD. I could take them to Melbourne and deliver them on my way to the funeral home.

All of that could wait. I went to my landline, not in the mood to play 'find the reception spot' with my mobile phone, and called Geoff and Lucy. It was such a relief to talk to someone who knew nothing about what had happened, and this wasn't the time to tell them. They were happy to have Mia for another day until I could collect her. At last I got to speak to Mia.

'Juddy, you have to come and push me on the swing,' she said.

'I will.'

'When? Today?'

'Tomorrow. I'll come and get you tomorrow. Are you having fun?'

'Bum isn't,' she said. 'Bum doesn't like broccoli. I told him not to eat it.'

I laughed. 'Is he eating his lettuce and tomato though?'

'If he has to,' she said mutinously. 'It's from the big shop though. It tastes yucky.'

A few more things she had to tell me and then it was off to watch the birds in the garden, after informing me they were 'lokareets'. I hung up, feeling a hundred per cent better. Things didn't seem so bad with a chirpy three-year-old in my life.

I was on my second coffee when Hawke and Barney arrived. I found them outside examining the Benz. Hawke was taking photos with his phone.

'The crime scene officers will be here later,' he said. 'They need to go to Mr Scott's house first.'

'He smelled of petrol,' I said.

'And you would know that because?' Barney said, trying to sound tough.

'Because I was there in his kitchen and I accused him of burning the pub and threatening me.' I gestured at the car. 'I suppose he did this, too. He was drunk when I got there. They'll probably find petrol and other evidence in his truck.' Barney opened his mouth and I forestalled him. 'Let's get this over with, shall we? Then you can go and work out who the man was in the pub.'

Hawke cleared his throat and didn't look at Barney. 'I believe someone is coming from Melbourne to follow up on that aspect.'

'Is he still alive?'

'Yes, the firefighters got him out before he inhaled too much smoke. He's got a fractured skull and a broken leg from the fall down the steps.'

That was more information than I expected to squeeze out of him. He rose slightly in my estimation; Barney never would. We went inside and finished the questions, with Barney thankfully being mostly quiet and letting Hawke lead. After they left, I debated about calling Connor, but I didn't want to hear his angry tone again, so I focused on the insurance companies instead and gradually ticked off all the jobs on my To Do list. Then I called Andre.

'Come and stay here,' I said. 'Please.'

'You just want a bodyguard,' he said with a laugh.

'And a chef and a dishwasher and…'

'How could I refuse then?' He laughed again. 'Lucky I'd parked my car away from the pub, eh? I'd left it at Joleen's so Sonny could give it a service for me.'

It was good to hear him being cheerful. I needed that. He arrived soon after, and he'd brought fish and chips from the local takeaway. We ate them critically. 'Not as good as mine,' Andre said. 'Chips aren't crispy enough but the batter is OK.'

'Your batter is definitely better,' I said. 'But these are yum anyway.' It was a relief to talk about something meaningless, except it reminded Andre that he wouldn't be cooking anything anytime soon.

'What the hell am I going to do with myself?' he said, rolling up the greasy paper and bashing it into a small ball. 'Do I have to go and look for a job in Bendigo?'

'Let's wait and see what the insurance assessors say. Did you drive past the pub on your way here?'

'Yeah.' He rubbed his eyes and sighed. 'There's more left of it than I thought. But it still looks fucking horrible. And depressing.'

'I know one thing you can do right now,' I said. 'Come to Melbourne with me. I need help.' The word 'help' almost stuck in my throat; when was the last time I'd ever truly asked someone for that? I'd always just gritted my teeth and soldiered on, no matter what.

'Of course!' he said. 'We've got to stick together. What do you need help with?'

I explained about my mother and the funeral, and he whistled. 'You mean you've had that to deal with as well as everything else? That's too much shit for one person. Time you backed a truck up and loaded some of it on and got it taken away.'

I burst out laughing. 'Andre, your metaphors really suck.'

'True. But I made you laugh.' He checked his phone. 'It's not even midday yet. We can go now. Barney Bubblehead and Hawkeye aren't coming back, are they?'

'I don't know. Can't we just leave?' I really wanted to. I didn't want to look at the shell of my Benz anymore, or feel like I had to lock every door and window of my house. 'Connor is really mad at me. I can't call him.' Then I had to explain about going to Scottie's house.

Andre whistled again. 'Totally understand why you did it, mate. But yeah, if he'd hit his head… Tell you what, I'll call him.' He found Connor in his Contacts and tapped to call, and I listened to his end of their brief conversation. He hung up and said, 'He was pretty snippy. But he said the funeral was clearly a priority, and he checked with Hawke. We're free to leave Candlebark but we have to stay in contact. They'll expect us to make formal statements very soon.'

That was all I needed to hear. 'Great, let's go as soon as I've packed a bag.'

He made a mournful face. 'I have no bags to pack.'

'We'll buy you new clothes in Melbourne, don't worry. The pub insurance will pay you back.'

That brightened him up and, after I'd called the funeral director to make an appointment, we were soon on the road. It felt brilliant to be driving away from disaster, free and footloose. We spent some of the trip fantasising about what kind of pub we'd build, what we'd have in it, and Andre's 'five-star menu'.

'Would you restore our burnt-out hulk?' Andre asked. 'I don't even know if it's heritage-listed.'

'Good question.' We crested the hill near Sunbury and there, on the horizon, was the city of Melbourne, skyscrapers poking up like broken palings in a fence. I pointed at it. 'You don't really want to live there again, do you?'

He didn't answer for a few moments, and I felt flickers of panic rise in my chest.

'No, I don't think so,' he finally said. I waited for more, but he changed the subject to what brand of undies was the best, and I had to tell myself not to worry with a very firm voice.

In Melbourne, we settled in to the Ascot Vale house and I popped next door to visit Margaret and thank her for her help.

'You do lead an exciting life,' she said. 'A few too many criminals, maybe.'

'Too exciting,' I agreed. 'There'll be no more of that.' But I didn't promise. I seemed to attract trouble like blowflies to an outdoor dunny. The thought weighed heavily inside me and, even though Margaret gave me a big hug and then a tin of shortbread, I couldn't shake it off.

A quick trip to Highpoint to buy Andre some clothes – he insisted on seven pairs of undies and socks as the minimum – and we were ready for the funeral director. I hoped he would be as helpful as the woman who'd organised Andy's funeral. Mr Gallop turned out to be very old, with a sombre voice that sounded almost fake and patches of pink on his pale cheeks.

The funeral was set for three days' time at 10am. I doubted I'd attend, but it seemed that it would all go ahead with their celebrant regardless. What would they do if I didn't turn up? I lied and said I had been very unwell and, if I was sick, could they please go ahead without me. The funeral director looked slightly horrified but he agreed all the same, as long as I signed everything and paid. Of course. Cheapest possible coffin, shortest possible service. Done.

I'd done my best for my mother. Hadn't I?

As I got back into my rental 4WD, I had another weird split feeling, as if the other me was getting into the back seat again. I tipped the rearview mirror up so I couldn't see anything except the roof, but I could hear her. 'Are you sure that's what you want?'

What I wanted was to see the old vulture burn in hell. 'If you don't let it go,' she said, 'you'll carry it like a cancer still. Is that what you want?'

I wanted to be rid of the memories, the ever-recurring image of my father taking his belt off and the welts on Andy's back and legs, my mother shaking her head and saying nothing.

'Andy got past it,' the other me said smugly. 'He went and visited her.'

'Shut the fuck up,' I muttered and started the engine.

'Are you OK?' Andre asked. He put a warm hand on mine as it gripped the steering wheel, white-knuckled. 'You're as white as a sheet.'

'I just... I just...' I burst into tears, horrifying jagged sobs exploding out of me, my chest aching and burning. I wrenched my hands back then pounded them on the steering wheel. The knife scar on my hand connected with the edge and it sent a searing rip of pain across my palm. I screamed and cradled my hand, but nothing helped. Nothing stopped the sobbing either. Andre hugged me tightly and let me get on with it, then fumbled with my bag and found me some tissues. By then, my jeans were wet and snot was dripping from my nose. I blew it loudly and wiped my face.

'Fuck my life,' I said. 'All of it.'

'You know we're both going to stagger to our feet and get on with things again, don't you?' he said. 'But you needed to have a meltdown. You've been holding everything in for way too long. I've been seeing a few cracks lately but I didn't want to say anything, in case it put more pressure on you.'

'Thanks, mate, for everything.' I blew my nose again and sighed. 'I wish having a good sook was the end of it. I still feel like there's more shit to come. That's what's freaking me out.'

'You've got me. You've got Connor. He'll come around. He's just busy making himself look good in front of Bubblehead.' He smiled. 'And you've got Mia.'

'I notice you didn't mention Heath.'

'I'll leave that one to you. Now, I think you need to go and see Mia.'

Before I could agree, my phone rang. It was Swan, and I braced myself for that next load of shit.

Something must be wrong with Emma.

24

I put Swan's call on speaker and signalled to Andre to keep quiet.

'Are you in Melbourne?' Swan asked. I said I was. 'Emma has been in contact with her father. She's flying over to Christchurch tomorrow.'

'God, that was fast.'

'She's scared. Really scared.' Swan huffed a breath. 'Can you come and talk to her? I think we've got one chance to find out the real truth here. We can't force her to stay. We don't have enough evidence yet to arrest Solomon for her mother's murder either.'

'I've got her possessions all boxed up in my car. I can bring them with me.'

'I asked her about those,' he said. 'We offered to send someone to Candlebark to get them but she said no, don't bother.'

That was odd. 'She's lucky I already had them with me.' I explained to him about the arson attack on the pub and my Benz.

'Shit. Have they caught who did it?'

'Keith Scott. He believed it was me who reported the meth lab on his farm.'

A bit of a stunned silence at his end, then, 'Does Heath know about all of this?'

'Probably not. I don't know.'

Swan let out a big sigh. 'Brendan Scott is going to be charged with murder as well. He shot the person in Candlebark, the one in the street the other night.'

'Why?'

'Guy was a dealer up from Melbourne, tried to scam them. Scott thought he was an undercover cop.'

'I'm… stunned. How stupid can you get?'

'Pretty stupid.' Swan almost laughed. Almost. 'So, are you doing OK?'

My eyes filled again and I blinked hard. Andre held my free hand again. 'Um, no. It's all been… you know. Pretty chaotic. And I had to come to Melbourne to sort out my mother's funeral.'

'Oh. Well, if you can't see Emma… but it would really help me.'

It seemed that even now, Swan couldn't bring himself to say please. Never mind. 'Is she still in the hotel?'

'Yes. Detective Constable Chandler or I can be there today with her if you want someone to help.'

'No, it's fine.' Swan made Emma clam up. Chandler didn't seem to be able to get past her defences either. 'I'll come and see her now, and bring her things.'

Andre and I were in the city in half an hour, and he decided to go shopping again when I said I thought it was better if I talked to Emma alone. I chose one box out of the back of the 4WD – the box with her and Kate's personal things in it. Upstairs, I checked in with the officer outside Emma's door and then knocked. I wasn't sure what to expect, and she seemed surprised to see me, but she let me in. The room was a mess, with snack food packets and empty drink cans everywhere and the bed unmade. She flopped down on the bed and continued watching the TV, ignoring me. I left the box by the door, picked up the rubbish bin and went around, collecting up the mess while I tried to judge her mood and decide how to approach her.

When the room was reasonable again, I sat in the chair at the little desk and tried to look motherly. Not something I was any good at so I dropped that idea. 'Swan tells me you're off to Kiwiland tomorrow.'

'Yeah.'

'Is your dad excited you're coming?'

She shrugged. 'Doubt it, but he doesn't have any choice really, does he?'

'You'd be surprised. A lot of men would say it's not their responsibility.' I pointed at the box. 'I brought up some of your things. Your personal things, not clothes and stuff.'

Her eyes slid sideways towards the box. 'Like what?'

'Some of your mum's things, for a start.'

'My monkey?'

I had to search my memory to remember that it was a stuffed toy. 'Yes, that's in there.'

She kept watching the TV, but her face was the show. Twitching, lip biting, blinking. She sat up, her arms around her legs, and rested her forehead on her knees. She stayed like that for several minutes and I didn't dare say a word. Something big was going on in her head and she needed some space. Finally, she unfolded herself, her face a mix of white and blotched red, and went to the box. Flipping back the top, she stuck in a hand and pulled out the stuffed monkey.

For a moment I thought she was going to hug it, but instead she threw it to me, and I caught it awkwardly. 'I'm giving it to you,' she said.

'Um, OK. Thanks.' I looked at the monkey – it was mauve and cute, not ugly and poo brown like Mia's old one. 'Why?'

'Turn it over.'

I obeyed, and examined it. Nothing out of the ordinary.

'Mum sewed it up really well. You'll have to use scissors to get inside it.'

'What's in there?'

'A phone.' She sucked in a raspy breath. 'A phone I never want to see again. What you do with it is up to you. Give it to Swan or your boyfriend. I don't care.'

'OK.' This was confusing, to say the least. 'What's on it?' I was guessing photos, but she shook her head.

'Let them work it out. Tell them the code is EFFU. But once I get to New Zealand, I'm never coming back. Ever. Not to testify. Nothing. They'll never get that guy who killed Mum. So you tell them –' Her voice caught on a sob. 'I'm never coming back and they can't make me.'

'Emma, can you please tell me what this is about?'

'No! I'm never saying anything. Ever! It got Mum killed, and nearly me and you as well. It's not worth it!' She thumped down on the bed and grabbed a pillow, holding it against her like a shield. 'You have to go now. I want you to go.'

'All right.' I stood slowly, clutching the monkey, and looked down at her. 'If you ever need anything, you let me know. I mean it. If it doesn't work out with your dad, you can come back and stay with me.'

'No, I can't,' she said sadly. She sounded like a ninety-year-old woman. I wanted to sit and give her a big hug, but I was pretty sure she'd shove me away. She glanced up at me. 'But thanks.' Then it was back to the TV like I no longer existed.

I left the room and went back down to my rental, sitting the monkey in the back footwell and covering it up with my jacket. Once upon a time I would have had that monkey on my lap, ripping it apart with whatever I could find that was sharp, and satisfying my curiosity. Those days were gone. After what Emma had said, I felt like shoving the monkey in the hotel dumpster and leaving it there to be taken to the tip.

It was half an hour yet before Andre was due back so I climbed out of the 4WD again and went to find a café. While dawdling over coffee, I played with my own phone. There wasn't much on it – my photos were nearly all of Mia, my Contacts list was tiny, and I had hardly any apps. I was a dinosaur, according to most people. I found one photo of Heath, taken when he wasn't looking, where he was staring into space. Probably thinking about a case. If people measured their lives by what was stored on their phones, mine was pretty small. I liked it that way.

I wondered what we really would do with the pub. If it was possible to rebuild, would we bother? Or take the insurance money and buy a pub somewhere else? I loved Candlebark, or I had until dead bodies started turning up everywhere. And people like Keith Scott and his son got into dealing tobacco and then ice. But there was Connor, who wasn't talking to me, and Joleen who was so good with Mia…

I shook my head. It was too soon to make decisions. Like launching into a new relationship on the rebound. I went back to the 4WD and found Andre waiting for me, arms laden with shopping bags. As we drove to Ascot Vale and he showed me what he'd bought, I tried to be interested in his new clothes but he soon worked out I wasn't in the mood and fell silent. He raised his eyebrows at the monkey I carried inside, and it was a relief to tell him what it was about. Thank God for a friend I could rely on.

'That's a bit ominous,' he said, frowning at the monkey who stared back at him without blinking. 'Are you going to open it up?'

'Do you think I should?'

'Shit, yeah!' He picked up the toy and shook it. 'It does feel heavier than you'd expect. Where are your scissors?'

'I don't know…'

'Judi, whatever is on that phone has been responsible for

Kate's death as well as the hunt for Emma. Don't forget the attack on you. I want to know, don't you?'

'Don't you think that once we know, we'll be targets, too?' I couldn't help thinking of what Andy had hidden, and I rubbed the scar on my hand. His secret had nearly got Mia and me killed as well. Bloody secrets. They were lethal!

'You're going to give it to Heath, aren't you?'

I nodded. 'That's the plan. But…'

'Do you wish now you had never seen what Andy left you?' Andre asked softly.

'No.' But it wasn't a definite no.

'Because?'

I considered his question carefully. 'Well, once I'd seen it, I knew what I was dealing with. And I guess that helped me decide what to do.' I thought about it for another few seconds, then I went to get the scissors and handed them to him. 'Just remember, Andre, that it's like Pandora's box. Once we open it and look, we can't take it back.'

'Yes, I know.'

But I could see he didn't really. He was practical and straightforward. Do this and then that. Finished. Like his time inside. He'd made a mistake, paid for it, moved on. The problem was that other people often wouldn't let him.

All the same, I did want to know. Information was power. I'd learned that and there was no point pulling back now. I'd always wonder, perhaps always regret it if I didn't look.

He snipped down the back seam of the monkey and dug his fingers into the stuffing. 'Got it.' The phone he pulled out was small and cheap, pink with sparkles on it. Probably the first phone Emma had been allowed to have. He turned it over and found the On button, pressed it and waited for the starting screen to come up. 'Oh. It needs a code to get in.'

'EFFU.' I suddenly wanted to take it out of his hands and

smash it. For all its pink sparkles, that phone gave me the creeps. He tapped in the code and the phone lit up.

'Not much on it. Not many apps, or else they've been deleted. Some music, half a dozen photos.' He held it out and I glimpsed images of Emma staring seriously into the lens, and one of her mum laughing. 'Nothing much here really. Weird for a young teenager.' He tapped a few more icons. 'Oh wait, there's a video, but it's sort of dark and light.' He peered at the screen. 'That's someone's ceiling and a lamp.'

Then the voice started.

'Hi, Emma. It's me. OK to come in?'

A muffled 'No.'

'Hey, don't be like that. You and me are friends, remember? Like your mum and me are friends.'

I frowned at Andre. 'Is this Kate's boyfriend?'

He shrugged.

The sound of a bed creaking and something moving. Emma's voice. 'Don't. Please.'

'Now, don't be like that. You know you like it.'

'I don't. Kabir, please.'

'Don't you make any noise now.'

'Don't! No! Kabir! I'll tell Mum this time. I will!'

His voice turned hard. 'No, you fucken won't. Stay still, you little bitch.'

'No! Stop!'

I leaned over to grab the phone off Andre but he'd already stopped the recording. He looked like he was going to faint, swaying slightly, his face as grey as ash. We both sat there in stunned silence, not looking at each other.

'Fuck,' he said. He stared at the phone like it was contaminated. It was. Contaminated with something horrific that had been inflicted on Emma and there was nothing we could do. It had already happened. 'What do we do?'

'I... I don't know. I have to think about it.' I got up, my bones feeling about a million years old, and began to pull the curtains and lower the blinds around the room. Melbourne never got completely dark anymore – there was always light that created a dusty gloom, but I needed to shut out the world completely, to make the house feel enclosed, a fortress against bad things. All the while knowing that was impossible. By the time I'd finished and checked the door and window locks, I still felt unsettled and – I had to acknowledge – afraid. I'd been here before.

Andre had found wine in the fridge and poured us a glass each. His was already half-finished. 'I don't know what to do with this,' he said. 'I want to go and kill that guy, whoever he is. Fucking exterminate him!'

'We don't know who he is,' I said. 'She called him Kabir. It could be a really common name.'

'I doubt it,' he said morosely.

'Look.' I laced my fingers together tightly, and the scar on my hand went white. 'This is what got Kate killed. We know that. And Emma hunted. We know that, too. This guy must know about the recording. He's trying to find it and to destroy anyone who could testify against him.' I couldn't shake the sickening sense of déjà vu.

'He raped a thirteen-year-old girl!' He drank the rest of his wine in one go and banged the glass back on to the table. 'He can't get away with that.'

'Emma told me today that she won't come back from New Zealand – ever – and that means she won't testify against him either. She totally understands the situation.'

'I don't care. We have to do something. You have to give this to Heath or Swan.'

'I will, don't worry.' I grimaced at him. 'But I reckon this happened in Sydney. Different jurisdiction and Victoria Police won't be able to do anything. Emma says there's a corrupt cop up there so I'm betting this won't go anywhere up there either.'

'Shit!' He got up and started pacing.

'Can we sit on this for tonight, please?' My head was aching and I really had had enough for one day. 'Tomorrow morning, we can talk about it and work out what to do.' I looked around the large, open lounge and shivered. Every house was starting to feel like a prison. Well, I wouldn't let it get the better of me. If I did, I'd never live anywhere again without looking over my shoulder. This had to stop. If nothing else, it had to stop for Mia's sake. This was really her house. I couldn't poison her against it, or make her afraid to be here.

'Get your nice new clothes on,' I told him. 'We're going out for dinner.'

'But –'

'No buts. We're doing it.' I showed him the spare bedroom, found him some clean sheets and a towel, and he disappeared into the bathroom. Just as I was ferreting through the wardrobe, looking for something clean to wear, my phone rang. It was Heath.

'Where are you?' he said. 'Swan told me you'd gone to see Emma. Any luck?' Not 'How are you? Are you OK? Let's get together.' Just his official voice.

'I'm in Ascot Vale,' I said nicely. 'Andre and I are about to go out to eat.' I wanted to ask him if he'd like to join us – I knew Andre wouldn't mind – but I wasn't sure I could go the whole evening without confessing about the phone. I was damn sure Andre wouldn't be able to.

'Oh, right.'

'He's been shopping for clothes,' I prattled on. 'He lost everything in the pub fire. He's had to buy undies as well.'

He let out a loud breath. 'Shit, I'm sorry. I haven't even talked to you about that. Or anything. I should have called.'

'It's all been very weird and horrible. I don't even know where to start to tell you about it.'

'I've heard a lot from Swanny. Don't feel like you need to debrief me or anything.'

Debrief him? I laughed, but it wasn't funny. 'No, I won't.' It settled my mind. 'Shall we meet for breakfast? Can you manage that?'

'Sure. What time?'

'Let's say eight. Around the corner at Chez Nous.' That'd give me time to do what I was planning.

'OK.' He hesitated, and I knew he was still thinking about crashing our dinner.

'See you then,' I said brightly and disconnected, then felt immediately guilty and dismayed. I was lying to him. And the last time I'd done that, he'd been really angry and our budding relationship had almost curled up and died right then and there.

This is not really a lie. I'm just putting off telling him until I'm ready.

That helped a bit. I found a clean T-shirt with satin edging that looked a little more dressy than my usual tops and dragged it over my head. A quick brush of my hair and I was ready. Andre and I walked to the Thai restaurant on Mt Alexander Road and had a lovely meal of roast duck red curry and Penang beef curry and my favourite coconut rice. We tried to keep the conversation light, but inevitably we ended up talking about the pub.

'I could do a Thai night,' Andre said, scooping up more coconut rice. 'This is amazing.'

'We might have to wait until the pub is rebuilt,' I said, laughing.

'I think,' he said, his face going all serious, 'I think we should look at reopening the pub in the old workshop in the main street. Just as a temporary measure. Transfer the alcohol licence

– that'd be a winner, surely. Run it like a licenced café. There's a café in Elwood that used to be a service station and garage. We could do that, too.'

And with that, we were off, brainstorming how to do it, what we'd need, what regulations we'd have to negotiate, what to call it. It made the evening fly, and by the time we staggered home, our stomachs full to bursting, it was starting to feel like our disasters might finally be behind us.

Until I looked at Emma's phone again. But by then, I'd decided what to do with it.

25

I waited until Andre had gone to bed and I could hear him snoring lightly, then I took my phone and Emma's and crept out to the 4WD. I'd read somewhere that inside a car was the best place to make recordings, because it acted like a little sound box. I just had to hope nobody roared past in a noisy car.

I set my own phone to record, and checked how to play Emma's video, made sure the sound on both was up reasonably high, and pressed Play and Record together on both phones. Then I sat there with my fingers in my ears and watched. I couldn't bear to listen to Emma and that bastard again. Andre was right about the video being of the ceiling of her room – she must have had the phone recording beside her bed, maybe in the top drawer.

Whose idea was that? I pondered while I waited, deaf to the voices, only hearing the ones in my head. It had sounded like it wasn't the first time this guy had raped her. I couldn't imagine Emma coming up with that idea on her own, which meant after the first time, she'd told Kate. That Kate had never gone to the police suggested she didn't trust them, that she knew they'd want evidence – more than a rape kit result.

But even after making the recording, she still didn't go to the police. Or... the next thought turned my guts to ice. Maybe she had. And the corrupt cop up there was somehow involved with this Kabir guy and tipped him off.

Either way, knowledge of the recording had got out. Kate had changed her name and she and Emma had gone on the run, trusting nobody, trying to hide in Candlebark. She'd changed Emma's name, too, but legal name changes were probably searchable. For a cop, it'd be easy to find out their new names. Something had flagged where they were – possibly her tax file number from working at the pub. I had no idea whether she'd have been able to get a new one of those.

And then it had all gone to shit. Perhaps Kate had expected someone to come and threaten her and make her hand over the recording. But the knowledge of the rape was still inside her head and inside Emma's. At any time, they could both testify. This bastard Kabir had decided they both had to be wiped off the earth.

The video on Emma's phone ended and I turned both off with shaking hands. So now I had the knowledge, too, as did Andre. Logic said neither of us could testify to any more than saying we'd seen and heard the video. In a court of law, it'd be laughed out of the room. So really we were no threat. Still...

I went back inside, checked all the locks again and crawled into bed. I'd copied the recording the way I had because I had no cord for Emma's phone, not even to recharge it. I could have bought one, but I didn't want to. It'd had enough power left to do what I wanted. I wasn't sure why I'd made a copy, but I didn't want to hand the phone over to Heath without doing so. Once the police had it, it could sink without a trace. I didn't want what happened to Emma to be brushed off, dismissed, put in the 'too hard' basket. And if it made its way back to Sydney, God knows what'd happen to it.

I got out of bed, turned Emma's phone on again and set the recording going but stopped it within a couple of seconds. Then I took photos of the phone as it was, showing the video of the ceiling and lamp, and the phone itself, front and back.

Only then could I get back into bed and have any hope of falling asleep.

Sometime in the early morning, I had a nightmare in which I was wearing different types of armour – a thick woollen vest, a Kevlar vest, a firefighter's jacket, all on top of each other. And there was my mother, forcing me into heavy metal armour like a knight from the Middle Ages, roughly forcing my arms through and my head, just like she used to with jumpers when I was little. I was begging her to stop, shouting that it hurt – and then I opened my eyes to see Andre leaning over me.

I gasped, 'What? What's wrong?' and fear leapt up through my stomach like a wild thing.

'You were shouting in your sleep. You woke me up.' His face was furrowed with concern.

'Uh, sorry.' I struggled to sit up, my head pounding. 'Had a bad dream.'

'Stay there, I'll make you some tea.' He went off to the kitchen, and came back with tea for both of us and sat beside me on the bed.

'So, have you decided what to do with Emma's phone?' he asked.

'I'm giving it to Heath – I'm meeting him for breakfast. Want to come?'

He made a mock-horror face. 'Barge in on the two lovebirds? I don't think so!'

My face warmed. 'Not much love-birding going on lately, I can tell you.'

'It's not like you've had time, is it? Too many disasters to deal with.' He peered out the window. 'Good God, the sun is coming up. I can't tell you the last time I saw the dawn. And it's rosy pink.'

'Good omen?'

We sat and watched the sun come up over the rooftops and

drank our tea, then I pottered around, having a shower and tidying up until it was time to meet Heath. As always, as I walked up the street, I felt full of what Mia would call 'bufferflies'. Heath was there before me – a good sign? – and stood and wrapped his arms around me when I reached the table.

'You smell good,' he murmured into my neck.

He did, too. I let myself sag against him for a few seconds and then we both pulled away at the same time. 'Busy day ahead?'

'I don't have to go in at all,' he said. 'Not a day off as such, but I'm owed a lot of time so…'

'Let's order then, so we can talk.' I grabbed a menu and buried my head in it. I could feel his eyes on me but he didn't say anything, just signalled to the wait staff that we were ready to order. He ordered eggs-something while I went for the café's famous fruit toast and a large double-shot latte.

When the café guy had taken our orders and gone, Heath leaned back and eyed me. 'Are we talking about work stuff or us stuff?'

'I guess it's work first.' I took Emma's phone out of my bag and placed it carefully on the table. 'This is Emma's. It has a recording on it of her being… raped.' I nearly said assaulted but I hated euphemisms. 'By some guy called Kabir.' I swallowed and coughed. The anger I felt about this was nearly choking me again. 'I'm giving it to you.'

'Right.' Heath picked up the phone but he didn't look happy. 'Audio? Video?' His work voice.

'It's a video but I think it was sitting in her drawer or beside her bed. You just see the ceiling and a lamp.'

'You've watched it.' Flat tone.

'A bit of it. I didn't know what it was.' Now I sounded defensive, which I hated. I went on the offensive. 'I think it happened in Sydney, so I guess you and Swan won't be able to do anything about it, and my guess is nobody in the NSW police is going to be interested.'

'Hang on!' He frowned at me. 'Emma is how old?'

'Fourteen now. Probably thirteen when it happened.'

'Of course we're going to do something about it! Jeez.' He ran his fingers through his short-cropped hair. 'Apart from anything else, her mother's murder happened in Victoria.'

'So you understand this is why Kate was killed and that guy was trying to kill Emma, too?' When he said yes, I added, 'How much use is it really, as evidence? I mean, was Kate murdered for nothing? These things go to court, he gets a really good defence lawyer, Kate's boyfriend was a drug dealer… Surely this Kabir knows he has a good chance of getting off?'

'I don't understand what your point is?'

Somebody delivered our coffees but I was so focused on trying to explain what I meant that I hardly noticed. 'Why kill Kate? And try to get rid of Emma? For a recording like this? Murder is a pretty over-the-top way to deal with an accusation of rape. Considering most cases never even make it to court.'

'Because it's a major crime, both here and NSW. Here the penalty for sex with an under-sixteen-year-old is fifteen years, up there it's sixteen years. Possibly even twenty if aggravated assault can be proven.' He shook his head. 'Here, he'd be charged with rape and with sexual penetration of a ten- to fourteen-year-old.'

'Oh. Right. Would this recording be enough? Wouldn't Emma still have to testify?'

'Well, yes, I think so.' He stirred sugar into his coffee, the spoon clinking over and over until I wanted to rip it out of his hand. 'But that offence didn't take place in Victoria, did it?'

'Pretty sure it's in Sydney.'

'Mmm.'

'What does *Mmm* mean?' My tone had turned snappish and he gave me a funny look.

'It's the motive for a murder that took place here, but the offence took place in another state. It's tricky.'

I reached for the phone and he put his hand over mine.

'Judi, please leave it with me. I'll do everything I can.'

'But what does that mean exactly?' I felt the old anger rise up, the way it had when they were going to accept somebody's fake confession for my brother's murder. To hell with convenience and procedure!

The other Judi loomed at my shoulder. 'Back off, or he'll get annoyed. Then maybe he really will bury the phone evidence.'

I closed my eyes and tried to force her away, but it wasn't working. My head was pounding again. But I couldn't let this go. My eyes sprung open.

'I'm not giving you the phone until you promise me you'll actually do something concrete. Get the NSW police to charge this guy. If you all let him get away with it…'

His face tightened and his eyes flashed. 'We don't *let* people get away with committing offences!'

OK, that just stuffed up our romantic breakfast then. Good on you, Judi.

Suddenly I was very glad I'd copied the recording. I pulled my hand back. 'All right, it's yours. There was no point me keeping it anyway.'

'Good. I think.' He eyed me suspiciously, but apparently decided to calm things down. 'I gather they've arrested someone for burning down the pub?'

'Keith Scott. He still stank of petrol when Connor went to his house.' I wasn't going to mention that Connor had followed me there.

Heath made a face. 'Yes, Swanny said my tip-off about the meth lab led to Scott's son being arrested.'

'Emma's tip-off.'

Our breakfasts slid on to the table in front of us. I was glad I'd ordered the toast – my stomach couldn't have coped with eggs right then. Heath started on his Eggs Benedict with obvious relish while I cut my toast into small pieces and ate them slowly.

Halfway through, Heath slowed down enough to talk again. 'I'm really sorry you've lost the pub.'

'We're all safe and well,' I said. 'That's what counts.' My words echoed in my head, and I had a flash of standing by the desk, watching the petrol flood under the door again.

The other Judi said, 'You're not safe and well really. Your life's gone to shit, and here you are ruining things with Heath. What's the matter with you?'

'Are you OK?' Heath asked. He put down his knife and fork and peered at me.

'What do you mean?'

'You've gone very pale and your hands are shaking.' He scooted his chair around and put his arms around me. I tried to relax into him again, but my body felt like planks of wood nailed together very precariously. At the same time my heart was racing so fast I was scared I was having a heart attack. I opened my mouth but no words came out.

Heath's voice came from a long way away. 'I think you're suffering from delayed shock.'

What's delayed about it?

26

Warm arms around me, his soothing voice. My whole body was rigid but I was gasping. 'Breathe, Judi. Long, slow breaths. Concentrate on your breathing. Come on, breathe in for four, out for four. Count with me.'

I vaguely heard someone say, 'Do you want some water?'

'Yes, thanks.' Then Heath was counting again, and I followed his voice, doing what he said. My heart slowed, and the dizziness receded. When the water came, I drank it in sips, and finally my body returned to me.

I turned to him. 'Don't tell me to go to the doctor.'

He laughed. 'Now I know you're OK again.'

'I'm fine. I just…' I took more breaths, then told him about the pub burning, seeing the petrol and the flames, climbing out on the balcony with Andre, and finding my Benz burned as well. 'It's all been a bit much.'

'Bit much?' He shook his head. 'It's been a bloody nightmare for you!'

I made a face. 'Yeah, well, that's the other thing. I've had to organise my mother's funeral on top of everything else.'

The expression on his face said it all, but he took my hand and covered it with his warm ones. 'Your hands are freezing. I'm sorry you've had to deal with all of this. I feel like I should've been here for you…'

'There's nothing you could've done,' I said. 'And you're here now.'

'Have you still got that rental car?'

'Yes. I suppose I'll have to buy something to replace the Benz.' I sighed. Another job to add to the list.

'Things are…' He stopped himself from saying quiet, which was like bringing hell down on the Homicide squad. 'I can take a couple of days off. How about I drive you and Mia back to Candlebark? And help with stuff?'

He didn't know I was nervous about going back to my house, let alone about facing the wreck of the pub. Even though Andre would be with me, to have Heath there would be like an amazing, unexpected gift. 'God, that would be wonderful!' I leaned over and kissed him and then he kissed me back, and seconds later I heard clapping. The café staff were all beaming at us and applauding, and my face flamed.

Heath grinned. 'We made their day.'

'You made mine. We should finish eating and get moving.'

'I have to take that phone in to Swan first.' He patted his pocket where he'd put Emma's phone. 'But then I'm all yours.'

Best words I'd heard for weeks.

I called Lucy and Geoff to let them know I'd be picking Mia up in a few hours. That made me even happier. Heath dropped me back at the house and I went inside to tell Andre what was happening, then I planned to pop in to see Margaret next door. But a visitor was waiting for me, sitting at the table with Andre, drinking tea. Chris Winter.

'What are you doing here?' I asked, the nervous churning in my stomach returning in an instant.

'I'm heading back to Sydney,' he said. 'Thought I'd say goodbye.'

That was definitely weird. 'Are you flying?'

'No, driving.' He smiled at me with his usual charm.

'Bit of a detour.' My tone was getting more and more terse.

'I wanted to explain a few things before I left.' The smile fell from his face and I saw a glimpse of the real Chris Winter, one I'd sensed before.

I sat down opposite him and said, 'Go right ahead.'

'I knew Kate and Emma in Sydney. I visited their house a few times, because I knew Mikey as well. Mikey Koslov was bad news.' He took a breath. 'It was a pleasure to help him along into gaol. But you didn't hear that from me.'

'And?'

'I was in love with Kate, actually. But as long as Mikey was around, I didn't have a chance. She couldn't get away from him. When he went inside, I helped Kate change her name and move to Candlebark.'

'And then you followed her there.' I frowned. 'Was it you who led that killer to her? Caused her death?'

'No! That's why I came. I'd heard there'd been a hit put out on her. I was trying to get in front of whoever was sent to get rid of her.' He ground his palms in his eye sockets. 'If I'd known it was Aidan… I could've taken him out somehow. But he's an ex-soldier, and a bloody psycho.'

I thought of the recording on the phone. 'Do you know why she was killed? Why they were after Emma as well?'

He nodded. 'It was about Emma.'

'About Emma being raped,' I said flatly.

His head jerked up and he stared at me. 'How did you know about that? You can't know about it. It's not…'

'Safe? Tell me about it.' I glanced at Andre who mouthed 'Phone?' at me. I shrugged. Should I tell this guy anything about the phone? I still didn't trust him.

'What is it?' Chris said sharply. 'What are you hiding?'

It didn't matter now – Heath had the phone – so I told him about it and what Emma had recorded on it. 'I've handed it over to police here. It's out of my hands now.'

Chris threw up his hands. 'Shit! You know it'll just disappear. Did Emma give you permission to do that?'

'More or less. She's left Australia. She's never going to testify, she says, so it's the phone or nothing.'

'Fuck!' Chris jumped up and paced a few times then tucked his hands under his arms and leaned against the bench. 'Look, the guy who raped Emma is the big boss of their gang. He's… I think he's got a thing for underage girls.'

'So this is the gang you're a member of?' I leaned back in my chair and eyeballed him. 'You know all this and you still hang out with them?'

'It's my…' He stopped himself, but I was bloody sure he was about to say 'job'. He breathed heavily for a while, then said, 'The Victorian police will make a fuss, but in the end they'll have to send that phone to Sydney. I reckon it'll disappear.'

'Emma said Kate was convinced this Kabir had a high-level cop in his pocket.'

Chris gaped at me. 'How do you know his name?'

'Emma says it clearly on the recording, several times.' She probably said more than that but I wasn't willing to listen to all of it.

'Shit, shit!' Chris began pacing again, muttering to himself. I'd made sure I hadn't looked at my bag once, where my own phone was. Andre and I glanced at each other. I wanted Chris to leave but he didn't seem in a hurry – what more did he want from us?

'Chris, we're going back to Candlebark today. I don't know what else –'

'There has to be a way,' he said. 'Can you get the phone back from Swan?'

'No! What the hell would you do with it anyway?'

He came back to the table. 'That recording would blow Kabir's world apart. He's got a wife and four daughters, all under ten. He's got family in his gang with young daughters, not to mention mates. This guy – he's the king because he puts himself above everyone else, like he's untouchable, never does anything wrong, holds all the power. That recording would be the end of him.'

'Are you sure?' Andre said. 'Seems to me that guys like that just blow off any accusations and move on.'

Chris shook his head. 'Nup, not this guy. And not if it's done right. For a start, his wife would leave him, and one of Kabir's biggest backers is his father-in-law. Why do you think he sent Solomon after Kate and Emma? He was bloody desperate to get rid of them and any evidence that proved he'd done it.' He shook his head again. 'A recording. Fuck, I bet he doesn't know it exists.'

'I think he does,' I said slowly. 'I think Kate threatened him with it. Leave her and Emma alone or she'd give it to the cops.'

Chris stared at me for a moment then he closed his eyes. 'Oh shit, Kate, what did you do that for? I could've… I could've fixed it for you.'

'I doubt it,' I said, and Andre nodded. 'He would've got rid of you as well. The thing is…' I took a breath. 'What does it mean that we've heard it? Andre and I thought our evidence would be hearsay and not relevant.'

What did it mean that I still had a copy? It was sounding more and more like I was carrying my death warrant around with me. Fuck. I was putting everyone around me in danger, just like Kate had. No, that wasn't fair. She was scared out of her mind. Well, so was I – again.

'True,' Chris said. 'If I had that phone…'

'What? You'd do what?' I scoffed at him. 'Get yourself killed for it? Or blackmail this Kabir and make some good money? And then get killed.'

Anger filled his face and his eyes narrowed at me. 'Don't

you bloody accuse me of making money out of Emma's bloody misery! I loved Kate. I still love her. I miss her every day. I'm glad Emma is leaving Australia. I hope she gets a new life and leaves all of this shit behind.'

If only it was that easy, but I left that one alone. 'You still haven't told us what you'd do with the recording.'

He didn't miss that I'd moved from saying 'phone' to 'recording' but he didn't pounce on it. 'I'd make sure that everyone around Kabir got a copy of it. His wife, his father-in-law, her brothers and all his gang members. That would ensure his downfall, and possibly his death.' He smiled grimly. 'And I'd make sure the right people in NSW police got a copy as well, along with the information that Vic Police have the phone. That way it can't possibly be ignored or shoved out of sight.'

'You could do all that? Who do you know up there?' I said. But I wasn't disbelieving him. He was confirming who I thought he was.

'Damn fucking right! I know exactly who to give it to. Now, can you get the phone back so I can make a copy of the recording?'

I glanced at Andre again, but he was no help – he had no idea what I'd done. This was completely up to me. And when I got right down to it, I knew I had to give it to him. If I kept it, I was putting Mia in danger as well as myself. I didn't want to live a life where I had to leave her with her grandparents all the time to keep her safe. No fucking way.

I tested it all in my head, to make sure there was no way the recording could be traced back to me. 'Where will you say you got it from?'

'I'll say Kate sent it to me. Before Aidan killed her. There'll be no comeback on you, I promise. Or on Emma.' His face twisted. 'I hate to blame it all on Kate, but I don't think she'll mind.'

'It won't compromise your… job?'

'Ha ha.' The laugh was a bit sarcastic, but he knew I knew. 'No. It's cool. Now...'

'I don't need to get it back,' I said slowly. 'I copied it on to my own phone.'

'What?' Andre was horrified. 'When?'

'Last night. I'm sorry, I should've told you.'

'Don't worry, I probably didn't really want to know,' he said, patting my arm.

Chris was clearly gobsmacked, then he said, 'I... are you going to give it to me?'

'I guess so. I wouldn't have told you otherwise.' I reached into my bag and pulled out my phone. 'How do we do this?'

'Can you email it to me?'

That took a bit of fiddling as I only had an old Gmail account I hadn't used for months, but finally, with Chris's help, I attached the file to an email and sent it to him. A few seconds later, his phone pinged and he downloaded the file.

'Don't listen to it here,' I said. 'I don't want to hear it again.'

He went out into the back garden and listened with his ear jammed to the phone. From where we sat, I could see his shoulders sag and his hand went to his face. Andre said, 'I'm glad you copied it. I think he means what he says.'

The little part of me that had hardened into making the decision grew bigger and harder. 'You know something? I can't afford to care any longer. I know that makes me cold-hearted, but I'm handing this over, once and for all. When he's gone, I'm deleting the recording from my phone.'

'Not cold-hearted,' he said. 'You're thinking of Mia, and all of us. I want to be safe as much as you do.'

Chris came back inside, his face grim. 'Thanks. You won't regret this. Get rid of it off your phone, OK?'

'For sure.' I hesitated, knowing I was my own worst enemy, but I couldn't help it. 'What were you doing "sleepwalking" around the streets? Did you know Brendan was going to shoot that drug dealer?'

'No,' Chris said. He didn't sound like he was faking the surprise. 'It's a habit, walking around places at night, watching. I heard them talking, arguing actually, but when he was shot the next night, I was tucked up in bed, snoring my head off.'

I didn't respond. Maybe he was lying, maybe he wasn't. I decided it didn't matter now.

'You probably won't hear from me again,' he said, with a wry grin. 'I guess that won't break your heart.'

I didn't reply to that one either. He left and Andre and I got our stuff together, ready to go back to Candlebark. I went and said goodbye to Margaret next door, and then Heath arrived. He'd even managed to borrow a car seat for Mia. We picked her up after dropping off my rental 4WD, and were on the road by lunchtime, Mia telling Andre in the back seat all about her swing and showing him her fingernails painted with sparkles. Time with her grandparents had worked out well.

All along the Calder Highway, I wrestled with whether to tell Heath about the recording and giving it to Chris Winter. I wanted to. One part of my brain said that relationships were built on truth and trust, but another part of my brain said that was the kind of crap people said who had no real secrets. I'd seen a few marriages go down the gurgler over the years because someone confessed an affair out of guilt. Unloading just to make yourself feel better was selfish in my book.

And I couldn't help remembering how angry he'd been with me about giving Andy's evidence to Graeme Nash. It had taken a while for us to get past that. At one point I hadn't thought we'd make it.

No, let it stay a secret. Andre wouldn't tell. And neither would I. Not until Heath and I were old and grey and too doddery to care about it anymore. That thought – seeing Heath grey and doddery – made me smile.

'What's got you so happy?' Heath asked.

'Thinking about what you'll look like when you're old.'

'Yeah, sure you are,' he said with a grin.

See? Tell a man the truth and he doesn't believe you anyway.

As we neared Candlebark, I sat up straighter in my seat. I could cope with seeing the burnt pub now, and all the paperwork and hassles that were coming. Andre's idea of using the old workshop as a temporary pub had me excited and ready to tackle it. When we pulled into my driveway and I found the wreck of the Benz was gone, and someone had cleaned the remnants away as well, I was able to relax and start to see my little house as a haven again.

But when Mia got out of the car and ran into the garden, shouting, 'Peas! Peas!' and pulling them off the plants, that was when I really felt like we'd turned a corner and were starting again. Weird. But perfect.

About the Author

Sherryl Clark has had 70 children's and YA books published in Australia, and several in the US and UK, plus collections of poetry and four verse novels. She has taught writing at Holmesglen TAFE and Victoria University Polytech. She completed a Master of Fine Arts program at Hamline University, Minnesota, and a PhD in creative writing at Victoria University. Her debut novel, *Trust Me, I'm Dead* was shortlisted for the CWA Debut Dagger Award.

@sherrylwriter

vervebooks.co.uk/**SherrylClark**